TROLLSLAYER

GOTREK GURNISSON turned and glared out into the darkness of the woods. 'Come out, little beastmen!' he bellowed. 'I have a gift for you.'

He laughed loudly and ran his thumb along the edge of the blade of his great two-handed axe. Felix saw that it drew blood. Gotrek began to suck his thumb.

The dwarf turned once more to the darkness. 'Come out!' he shouted. 'I care not if all the powers of evil walk the woods this night. I will face any challenger.'

Only a madman would so tempt fate and the dark powers on Geheimnisnacht, Night of Mystery, in the darkest reaches of the forest, Felix Jaeger decided.

He could make out chanting in the flinty, guttural tongue of the Mountain Dwarfs, then once more in Reikspiel, he heard: 'Send me a champion!

For a second there was silence. Condensation from the clammy mist ran down his brow. Then – from far, far off – the sound of galloping horses rang out in the quiet night.

'Good!' Gotrek roared. 'Good!'

A WARHAMMER NOVEL

Gotrek and Felix

TROLLSLAYER

By William King

A BLACK LIBRARY PUBLICATION

Games Workshop Publishing
Willow Road, Lenton,
Nottingham, NG7 2WS, UK

First US edition, March 2000

10 9 8 7 6 5 4 3 2

Distributed by Simon & Schuster
1230 Avenue of the Americas
New York, NY 10020, USA

Cover illustration by John Gravato

ISBN 0-671-78373-4

Set in ITC Giovanni

Printed and bound in Great Britain by
Omnia Books Limited, Glasgow

See the Black Library on the Internet at
http://www.blacklibrary.co.uk

Find out more about Games Workshop
and the world of Warhammer at
http://www.games-workshop.com

CONTENTS

GEHEIMNISNACHT

'After the terrible events and nightmare adventures we endured in Altdorf, my companion and I fled southwards, following no path more certain than that chosen for us by blind chance. We took whatever means of transport presented itself: stagecoach, peasant cart, drayage wagon, resorting to our own two feet when all else failed.

'It was a difficult and fear-filled time for me. At every turning, it seemed, we stood in imminent danger of arrest and either imprisonment or execution. I saw sheriffs in every tavern and bounty killers behind every bush. If the Trollslayer suspected that things might have been otherwise, he never bothered to communicate this information to me.

'To one as ignorant of the true state of our legal system as I then was, it seemed all too possible that the entire apparatus of our mighty and extensive state might be bent to the apprehension of two fugitives such as ourselves. I did not then have any idea of quite how feebly and

randomly the rule of law was applied. It was indeed a pity
that all those sheriffs and all those bounty killers who
peopled my imagination did not, in fact, exist – for
perhaps then evil would not have flourished quite so
strongly within the boundaries of my homeland.

'The extent and nature of the evil was to become very
clear to me one dark evening after boarding a southbound
stagecoach, on what is perhaps the most ill-omened night
in our entire calendar...'

—From *My Travels with Gotrek, Vol. II,* by Herr
Felix Jaeger (Altdorf Press, 2505)

'DAMN ALL MANLING coach drivers and all manling women,'
Gotrek Gurnisson muttered, adding a curse in dwarfish.

'You did have to insult the lady Isolde, didn't you?' Felix
Jaeger said peevishly. 'As things are, we're lucky they didn't just
shoot us. If you can call it "lucky" to be dumped in the
Reikwald on Geheimnisnacht Eve.'

'We paid for our passage. We were just as entitled to sit inside
as her. The drivers were unmanly cowards,' Gotrek grumbled.
'They refused to meet me hand to hand. I would not have
minded being spitted on steel, but being blasted with buckshot
is no death for a Trollslayer.'

Felix shook his head. He could see that one of his companion's black moods was coming on. There would be no arguing
with him and Felix had plenty of other things to worry about.
The sun was setting, giving the mist-covered forest a ruddy hue.
Long shadows danced eerily and brought to mind too many
frightening tales of the horrors to be found under the canopy
of trees.

He wiped his nose with the edge of his cloak then pulled the
Sudenland wool tight about him. He sniffed and looked at the
sky where Morrslieb and Mannslieb, the lesser and greater
moons, were already visible. Morrslieb seemed to be giving off
a faint greenish glow. It wasn't a good sign.

'I think I have a fever coming on,' Felix said. The Trollslayer
looked up at him and chuckled contemptuously. In the last
rays of the dying sun, his nose-chain was a bloody arc running
from nostril to earlobe.

'Yours is a weak race,' Gotrek said. 'The only fever I feel this eve is the battle-fever. It sings in my head.'

He turned and glared out into the darkness of the woods. 'Come out, little beastmen!' he bellowed. 'I have a gift for you.'

He laughed loudly and ran his thumb along the edge of the blade of his great two-handed axe. Felix saw that it drew blood. Gotrek began to suck his thumb.

'Sigmar preserve us, be quiet!' Felix hissed. 'Who knows what lurks out there on a night like this?'

Gotrek glared at him. Felix could see the glint of insane violence appear in his eyes. Instinctively Felix's hand strayed nearer to the pommel of his sword.

'Give me no orders, manling! I am of the Elder Race and am beholden only to the Kings Under the Mountain, exile though I be.'

Felix bowed formally. He was well schooled in the use of the sword. The scars on his face showed that he had fought several duels in his student days. He had once killed a man and so ended a promising academic career. But still he did not relish the thought of fighting the Trollslayer. The tip of Gotrek's crested hair came only to the level of Felix's chest but the dwarf outweighed him and his bulk was all muscle. And Felix had seen Gotrek use that axe.

The dwarf took the bow as an apology and turned once more to the darkness. 'Come out!' he shouted. 'I care not if all the powers of evil walk the woods this night. I will face any challenger.'

The dwarf was working himself up to a pitch of fury. During the time of their acquaintance Felix had noticed that the Trollslayer's long periods of brooding were often followed by brief explosions of rage. It was one of the things about his companion that fascinated Felix. He knew that Gotrek had become a Trollslayer to atone for some crime. He was sworn to seek death in unequal combat with fearsome monsters. He seemed bitter to the point of madness – yet he kept to his oath.

Perhaps, thought Felix, I too would go mad if I had been driven into exile among strangers not even of my own race. He felt some sympathy for the crazed dwarf. Felix knew what it was like to be driven from home under a cloud. The duel with Wolfgang Krassner had caused quite a scandal.

At that moment, however, the dwarf seemed bent on getting them both killed, and he wanted no part of it. Felix continued to plod along the road, casting an occasional worried glance at the bright full moons. Behind him the ranting continued.

'Are there no warriors among you? Come feel my axe. She thirsts!'

Only a madman would so tempt fate and the dark powers on Geheimnisnacht, Night of Mystery, in the darkest reaches of the forest, Felix decided.

He could make out chanting in the flinty, guttural tongue of the Mountain Dwarfs, then once more in Reikspiel, he heard: 'Send me a champion!'

For a second there was silence. Condensation from the clammy mist ran down his brow. Then – from far, far off – the sound of galloping horses rang out in the quiet night.

What has that maniac done, Felix thought, has he offended one of the Old Powers? Have they sent their daemon riders to carry us off?

Felix stepped off the road. He shuddered as wet leaves fondled his face. They felt like dead men's fingers. The thunder of hooves came closer, moving with hellish speed along the forest road. Surely only a supernatural being could keep such breakneck pace on the winding forest road? He felt his hand shake as he unsheathed his sword.

I was foolish to follow Gotrek, he thought. Now I'll never get the poem finished. He could hear the loud neighing of horses, the cracking of a whip and mighty wheels turning.

'Good!' Gotrek roared. His voice drifted from the trail behind. 'Good!'

There was a loud bellowing and four immense jet horses drawing an equally black coach hurtled past. Felix saw the wheels bounce as they hit a rut in the road. He could just make out a black-cloaked driver. He shrank back into the bushes.

He heard the sound of feet coming closer. The bushes were pulled aside. Before him stood Gotrek, looking madder and wilder than ever. His crest was matted, brown mud was smeared over his tattooed body and his studded leather jerkin was ripped and torn.

'The snotling-fondlers tried to run me over!' he yelled. 'Let's get after them!'

He turned and headed up the muddy road at a fast trot. Felix noted that Gotrek was singing happily in Khazalid.

* * *

FURTHER DOWN THE Bogenhafen road the pair found the Standing Stones Inn. The windows were shuttered and no lights showed. They could hear a neighing from the stables but when they checked there was no coach, black or otherwise, only some skittish ponies and a peddler's cart.

'We've lost the coach. Might as well get a bed for the night,' Felix suggested. He looked warily at the smaller moon, Morrslieb. The sickly green glow was stronger. 'I do not like being abroad under this evil light.'

'You are feeble, manling. Cowardly too.'

'They'll have ale.'

'On the other hand, some of your suggestions are not without merit. Watery though human beer is, of course.'

'Of course,' Felix said. Gotrek failed to spot the note of irony in his voice.

The inn was not fortified but the walls were thick, and when they tried the door they found it was barred. Gotrek began to bang it with the butt of his axe-shaft. There was no response.

'I can smell humans within,' Gotrek said. Felix wondered how he could smell anything over his own stench. Gotrek never washed and his hair was matted with animal fat to keep his red-dyed crest in place.

'They'll have locked themselves in. Nobody goes abroad on Geheimnisnacht. Unless they're witches or daemon-lovers.'

'The black coach was abroad,' Gotrek said.

'Its occupants were up to no good. The windows were curtained and the coach bore no crest of arms.'

'My throat is too dry to discuss such details. Come on, open up in there or I'll take my axe to the door!'

Felix thought he heard movement within. He pressed an ear to the door. He could make out the mutter of voices and what sounded like weeping.

'Unless you want me to chop through your head, manling, I suggest you stand aside,' Gotrek said to Felix.

'Just a moment. I say: you inside! Open up! My friend has a very large axe and a very short temper. I suggest you do as he says or lose your door.'

'What was that about "short"?' Gotrek said touchily.

From behind the door came a thin, quavering cry. 'In the name of Sigmar, begone, you daemons of the pit!'

'Right, that's it,' Gotrek snapped. 'I've had enough.'

He drew his axe back in a huge arc. Felix saw the runes of its blade gleam in the Morrslieb light. He leapt aside.

'In the name of Sigmar!' Felix shouted. 'You cannot exorcise us. We are simple, weary travellers.'

The axe bit into the door with a chunking sound. Splinters of wood flew from it. Gotrek turned to Felix and grinned evilly up at him. Felix noted the missing teeth.

'Shoddily made, these manling doors,' Gotrek said.

'I suggest you open up while you still have a door,' Felix called.

'Wait,' the quavering voice said. 'That door cost me five crowns from Jurgen the carpenter.'

The door was unlatched. It opened. A tall, thin man with a sad face framed by lank, white hair stood there. He had a stout club in one hand. Behind him stood an old woman who held a saucer that contained a guttering candle.

'You will not need your weapon, sir. We require only a bed for the night,' Felix said.

'And ale,' the dwarf grunted.

'And ale,' Felix agreed.

'Lots of ale,' Gotrek said. Felix looked at the old man and shrugged helplessly.

Inside, the inn had a low common room. The bar was made of planks stretched across two barrels. From the corner, three armed men who looked like travelling peddlers watched them warily. They each had daggers drawn. The shadows hid their faces but they seemed worried.

The innkeeper hustled the pair inside and slid the bars back into place. 'Can you pay, Herr Doktor?' he asked nervously. Felix could see the man's Adam's apple moving.

'I am not a professor, I am a poet,' he said, producing his thin pouch and counting out his few remaining gold coins. 'But I can pay.'

'Food,' Gotrek said. 'And ale.'

At this the old woman burst into tears. Felix stared at her.

'The hag is discomfited,' Gotrek said.

The old man nodded. 'Our Gunter is missing, on this of all nights.'

'Get me some ale,' Gotrek said. The innkeeper backed off. Gotrek got up and stumped over to where the peddlers were sitting. They regarded him warily.

'Do any of you know about a black coach drawn by four black horses?' Gotrek asked.

'You have seen the black coach?' one of the peddlers asked. The fear was evident in his voice.

'Seen it? The bloody thing nearly ran me over.' A man gasped. Felix heard the sound of a ladle being dropped. He saw the innkeeper stoop to pick it up and begin refilling the tankard.

'You are lucky then,' the fattest and most prosperous-looking peddler said. 'Some say the coach is driven by daemons. I have heard it passes here on Geheimnisnacht every year. Some say it carries wee children from Altdorf who are sacrificed at the Darkstone Ring.'

Gotrek looked at him with interested. Felix did not like the way this was developing.

'Surely that is only a legend,' he said.

'No, sir,' the innkeeper shouted. 'Every year we hear the thunder of its passing. Two years ago Gunter looked out and saw it, a black coach just as you describe.'

At the mention of Gunter's name the old woman began to cry again. The innkeeper brought stew and two great steins of ale.

'Bring beer for my companion too,' Gotrek said. The landlord went off for another stein.

'Who is Gunter?' Felix asked when he returned. There was another wail from the old woman.

'More ale,' Gotrek said. The landlord looked in astonishment at the empty flagons.

'Take mine,' Felix said. 'Now, mein host, who is Gunter?'

'And why does the old hag howl at the very mention of his name?' Gotrek asked, wiping his mouth on his mud-encrusted arm.

'Gunter is our son. He went out to chop wood this afternoon. He has not returned.'

'Gunter is a good boy,' the old woman sniffled. 'How will we survive without him?'

'Perhaps he is simply lost in the woods?'

'Impossible,' the innkeeper said. 'Gunter knows the woods round here like I know the hairs on my hand. He should have been home hours ago. I fear the coven has taken him, as a sacrifice.'

'It's just like Lotte Hauptmann's daughter, Ingrid,' the fat peddler said. The innkeeper shot him a dirty look.

'I want no tales told of our son's betrothed,' he said.

'Let the man speak,' Gotrek said. The peddler looked at him gratefully.

'The same thing happened last year, in Hartzroch, just down the road. Goodwife Hauptmann looked in on her teenage daughter Ingrid just after sunset. She thought she heard banging coming from her daughter's room. The girl was gone, snatched by who-knows-what sorcerous power from her bed in a locked house. The next day the hue and cry went up. We found Ingrid. She was covered in bruises and in a terrible state.'

He looked at them to make sure he had their attention. 'You asked her what happened?' Felix said.

'Aye, sir. It seems she had been carried off by daemons, wild things of the wood, to Darkstone Ring. There the coven waited with evil creatures from the forests. They made to sacrifice her at the altar but she broke free from her captors and invoked the good name of blessed Sigmar. While they reeled she fled. They pursued her but could not overtake her.'

'That was lucky,' Felix said dryly.

'There is no need to mock, Herr Doktor. We made our way to the stones and we did find all sorts of tracks in the disturbed earth. Including those of humans and beasts and cloven-hoofed daemons. And a yearling infant gutted like a pig upon the altar.'

'Cloven-hoofed daemons?' Gotrek asked. Felix didn't like the look of interest in his eye. The peddler nodded.

'I would not venture up to Darkstone Ring tonight,' the peddler said. 'Not for all the gold in Altdorf.'

'It would be a task fit for a hero,' Gotrek said, looking meaningfully at Felix. Felix was shocked.

'Surely you cannot mean—'

'What better task for a Trollslayer than to face these daemons on their sacred night? It would be a mighty death.'

'It would be a stupid death,' Felix muttered.

'What was that?'

'Nothing.'

'You are coming, aren't you?' Gotrek said menacingly. He was rubbing his thumb along the blade of his axe. Felix noticed that it was bleeding again.

He nodded slowly. 'An oath is an oath.'

The dwarf slapped him upon the back with such force that he thought his ribs would break. 'Sometimes, manling, I think you must have dwarf blood in you. Not that any of the Elder race would stoop to such a mixed marriage, of course.' He stomped back to his ale.

'Of course,' his companion said, glaring at his back.

FELIX FUMBLED IN his pack for his mail shirt. He noticed that the innkeeper and his wife and the peddlers were looking at him. Their eyes held something that looked close to awe. Gotrek sat near the fire drinking ale and grumbling in dwarfish.

'You're not really going with him?' the fat peddler whispered. Felix nodded.

'Why?'

'He saved my life. I owe him a debt.' Felix thought it best not to mention the circumstances under which Gotrek had saved him.

'I pulled the manling out from under the hooves of the Emperor's cavalry,' Gotrek shouted.

Felix cursed bitterly. The Trollslayer has the hearing of a wild beast as well as the brains of one, he thought to himself, continuing to pull on the mail shirt.

'Aye. The manling thought it clever to put his case to the Emperor with petitions and protest marches. Old Karl Franz chose to respond, quite sensibly, with cavalry charges.'

The peddlers were starting to back away.

'An insurrectionist,' Felix heard one mutter.

Felix felt his face flush. 'It was yet another cruel and unjust tax. A silver piece for every window, indeed. To make it worse, all the fat merchants bricked up their windows and the Altdorf militia went around knocking holes in the side of poor folks' hovels. We were right to speak out.'

'There's a reward for the capture of insurrectionists,' the peddler said. 'A big reward.'

Felix stared at him. 'Of course, the Imperial cavalry were no match for my companion's axe,' he said. 'Such carnage! Heads, legs, arms everywhere. He stood on a pile of bodies.'

'They called for archers,' Gotrek said. 'We departed down a back alley. Being spitted from afar would have been an unseemly death.'

The fat peddler looked at his companions then at Gotrek, then at Felix, then back at his companions. 'A sensible man keeps out of politics,' he said to the man who had talked of rewards. He looked at Felix. 'No offence, sir.'

'None taken,' Felix said. 'You are absolutely correct.'

'Insurrectionist or no,' the old woman said, 'may Sigmar bless you if you bring my little Gunter back.'

'He is not little, Lise,' the innkeeper said. 'He is a strapping young man. Still, I hope you bring my son back. I am old and I need him to chop the wood and shoe the horses and lift the kegs and–'

'I am touched by your paternal concern, sir,' Felix interrupted. He pulled his leather cap down on his head.

Gotrek got up and looked at him. He beat his chest with one meaty hand. 'Armour is for women and girly elves,' he said.

'Perhaps I had best wear it, Gotrek. If I am to return alive with the tale of your deeds – as I did, after all, swear to do.'

'You have a point, manling. And remember that is not all you swore to do.' He turned to the innkeeper. 'How will we find the Darkstone Ring?'

Felix felt his mouth go dry. He fought to keep his hands from shaking.

'There is a trail. It runs from the road. I will take you to its start.'

'Good,' Gotrek said. 'This is too good an opportunity to miss. Tonight I will atone my sins and stand among the Iron Halls of my fathers. Great Grungni willing.'

He made a peculiar sign over his chest with his clenched right hand. 'Come, manling, let us go.' He strode out the door.

Felix picked up his pack. At the doorway the old woman stopped him and pressed something into his hand. 'Please, sir,' she said. 'Take this. It is a charm to Sigmar. It will protect you. My little Gunter wears its twin.'

And much good it's done him, Felix was about to say, but the expression on her face stopped him. It held fear, concern and perhaps hope. He was touched.

'I'll do my best, frau.'

Outside, the sky was bright with the green witchlight of the moons. Felix opened his hand. In it was a small iron hammer on a fine-linked chain. He shrugged and hung it round his neck. Gotrek and the old man were already moving down the road. He had to run to catch up.

* * *

'WHAT DO YOU think these are, manling?' Gotrek said, bending close to the ground. Ahead of them, the road continued on towards Hartzroch and Bogenhafen. Felix leaned on the league marker. This was the edge of the trail. Felix hoped the innkeeper had returned home safely.

'Tracks,' he said. 'Going north.'

'Very good, manling. They are coach tracks and they take the trail north to the Darkstone Ring.'

'The black coach?' Felix said.

'I hope so. What a glorious night! All my prayers are answered. A chance to atone and to get revenge on the swine who nearly ran me over.' Gotrek cackled gleefully but Felix could sense a change in him. He seemed tense, as if suspecting that his hour of destiny were arriving and he would meet it badly. He seemed unusually talkative.

'A coach? Does this coven consist of noblemen, manling? Is your Empire so very corrupt?'

Felix shook his head. 'I don't know. It may have a noble leader. The members are most likely local folk. They say the taint of Chaos runs deep in these out of the way places.'

Gotrek shook his head and for the first time ever he looked dismayed. 'I could weep for the folly of your people, manling. To be so corrupted that your rulers could sell themselves over to the powers of darkness, that is a terrible thing.'

'Not all men are so,' Felix said angrily. 'True, some seek easy power or the pleasures of the flesh, but they are few. Most people keep the faith. Anyway, the Elder Race are not so pure. I have heard tales of whole armies of dwarfs dedicated to the Ruinous Powers.'

Gotrek gave a low angry growl and spat on the ground. Felix gripped the hilt of his sword tighter. He wondered whether he had pushed the Trollslayer too far.

'You are correct,' Gotrek said, his voice soft and cold. 'We do not lightly talk about such things. We have vowed eternal war against the abominations you mention and their dark masters.'

'As have my own people. We have our witch hunts and our laws.'

Gotrek shook his head. 'Your people do not understand. They are soft and decadent and live far from the war. They do not understand the terrible things which gnaw at the roots of the world and seek to undermine us all. Witch hunts? Hah!' He spat on the ground. 'Laws! There is only one way to meet the threat of Chaos.'

He brandished his axe meaningfully.

THEY TRUDGED WEARILY through the forest. Overhead, the moons gleamed feverishly. Morrslieb had become ever brighter, and now its green glow stained the sky. A light mist had gathered and the terrain they moved through was bleak and wild. Rocks broke through the turf like plague spots breaking through the skin of the world.

Sometimes Felix thought he could hear great wings passing overhead, but when he looked up he could see only the glow in the sky. The mist distorted and spread so that it looked as though they walked along the bed of some infernal sea.

There was a sense of wrongness about this place, Felix decided. The air tasted foul and the hairs on the nape of his neck constantly prickled. Back when he had been a boy in Altdorf he had sat in his father's house and watched the sky grow black with menacing clouds. Then had come the most monstrous storm in living memory. Now he felt the same sense of anticipation. Mighty forces were gathering close to here, he was certain. He felt like an insect crawling over the body of a giant that could at any moment awake and crush him.

Even Gotrek seemed oppressed. He had fallen silent and did not even mumble to himself as he usually did. Now and again he would stop and motion for Felix to stand quiet then he would stand and sniff the air. Felix could see that his whole body tensed as if he strained with every nerve to catch the slightest trace of something. Then they would move on.

Felix's muscles all felt tight with tension. He wished he had not come. Surely, he told himself, my obligation to the dwarf does not mean I must face certain death. Perhaps I can slip away in the mist.

He gritted his teeth. He prided himself on being an honourable man, and the debt he owed the dwarf was real. The dwarf had risked his life to save him. Granted, at the time he had not known Gotrek was seeking death, courting it as a man courts a desirable lady. It still left him under an obligation.

He remembered the riotous drunken evening in the taverns of the Maze when they had sworn blood-brothership in that curious dwarfish rite and he had agreed to help Gotrek in his quest.

Gotrek wished his name remembered and his deeds recalled. When he had found out that Felix was a poet the dwarf had asked Felix to accompany him. At the time, in the warm glow of beery camaraderie, it had seemed a splendid idea. The Trollslayer's doomed quest had struck Felix as excellent material for an epic poem, one that would make him famous.

Little did I know, Felix thought, that it would lead to this. Hunting for monsters on Geheimnisnacht. He smiled ironically. It was easy to sing of brave deeds in the taverns and playhalls where horror was a thing conjured by the words of skilled craftsmen. Out here though it was different. His bowels felt loose with fear and the oppressive atmosphere made him want to run screaming.

Still, he tried to console himself, this is fit subject matter for a poem. If only I live to write it.

THE WOODS BECAME deeper and more tangled. The trees took on the aspect of twisted, uncanny beings. Felix felt as if they were watching him. He tried to dismiss the thought as fantasy but the mist and the ghastly moonlight only stimulated his imagination. He felt as if every pool of shadow contained a monster.

Felix looked down at the dwarf. Gotrek's face held a mixture of anticipation and fear. Felix had thought him immune to terror but now he realised it was not so. A ferocious will drove him to seek his doom. Feeling that his own death might be near at hand, Felix asked a question that he had long been afraid to utter.

'Herr Trollslayer, what was it you did that you must atone for? What crime drives you to punish yourself so?'

Gotrek looked up to him, then turned his head to gaze off into the night. Felix watched the cable-like muscles of his neck ripple like serpents as he did so.

'If another man asked me that question I would slaughter him. I make allowances for your youth and ignorance and the friendship rite we have undergone. Such a death would make me a kin-slayer. That is a terrible crime. Such crimes we do not talk about.'

Felix had not realised the dwarf was so attached to him. Gotrek looked up at him as if expecting a response.

'I understand,' Felix said.

'Do you, manling? Do you really?' The Trollslayer's voice was as harsh as stones breaking.

Felix smiled ruefully. In that moment he saw the gap that separated man from dwarf. He would never understand their strange taboos, their obsession with oaths and order and pride. He could not see what would drive the Trollslayer to carry out his self-imposed death sentence.

'Your people are too harsh with themselves,' he said.

'Yours are too soft,' the Trollslayer replied. They fell into silence. Both were startled by a quiet, mad laugh. Felix turned, whipping up his blade into the guard position. Gotrek raised his axe.

Out of the mists something shambled. Once it had been a man, Felix decided. The outline was still there. It was as if some mad god held the creature close to a daemonic fire until flesh dripped and ran, then had left it to set in a new and abhorrent form.

'This night we will dance,' it said, in a high-pitched voice that held no hint of sanity. 'Dance and touch.'

It reached out gently to Felix and stroked his arm. Felix recoiled in horror as fingers like clumps of maggots rose towards his face.

'This night at the stone we will dance and touch and rub.' It made as if to embrace him. It smiled, showing short, pointed teeth. Felix stood quietly. He felt like a spectator, distanced from the event that was happening. He pulled back and put the point of his sword against the thing's chest.

'Come no closer,' Felix warned. The thing smiled. Its mouth seemed to grow wider, it showed more small sharp teeth. Its lips rolled back till the bottom half of the face seemed all wet glistening gum and the jaw sank lower like that of a snake. It pushed forward against the sword till beads of blood glistened on its chest. It gave a gurgling, idiotic laugh.

'Dance and touch and rub and eat,' it said, and with inhuman swiftness it writhed around the sword and leapt for Felix. Swift as it was, the Trollslayer was swifter. In mid-leap his axe caught its neck. The head rolled into the night; a red fountain gushed.

This is not happening, thought Felix.

'What was that? A daemon?' Gotrek asked. Felix could hear the excitement in his voice.

'I think it was once a man,' Felix said. 'One of the tainted ones marked by Chaos. They are abandoned at birth.'

'That one spoke your tongue.'

'Sometimes the taint does not show till they are older. Relatives think they are sick and protect them till they make their way to the woods and vanish.'

'Their kin protect such abominations?'

'It happens. We don't talk about it. It is hard to turn your back on people you love even if they change.'

The dwarf stared at him in disbelief, then shook his head.

'Too soft,' he said. 'Too soft.'

THE AIR WAS still. Sometimes Felix thought he sensed presences moving in the trees about him and froze nervously, peering into the mist, searching for moving shadows. The encounter with the tainted one had brought home to him the danger of the situation. He felt within him a great fear and a great anger.

Part of the anger was directed at himself for feeling the fear. He was sick and ashamed. He decided that whatever happened he would not repeat his error, standing like a sheep to be slaughtered.

'What was that?' Gotrek asked. Felix looked at him.

'Can't you hear it, manling? Listen! It sounds like chanting.' Felix strained to catch the sound but heard nothing. 'We are close, now. Very close.'

They pushed on in silence. As they trudged through the mist Gotrek became ever more cautious and left the trail, using the long grass for cover. Felix joined him.

Now he could hear the chanting. It sounded as though it was coming from scores of throats. Some of the voices were human, others were deep and bestial. There were male voices and female voices mingled with the slow beat of a drum, the clash of cymbals and discordant piping.

Felix could make out one word only, repeated over and over till it was driven into his consciousness. The word was 'Slaanesh'.

Felix shuddered. Slaanesh, dark lord of unspeakable pleasures. It was a name that conjured up the worst depths of depravity. It was whispered in the drug dens and vice houses of Altdorf by those so jaded that they sought pleasures beyond human understanding. It was a name associated with corruption and excess and the dark underbelly of Imperial society. For

those who followed Slaanesh no stimulation was too bizarre,
no pleasure forbidden.

'The mist covers us,' Felix whispered to the Trollslayer.

'Hist! Be quiet. We must get closer.'

They crept forward slowly. The long wet grass dragged at
Felix's body, and soon he was damp. Ahead he could see bea-
cons burning in the dark. The scent of blazing wood and
cloying sickly-sweet incense filled the air. He looked around,
hoping that no latecomer would blunder into them. He felt
absurdly exposed.

Inch by inch they advanced. Gotrek dragged his battleaxe along
behind him and once Felix touched its sharp blade with his fingers. He cut himself and fought back a desire to scream out.

They reached the edge of the long grass and found themselves staring at a crude ring of six obscenely-shaped stones
amid which stood a monolithic slab. The stones glowed
greenly with the light of some luminous fungus. On top of
each was a brazier which gave off clouds of smoke. Beams of
pallid, green moonlight illuminated a hellish scene.

Within the ring danced six humans, masked and garbed in
long cloaks. The cloaks were thrown back over one shoulder
revealing naked bodies, both male and female. On one hand
the revellers each wore finger cymbals which they clashed, in
the other they carried switches of birch with which they each
lashed the dancer in front.

'Ygrak tu amat Slaanesh!' they cried

Felix could see that some of the bodies were marked by
bruises. The dancers seemed to feel no pain. Perhaps it was the
narcotic effect of the incense.

Around the stone ring lolled figures of horror. The drummer
was a huge man with the head of a stag and cloven hooves.
Near him sat a piper with the head of a dog and hands with
suckered fingers. A large crowd of tainted women and men
writhed on the ground nearby.

Some of their bodies were subtly distorted: men who were
tall with thin, pin heads; short, fat women with three eyes and
three breasts. Others were barely recognisable as once having
been human. There were scale-covered man-serpents and wolf-
headed furred beasts mingling with things that were all teeth
and mouth and other orifices. Felix could barely breathe. He
watched the entire proceeding with mounting fear.

The drums beat faster, the rhythmic chanting increased in pace, the piping became ever louder and more discordant as the dancers became more frenzied, lashing themselves and their companions until bloody weals became visible. Then there was a clash of cymbals and all fell silent.

Felix thought they had been spotted, and he froze. The smoke of the incense filled his nostrils and seemed to amplify all his senses. He felt even more remote and disconnected from reality. There was a sharp, stabbing pain in his side. He was startled to realise that Gotrek had elbowed him in the ribs. He was pointing to something beyond the stone ring.

Felix struggled to see what loomed in the mist. Then he realised that it was the black coach. In the sudden, shocking silence he heard its door swing open. He held his breath and waited to see what would emerge.

A figure seemed to take shape out of the mist. It was tall and masked, and garbed in layered cloaks of many pastel colours. It moved with calm authority and in its arms it carried something swaddled in brocade cloth. Felix looked at Gotrek but he was watching the unfolding scene with fanatical intensity. Felix wondered if the dwarf had lost his nerve at this late hour.

The newcomer stepped forward into the stone circle.

'Amak tu amat Slaanesh!' it cried, raising its bundle on high. Felix could see that it was a child, though whether living or dead he could not tell.

'Ygrak tu amat Slaanesh! Tzarkol taen amat Slaanesh!' The crowd responded ecstatically.

The cloaked man stared out at the surrounding faces, and it seemed to Felix that the stranger gazed straight at him with calm, brown eyes. He wondered if the coven-master knew they were there and was playing with them.

'Amak tu Slaanesh!' the man cried in a clear voice.

'Amak klessa! Amat Slaanesh!' responded the crowd. It was clear to Felix that some evil ritual had begun. As the rite progressed, the coven-master moved closer to the altar with slow ceremonial steps. Felix felt his mouth go dry. He licked his lips. Gotrek watched the events as if hypnotised.

The child was placed on the altar with a thunderous rumble of drum beats. Now the six dancers each stood beside a pillar, legs astride it, clutching at the stone suggestively. As the ritual

progressed they ground themselves against the pillars with
slow sinuous movements.

From within his robes the master produced a long wavy-
bladed knife. Felix wondered whether the dwarf was going to
do something. He could hardly bear to watch.

Slowly the knife was raised, high over the cultist's head. Felix
forced himself to look. An ominous presence hovered over the
scene. Mist and incense seemed to be clotting together and
congealing, and within the cloud Felix thought he could make
out a grotesque form writhe and begin to materialise. Felix
could bear the tension no longer.

'No!' he shouted.

He and the Trollslayer emerged from the long grass and
marched shoulder-to-shoulder towards the stone ring. At first
the cultists didn't seem to notice them, but finally the
demented drumming stopped and the chanting faded and the
cult-master turned to glare at them, astonished.

For a moment everyone stared. No one seemed to understand what was happening. Then the cult-master pointed the
knife at them and screamed; 'Kill the interlopers!'

The revellers moved forward in a wave. Felix felt something
tug at his leg and then a sharp pain. When he looked down he
saw a creature, half woman, half serpent, gnawing at his ankle.
He kicked out, pulling his leg free and stabbed down with his
sword.

A shock passed up his arm as the blade hit bone. He began
to run, following in the wake of Gotrek who was hacking his
way towards the altar. The mighty double-bladed axe rose and
fell rhythmically and left a trail of red ruin in its path. The
cultists seemed drugged and slow to respond but, horrifyingly,
they showed no fear. Men and women, tainted and untainted,
threw themselves towards the intruders with no thought for
their own lives.

Felix hacked and stabbed at anyone who came close. He put
his blade under the ribs and into the heart of a dog-faced man
who leapt at him. As he tried to tug his blade free a woman
with claws and a man with mucous-covered skin leapt on him.
Their weight bore him over, knocking the wind from him.

He felt the woman's talons scratch at his face as he put his
foot under her stomach and kicked her off. Blood rolled down
into his eyes from the cuts. The man had fallen badly, but

leapt to grab his throat. Felix fumbled for his dagger with his left hand while he caught the man's throat with his right. The man writhed. He was difficult to grip because of his coating of slime. His own hands tightened inexorably on Felix's throat in return and he rubbed himself against Felix, panting with pleasure.

Blackness threatened to overcome the poet. Little silver points flared before his eyes. He felt an overwhelming urge to relax and fall forward into the darkness. Somewhere far away he heard Gotrek's bellowed war-cry. With an effort of will Felix jerked his dagger clear of its scabbard and plunged it into his assailant's ribs. The creature stiffened and grinned, revealing rows of eel-like teeth. He gave an ecstatic moan even as he died.

'Slaanesh, take me,' the man shrieked. 'Ah, the pain, the lovely pain!'

Felix pulled himself to his feet just as the clawed woman rose to hers. He lashed out with his boot, connected with her jaw. There was a crunch, and she fell backwards. Felix shook his head to clear the blood from his eyes.

The majority of the cultists had concentrated on Gotrek. This had kept Felix alive. The dwarf was trying to hack his way towards the heart of the stone circle. Even as he moved, the press of bodies against him slowed him down. Felix could see that he bled from dozens of small cuts.

The ferocious energy of the dwarf was terrible to see. He frothed at the mouth and ranted as he chopped, sending limbs and heads everywhere. He was covered in a filthy matting of gore, but in spite of his sheer ferocity Felix could tell the fight was going against Gotrek. Even as he watched, a cloaked reveller hit the dwarf with a club and Gotrek went down under a wave of bodies. So he has met his doom, thought Felix, just as he desired.

Beyond the ruck of the melee, the cult-master had regained his composure. Once more he began to chant, and raised the dagger on high. The terrible shape that had been forming from the mist seemed once again to coalesce.

Felix had a premonition that if it took on full substance they were doomed. He could not fight his way through the bodies that surrounded the Trollslayer. For a long moment he watched the curve-bladed knife reflecting the Morrslieb light.

Then he drew back his own dagger. 'Sigmar guide my hand,' he prayed and threw. The blade flew straight and true to the throat of the High Priest, hitting beneath the mask where flesh was exposed. With a gurgle, the cult-master toppled backwards.

A long whine of frustration filled the air and the mist seemed to evaporate. The shape within the mist vanished. As one, the cultists looked up in shock. The tainted ones turned to stare at him. Felix found himself confronted by the mad glare of dozens of unfriendly eyes. He stood immobile and very, very afraid. The silence was deathly.

Then there was an almighty roar and Gotrek emerged from amidst the pile of bodies, pummelling about him with ham-sized fists. He reached down and from somewhere retrieved his axe. He shortened his grip on the haft and laid about him with its shaft. Felix scooped up his own sword and ran to join him. They fought through the crush until they were back to back.

The cultists, filled with fear at the loss of their leader, began to flee into the night and mist. Soon Felix and Gotrek stood alone under the shadows of the Darkstone Ring.

Gotrek looked at Felix balefully, blood clotted in his crested hair. In the witch-light he looked daemonic. 'I am robbed of a mighty death, manling.'

He raised his axe menacingly. Felix wondered if he were still berserk and about to chop him down in spite of their binding oath. Gotrek began to advance slowly towards him. Then the dwarf grinned. 'It would seem the gods preserve me for a greater doom yet.'

He planted his axe hilt first into the ground and began to laugh till the tears ran down his face. Having exhausted his laughter, he turned to the altar and picked up the infant. 'It lives,' he said.

Felix began to inspect the corpses of the cloaked cultists. He unmasked them. The first one was a blonde haired-girl covered in weals and bruises. The second was a young man. He had an amulet in the shape of a hammer hanging almost mockingly round his neck.

'I don't think we'll be going back to the inn,' Felix said sadly.

* * *

ONE LOCAL TALE tells of an infant found on the steps of the temple of Shallya in Hartzroch. It was wrapped in a blood-soaked cloak of Sudenland wool, a pouch of gold lay nearby, and a steel amulet in the shape of a hammer was round its neck. The priestess swore she saw a black coach thundering away in the dawn light.

The natives of Hartzroch tell another and darker tale of how Ingrid Hauptmann and Gunter, the innkeeper's son, were slain in some horrific sacrifice to the Dark Powers. The road wardens who found the corpses up by the Darkstone Ring agreed it must have been a terrible rite. The bodies looked as if they had been chopped up with an axe wielded by a daemon.

WOLF RIDERS

'I cannot quite remember exactly how and when the
decision to head southwards in search of the lost gold of
Karak Eight Peaks was made. Alas, like so many of the
important decisions made during that period of my life, it
was taken in a tavern under the influence of enormous
quantities of alcohol. I do seem to remember an ancient
and toothless dwarf mumbling about "gold", and I
distinctly remember the insane gleam which entered into
my companion's eyes when it was described to him.

'It was perhaps typical of my companion that on no more
than this slim provocation, he was willing to risk life and
limb in the wildest and most barren places imaginable. Or
perhaps it was typical of the effect of "gold fever" on all
his people. As I was later to see, the lure of that glittering
metal had a terrifying and potent power over the minds of
all of that ancient race.

'In any event, the decision to travel beyond the Empire's
southernmost borders was a fateful one, and it led to

meetings and adventures the dreadful consequences of which haunt me still...'

—From *My Travels with Gotrek, Vol. II*, by Herr Felix Jaeger (Altdorf Press, 2505)

'HONESTLY, GENTLEMEN, I don't want any trouble,' Felix Jaeger said sincerely. He spread his empty hands wide. 'Just leave the girl alone. That's all I ask.'

The drunken trappers laughed evilly.

'Just leave the girl alone,' one of them mimicked in a high-pitched, lisping voice.

Felix looked around the trading post for support. A few hardy fellows clad in the heavy furs of mountain men looked at him with drink-fuddled eyes. The store owner, a tall, stooped man with lank hair, turned and began stacking bottles of preserves on the rough wooden shelving. There were no other customers.

One of the trappers, a huge man, loomed over him. Felix could see the particles of grease stuck in his beard. When he opened his mouth to speak, the smell of cheap brandy overwhelmed even the odour of the rancid bear fat which the trappers covered themselves with against the cold. Felix winced.

'Hey, Hef, I think we got a city boy here,' the trapper said. 'He speaks right nice.'

The one called Hef looked up from the table against which he had pinned the struggling girl.

'Aye, Lars, right pretty he talks, and all that nice golden hair, like cornstalks. Could almost take him for a girl himself.'

'When I come off the mountains anything looks good. I tell you what: you take the girl. I'll have this pretty boy.'

Felix felt his face flush. He was getting angry. He hid his anger with a smile. He wanted to avoid trouble if he could. 'Come on, gentlemen, there's no need for this. Let me buy you all a drink.'

Lars turned to Hef. The third mountain man guffawed. 'He has money too. My luck's in tonight!'

Hef smirked. Felix looked around desperately as the big man advanced on him. Damn, where was Gotrek? Why was the dwarf never around when a man needed him? He turned to face Lars. 'All right, I'm sorry I interfered. I'll just leave you gentlemen to it.'

He saw Lars relax somewhat, letting down his guard as he advanced. Felix let him come closer. He watched the trapper spread his arms as if he were about to hug him. Felix suddenly jabbed his knee hard into Lars's groin. With a whoosh like a blacksmith's bellows, all of the air ran out of the big man. He doubled over with a whimper. Felix grabbed his beard and pulled the man's head down to meet his knee.

He heard teeth break, and the trapper's head snapped backwards. Lars fell on the floor gasping for breath and clutching at his groin.

'What in the name of Taal?' Hef said. The big trapper lashed out at Felix and the force of the blow sent him reeling across the room into a table. He tipped over a tankard of ale.

'Sorry,' Felix apologised to the drink's startled owner. Felix struggled to lift the table and hurl it at his assailant. He strained until he thought the muscles in his back would crack.

The drunk looked at him and smiled wickedly. 'You can't lift it. It's nailed to the floor. In case of fights.'

'Thanks for telling me,' Felix said, feeling someone grab him by the hair and slam his head into the table. Pain smashed through his skull. Black spots danced before his eyes. His face felt wet. I'm bleeding, he thought then realised it was just the spilled beer. His head was smashed into the table a second time. As if from very far away he heard footsteps approaching.

'Hold him, Kell. We're gonna have us some fun for what he did to Lars.' He recognised the voice as belonging to Hef.

Desperately Felix jabbed backward with his elbow, ramming it into the hard muscle of Kell's stomach. The grip on his hair loosened somewhat. Felix tore free and he turned to face his assailants. With his right hand he frantically fumbled for the beer stein. Through a haze he saw the two gigantic trappers closing in. The girl was gone – Felix saw the door close behind her. He could hear her start shouting for help. Hef was loosening a knife in his belt. Felix's fingers closed over the handle of the stein. He lashed out and hit Kell square in the face with it. The trapper's head snapped around, then he spat blood and turned back to Felix, smiling moronically.

Fingers, muscled like steel bands, grabbed Felix's wrist. The pressure forced him reluctantly to drop the stein. Despite frantic resistance, Felix's arm was inexorably forced up his back by Kell's superior strength. The smell of bear fat and body odour was almost overpowering. Felix snarled and tried to writhe free but his struggles were fruitless.

Something sharp jabbed into his throat. Felix looked down. Hef brandished a long-bladed knife at his throat. Felix smelled its well-oiled steel. He saw his own red blood trickle down its central channel. Felix froze. All Hef had to do was lean forward and Felix would be walking in the kingdom of Morr.

'That was downright unfriendly, boy,' Hef said. 'Old Lars was only bein' affectionate and you had to go and bust his teeth. Now what you reckon we should do about that, we bein' his friends n'all?'

'Kill the thnotling fondler,' Lars gasped. Felix felt Kell push his arm further up his back until he feared it would break. He moaned in pain.

'Reckon we'll just do that,' Hef said.

'You can't,' the trader behind the bar whined. 'That'd be murder.'

'Shut up, Pike! Who asked you?'

Felix could see they meant to do it. They were full of drunken violence and ready to kill. Felix had just given them the excuse they needed.

'Been a long time since I killed me a pretty boy,' Hef said, pushing his knife forward just a fraction. Felix grimaced with the pain. 'Gonna beg, pretty boy? Gonna beg for your life?'

'Go to hell,' Felix said. He would have liked to spit but his mouth felt dry and his knees were weak. He was shaking. He closed his eyes.

'Not so polite now, city boy?' Felix felt thick laughter rumble in Kell's throat. What a place to die, he thought incongruously, some hell-spawned outpost in the Grey Mountains.

There was a blast of chill air and the sound of a door opening.

'The first one to hurt the manling dies instantly,' said a deep voice that grated like stone crushed against stone. 'The second one I take my time over.'

Felix opened his eyes. Over Hef's shoulders he could see Gotrek Gurnisson, the Trollslayer. The dwarf stood silhouetted in the doorway, his squat form filling it widthwise. He was only the height of a boy of nine years but he was muscled like two strong men. Torch light illuminated the strange tattoos that covered his half-naked body and turned his eye sockets into shadowy caves from which mad eyes glittered.

Hef laughed, then spoke without turning round. 'Get lost, stranger, or we'll deal with you after we've finished your friend.'

Felix felt the grip on his arm relax. Over his shoulder, Kell's hand pointed to the doorway.

'That so?' Gotrek said, stomping into the room, shaking his head to clear the snow from his huge crest of orange-dyed hair. The chain that ran from his nose to his right ear jingled. 'By the time I've finished with you, you'll sing as high as a girly elf.'

Hef laughed again and turned around to face Gotrek. His laughter died into a sputtering cough. Colour drained from his face until it was corpse-white. Gotrek grinned nastily at him, revealing missing teeth, then he ran his thumb across the blade of the great two-handed axe that he carried in one ham-sized fist. Blood dripped freely from the cut but the dwarf just grinned more wider. The knife in Hef's hand clattered to the floor.

'We don't want no trouble,' Hef said. 'Leastwise, not with a Trollslayer.'

Felix didn't blame him. No sane man would cross a member of that doomed and death-seeking berserker cult. Gotrek glared at them, then lightly tapped the hilt of his axe against the floor. While Kell was distracted, Felix seized the opportunity to put some ground between himself and the mountain man.

Hef was starting to panic. 'Look, we don't want no trouble. We was just funnin'.'

Gotrek laughed evilly. 'I like your idea of fun. I think I'll have some myself.'

The Trollslayer advanced towards Hef. Felix saw Lars pick himself up and start crawling towards the door, hoping to slip past the Trollslayer while he was distracted. Gotrek brought his boot down on Lars's hand with a crunch that made Felix wince. It was not Lars's night, he decided.

'Where do you think you're going? Better stay with your friends. Two against one is hardly fair odds.'

Hef had broken down completely. 'Don't kill us,' he pleaded. Kell, meanwhile, had moved away, bringing him close to Felix again. Gotrek had moved right in front of Hef. The blade of the Slayer's axe lay against Hef's throat. Felix could see the runes on the ancient blade glinting redly in the torchlight.

Slowly Gotrek shook his head. 'What's the matter? There's three of you. You thought they were good enough odds against the manling. Stomach gone out of you?'

Hef nodded numbly; he looked as if he was about to cry. In his eyes Felix could see a superstitious terror of the dwarf. He seemed ready to faint.

Gotrek pointed to the door. 'Get out!' he roared. 'I'll not soil my blade on cowards like you.'

The trappers scurried for the door, Lars limping badly. Felix saw the girl step aside to let them by. She closed the door behind them.

Gotrek glared at Felix. 'Can't I even stop to answer a call of nature without you getting yourself into trouble?'

'PERHAPS I SHOULD escort you back,' Felix said, inspecting the girl closely. She was small and thin; her face would have been plain except for the large dark eyes. She tugged her cloak of coarse Sudenland wool about her and hugged the package she had purchased in the trading post to her chest. She smiled shyly up at him. The smile transformed that pale hungry face, Felix thought, gave it beauty.

'Perhaps you could, if it's not too much trouble.'

'No trouble whatsoever,' he said. 'Maybe those ruffians are still lurking about out there.'

'I doubt that. They seemed too afraid of your friend.'

'Let me help you with those herbs, then.'

'The mistress told me to get them specifically. They are for the relief of the frostbitten. I would feel better if I carried them.'

Felix shrugged. They stepped out into the chill air, breath coming out in clouds. In the night sky the Grey Mountains loomed like giants. The light of both moons caught on their snow-capped peaks so that they looked like islands in the sky, floating above a sea of shadow.

They walked through the squalid shanty-town which surrounded the trading post. In the distance Felix saw lights, heard lowing cattle and the muffled hoofbeats of horses. They were heading towards a campsite where more people were arriving.

Gaunt, hollow-cheeked soldiers, clad in tattered tunics on which could be seen the sign of a grinning wolf, escorted carts drawn by thin oxen. Tired looking drivers in the garb of peasants gazed at him. Women sat beside the drivers with shawls drawn tight, headscarves all but obscuring their features. Sometimes children peeked out over the back of the carts to stare at them.

'What's going on?' Felix asked. 'It looks like a whole village on the move.' The girl looked at the carts and then back at him.

'We are the people of Gottfried von Diehl. We follow him into exile, to the land of the Border Princes.'

Felix paused to look north. More carts were coming down the trail, and behind them were stragglers, limping on foot, clutching at thin sacks as if they contained all the gold of Araby. Felix shook his head, puzzled.

'You must have come through Blackfire Pass,' he said. He and Gotrek had come by the old dwarf routes under the mountain. 'And it's late in the season for that. The first blizzards must already be setting in up there. The pass is only open in the summer.'

'Our liege was given until year's end to leave the Empire.' She turned and began walking into the ring of wagons that had been set up to give some protection from the wind. 'We set out in good time but there was a string of accidents that slowed us down. In the pass itself we were caught by an avalanche. We lost many people.'

She paused, as if remembering some personal grief.

'Some say it was the "Von Diehl Curse". That the baron can never outrun it.'

Felix followed her. On the fires sat a few cooking pots. There was one huge cauldron from which steam emerged. The girl pointed to it.

'The mistress's cauldron. She will be expecting the herbs.'

'Is your mistress a witch?' Felix asked. She looked at him seriously.

'No, sir. She is a sorceress with good credentials, trained in Middenheim itself. She is the baron's adviser in matters magical.'

The girl moved towards the steps of a large caravan, covered in mystical signs. She began to climb the stairs. She halted, hand poised on the handle of the door, then she turned to face Felix.

'Thank you for your help,' she said.

She leaned forward and kissed him on the cheek then turned to open the door. Felix laid his hand on her shoulder, restraining her gently.

'A moment,' he said. 'What is your name?'

'Kirsten,' she said. 'And yours?'

'Felix. Felix Jaeger.'

She smiled at him again before she vanished inside the caravan. Felix stood looking at the closed door, slightly bemused. Then, feeling as if he was walking on air, he strolled back to the trading post.

'ARE YOU MAD?' Gotrek Gurnisson demanded. 'You want us to travel with some renegade duke and his rag-tag entourage. Have you forgotten why we've come here?'

Felix looked around to see that no one was looking at them. Not much chance of that, he decided. He and the Trollslayer nursed their beer in the darkest recess of the trading post. A few drunks lay snoring on the trestle tables and the sullen glowers of the dwarf kept the casually curious at bay.

Felix leaned forward conspiratorially. 'But look, it makes perfect sense. We are heading through the Border Princes and so are they. It will be safer if we ride with them.'

Gotrek looked at Felix dangerously. 'Are you implying I fear some peril on this road?'

Felix shook his head. 'No. All I'm saying is that it would make our journey easier and we might get paid for our efforts if the baron could be persuaded to take us on as mercenaries.'

Gotrek brightened at the mention of money. All dwarfs are misers at heart, thought Felix. Gotrek appeared to consider for a second, then shook his head.

'No. If this baron has been exiled he's a criminal and he's not getting his hands on my gold.'

He ducked his head and looked around with paranoid shiftiness. 'That treasure is ours, yours and mine. Mostly mine, of course, since I'll do the bulk of the fighting.'

Felix felt like laughing. There was nothing worse than a dwarf in the throes of gold-lust.

'Gotrek, we don't even know if there is any treasure. All we've got to go on are the ramblings of some senile old prospector who claims to have seen the lost horde of Karak Eight Peaks. Faragrim couldn't remember his own name half the time.'

'Faragrim was a dwarf, manling. A dwarf never forgets the sight of gold. You know the problem with your people? You have no respect for your elders. Among my people Faragrim is treated with respect.'

'No wonder your people are in such dire straits then,' Felix muttered.

'What was that?'

'Nothing. Just answer me this. Why didn't Faragrim return for the treasure himself? He's had eighteen years.'

'Because he showed proper fiscal caution–'

'Meanness, you mean.'

'Have it your way, manling. He was crippled by the guardian. And he could never find anybody he could trust.'

'Why suddenly tell you then?'

'Are you implying I am not trustworthy, manling?'

'No. I think he wanted rid of you, he wanted you out of his tavern. I think he invented the cock-and-bull story about the world's largest treasure guarded by the world's largest troll because he knew you would fall for it. He knew it would put a hundred leagues between you and his ale cellar.'

Gotrek's beard bristled and he growled angrily. 'I am not such a fool, manling. Faragrim swore to the truth on the beards of all his ancestors.'

Felix groaned loudly. 'And no dwarf has ever broken an oath, I suppose?'

'Well, very rarely,' Gotrek admitted. 'But I believe this one.'

Felix saw that it was no use. Gotrek wanted the story to be true, so for him it was true.

He's like a man in love, thought Felix, unable to see his beloved's frailties for the wall of illusions he has built around her. Gotrek stroked his beard and stared into space, lost in contemplation of the troll-guarded horde. Felix decided to play his trump card.

'It would mean we wouldn't have to walk,' he said.

'What?' Gotrek grunted.

'If we sign on with the baron. We could hitch a ride on a cart. You're always complaining that your feet hurt. This is your chance to give them a rest.

'Just think about it,' he added enticingly. 'We get paid and you don't get sore feet.'

Gotrek appeared to contemplate this once more. 'I can see I'll get no peace unless I agree to your scheme. I'll go along with it on one condition.'

'What's that?'

'No mention of our quest. Not to anybody.'

Felix agreed. Gotrek raised one bushy eyebrow and looked at him cunningly.

'Don't think I don't know why you're so keen to travel with this baron, manling.'

'What do you mean?'

'You're enamoured of that chit of a girl you left here with earlier, aren't you?'

'No,' Felix spluttered. 'Whatever gave you that idea?'

Gotrek laughed uproariously, waking several slumbering drunks.

'Then why has your face gone all red, manling?' he shouted triumphantly.

FELIX KNOCKED ON the door of the caravan he had been told belonged to the baron's master-of arms.

'Come in,' a voice said. Felix opened the door and his nostrils were assailed with the smell of bear fat. Felix reached for the hilt of his sword.

Inside the caravan, five men were crowded. Three Felix recognised as the trappers he had met the previous evening. Of the others, one was young, richly dressed and fine featured, hair cut short in the fashion of the warrior nobility. The other was a tall, powerfully built man clad in buckskins. He was tanned and appeared to be in his late twenties although his hair was silver grey. He had a quiver of black-fletched arrows slung over his back and a powerful longbow lay near his hand. There seemed to be a family resemblance between the two men.

'Thatsh tha bashtard,' Lars said through his missing teeth. The two strangers exchanged looks.

Felix stared at them warily. The grey-haired man inspected him, casually assessing him.

'So you're the young man who broke the teeth of one of my guides,' he said.

'One of your guides?'

'Yes, Manfred and I hired them last season to steer us across the lowlands, along Thunder River.'

'They're mountain men,' Felix said, stalling for time, wondering how much trouble he was in.

'They're trappers,' the well-dressed youth said, in a cultured accent. 'They cross the lowlands in search of game too.'

Felix spread his hands. 'I didn't know.'

'What do you want here?' Greyhair asked.

'I'm looking for work, as a hired blade. I was looking for the baron's master-of arms.'

'That's me,' Greyhair said. 'Dieter. Also the Baron's Chief Forester, Master Of Hounds and Falconer.'

'My uncle's estate has fallen on rather hard times,' the young man said.

'This is Manfred, nephew and heir to Gottfried von Diehl, Baron of the Vennland Marches.'

'Former baron,' Manfred corrected. 'Since Countess Emmanuelle saw fit to banish my uncle and confiscate our lands rather than punish the real malefactors.'

He noted Felix's quizzical look. 'Religious differences, you know? My family come from the north and follow blessed Ulric. All our southern neighbours are devout Sigmarites. In these intolerant times it was all the excuse they needed to seize the lands they coveted. Since they were Countess Emmanuelle's cousins we get exiled for starting a war.'

He shook his head in disgust. 'Imperial politics, eh?'

Dieter shrugged. He turned to the mountain men. 'Wait outside,' he said. 'We have business to conduct with Herr…?'

'Jaeger. Felix Jaeger.'

The trappers filed past. Lars gave Felix a hate-filled look as he came abreast. Felix looked straight into his blood-shot eyes. Their gazes locked for a second, then the trappers were gone, leaving only the whiff of bear fat hanging in the air.

'I fear you have made an enemy there,' Manfred said.

'I'm not worried.'

'You should be, Herr Jaeger. Such men hold grudges,' Dieter said. 'You say you are seeking employment?'

Felix nodded. 'My companion and I–'

'The Trollslayer?' Dieter raised an eyebrow.

'Gotrek Gurnisson, yes.'

'If you want a job, you've got one. The Border Princes are a violent place and we could do with two such warriors. Unfortunately we cannot afford to pay much.'

'My uncle's estates are now poor,' Manfred explained.

'We do not require much more than bed, board and carriage,' Felix said.

Dieter laughed. 'Just as well really. You can travel with us if you wish. If we are attacked you'll have to fight.'

'We are employed?'

Dieter handed him two gold coins. 'You have taken the baron's crown. You are with us.' The grey-haired man opened the door. 'Now, if you excuse us, I have a journey to plan.'

Felix bowed to each of them and exited.

'Just a second.'

Felix turned and saw Manfred jump down from the caravan after him. The young noble smiled.

'Dieter is a brusque man but you will get used to him.'

'I'm sure I will, milord.'

'Call me Manfred. We are on the frontier, not at the Court of the Countess of Nuln. Rank has less meaning here.'

'Very well, milor– Manfred.'

'I just wanted to tell you that you did the right thing last night. Standing up for the girl, even if she is the servant of that witch. I appreciate it.'

'Thank you. May I ask a question?'

Manfred nodded. Felix cleared his throat. 'The name of Manfred von Diehl is not unknown among the scholars of Altdorf, my home city. As a playwright.'

Manfred beamed broadly. 'I am he. By Ulric, an educated man! Who would have thought to find one here? I can tell you and I are going to get along, Herr Jaeger. Have you seen Strange Flower? Did you like it?'

Felix considered his answer carefully. He had not cared for the play, which dealt with the degeneration of a noblewoman into madness when she found out that she was a mutant, devolving to beasthood. Strange Flower was lacking that open-hearted humanity to be found in the works of the Empire's greatest playwright, Detlef Sierck. However, it had been very topical in these dark days when the number of mutations was apparently increasing. It had been banned by Countess Emmanuelle, Felix remembered.

'It was very powerful, Manfred. Very haunting.'

'Haunting, very good! Very good indeed! I must go now, visit my ailing uncle. I hope to talk to you again before the journey is complete.'

They bowed and the nobleman turned and walked away.

Felix stared after him, unable to reconcile this amiable eccentric young nobleman and the brooding, Chaos-haunted images of his work. Among the cognoscenti of Altdorf,

Manfred von Diehl was known as a brilliant playwright – and
a blasphemous one.

BY MID-MORNING the exiles were ready to leave. At the front of
the long, straggling line, Felix could see a tired-looking, white-
haired old man, clad in a cloak of sable skin and mounted on
a black charger. He rode under the unfurled wolf banner that
was held by Dieter. Beside him Manfred leaned over to say
something to the old man. The baron gestured and the whole
caravan of his people began to roll forward.

Felix felt a thrill pass through him at the sight of it all. He
drank in the spectacle of the line of wagons and carts with their
armed escort of mounted and armoured warriors. He clambered aboard the supply wagon that he and Gotrek had
commandeered from a crabbed old servant dressed in baronial
livery.

Around them the mountains jutted skyward like grey giants.
Trees dotted their sides and streams ran like quicksilver down
their flanks towards the source of Thunder River. Rain, mingled
with snow, softened the harsh outline of the landscape and lent
it a wild loveliness.

'Time to go again,' Gotrek moaned, clutching his head, eyes
bleary and hung-over.

They rumbled forward, taking their place in the line. Behind
them men-at-arms shouldered their crossbows, drew their
cloaks tight about themselves and began to march. Their oaths
mingled with the curses and the whipcracks of the drivers and
the lowing of the oxen. A baby started crying. Somewhere
behind them a woman began to sing in a low musical voice.
The child's squalling quietened. Felix leaned forward, hoping
to catch sight of Kirsten among the people trudging through
the sleet towards the rolling hills that unfolded below them
like a map.

He felt almost at peace, drawn in to all that human motion,
as if he were being borne by a river towards his goal. He already
felt part of this small itinerant community, a sensation he had
not enjoyed for a long time. He smiled, but was drawn from his
reverie by Gotrek's elbow in his ribs.

'Keep your eyes peeled, manling. Orcs and goblins haunt
these mountains and the lands below.'

Felix glared at him, but when he gazed once more at his

surroundings it was not to appreciate their wild beauty. He was
keeping watch for possible ambush sites.

FELIX LOOKED BACK at the mountains. He was not sorry to be
leaving those bleak highlands. Several times they had been
assaulted by green-skinned goblins whose shields bore the sign
of a crimson claw. The wolf-riders had been beaten back, but
with casualties. Felix was red-eyed from lack of sleep. Like all
the warriors, he had taken double stints on watch, for the
raiders attacked at night. Only Gotrek seemed to be disappointed by the lack of pursuit.

'By Grungni,' the dwarf said. 'We won't see them again, not
since Dieter shot their leader. They're all cowards without the
big bully-boys to put fire in their bellies. Pity! Nothing beats
the slaughter of a few gobbos for working up an appetite.
Healthy exercise is good for the digestion.'

Felix gave him a jaundiced look. He jerked a thumb towards
a covered wagon from which Kirsten and a tall middle-aged
woman descended. 'I'm sure the wounded in that cart would
disagree with your idea of healthy exercise, Gotrek.'

The dwarf shrugged. 'In this life, manling, people get hurt.
Just be glad it wasn't your turn.'

Felix had had enough. He clambered down from the seat of
the wagon and dropped off onto the muddy ground.

'Don't worry, Gotrek. I intend to be around to complete your
saga. I wouldn't want to break a sworn oath, would I?'

Gotrek stared at him, as if suspecting a hint of sarcasm. Felix
made his expression carefully bland. The dwarf took the idea of
Felix's composition seriously; he wanted to be the hero of a
saga after his death, and he kept the educated Felix around to
make sure of it. Shaking his head, Felix walked over to where
Kirsten and her mistress stood.

'Good day, Frau Winter. Kirsten.' The two women surveyed
him wearily. A frown crossed the sorceress's long face, although
no expression seemed to flicker in her hooded, reptilian eyes.
She adjusted one of the raven's feathers pinned in her hair.

'What's good about it, Herr Jaeger? Two more men dead from
wounds. Those arrows were poisoned. By Taal, I hate those
wolf-riders.'

'Where's Doctor Stockhausen? I thought he would be helping
you.'

The older woman smiled – a little cynically, Felix thought.

'He's seeing to the baron's heir. Young Manfred got his arm nicked. Stockhausen would rather let good men die than have little Manfred injured.'

She turned and walked away. Her hair and cloak fluttered in the breeze.

'Pay no attention to the mistress,' Kirsten said. 'Master Manfred lampooned her in one of his plays. She's always resented it. She's a good woman really.'

Felix looked at her, wondering why his heartbeat seemed so loud and his palms so sweaty. He remembered Gotrek's words back in the tavern, and felt his face flush. All right, he admitted, he found Kirsten attractive. What was wrong with that? Maybe the fact that she might not be attracted to him. He looked around, feeling tongue-tied, trying to think of something to say. Nearby, children were playing soldiers.

'How are you?' he asked eventually.

She looked a little shaky. 'Fine. I was afraid last night, with the howling of the wolves and the arrows coming down, but now… Well, during the day it all seems so unreal.'

Behind them, from the wagon, came the groans of a man in agony. She turned momentarily to look, then hardness passed across her face and settled like a mask.

'It's not nice working with the wounded,' Felix said.

She shrugged. 'You get used to it.'

Felix was chilled to see that expression on the face of a woman her age. It was one he had seen on the faces of mercenaries, men whose profession was death. Looking around, he could see children playing near the cart of the wounded. One was firing an imaginary crossbow; another gurgled, clutched his chest and fell over. Felix felt isolated and suddenly very far from home. The safe life of poet and scholar he had left back in the Empire seemed to have happened to someone else a long time ago. The laws and their enforcers he had taken for granted had been left behind at the Grey Mountains.

'Life is cheap here, isn't it?' he said. Kirsten looked at him and her face softened. She linked her arm with his.

'Come, let's go where the air is cleaner,' she said.

Behind them the shrieks of the playing children mingled with the groans of the dying men.

* * *

FELIX CAUGHT SIGHT of the town as they emerged from the hills. It was late afternoon. To the left, the east, he could see the curve of the fast-flowing Thunder River and beyond that the mighty peaks of the World's Edge Mountains. South he could see another range of hills marching bleakly into the distance. They were bare and foreboding and something about them made Felix shudder.

In a valley between the two ranges nestled a small walled town. White shapes that could have been sheep were being herded through the gates. Felix thought he saw some figures moving on the walls, but at this distance he could not be sure.

Dieter beckoned for him to approach. 'You are fair-spoken,' he said. 'Ride down and make parlay. Tell the people there that we mean them no harm.'

Felix just looked at the tall, gaunt man. What he means, thought Felix, is that I am expendable, just in case the people aren't friendly. Felix considered telling him to go to hell. Dieter must have guessed his thoughts.

'You took the baron's crown,' he said plainly.

It was true, Felix admitted. He also considered taking a hot bath and drinking in a real tavern, sleeping with a roof over his head – all the luxuries that even the most primitive frontier town could offer. The prospect was very tempting.

'Get me a horse,' he said. 'And a truce banner.'

As he clambered up on to the skittish war-horse, he tried not to think about what suspicious people armed with bows might do to the messenger of a potential enemy.

A CROSSBOW BOLT hissed through the air and stuck quivering in the earth in front of the hooves of his steed. Felix struggled to control the animal, as it reared. At times like these he was glad his father had insisted that riding be part of the education of a wealthy young gentleman of means.

'Come no closer, stranger, or, white banner or no, I'll have you filled full of bolts.' The voice was coarse but powerful. Its owner was obviously used to giving commands and having them obeyed. Felix wrestled his steed back under control.

'I am the herald of Gottfried von Diehl, Baron of the Vennland Marches,' Felix called. 'We mean no harm. We seek only shelter from the elements and to renew our supplies.'

'Well you can't do that here! Tell your Baron Gottfried that if he's so peaceful he can march on. This is the freistadt of Akendorf and we want no truck with nobles.'

Felix studied the man who shouted at him from the gate tower. Beneath a peaked metal cap his face was keen and intelligent. He was flanked by two men whose crossbows were pointed unwaveringly at Felix. Felix felt his mouth go dry and sweat run clammily down his back. He was wearing his mail shirt but he doubted it would be much good against their quarrels at such close range.

'Sir, in the name of Sigmar, we seek only common hospitality…'

'Begone, boy, you'll get no hospitality in Akendorf nor in any other town in these lands. Not travelling with twenty armed knights and fifty men-at-arms.'

Felix wondered at the quality of scouts the freistadt must have, to know the numbers of their force so exactly. He saw the pattern of things in this land. The baron's force was too powerful for any local warlord to open his town gates to them. It would be a threat to any ruler's position in these isolated towns. Yet Felix doubted whether the baron's force was strong enough to take a walled fort against determined resistance.

'We have wounded,' he shouted. 'Will you at least take them?'

For the first time the man in the tower looked apologetic. 'No. You brought those extra mouths here. You can feed them.'

'In the name of Shallya, mistress of mercy, you must help them.'

'I must do nothing, herald. I rule here, not your baron. Tell him to follow Thunder River south. Taal knows, there is enough unclaimed land there. Let him clear his own estate or claim one of the abandoned forts.'

Felix dispiritedly brought his horse around. He was keenly aware of the weapons pointed at his back.

'Herald!' the lord of Akendorf cried. Felix turned in the saddle to look at him. In the fading light the man's face held a look of concern.

'What?'

'Tell the baron on no account to enter the hills to the south. Tell him to stay by Thunder River. I would not have it on my conscience that he ventured into the Geistenmund Hills unwarned.'

Something in the man's tone made the hairs on the back of Felix's neck prickle.

'Those hills are haunted, herald, and no man should dare them, on peril of his immortal soul.'

'THEY WILL NOT let us past their gates. It's that simple,' Felix concluded, looking round the faces that circled the fire. The baron gestured for him to sit down with a faint movement of his left hand, then turned his rheumy gaze to Dieter.

'We cannot take Akendorf, at least not without great loss of life. I am no expert on sieges but even I can see that,' the grey-haired man said. He leaned forward and put another branch on the fire. Sparks drifted upwards into the cold night air.

'You are saying we must continue on,' the baron said. His voice was weak and reminded Felix of the crackle of dry leaves.

Dieter nodded.

'Perhaps we should go west,' Manfred said. 'Seek out land there. That way we could miss the hills, assuming there is anything there to fear.'

'There is,' the trapper, Hef, said. Even in the cheery glow of the fire his features looked pale and strained.

'Going west is a foolish idea anyway,' Frau Winter said. Felix saw that she was glaring right at Manfred.

'Oh, how so?' he asked.

'Use your brain, boy. The mountains to the east are the haunt of goblins, now that the dwarf realm is sundered. So the best land will be that furthest away from Thunder River, safest from raids. It will be held by the strongest of the local rulers. Any place to the west will be better defended than Akendorf.'

'I know my geography,' Manfred sneered. He looked around the fire, meeting the gaze of every watcher. 'If we continue south we will come to Blood River, where the wolf-riders are thicker than worms in a corpse.'

'In every direction lies peril,' the old baron wheezed. He looked straight at Felix and his blue eyes were very piercing. 'Do you think that the Lord of Akendorf warned us to keep to the river simply to make us a tempting target for any raiding greenskins?'

Felix considered for a moment, weighing his judgement. How could he be expected to tell whether the man had been lying or not on the basis of a few minutes' conversation? Felix was acutely conscious that he would influence the destiny of everyone in the caravan by what he said. For the first time in his life he felt a vague glimmer of the responsibilities of leadership. He took a deep breath.

'The man seemed sincere, Herr Baron.'

'He was tellin' the truth,' Hef said, tamping some smokeweed into the bowl of his pipe. Felix noted the way the man's fingers played nervously with its stem. Hef leaned forward and pulled a twig from the fire, using it to light his pipe before continuing.

'The Geistenmund Hills are an evil place. Folk say that centuries ago sorcerers came out of Bretonnia, necromancers exiled by the Sun King. They found the barrows of the folk who passed here in Elder days and used their spells to raise an army. Came very near to conquering the whole of the Border Princes afore the local lords made alliance with the dwarfs of the mountains and threw them back.'

Felix felt a shiver pass up his spine. He fought an urge to look back over his shoulder into the shadows.

'Folk say that the sorcerers and their allies retreated into the barrows. These were sealed with dwarf stonework and powerful runes by the victors.'

'But that was centuries ago,' Frau Winter said. 'Strong though their sorceries were, can they endure?'

'I don't know, mistress. But tomb robbers never return from the Geistenmunds. Some nights, unnatural lights can be seen in the hills and when both moons are full the dead lie unquiet in their tombs. They come to take the living so that their blood can renew the life of their dark lords.'

'Surely that is nonsense,' Dr Stockhausen said.

Felix himself was not so sure. The previous year on Geheimnisnacht he had seen terrible things. He pushed the memory back from his mind.

'If we go west we face certain peril and no surety of finding haven,' the baron said, his face made gaunt and angular by the underlight of the fire. 'South it is claimed we will find clear land, guarded though it may be by a sorcerous foe. I think we should brave the southward way. It may be clear. We will follow Thunder River.'

His voice held no great hope. He sounded like a man who had resigned himself to his fate. Does the baron court death, wondered Felix? In the atmosphere created by the trapper's dark tale Felix could almost believe it. He made a mental note to find out more about the von Diehl curse. Then he noticed

the face of Manfred. The young noble was staring raptly into
the fire, a look almost of pleasure on his face.

'I BELIEVE I have found the inspiration for a new play,' Manfred
von Diehl said enthusiastically. 'That delightful story the trapper told last night will be its core.'

Felix looked at him dubiously. They were walking along the
west side of the caravan, keeping between the wagons and the
ominous, barren hills.

'It may be more than a simple trapper's tale, Manfred. There
is some truth to many old legends.'

'Quite so! Quite so! Who should know that better than I? I
think I shall call this play Where the Dead Men Walk. Think of
it: silver rings clinking on bony fingers, the parchment skins of
the restless dead glistening in the witchlight. Imagine a king
who lies in state untouched by the worms and who rises every
year to seek blood to prolong his shadowy reign.'

Looking at those brooding, blasted heights, Felix found it
only too easy to imagine such things. Among the four hundred
who followed Baron von Diehl, only three people dared enter
the hills. During the day Doctor Stockhausen and Frau Winter
would search among the mossy boulders on the rubble-strewn
slopes for herbs. Sometimes they would encounter Gotrek
Gurnisson if they returned late. The Trollslayer prowled the
hillside by night, as if daring the powers of darkness to touch
him.

'Think,' Manfred said in a conspiratorial whisper. 'Think of
lying sleeping in your bed and hearing the soft pad of
approaching feet and no breathing whatsoever except your
own... You could lie there listening to your heart pound and
know that no heartbeat tolled within the chest of the
approaching–'

'Yes,' Felix said hurriedly. 'I'm sure it will be an excellent
work. You must let me read it when it is complete.'

He decided to change the subject, tried to think of one that
would appeal to this strange young man. 'I was thinking perhaps of writing a poem myself. Could you tell me more of the
von Diehl curse?'

Manfred's face froze. His glittering look made Felix shiver,
then Manfred shook his head and smiled and became his old
affable self.

'There is little to tell.' He giggled lightly. 'My grandfather was a very devout man. Always burning witches and mutants to prove it. One Hexensnacht he roasted a pretty maid called Irina Trask. All his subjects came to watch, for she was a beauty. As the flames rose about her, she called on the powers of hell to avenge her, to bring death to my grandfather and the wrath of Chaos to his heirs and followers and all of their children. The darkness and its children will take you all, she said.'

He fell silent and stared gloomily towards the hills. Felix prompted him. 'What happened?'

'Shortly thereafter my grandfather was killed while out hunting, by a pack of beastmen. There was a quarrel amongst his sons. The eldest, Kurt, was heir. My father and his brother rebelled and ousted him. Some folk say that Kurt became a bandit and was killed by a warrior of Chaos. Others claim that he headed north and met a much darker fate.

'My father inherited the barony and married my mother, Katerina von Wittgenstein.' Felix stared at him. The Wittgensteins were a family with a dark reputation, shunned by normal society. Manfred ignored his stare.

'Uncle Gottfried became their warleader. My mother died giving birth to me, and my father disappeared. Gottfried seized power. Since then we have been dogged by ill-luck.'

Felix could see a figure approaching downslope. It was Frau Winter. She seemed to be in a great hurry.

'Disappeared?' Felix said distractedly.

'Aye, vanished. It wasn't until much later I found out what had happened to him.'

Frau Winter approached, glaring at Manfred. 'Bad news,' she said. 'I've discovered an opening on the hillside up there. It is barred by runes, but I sense a terrible danger lies beyond it.'

Something in her tone compelled belief. She swirled on down into the camp. Manfred glared daggers at her back.

Felix looked over at him. 'There is no love lost between you two, is there?'

'She hates me, has done ever since uncle named me heir. She thinks her son should be the next baron.'

Felix raised an eyebrow.

'Oh yes, didn't you know? Dieter is her son. He's my father's bastard offspring.'

* * *

MOONLIGHT DAPPLED the waters of Thunder River. It gleamed like liquid silver. Old gnarled trees hung over the banks at this point, reminding Felix of waiting trolls. Nervously, he looked about. There was something in the air tonight, he decided; a tension, a feeling that something was not right.

He had to fight to control the sensation that somewhere something evil stirred, hungry for his life, for the lives of all the people of Baron Gottfried's entourage.

'Is there something wrong, Felix? You seem very distracted tonight,' Kirsten said.

He looked over to her and smiled, finding pleasure in her presence. Normally he enjoyed their nightly walks by the river but tonight foreboding came between them.

'No. Just tired.' He couldn't restrain a glance in the direction of the nearby hills. By the light of the moons the opening looked very like a gaping maw.

'It's this place, isn't it? There's something unnatural about it. I can feel it. It's like when Frau Winter does one of her dangerous spells. The hair on the back of my neck prickles. Only this is much worse.'

Felix saw terror surface in her face then disappear again. She looked out over the water. 'Something old and evil dwells below those hills, Felix. Something hungry. We could die here.'

Felix took her hand. 'We're quite safe. We're still by the river.'

His voice quivered and his words did not come across reassuringly. He sounded like a scared boy. They were both shaking.

'Everyone in the camp is afraid, except your friend Gotrek. Why is he so fearless?'

Felix laughed quietly. 'Gotrek is a Trollslayer, sworn to seek death to atone for some crime. He's an exile from his home, family and friends. He has no place in this world. He is brave because he has nothing to lose. He can only regain his honour by dying honourably.'

'Why do you follow him? You seem like a sensible man.'

Felix considered his reply carefully. He had never really questioned his motives that closely. Under the gaze of Kirsten's dark eyes it suddenly became important for him to know.

'He saved my life. We pledged blood-loyalty after that. At the time I did not know what the ritual meant but I've stuck to it.'

He had given the barest facts, the truth in a sense, but not an explanation. He paused and stroked the old scar on his right cheek. He wanted to be honest.

'I killed a man in a duel. It caused a scandal. I had to give up my life as a student, my father disinherited me. I was full of anger, got into trouble with the law. At the time I met Gotrek I had no goals, I was just drifting. Gotrek's purpose was so strong I just got sucked along behind him. It was easier to follow him than to start a new life. Something about his self-destructive madness appealed to me.'

She looked at him questioningly. 'It doesn't any more?'

He shook his head. 'What about you? What brings you along Thunder River?'

They approached a tumbled tree. Felix gave Kirsten a hand up onto the bole, then jumped up beside her himself. She smoothed the folds of her long peasant skirt, tucked a lock of her hair behind one ear. Felix thought she looked very lovely in the light of the twin moons, with the mist beginning to rise.

'My parents were vassals of Baron Gottfried's, serfs back in Diehlendorf. They indentured me to Frau Winter. They died back in the avalanche, along with my sisters.'

'I'm sorry,' Felix said. 'I didn't know.'

She shrugged fatalistically. 'There has been so much death along the way. I'm just grateful to be here.'

She was quiet for a long moment and when she spoke again her voice was soft. 'I miss them.'

Felix could think of nothing to say, so he kept quiet.

'You know, my grandmother never travelled more than a mile from Diehlendorf in her life. She never even saw the inside of that bleak old castle. All she knew was her hut and the strips of fields where she laboured. Already I've seen mountains and towns and this river. I've travelled further than she ever dreamed. In a way I'm glad.'

Felix looked at her. Along the shadowy planes of her cheeks he could see a teardrop glisten. Their faces were very close. Behind her, tendrils of mist drifted from the surface of the river. It had thickened quickly. He could barely see the water. Kirsten moved closer.

'If I hadn't come I wouldn't have met you.'

They kissed, unskilfully, tentatively. Lips barely brushed lips. Felix leaned forward and took her long hair in his hands. They leaned into each other, holding one another hungrily as the kiss deepened. Passionately their hands began to wander, exploring each other's bodies through the thick layers of clothing.

They leaned over too far. Kirsten screamed slightly as they fell off the tree trunk onto the soft wet earth.

'My cloak's all muddy,' Felix said.

'Perhaps you'd better take it off. We can lie on it. The ground's all wet.'

Under the shadow of the deathly hills they made love in the mist and moonlight.

'WHERE HAVE YOU been, manling, and why are you looking so pleased with yourself?' Gotrek asked surlily.

'Down by the river,' Felix replied innocently. 'Just walking.'

Gotrek raised one bushy eyebrow. 'You picked a bad night just to go walking. See the way this mist thickens. I smell sorcery.'

Felix looked at him, feeling fear creep though his bones. His hand went to the hilt of his sword. He remembered the mist that had covered the moors around the Darkstone Ring a year before, and what it had hidden. He glanced over his shoulder into the darkness.

'If that's true we should tell Dieter and the baron.'

'I've already informed the duke's henchman. The guard has been doubled. That's all they would do.'

'What are we going to do?'

'Get some sleep, manling. It will be your watch soon.'

Felix lay down in the back of the wagon on top of some sacks of grain. He pulled his cloak tight about him. Try as he might, sleep was a long time coming. He kept thinking of Kirsten. When he stared at Morrslieb, the lesser moon, it seemed he could see the outline of her face. The mist grew thicker, muffling all sound except Gotrek's quiet breathing.

When sleep finally came, he dreamed dark dreams in which dead men walked.

IN THE DISTANCE a horse whinnied uneasily. A huge hand was clamped over Felix's mouth. He struggled furiously, wondering whether Lars had come back for revenge.

'Hist, manling! Something comes. Be very quiet.'

Felix came groggily to full wakefulness. His eyes felt dry and tired; his muscles ached from the mattress of sacks. He felt weary and lacking in energy.

'What is it, Gotrek?' he asked softly. The Trollslayer gestured for him to be quiet and sniffed at the air.

'Whatever it is, it's been dead a long time.'

Felix shivered and drew his cloak tight. He felt fear begin to churn in the pit of his stomach. As the meaning of the dwarf's words sank in, he had to fight to restrain the terror.

Felix peered out into the mist. It cloaked the land, obscuring vision at more than a spear's length. If Felix strained every sense he could just make out the wagon opposite. He cast a glance back over his shoulder, fearful that some frightful denizen of the dark might be creeping up behind him.

His heartbeat sounded loud in his ears and he remembered Manfred's words. He pictured bony hands reaching out to grab him and carry him off to a deep dark tomb. His muscles felt as if they had frozen in place. He had to struggle to get them to move, to reach for the hilt of his sword.

'I'm going to take a look around,' Gotrek whispered. Before Felix could argue or follow, the dwarf dropped noiselessly off the cart and vanished into the gloom.

Now Felix felt totally alone. It was like waking from one nightmare to find himself in a worse one. He was isolated in the dark and clammy mist. He knew that just outside the range of his perception hungry, uncanny creatures lurked. Some primitive sense told him so. He knew that to stir from the cart meant death.

Yet Kirsten was out there, sleeping in Frau Winter's carriage. He pictured her lying in bed as terrible pressure was exerted on the caravan's door and slowly the timber buckled inwards, to reveal–

He drew his blade and leapt from the cart. The soft thud of his feet rang as loud as the tolling of a bell to his fear-honed senses. He strained to pick out details in the mist as he moved through the outer ring of wagons to where he knew Kirsten was.

Every step seemed to take eternity. He cast wary glances about him, fearful that something was creeping up stealthily behind. He skirted pockets of deep shadow. He wanted to cry out loud to alert the camp, but something instinctively stopped

him. To do so would be to attract the attention of the terrible
watchers – and that would mean death.

A figure loomed out of the shadows, and Felix brought his
sword up. His heart was in his mouth until he noticed the figure was wearing leather armour and a metal cap. A guard, he
thought, relaxing. Thank Sigmar. But when the figure turned,
Felix almost screamed.

Its face had no flesh. Greenish light flickered in its empty
sockets. Age-rotten teeth smirked from the fleshless, lipless
mouth. He saw that the helm which he had originally taken for
a guard's was verdigrised bronze and inscribed with runes
which hurt the eye. The smell of mould and rotten leather rose
from the thing's tunic and tattered cloak.

It lashed out at him with its rusty blade. Felix stood frozen
for a moment and then, acting on reflex, flung himself to one
side. The thing's sword nicked his ribs. Pain seared his side. He
noticed the movement of ancient tendons under the paper-thin
skin of the hand which held the weapon. He countered with a
high blow to the neck, his body responding with trained discipline even as his mind reeled in horror.

His blade crashed through the thing's neck with a cracking of
severed vertebrae. His return blow chopped through its chest
like a butcher's cleaver through a bone. The skeletal warrior fell
like a marionette with its strings cut.

As if Felix's blows were a signal, the night came alive with
shadowy figures. He heard wood splinter and animals scream
in terror, as if whatever spell had held them mute was broken.
Somewhere off in the night Gotrek Gurnisson bellowed his war
chant.

Felix rushed through the mist, almost colliding with Dieter
as he tumbled out of a wagon. The big man was fully dressed
and clutched a hand-axe.

'What's going on?' he shouted, through the cacophony of
screams.

'Attackers... dead things from under the hills,' Felix said. The
words came out in jerky gasps.

'Foes!' Dieter shouted. 'To me, men. Rally to me!' He gave
out a wolf-like war-cry. From about them came a few weak
answering howls. Felix charged on, seeking Kirsten's home.
From the shadowy gap between two wagons, figures leapt out,
striking at him with long, wickedly curved blades.

He writhed aside from one and parried the other. Two more skeletal creatures leered at him. He chopped at one's leg. It fell over as his blade broke through the knee. Mind numbed with horror, he fought almost mechanically, leaping over the blow of the one on the ground then bringing his heel down to break its spine. Blows flickered between him and the other until he chopped it to pieces.

He saw two of the fiends battering though the door of Frau Winter's wagon just as he had feared. From inside came the sound of chanting, which he assumed was a prayer. He prepared himself to charge but his eyes were dazzled by a sudden blueish flash. Chain lightning flickered and a rank smell of ozone filled the air, overcoming even the stench of rot. When Felix's sight cleared he saw the charred remains of two skeletons lying near the caravan's steps.

In the doorway Frau Winter stood calm and unafraid, a nimbus of light emerging from her left hand. She looked over at Felix and gave him an encouraging nod.

Behind her was Kirsten, who pointed mutely over his shoulder. He whirled and saw a dozen undead warriors rushing towards him. He heard Dieter and his men run up to meet them. Then he joined the rush.

For Felix the night became howling chaos as he hacked his way round the camp in search of Gotrek. At one point the mist cleared and he pushed some quivering children under a wagon away from the bodies of their dead parents. The man lay in a night shirt, the woman close by, a broom handle clutched in one hand like a spear. Felix heard a sound and turned to face a skeletal giant bearing down at him. Somehow he survived.

Felix fought back to back with Dieter until they stood among a pile of mouldering bones. The battle surged away from him as the mist closed in and for a long moment he stood alone, listening to the screams of the dying.

A passing figure lashed out at him and they exchanged blows. Felix saw that it was Lars, a grin frozen on his face revealing missing teeth, terror froth foaming from his mouth. Berserkly he hacked at Felix. The man was mad with fear.

'Bathtard!' he hissed, chopping at Felix with a blow which would have felled a tree. Felix ducked underneath the blow and lunged forward, taking him through the heart. Lars sobbed as he died. Felix wondered how crazed Lars really had been. If the trapper had killed Felix it could have been blamed on the attackers. He returned to the fray.

He rounded a corner to find a score of undead warriors being driven back by the furious onslaught of Gotrek's axe. Blue chain lightning flickered and the area about him was suddenly clear. He looked about for Frau Winter to offer his thanks but she was gone, vanished into the mists. He turned to see Gotrek standing astonished, his jaw hanging open.

Sometime before dawn, their assailants retreated back towards the hills, leaving Baron von Diehl's warriors to contemplate their ruined wagons and the bodies of their dead.

IN THE EARLY morning light, Felix watched warily as Gotrek inspected the rubble of the old stone arch. The stench of dank air and mouldering bones that came from within made Felix want to gag. He turned to stare down the hillside, to where the surviving exiles were building funeral pyres for the dead out of the remains of ruined wagons. Nobody wanted to bury them so close to the hills.

Felix heard Gotrek grunt with grim satisfaction, and turned to look at him. The dwarf was running his hand expertly along the broken stones with their faint webwork of old runes. Gotrek looked up and grinned savagely.

'No doubt about it, manling: the runes guarding the entrance were broken from the outside.'

Felix looked at him. Suspicion blossomed. He was very afraid. 'It looks as though someone has been giving the von Diehl curse a helping hand,' he whispered.

RAIN LASHED DOWN from the grey sky. The cart rumbled southward. Beside the caravan the waters of Thunder River tumbled headlong towards their goal. The rain-swollen river constantly threatened to burst its banks. Felix jerked the reins; the oxen lowed and redoubled their efforts to move on the muddy ground.

Beside him Kirsten sneezed. Like almost everyone else, she was pale and ill-looking. The strain of the long journey and the worsening weather had made them all prey to disease.

No town would take them in. Armed warriors had threatened battle unless they moved on to untenanted land. The trail had become interminable. It seemed as if they had been riding forever and would never come to rest. Even the knowledge that someone in the train had freed the undead beneath the hills has ceased to be alarming, fading into cold suspicion when no culprit could be found.

Felix looked at Gotrek guiltily, expecting Kirsten's sneeze to produce his usual crass comments about human frailty, but the Trollslayer was silent, staring towards the World's Edge Mountains with a fixity of purpose unusual even for him.

Felix wondered when he would pluck up the courage to tell Gotrek that he wasn't continuing onwards with him, that he was settling down with Kirsten. He was worried about what the dwarf's reaction would be. Would Gotrek simply dismiss it as another example of human faithlessness – or would he turn violent?

Felix felt miserable. He was fond of the Trollslayer, for all his black moods and bitter comments. The thought of Gotrek wandering off to meet a lonely doom disturbed him. But he loved Kirsten and the thought of being parted from her was painful to him. Perhaps Gotrek sensed this and it was the reason for his withdrawn mood. Felix reached over and squeezed the girl's hand.

'What are you looking for, Herr Gurnisson?' Kirsten asked the dwarf. Gotrek did not turn to look at her but continued to stare longingly at the mountains. At first it seemed as if the Trollslayer would not reply but eventually he pointed to the outline of one cloud-swathed mountain.

'Karaz-a-Karak,' he said. 'The Everpeak. My home.' His voice was softer than Felix had ever heard it and it held a depth of longing that was heart-breaking. Gotrek turned to look at them and his face held such a look of dumb, brute misery that Felix had to look away. The dwarf's crest of hair was flattened by the rain and his face was bleak and weary. Kirsten reached past to adjust Gotrek's cloak about his shoulders, as she would have done for a lost child.

Gotrek tried to give her his ferocious, insular scowl but he could not hold it and he just smiled sadly, revealing his missing teeth. Felix wondered whether the dwarf had come all this way just for that fleeting glimpse of the mountain. He noticed a drop of water hanging from the end of the Trollslayer's nose. It might have been a teardrop or it might just have been rain.

They continued southward.

* * *

'WE CAN'T LEAVE them just yet,' Felix said, cursing himself for being such a coward.

Gotrek turned and looked towards the tumbled-down fortified mansion which they had found. He could see smoke rising in plumes from the chimneys of the recently cleared building.

'Why not, manling? They've found clear ground, cultivatable land and the ruins of that old fort. With a little work it should prove quite defensible.'

Felix strove desperately to find a reason. He was surprised that he was trying so hard to delay the moment when he had to tell Gotrek of their parting. The way Gotrek looked at him disapprovingly reminded him of his father at his sternest. He felt once more the need to make excuses, and he hated himself for it.

'Gotrek, we're only a hundred miles north of where the Thunder River flows into Blood River. Beyond that is the Badlands and a horde of wolf-riders.'

'I know that, manling. We'll have to cross there on our way to Karak Eight Peaks.'

Tell him. Just say it, Felix argued with himself. But he couldn't.

'We can't go just yet. You've seen the bodies we found in the mansion. Bones cracked for the marrow. The walls have been burned. Dieter has found the spoor of wolf-riders nearby. The place is not defensible. With your help, with the help of a dwarf, it could be made so.'

Gotrek laughed. 'I don't know why you think that.'

'Because dwarfs are good with stone and fortifications. Everyone knows that.'

Gotrek glanced back at the mansion thoughtfully. He seemed to be remembering a former life. A frown creased his brow and he rested his forehead against the shaft of his axe.

'I don't know,' he said eventually, 'that even a dwarf could make this place defensible. Typical human workmanship, manling. Shoddy, very shoddy.'

'It could be made safe. You know it could, Gotrek.'

'Perhaps. It has been a long time since I worked with stone, manling.'

'A dwarf never forgets such things. And I'm sure the baron will pay handsomely for your services.'

Gotrek sniffed suspiciously. 'It had better be more than he pays his mercenaries.'

Felix grinned. 'Come on. Let's find out.'

UNABLE TO SLEEP, Felix got up quietly. He dressed quickly, not wanting to wake Kirsten. He gently rearranged the cloaks that they used as blankets about her so that she would not get cold, then kissed her lightly on the forehead. She stirred but did not awake. He lifted his sword from where it lay by the entrance of their hut and stepped out into the cold night air. Winter was coming, Felix thought, watching his breath cloud.

By the moons' light he picked his way through the cluster of hovels which lay in the lee of the new wooden walls surrounding the mansion. He felt at peace for the first time in a long while. Even the night-time noise of the camp was reassuring. The fort had been completed before the first snows; it looked as if the settlers would have enough grain to last the winter and seed a new crop in the spring.

He listened to the cattle lowing and the measured tread of the sentry on the walls. He looked up and saw that a light still gleamed in the window of Manfred's room. Felix thought about his convoluted destiny. *Not a place I would ever have imagined myself settling down, a fortified village on the edge of nowhere. I wonder what my father would think if he could see me now, about to become a farmer. He'd probably die of mortification.* Felix smiled.

It was exciting to be here. *There was a sense of something about to begin, a community still taking shape. And I will have a place in shaping that community,* he thought. *This is the perfect place to start a new life.*

He walked on towards the guard tower, where he knew he would find Gotrek. The dwarf was unable to sleep, restless and ready to move on. He liked to while away the night watches in the tower he himself had designed.

Felix clambered up the ladder and through the trapdoor in the floor of the guardroom. He found Gotrek staring out into the night. The sight of the dwarf made Felix nervous but he steeled himself, determined to tell the dwarf the truth.

'Can't sleep either, eh, manling?'

Felix managed a nod. When he had rehearsed his speech to himself it all had seemed simple. He would explain the situation rationally, tell Gotrek he was staying with Kirsten and await the dwarf's response. Now it was more difficult, his tongue felt thick and it was as if the words had stuck in his throat.

He found himself flinching inwardly at all the accusations he imagined Gotrek would make: that he was a coward and an oathbreaker; that this was the thanks a dwarf got for saving a man's life. Felix had to admit that he had sworn an oath to follow Gotrek and record his doom. Certainly, he had sworn it while drunk and full of gratitude to a dwarf who had just pulled him from under the hooves of the Emperor's cavalry, but an oath was still an oath, as Gotrek was wont to point out.

He moved over to stand beside the Trollslayer. They stared out over the ditch that surrounded the outer wall and which was sided with sharpened stakes. The only easy way over it was the bridge of earth that this tower overlooked.

'Gotrek…'

'Yes, manling?'

'You've built well,' Felix said.

Gotrek looked up and smiled grimly. 'We'll soon find out,' he said. Felix looked to where the Trollslayer pointed. The fields were dark with wolf-riders. Gotrek raised the alarm horn to his lips and sounded a blast.

FELIX DUCKED AS an arrow splintered into the wood of the parapet in front of him. He reached down and took a crossbow from the fingers of the dead guard. The man lay with an arrow through his throat. Felix fumbled for a quarrel and strained to cock the weapon. He eventually slipped a bolt into place.

He leapt up. Fire arrows flashed overhead like falling stars. From behind him came the stench of burning. Felix looked down from the parapet. Wolf-riders circled the camp as a wolf-pack circles a herd of cattle. He could see the green skin of the riders glistening in the light of their burning arrows. The flames highlighted their jaundiced eyes and yellowish tusks.

There must be hundreds of them, Felix thought. He thanked Sigmar for the ditch and the spikes and the wooden walls that Gotrek had made them build. At the time it had seemed needless labour and the dwarf had been roundly cursed. Now it seemed barely adequate provision.

Felix aimed at a wolf-rider who was drawing a bead on the tower with one pitch-soaked arrow. He pulled the trigger on the crossbow. The bolt blurred across the night and took the goblin in the chest. It fell backwards in the saddle. Its blazing arrow was launched directly into the sky, as if aimed at the moons.

Felix ducked back and reloaded. With his back to the parapet he could see down into the courtyard. A human chain of women and children carried buckets from the rain-barrels to the flaming hovels, struggling vainly to extinguish the fires. He saw one old woman go down and others flinch as arrows fell around them like dark rain.

Felix turned and fired again, missing. The night was filled with a cacophony of sound. The screams of the dying, the howling of wolves, the deadly cutting whisper of arrows and crossbow bolts. He heard Gotrek singing happily in dwarfish and somewhere far-off the baron's dry, rasping voice giving orders in a firm, calm voice. Dogs barked, horses whinnied in terror, children cried. Felix wished he were deaf.

He heard the scratching of claws on wood nearby and lurched to his feet. He looked over the parapet and almost lost his face. The jaws of a wolf snapped shut below him. The creature had leapt the ditch, ignoring the stakes which were covered by the bodies of its fallen comrades.

He smelled the stench of its breath as it fell, saw its rider hanging on grimly as it gathered itself for another spring. Felix let fly with a crossbow bolt. It thunked into the creature's chest, and the wolf fell. Its rider rolled clear and scuttled off into the night.

Felix saw Frau Winter climb up into the watchtower, to stand at Gotrek's shoulder. He hoped she would do something. In the howling chaos of the night it was impossible to tell, but Felix sensed that things were not going well for the defenders. The ditch seemed to be filling with the bodies of their attackers, and the guards were falling like flies to the incessant barrages of arrows in spite of the protection of the parapet.

When Felix looked again, he saw a group of heavily armoured orcs, bearing a sharpened tree trunk, racing towards the gate. A few crossbow bolts landed among them but others were deflected by the shields of those who ran alongside the rammers. He heard the juddering sound of the tree's impact on the gate.

Felix fumbled for his sword, preparing to leap from the walls into the courtyard and hold the gate. If it fell, all he could do was sell his life dearly; they were too badly outnumbered to delay the besiegers long. He felt fear twist in his gut. He hoped Kirsten was safe.

Frau Winter's calm, clear voice rang out. She chanted like a priest at prayer. Then the lightning came.

Searing blue light leapt through the night. The air stank of ozone. The hair on the back of Felix's neck prickled. He tried to watch as the lightning flashed among the ram-carriers. He heard them scream. Some danced back, capering like clowns, dropping the treetrunk. They fell to earth, bodies smouldering. The disgusting burned-meat smell of scorched flesh filled the air.

Again and again the lightning lashed out. Wolves howled fearfully, the hail of arrows slackened, the sickening smell increased. Felix looked at Frau Winter. Her face was drawn and pale, her hair stood upright. As her face alternated black and blue in the nightmarish flashes, she looked daemonic. He had not suspected any human being could wield such power.

The wolf-riders and the orc infantry retreated, howling in terror, to beyond the reach of those appalling thunderbolts. Felix felt relieved. Then he noticed, off in the distance, a glow of light.

He peered into the darkness, making out an old greenskin shaman. A red nimbus played around his skull, illuminating the wolfskin head-dress and the bone-staff he held in one gnarled claw. A beam of blood-coloured light flickered from his head and lashed out at Frau Winter.

Felix saw the sorceress moan and totter back. Gotrek reached out to support her. He watched her grimace in pain, her face a pale mask. She gritted her teeth, and sweat beaded her brow. She seemed to be locked in a supernatural contest of wills with the old shaman.

The wolf-riders rallied around their braver leaders. Cautiously they began to return, although their renewed attacks lacked the wild ferocity of their initial onslaught. All through the night the struggle continued.

IN THE FIRST light of dawn, Felix approached Gotrek where he stood with Manfred, Dieter and Frau Winter. The woman looked weary beyond endurance. People crowded around her, gazing at her in awe.

'How are we doing?' Felix asked Gotrek.

'As long as she holds out, we can. If she can call the lightning.' Manfred looked at Gotrek and nodded agreement.

There was a commotion from the other side of the courtyard.

'Frau Winter, come quickly, Doctor Stockhausen called. 'The baron has been gravely wounded. An arrow, maybe poisoned.' Wearily, the sorceress walked into the mansion. From the crowd Felix saw Kirsten move to help her. He smiled at her, glad they were both alive.

WITH A SOUND like sudden thunder, the gate rocked back on its hinges. Another blow like that and it will fall, Felix thought. He looked over at Gotrek who was testing the edge of his axe experimentally with his thumb. On this second night of the siege the Trollslayer was looking forward to the hand-to-hand combat to come. Felix felt a tug on his shoulder. It was Hef. The big man looked deathly afraid.

'Where is Frau Winter?' he asked. He nodded at the gate. 'That's no battering ram. That's the staff of that old devil. He'll have all our heads for his lodge afore the night's out unless the witch can stop him!'

Felix looked from Hef to the rest of the pitifully depleted band of defenders. He saw tired warriors; wounded men who could barely carry a sword, teenage boys and girls armed with pitchforks and other improvised weapons. From outside the howling of the wolves was deafening. Only Gotrek looked calm.

'I don't know where she is. Dieter went to get her ten minutes ago.'

'Well, he's takin' his time 'bout it.'

'All right,' Felix said. 'I'll go and get her.'

'I'll come with you,' Hef said.

'Oh no you won't,' Gotrek said loudly. 'I trust the manling to return. You'll stay here. The gobbos will pass this gate over our dead bodies.'

Felix made for the mansion. He knew that Kirsten was with the sorceress. If things went as badly as he feared, he would at least see her before the end.

He had barely reached the door when he heard a splintering sound from behind him and the heart-stopping crash of the gate falling in. He heard Gotrek bellow his war-cry, and the screams of terror from some of the warriors. Felix turned and saw a terrible sight.

In the gateway, mounted on a great white wolf, was the shaman. Around his head crackled a halo of ruddy light. It played from the tip of his bone staff, staining the faces of all around like blood. From the wall a quarrel flashed but it was turned aside by some force before it could hit the sorcerer.

Flanking the shaman were six mighty orcs, mail-clad, axe-armed and fierce. Beyond them was a sea of green faces and wolves. Gotrek laughed aloud and charged for them. The last thing Felix saw before he stepped inside was the Trollslayer running forward, axe held high, beard bristling, towards the source of that terrible light.

Inside, the mansion was strangely quiet, the roar of sound outside muffled by the stone-walls. Felix ran through the corridor, shouting for Frau Winter, his voice ringing eerily in the quiet halls.

He found the bodies in the main hall. Frau Winter had been stabbed through the chest several times. Her clean, grey dress was red. She had a look of surprise on her face, as if death had taken her unawares. How had the goblins got inside? Felix thought crazily. But he knew no goblin had done this.

Another body lay near the door, stabbed through the back as she had struggled to open it. Not wanting, not daring to believe it, Felix advanced, heart in his mouth. Gently he turned Kirsten's body over. He felt a brief flicker of hope as her eyes opened, then noticed the trickle of blood from her mouth.

'Felix,' she sighed. 'Is that you? I knew you'd come.'

Her voice was weak and blood frothed from her lips as she spoke. He wondered how long she had lain there.

'Don't talk,' he said. 'Rest.'

'Can't. Have to talk. I'm glad I came down Thunder River. Glad I met you. I love you.'

'I love you too,' he said, for the first time, then he noticed her eyes were closed. 'Don't die,' he said, rocking her gently in his arms. He felt her body go limp and his heart turned to ash. He laid her down gently, tears in his eyes, then he looked towards the door she had tried to open and cold fury filled him. Felix stood and raced down the corridor.

* * *

DIETER'S BODY LAY in the doorway to the baron's room. The side of the big man's head had been caved in. Felix pictured him rushing through the doorway in anger and being hit from the side by his prepared enemy.

Felix sprang over the body like a tiger, rolling as he hit the ground and leaping to his feet. He surveyed the room. The old baron lay in bed, a knife through his heart, blood soaking the bandages on his chest and the sheets of the bed.

Felix glared over at the chair in which Manfred sat, his gore-smeared sword red across his lap.

'The curse is fulfilled at last,' the playwright said in a tight voice that held the shrill edge of hysteria. He looked up and Felix shuddered. It was as if Manfred's face were a mask through which something else stared, something alien.

'I knew it was my destiny to fulfil the curse,' Manfred said as if passing the time of day. 'Knew it from the moment I killed my father. Gottfried had him imprisoned when he started to change. Locked him up in the old tower, took him all his food himself. No one else was allowed into that tower except Gottfried and Frau Winter. Nobody else went there until the day I did. Ulric knows, I wish I hadn't.'

He rose to his feet gripping the hilt of his sword. Felix watched him, hypnotised by his own hatred.

'I found my father there. There was still a family resemblance in spite of the way he had… changed. He still recognised me, called me "Son" in a horrid rasping voice. He begged me to kill him. He was too cowardly to do it himself. So was Gottfried. He thought he was doing my father a kindness, by keeping him alive. Keeping alive a mutant.'

Manfred began to edge closer. Felix noticed the blood dripping from his blade, speckling the floor. He felt dizzy and tired. The mad young aristocrat became the centre of his world.

'As I felt the old man's blood flow over my knife, everything changed. I saw things clearly for the first time. I saw the way Chaos taints all things, twisting and corrupting them as it had done to my father's body. I knew that I was his son and that within me, carried in my blood, was the mark of daemons. I was the agent of Chaos, spawn of its loins. I was a child of darkness. It was my destiny to destroy the von Diehl line. As I have done.'

He laughed. 'The exile was the perfect opportunity, hell-sent. The avalanche was mine, a good start. I thought I had failed

when I released the undead and they didn't succeed in destroy-
ing my uncle and his followers. But now nothing can save you.
Darkness will take you all. The curse is complete.'

'Not yet,' Felix said, his voice choked with hatred. 'You're a
von Diehl and you're still alive. I haven't killed you yet.'

Insane laughter rang out. Once more Felix felt as if he was
staring at some devil in human flesh.

'Herr Jaeger, you do have a sense of humour. Very good! I
knew you would be amusing. But how can you slay the spawn
of Chaos?'

'Let us find out,' Felix said, springing forward to the attack.
Viperishly swift, Manfred's blade rose to parry then began the
counter. Swordstrokes flickered like lightning between them.
Steel rang on steel. Felix's sword-arm was numb from the force
of Manfred's blows. The nobleman had the strength of a
maniac.

Felix gave ground. Normally, cold fear of Manfred's insanity
would have paralysed him but now he was so filled with rage
and hate that there was no room for terror. His world was
empty. He lived only to kill Kirsten's murderer. It was his one
remaining desire.

Two madmen fought in the baron's chamber. Manfred
advanced with cat-like grace, smiling confidently, as if amused
by some mild witticism. His blade wove a web of steel that was
slowly tightening around Felix. His eyes glittered, cold and
inhuman.

Felix felt the stone of the wall at his back. He lunged forward, striking at Manfred's face. Manfred parried with lazy
ease. They stood vis-a-vis, blades locked, faces inches from
each other. They pushed with all their strengths, each searching for advantage. Muscles stood out in Felix's neck, his arm
burned with fatigue as slowly, inexorably Manfred pushed
back his arm, bringing his razor-sharp blade into contact with
Felix's face.

'Goodbye, Herr Jaeger,' Manfred said casually.

Felix brought the heel of his boot down on Manfred's instep,
crunching into the foot with all his strength and weight. He felt
bone splinter, saw the nobleman's face twist in agony, felt the
pressure ease. He brought his blade forward, slicing across
Manfred's neck. The playwright tottered back and Felix's thrust
took him through the heart.

Manfred fell to his knees and stared up at Felix with blank uncomprehending eyes. Felix pushed him over with his boot and spat on his face.

'Now the curse is fulfilled,' he said.

MIND CLEAR AND unafraid, Felix stepped out into the cold night air, expecting to find the wolf-riders and death. He no longer cared. He welcomed it. He had come to understand Gotrek thoroughly. He had nothing worth living for. He was beyond all fear.

Kirsten, I will be with you soon, he thought.

In the gateway he saw Gotrek, standing amidst a pile of bodies. Blood flowed from the dwarf's appalling wounds. He was slumped forward, supporting himself on his axe, barely able to keep upright. Nearby Felix saw the bodies of Hef and the other defenders.

Gotrek turned to look at him and Felix could see that one eye was missing, torn from its socket. The dwarf staggered dizzily, fell forward and slowly and painfully tried to pull himself upright.

'What kept you, manling? You missed a good fight.'

Felix moved towards him. 'So it seems.'

'Damn gobbos are all yellow-eyed cowards. Kill their leaders and the rest turn tail and run.' He laughed painfully. 'Course... I had to kill a score or so of them before they agreed.'

'Of course,' Felix said, looking towards the pile of dead wolves and orcs. He could make out the wolf head-dress of the shaman.

'Damnedest thing,' Gotrek said. 'I can't seem to stand up.'

He closed his eye and lay very still.

FELIX WATCHED THE small line of stragglers begin to trek northwards under the watchful eyes of the few remaining soldiers. Felix thought that they might be taken in by one of the settlements now that they were no longer being escorted by the baron's full force. For the sake of the children he hoped so.

He turned to the mass grave, the barrow in which they had buried the bodies. He thought about the future he had buried with them. He was landless and homeless again. He settled the weight of the pack on his shoulders and turned to look at the distant mountains.

'Goodbye,' he said. 'I'll miss you.'

Gotrek rubbed at his new eye-patch irritably, then blew his nose. He hefted his axe. Felix noticed that his wounds were pink and barely healed.

'There's trolls in those mountains, manling. I can smell them!'

When Felix spoke his voice was flat and devoid of all emotion. 'Let us go and get them.'

He and Gotrek exchanged a look full of mutual understanding. 'We'll make a Trollslayer out of you yet, manling.'

Wearily the two of them set out towards the dark promise of the mountains, following the bright thread of Thunder River.

THE DARK BENEATH
THE WORLD

'After the dire events at Fort von Diehl, we set off with heavy hearts towards the mountains and Karak Eight Peaks. It was a long, hard journey, one not made any easier by the wildness of the country that we passed through. The hunger, the hardships and the constant threat of marauding greenskins did little to improve my state of mind, and it may be that I was perhaps particularly susceptible when I first looked on the fading grandeur of that ancient ruined city of the dwarfs, lost amid those distant peaks for all those long ages. In any case, I now recall that I had a terrible sense of foreboding about what we would find there and, as was usually the case, my fears were to prove amply justified...'

—From *My Travels with Gotrek, Vol. II*, by Herr
Felix Jaeger (Altdorf Press, 2505)

A SCREAM ECHOED through the cold mountain air. Felix Jaeger ripped his sword from its scabbard and stood ready.

Snowflakes fell; a chill wind stirred his long blond hair. He threw his red woollen cloak back over his shoulder, leaving his sword arm unobstructed. The bleak landscape was a perfect site for an ambush; pitted and rocky, harsher than the face of the greater moon, Mannslieb.

He glanced left, upslope. A few stunted pines clutched the mountainside with gnarled roots. Downslope, to the right, lay an almost sheer drop. Neither direction held any sign of danger. No bandits, no orcs, none of the darker things that lurked in these remote heights.

'The noise came from up ahead, manling,' Gotrek Gurnisson said, rubbing his eye patch with one huge, tattooed hand. His nose chain jingled in the breeze. 'There's a fight going on up there.'

Uncertainty filled Felix. He knew Gotrek was correct; even with only one eye the dwarf's senses were keener than his own. The question was whether to stand and wait or push forward and investigate. Potential enemies filled the World's Edge Mountains. The chances of finding friends were slim. His natural caution inclined him towards doing nothing.

Gotrek charged up the scree-strewn path, enormous axe held high above his red-dyed crest of hair. Felix cursed. For once why couldn't Gotrek remember that not everyone was a Trollslayer?

'We didn't all swear to seek out death in combat,' he muttered, before following slowly, for he lacked the dwarf's sure-footedness over the treacherous terrain.

FELIX TOOK IN the scene of carnage with one swift glance. In the long depression, a gang of hideous, green-skinned orcs battled a smaller group of men. They fought across a fast-flowing stream which ran down the little valley before disappearing over the mountain edge in a cloud of silver spray. The waters ran red with the blood of men and horses. It was easy to imagine what had happened: an ambush as the humans crossed the water.

In mid-stream, a huge man in shiny plate-mail battled with three brawny, bow-legged assailants. Wielding his two-handed blade effortlessly, he feinted a blow to his left then beheaded a different foe with one mighty swing. The force of his blow almost overbalanced him. Felix realised the stream bed must be slippery.

On the nearer bank a man in dark brocaded robes chanted a spell. A ball of fire blazed in his left hand. A dark-haired warrior in the furred hat and deerskin tunic of a trapper protected the sorcerer from two screaming orcs, using only a longsword held in his left hand. As Felix watched, a blond man-at-arms fell, trying to hold in entrails released by a scimitar slash to his stomach. As he went down, burly half-naked savages hacked him to pieces. Only three of the ambushed party now stood. They were outnumbered five to one.

'Orcish filth! You dare to soil the sacred approach to Karak Eight Peaks. Uruk mortari! Prepare to die,' Gotrek screamed, charging down into the melee.

An enormous orc turned to face him. A look of surprise froze forever on its face as Gotrek lopped off its head with one mighty stroke. Emerald blood spattered the Trollslayer's tattooed body. Raving and snarling, the dwarf ploughed into the orcs, hewing left and right in a great double arc. Dead bodies lay everywhere his axe fell.

Felix half-ran, half-slid down the scree. He fell at the bottom. Wet grass tickled his nostrils. He rolled to one side as a scimitar-wielding monster half again his bulk chopped down at him. He sprang to his feet, ducked a cut that could have chopped him in two and lopped off an earlobe with his return blow.

Startled, the orc clutched at its wound, trying to stop the blood flowing down its face. Felix seized his chance and stabbed upwards through the bottom of the creature's jaw into its brain.

As he struggled to free his blade another monster leapt on him, swinging its scimitar high over its head. Felix let go of his weapon and moved to meet his attacker. He grabbed its wrists as he was overborne. Fetid breath made him gag as the orc fell on top of him. The thing dropped its weapon and they wrestled on the ground, rolling down into the stream.

Copper rings set in the orc's flesh scraped him as the thing sought to bite his throat with its sharp tusks. Felix writhed to avoid having his windpipe torn out. The orc pushed his head underwater. Felix looked up through stinging eyes and saw the strangely distorted face leering down at him. Bitterly cold water filled his mouth. There was no air in his lungs. Frantically he shifted his weight, trying to dislodge his attacker. They rolled and suddenly Felix was astride the orc, trying to push its head under the stream in turn.

The orc grabbed his wrists and pushed. Locked in a deadly embrace they began to roll through the freezing water. Again and again Felix's head went under, again and again he floundered gasping to the surface. Sharp rocks speared his flesh. Realisation of his peril flashed through his mind as the current and their own momentum carried them towards the cliff edge. Felix tried to break free, giving up all thoughts of drowning his opponent.

When next his head broke surface, he looked for the cloud of spray. To his horror it was only a dozen paces away. He redoubled his efforts to escape but the orc held on like grim death and they continued their downward tumble.

Maybe ten feet now. Felix heard the rumble of the fall, felt the distorted currents of the turbulent water. He drew back his fist and smashed the orc in the face. One of its tusks broke but it would not let go.

Five feet to go. He lashed out once more, bouncing the orc's head off the stream bottom. Its grip loosened. He was almost free.

Suddenly he was falling, tumbling through water and air. He frantically grabbed for something, anything, to hold. His hand smashed into the rock and he struggled for a grip on the slippery streambed. The pressure of the freezing water on his head and shoulders was almost intolerable. He risked a downward look.

A long way below he saw the valleys in the foothills. So great was the drop that copses of trees looked like blotches of mould on the landscape. The falling orc was a receding, screaming greenish blob.

With the last of his strength Felix flopped over the edge, pushing against the current with cold-numbed fingers. For a second he thought he wasn't going to make it, then he was face down on the edge of the stream, gasping in bubbling water.

He crawled out onto the bank. The orcs, their leaders dead, had been routed. Felix pulled off his sodden cloak, wondering whether he was going to catch a chill from the frigid mountain air.

'BY SIGMAR, THAT was well done! We were sore pressed there,' the tall, dark-haired man said. He made the sign of the hammer over his chest as he spoke. He was handsome in a coarse way. His armour, although dented, was of the finest quality. The intensity of his stare made Felix uneasy.

'It would seem we owe you gentlemen our lives,' the sorcerer said. He, too, was richly dressed. His brocaded robes were trimmed with gold thread; scrolls covered in mystical symbols were held by rings set in it. His long blond hair was cut in a peculiar fashion. From the centre of his flowing locks rose a crest not unlike Gotrek's, save for the fact that it was undyed and cropped short. Felix wondered if it was the mark of some mystical order.

The armoured man's laughter boomed out. 'It is the prophecy, Johann. Did not the god say one of our ancient brethren would aid us! Sigmar be praised! This is a good sign indeed.'

Felix looked over at the trapper. He spread his hands and shrugged helplessly. A certain cynical humour was apparent in the way he raised an eyebrow.

'I am Felix Jaeger, of Altdorf, and this is my companion Gotrek Gurnisson, the Trollslayer,' Felix said, bowing to the knight.

'I am Aldred Keppler, known as Fellblade, Templar Knight of the Order of the Fiery Heart,' the armoured man said.

Felix suppressed a shudder. In his homeland the Empire, the order was famed for the fanatic zeal with which they pursued their crusade against the goblin races – and those humans they considered heretics.

The knight gestured to the sorcerer. 'This is my adviser on matters magical: Doctor Johann Zauberlich of the University of Nuln.'

'At your service,' Zauberlich said, bowing.

'I am Jules Gascoigne, once of Quenelles in Bretonnia. Although that was many a year ago,' the fur-clad man said. He had a Bretonnian accent.

'Herr Gascoigne is a scout. I engaged him to guide us through these mountains,' Aldred said. 'I have a great work to perform at Karak Eight Peaks.'

Felix and Gotrek exchanged glances. Felix knew the dwarf would rather they travelled alone in search of the lost treasure of the ancient dwarf city. However, parting company from their chance-met companions would only arouse suspicion.

'Perhaps we should join forces,' Felix said, hoping Gotrek would follow his line of reasoning. 'We too are bound for the city of the eight peaks, and this road is far from safe.'

'A capital suggestion,' the sorcerer said.

'Doubtless your companion, he goes to visit his kin,' Jules said, oblivious to the dagger-stare Gotrek gave him. 'There still is a small outpost of Imperial dwarfs there.'

'We had best bury your companions,' Felix said to fill the silence.

'WHY SO GLUM, friend Felix? Is it not a lovely night?' Jules Gascoigne asked sardonically, blowing on his hands to warm them against the bitter cold. Felix pulled his spare cloak up over his knees and extended his hands towards the small fire Zauberlich had lit with a muttered word of power. He looked over at the Bretonnian, his face turned into a daemonic mask by the firelight.

'These mountains are chill and daunting,' Felix replied. 'Who knows what perils they hide?'

'Who indeed? We are close to the Darklands. Some say that is the very spawning ground of orcs and all other greenskin devils. Also, I have heard tales that these mountains are haunted.'

Felix gestured towards the fire. 'Do you think we should have lit this?' From nearby came Gotrek's reassuring snores and the regular rhythmic breathing of the others.

Jules chuckled. 'It is a choice between evils, no? I have seen men freeze to death on nights like this. If anything attacks us, it is best that we have light to see by. The greenskins may be able to spot a man in the dark but we cannot, eh? No, I do not think the fire makes much difference. However, I do not think this why you are sad.'

He looked at Felix expectantly. Without really knowing why, Felix told the whole sorry tale of how he and Gotrek had joined the von Diehl expedition to the Border Princes. Von Diehl and his retainers had sought peace in a new land and found only terrible death. He told of his meeting with his beloved Kirsten. The Bretonnian listened sympathetically. When Felix finished telling of Kirsten's death, Jules shook his head.

'Ah, it is a sorry world we live in, is it not?'

'It is indeed.'

'Do not dwell on the past, my friend. It cannot be altered. In time all wounds heal.'

'It doesn't seem that way to me.'

They fell into silence. Felix looked over at the sleeping dwarf. Gotrek sat like a gargoyle, immobile, eyes shut but axe in hand. Felix wondered how the dwarf would take the scout's advice. Gotrek, like all dwarfs, constantly brooded on the lessons of the past. His sense of history drove him inexorably towards his future. He claimed that men had imperfect memories, that dwarfs' were better.

Is that why he seeks his doom, Felix wondered? Does his shame burn in him as strong now as at the moment he committed whatever crime he seeks to atone for? Felix pondered upon what it must be like to live with the past intruding so strongly into the present that it could never be forgotten. I would go mad, he decided.

He inspected his own grief and tried to recall it new-minted. It seemed that it had diminished by a particle, had been eroded by time and would continue to be so. He felt no better, knowing that he was doomed to forget, to have his memories become pale shadows. Perhaps the dwarfs' way was better, he thought. Even the time he had spent with Kirsten seemed paler, more colourless.

DURING HIS WATCH, Felix thought he saw a greenish witchlight high up on the mountain above them. As he stared he felt a sense of dread. The light drifted about as if seeking something. In its midst was a vaguely human form. Felix had heard tales of the daemons haunting these mountains. He looked over at Gotrek, wondering whether he should wake him.

The light vanished. Felix watched for a long time but he saw no further sign. Perhaps it had been an after-image of the fire or a trick of the light and a tired mind. Somehow he doubted it.

IN THE MORNING he dismissed his suspicions. The party followed the road round the shoulder of the mountain and suddenly a new land lay spread out before them under the steel grey, overcast sky. They looked down into a long valley nestled in a basin between eight mountains. The peaks rose like the talons of a giant claw. In their palm lay a city.

Huge walls blocked the valley's entrance, built from blocks of stone taller than a man. Within the walls, next to a silver lake, sat a great keep. A town nestled beneath it. Long roads ran from the fortress to lesser towers at the base of each mountain. Drystone dykes criss-crossed the valley, creating a patchwork of overgrown fields.

Gotrek nudged Felix in the ribs and pointed towards the peaks.

'Behold,' he said, a hint of wonder in voice. 'Carag Zilfin, Carag Yar, Carag Mhonar and the Silverhorn.'

'Those are the eastern mountains,' Aldred said. 'Carag Lhune, Carag Rhyn, Carag Nar and the White Lady guard the western approach.'

Gotrek looked at the Sigmarite respectfully. 'You speak truthfully, Templar. Long have these mountains haunted my dreams. Long have I wished to stand in their shadow.'

Felix looked down on the city. There was a sense of enduring strength about the place. Karak Eight Peaks had been built from the bones of mountains to endure till the end of the world.

'It is truly beautiful,' he said.

Gotrek looked at him with fierce pride. 'In ancient times, this city was known as the Queen of the Silver Depths. It was the fairest of our realms and we grieved its fall most sorely.'

Jules stared down at the massive walls. 'How could it have fallen? All the armies of all the kings of men could be stood off in these mountains. Those fields could feed the population of Quenelles.'

Gotrek shook his head and stared down into the city as intensely as if he were staring back into elder days.

'In pride we built Eight Peaks, at the zenith of our ancient power. It was a wonder to the world; more beautiful than Everpeak, open to the sky. A sign of our wealth and power, strong beyond the measure of dwarfs or elves or men. We thought it would never fall and the mines it guarded would be ours forever.'

The Trollslayer spoke with a bitter, compelling passion that Felix had never heard in his voice before.

'What fools we were,' Gotrek said. 'What fools we were. In pride we built Eight Peaks, sure of our mastery of stone and the dark beneath the world. Yet even as we built the city, the seeds of its doom were planted.'

'What happened?' Felix asked.

'Our quarrel with the elves began; we scourged them from the forests and drove them from the lands. After that who were we to trade with? Commerce between our races had been the source of much wealth, tainted though it was. Worse, the cost in lives was more grievous than the cost to our merchants. The finest warriors of three generations fell in that bitter struggle.'

'Still, your folk now controlled all the land between the World's Edge Mountains and the Great Sea,' Zauberlich said with a pedant's smugness. 'So claims Ipsen in his book Wars of the Ancients.'

The acid of Gotrek's laughter could have corroded steel. 'Did we? I doubt it. While we had warred with our faithless allies, the dark gathered its strength. We were weary of war when the black mountains belched forth their clouds of ash. The sky was overcast and the sun hid its face. Our crops died and our cattle sickened. Our people had returned to the safety of their cities; and from the very heart of our realm, from the place we imagined ourselves strongest, our foes burst forth.'

He stopped speaking and in the silence Felix imagined he heard the caw of some distant bird.

'From tunnels far below any we had ever dug, our enemies struck into the core of our fortresses. Through mines that had been the source of our wealth poured armies of goblins and rat-like skaven and things far, far worse.'

'What did your people do?' Felix asked.

Gotrek spread his arms wide and looked into their faces. 'What could we do? We took up our weapons and went again to war. And a terrible war it was. Our battles with the elves had taken place under the sky, through field and forest. The new war was fought in cramped spaces in the long dark, with dreadful weapons and a ferocity beyond your imagining. Shafts were collapsed, corridors scoured with firethrowers, pits flooded. Our foes responded with poison gas and vile sorcery and the summoning of daemons. Beneath where we now stand we fought with every resource we could muster, with all our weapons and all the courage desperation brings. We fought and we lost. Step by step we were driven from our homes.'

Felix looked down at the placid city. It seemed impossible that what Gotrek described could ever have happened and yet there was something in the Trollslayer's voice that compelled belief. Felix imagined the desperate struggle of those long-ago dwarfs, their fear and bewilderment as they were pushed from the place they had believed was theirs. He pictured them fighting their doomed struggle with more than human tenacity.

'In the end it became obvious that we could not hold the city, and so the tombs of our kings and the treasure-vaults were sealed and hidden by cunning devices. We abandoned this place to our foes.'

Gotrek glared at them. 'Since then we have not been so foolish as to believe any place is secure from the dark.'

ALL THROUGH THE long day, as they approached the wall, Felix realised how much the old structures had suffered. What, from a distance, gave the impression of ageless strength and sureness became, on closer inspection, just as ruined as the road upon which they travelled.

The curtain wall blocking the road into the valley was four times as tall as a man and passed between steep, sheer cliffs. Signs of neglect were obvious. Moss grew between the cracks of the great stone blocks. The stones were pitted by rain channels and mottled with yellow lichen. Some were blackened as if by great swathes of fire. A huge section of the wall had tumbled away.

His companions were silent. The desolation cast a pall over the whole party. Felix felt depressed and on edge. It was as if the spirits of antiquity watched over them, brooding over the tumbled remains of ancient grandeur. Felix's hand never strayed far from the hilt of his sword.

The cracked valves of the ancient gate had been wedged open. Someone had made a half-hearted attempt to clear the sign of the hammer and crown over eight peaks carved into the stone. Already the lichen was growing back into place.

'Someone has been here recently,' Jules said, studying the gates closely.

'I can see how you earned your reputation as a scout,' Gotrek said sarcastically.

'Stay where you are,' boomed out an unfamiliar voice. 'Unless you want to be filled with crossbow bolts.'

Felix looked up at the parapet. He saw the helmeted heads of a dozen dwarfs looking down through the battlements. Each pointed a loaded crossbow at them.

'Welcome to Karak Eight Peaks,' their grey-bearded leader said. 'I hope you have good reason for trespassing on the domain of Prince Belegar.'

UNDER GREY-WHITE clouds they marched through the city. It was a scene from after the day of judgement when the forces of Chaos returned to claim the world. Houses had tumbled and fallen into the streets. A fusty, rotten smell came from many of the buildings. Evil-looking ravens cawed from the remains of old chimneys. Clouds of more of the gaunt, black birds soared above them.

The score of dwarf warriors accompanying them were constantly on the alert. They scanned the doorways as if expecting ambush at any moment. Their crossbows were loaded and ready. They gave every impression of being in the middle of a battlefield.

Once they halted. The leader gestured for silence. Everyone stood listening. Felix thought he heard a scuttling sound but wasn't sure. He strained his eyes against the early evening gloom but could see no sign of trouble. The company leader gestured. Two of the armoured dwarfs moved cautiously towards the corner and glanced around. The rest formed into a square. After a long, tense moment, the scouts gave the all-clear.

The quiet was broken by Gotrek's laughter. 'Scared of a few goblins?' he asked.

The leader glared at him. 'There are worse things than goblins abroad on nights like this. Be assured of it,' he said.

Gotrek ran his thumb down the blade of his axe, drawing blood. 'Bring them on,' he roared. 'Bring them on!'

His shout echoed once through the ruins before it was muffled and swallowed by the ominous silence. After that even Gotrek was quiet.

THE CITY WAS larger than Felix had imagined; perhaps even the size of Altdorf, greatest city of the Empire. Most of it was ruined, devastated by ancient wars.

'Surely your own people did not cause all this damage. Some of it seems quite recent,' Felix said.

'Gobbos,' Gotrek replied. 'It is the curse of their kind that when they have no one else to fight they fight amongst themselves. Doubtless after the city fell it was divided up among various warlords. Sure as elvish treachery, they'd fall out over the division of spoils.

'In addition there have been many attempts to recapture the city by my kin and men from the Border Princes. There's still a motherlode of silver down there.'

He spat. 'No attempt to hold the city has ever lasted. The dark has lain here. Where once the darkness has been can never again be truly free of it.'

They entered an area where the buildings had been partially repaired and which now seemed abandoned again. An attempt to re-colonise the city had failed, defeated by the sheer immensity of the ruins. Under the walls of the great keep, the dwarfs seemed more relaxed. Their leader grumbled the occasional order to keep alert.

'Remember Svensson,' he said. 'He and his men were killed while on the path to the great gate.'

The dwarfs immediately reverted to their stern watchfulness. Felix kept his hand near his sword.

'This is not a healthy place,' Jules Gascoigne whispered.

As soon as they were through it, the keep's great gate closed with a crash like the fall of towers.

THE HALL WAS bleak, its walls covered by threadbare tapestries. It was lit by strange glowing gems that hung from a chandelier in the ceiling. On a throne of carved ivory inlaid with gold sat an aged dwarf, flanked by lines of mailed, blue-tunicked warriors. He gazed down with rheumy eyes, his glance flickering from the Trollslayer to the humans. Beside the ancient, a purple-robed female dwarf watched the whole proceeding with a strange, serene intensity. From a chain around her neck dangled an iron-bound book.

Felix thought he detected strain in the faces of these dwarfs. Perhaps dwelling in the haunted and run-down city had sapped their morale. Or perhaps it was something more; they seemed constantly to look over their shoulders. They started at the slightest noise.

'State your business, strangers,' the aged dwarf said in a deep, proud, brittle voice. 'Why have you come here?'

Gotrek glared back at him loutishly. 'I am Gotrek Gurnisson, once of Everpeak. I have come to hunt troll in the dark beneath the world. The manling Felix Jaeger is my blood-brother, a poet and rememberer. Do you seek to deny me my right?'

As he said the final sentence Gotrek hefted his axe. The dwarfish soldiers raised their hammers.

The ancient laughed. 'No, Gotrek Gurnisson, I do not. Your path is an honourable one and I see no reason to stand in it. Although your choice of brethren is an ill one.'

The dwarf soldiers began to mutter amongst themselves. Felix felt baffled. It seemed as if Gotrek had broken some incomprehensible taboo.

'There is precedent,' the robed dwarfess said. The sounds of consternation stopped. Felix expected her to speak further, to expand on what she had said but she did not. It seemed enough to the dwarfs that she had spoken.

'You both may pass, Gotrek, son of Gurni. Be careful of the gate you choose into the dark and beware, lest your courage fail you.' His voice held no hint of concern, only bitterness and secret shame.

Gotrek nodded curtly to the dwarf lord and withdrew to the back of the hall. Felix gave his best courtly bow, then followed the Trollslayer.

'State your business, strangers,' the ruler continued. Aldred went down on one knee before the throne and the others followed suit.

'I have come on a matter concerning my faith and an ancient pledge of aid between your folk and mine. My tale is a complex one and may take some time to tell.'

The dwarf laughed nastily. Once again Felix sensed some secret knowledge that ate at the aged dwarf-lord. 'Speak on. We are rich in no other commodity but time. We can spend it freely.'

'Thank you. Am I correct in assuming that you are the same Prince Belegar who led the expedition to reclaim this city from the greenskins twenty years ago?'

Belegar nodded. 'You are correct.'

'Your guide was a dwarfish prospector called Faragrim, who found many secret ways back into the city below the Eight Peaks.'

Once again the old dwarf nodded. Felix and Gotrek exchanged looks. It had been Faragrim who had told Gotrek about the troll-guarded treasure beneath the mountains.

'Your expedition was accompanied by a young knight of my order, a companion of Faragrim in his adventuring days. His name was Raphael.'

'He was a true man and a foe of our enemies,' Belegar said. 'He went with Faragrim on his last expedition into the depths and never returned. When Faragrim refused to seek him, I dispatched runners but they could not find his body.'

'It is good to know you honoured him, although I am downcast to learn that the blade which he bore was lost. It was a weapon of power and of great importance to my order.'

'You are not the first who has come here to retrieve it,' the dwarf woman said.

Aldred smiled. 'Nevertheless I have sworn a vow to return the sword, Karaghul, to the chapter house of my order. I have cause to believe I will succeed.'

Belegar raised an eyebrow.

'Before setting out on my quest I fasted for two weeks and scourged my body with purgatives and the lash. On Sigmarzeit last I was favoured with a vision. My lord appeared before me. He said he looked with favour on my mission and that the time was near for the enchanted blade to be drawn again.

'Further – he told me that I would be aided in my quest by one of our ancient brethren. I interpret this as meaning a dwarf, for so are your people always referred to in the Unfinished Book.

'I beseech you, noble Belegar, do not oppose my mission. My brother Raphael honoured the ancient vow of our faith, never to refuse aid to a dwarf, when he fell. It would be a mark of respect to allow me to recover his blade.'

'Well spoken, man,' Belegar said. Felix could see he was moved, as dwarfs invariably were by talk of honour and ancient oaths. Still there was a hint of bright malice in Belegar's gaze when he spoke again. 'I grant your petition. May you have more luck than your predecessors.'

Aldred rose and bowed. 'Could you provide us with a guide?'

Once again Belegar laughed and there was a strange, wild quality to his mirth. He cackled nastily. 'I am sure Gotrek Gurnisson would be prepared to aid a quest so similar to his own.'

Belegar rose from the throne and the robed woman moved to support him. He turned to hobble from the room. As he reached the rear exit of the chamber he turned and said, 'You are dismissed!'

FROM THE WINDOW of the tower where the dwarfs had housed them, Felix looked down at the cobbled street. Outside snow had begun to fall in feathery flakes. Behind him the others argued quietly.

'I don't like it,' Zauberlich said. 'Who knows how vast an area lies below ground? We could search from now till the end of the world and not find the blade. I had thought the dwarfs guarded the blade.'

'We must trust to faith,' Aldred replied, calmly and implacably. 'Sigmar wishes the blade to be found. We must trust that he will guide our hands to it.'

An undertow of hysteria was evident in Zauberlich's voice. 'Aldred, if Sigmar wished the blade returned, why did he not place it in the hands of the three of your brethren who preceded us?'

'Who am I to guess the Blessed Lord's motives? Perhaps the time was not right. Perhaps this is a test of our faith. I will not be found lacking. You do not have to accompany us if you do not wish.'

Off amongst the ruins, Felix spied a cold green light. The sight of it filled him with dread. He beckoned for Jules to come over and take a look. By the time the Bretonnian arrived at the window there was nothing to be seen. The scout gave him a quizzical look.

Embarrassed, Felix looked back at the discussion. Am I going mad, he wondered? He tried to dismiss the green light from his mind.

'Herr Gurnisson, what do you think?' Zauberlich asked. He turned to beseech the Trollslayer.

'I will be going down into the dark anyway,' Gotrek said. 'It does not bother me what you do. Settle your own quarrels.'

'We have already lost three-quarters of the people we set out with,' Zauberlich said, glancing from Jules Gascoigne to Aldred. What purpose would it serve to throw away our own lives?'

'What purpose would it serve to give up, save to make our comrades' sacrifice meaningless?' replied the Templar. 'If we give up now their deaths will be in vain. They believed that we should find Karaghul. They gave their lives willingly enough.'

The Templar's fanaticism made Felix uneasy. Aldred talked too casually of men laying down their lives. Yet he also had a calm certainty that gave his words a compelling urgency. Felix knew warriors would follow such a man.

'You took the same oath as everyone else, Johann. If you wish to foreswear yourself now so be it, but the consequences will be on your own eternal soul.'

Felix felt a wry sympathy for the mage. He himself had sworn to follow Gotrek while drunk, in a warm tavern in a civilised city, after the dwarf had saved his life. Peril had seemed remote then. He shook his head. It was easy to swear such oaths when you had no idea of the consequences. It was another to keep them when the path led to dismal places like Karak Eight Peaks.

Felix heard approaching footsteps. There was a knock and the door creaked open to reveal the female dwarf who had stood beside Belegar in the throne room. 'I've come to warn you,' she said in her low, pleasant voice.

'Warn us about what?' Gotrek enquired curtly.

'There are terrible things loose in the depths. Why do you think we live in such fear?'

'I think you had better come in,' the Trollslayer said.

'I AM MAGDA Freyadotter. I keep the Book of Remembering at the temple of Valaya. I speak with the voice of Valaya, so you will know that what I say is truth.'

'Accepted,' Gotrek Gurnisson said. 'Speak truth then.'

'In the darkness, unquiet spirits walk.' She paused and looked around at them. Her gaze rested on the Trollslayer and lingered.

'When first we came here we numbered five hundred, with a few mannish allies. The only perils we faced were the orcs and their followers. We cleared this keep and parts of the upper city as a prelude to reclaiming our ancient mines.

'We made forays into the depths, seeking the vaults of our ancestors, knowing that if we could find them word would spread among the kinsfolk and more would flock here.'

Felix understood the strategy. Word of a treasure find would lure more dwarfs here. He felt a little guilty. It had brought himself and Gotrek.

'We sent expeditions into the depths in search of the old

places. Things had changed from the ancient plans we memorise as children. Tunnels had collapsed, ways were blocked, foul new passages dug by orcs inter-connected with our own.'

'Did the dwarf Faragrim lead any of these expeditions?' Gotrek asked.

'Yes he did,' Magda replied.

Gotrek looked at Felix. 'That much of what he claimed is true then,' the Trollslayer said.

'Faragrim was bold and sought deeper and further than all others. What did he tell you?'

Gotrek studied his feet. 'That he had encountered the mightiest troll he had ever seen – and fled.'

Dwarfs are not good at lying, thought Felix. It seemed impossible that the priestess could not tell he was hiding something. But Magda didn't appear to notice anything amiss.

Felix thought back to the night in distant Nuln, in the Eight Peaks tavern, when the awesomely drunken Faragrim had poured out his tale to Gotrek. The dwarfs had been so inebriated that they had even seemed to forget there was a human present and had talked excitedly in a mixture of Reikspiel and Khazalid. At the time Felix assumed the dwarfs were only attempting to outdo each other in telling tall tales. Now he wasn't sure.

'So that is what terrified him – we thought it was the ghosts,' Magda said. 'One day he returned from the depths. His beard had turned pure white. He spoke no word but simply departed.'

'You spoke of terrors in the depths,' Zauberlich interrupted.

'Yes. Our patrols below soon spoke of encountering ghosts of ancient kin. The spirits howled and wailed and begged us to free them from the bondage of Chaos. Soon our early successes were reversed. What dwarf can bear the sight of kinsmen torn from the bosom of the ancestral spirits? Our forces lost heart. Prince Belegar led a mighty expedition to seek the source of the evil. His force was destroyed by the lurkers in the depths. Only he and a few trusted retainers returned. They have never spoken of what they found. Most of our surviving folk departed to their homelands. Now barely a hundred of us are left to hold this keep.'

The colour drained from Gotrek's face. Felix had never seen

the Trollslayer display such fear before. Gotrek could face any living creature boldly but this talk of ghosts had leeched away his courage. The worship of their ancestors must be very important to his people, thought Felix with sudden insight.

'I have warned you now,' the priestess said. 'Do you still wish to go below?'

Gotrek stared off into the fire. All eyes in the room were on him. Felix felt that if Gotrek abandoned his quest then even Aldred might give up. The Templar seemed convinced that the Trollslayer was the dwarf of his prophecy.

Gotrek clutched his axe so tightly that his knuckles were white. He took a deep breath. He seemed to will himself to speak.

'Man or spirit, alive or dead, I fear it not,' he said quietly in a voice that was not convincing. 'I will go below. There is a troll I have to meet.'

'Well spoken,' Magda said. 'I will lead you the entrance of the realm below.'

Gotrek bowed. 'It would be an honour.'

'Tomorrow then,' she said and rose to go.

Gotrek held the door for her. After she had departed he slumped into the chair. He laid down his axe and clutched at the armrests as if he feared he would fall over. He looked very afraid.

A HUGE DOORWAY gaped in the side of the mountain. Above it, rising from the rock, was a great window cut through the rock. The window was roofed with red-slate tiles, many of which had fallen in. It was as if a keep had been built and then sunk beneath the earth so that only the tallest parts protruded above the ground.

'This is the Silvergate,' Magda said. 'The Silverway runs to the Upper Granaries and the Long Stairs. I believe the Way is clear. After that, beware!'

'Thank you,' Felix said. Gotrek nodded to the priestess. Aldred, Jules and Zauberlich bowed. The men looked very sombre.

They began to check their lanterns and the supply of oil. They had plenty of provisions. All their weapons were oiled and ready.

Magda reached within the sleeves of her robe. She produced a tube of parchment and handed it to Gotrek. He unrolled it, gave it a quick glance and bowed from the waist until his crest touched the ground.

'May Grungni, Grimnir and Valaya watch over you all,' Magda said and made a peculiar sign of benediction over them.

'The blessing of Sigmar upon you and your clan,' Aldred Fellblade replied.

'Let's go,' Gotrek Gurnisson said. They hefted their gear and passed under the arch. Felix could see that it was marked with old dwarf runes that time had yet to erode.

As they passed below, they were cast into shadow and chill. Felix could not repress a shiver.

Light from the great window illumined the way down into the gloom. Felix marvelled at the precision of dwarfish engineering. At the brow of the slope he turned and looked back. The priestess and her escort stood there. He waved to her and she raised an arm in farewell. Then they began the downward way and the lands above were hidden from view. Felix wondered if any of them would ever see daylight again.

'WHAT DID THE priestess give you, Herr Gurnisson?' Johann Zauberlich asked. Gotrek thrust the document into the magician's hand.

'It's a map of the city copied from the master-map in the temple of Valaya the Rememberer. It covers all the ground that Prince Belegar's expeditions explored.'

By the light of the glowing crystals overhead the sorcerer inspected it, then scratched his head. Felix looked over his shoulder and saw only a scrawl of tiny runes connected with lines in different coloured ink. Some of the lines were thick, others were thin and some were dotted.

'It is like no map I've ever seen,' the mage said. 'I can't make head nor tail of it.'

Gotrek's lips curled into a sneer. 'I would be surprised if you could. It's written in the rune-code of the Engineers' Guild.'

'We are in your hands, Herr Gurnisson, and Sigmar's,' the Templar said. 'Lead on.'

FELIX TRIED TO count the number of steps he took but gave up at eight hundred and sixty-two. He had noted the passages leading off the Silverway and began to have some idea of the scale of the dwarf city. It was like the floating mountains of ice

that mariners reported in the Sea of Claws. Nine-tenths of it
was below the surface. The scale overwhelmed any of the
works of man Felix had ever seen. It was a humbling
experience.

The way passed many openings in the wall. Some were still
partially bricked up. The brickwork looked recent. Something
had chipped through it using very crude tools. There was a
smell of rot in the air.

'Grain silos,' Gotrek explained. 'Used to feed the city in winter. Looks like gobbos have been at Belegar's stores though.'

'If there are any greenskins near, they will soon taste my
steel,' Aldred Fellblade said.

Jules and Felix exchanged worried looks. They were not as
keen as the Templar and the Trollslayer to get to grips with
whatever dwelled down here.

FELIX LOST TRACK of time but he guessed it was half an hour
before they left the Silverway and entered a hallway as large as
the Koenigspark in Altdorf. It was lit by great slots in the ceiling. Motes of dust danced in a dozen columns of light taller
than the towers of Nuln. The sound of their steps echoed, disturbing strange shadowy, fluttering things that lurked by the
ceiling.

'The Square of Merscha,' Gotrek said, in a voice that held a
note of wonder. He gazed into the hall with a strange mixture
of hatred and pride. 'Where Queen Hilga's personal troops
turned and stood off an army of goblins a hundred times their
number. They gave the Queen and many of the citizens time to
escape. Never did I expect to lay eyes on it. Walk carefully. Every
stone has been sanctified with the blood of heroes.'

Felix looked at the Trollslayer. He saw a new person. Since
they had entered the city Gotrek had changed. He stood taller,
prouder. He no longer cast furtive looks around and muttered
to himself. For the first time since Felix had met him the dwarf
seemed at ease. It's as if he's come home, thought Felix.

Now it's we men who are out of place, he realised, suddenly
aware of the immense weight of stone which lay between him
and the sun. He had to fight against the fear that the whole
mountain, held in place only by the fragile craft of those
ancient dwarfs, would fall in on him, burying him forever. He
sensed the closeness of the dark, of the old places beneath the

mountains that had never known daylight. The seeds of terror were planted in his heart.

He looked out across a square larger than any structure he had ever known and he knew that he could not cross it. Absurdly, far below the surface of the earth, he began to feel agoraphobic. He did not want to pass below that vaulted ceiling for fear that the artificial sky would fall. He felt dizzy and his breathing came in ragged gasps.

A reassuring hand fell on his shoulder. Felix looked down to see that Gotrek stood by him. Slowly the urge to run back up the Silverway passed and he felt some semblance of calm return. He looked back out over the square of Merscha, overcome with awe.

'Truly, yours are a mighty people, Gotrek Gurnisson,' he said.

Gotrek looked up at him and there was sadness in his eyes. 'Aye, manling, that we were, but the craft which created this hall is beyond us now. We no longer have the number of masons needed to build it.'

Gotrek turned and looked back into the hall then, he shook his head. 'Ach, manling, you have some inkling of how far we have fallen. The days of our glory are behind us. Once we created all of this. Now we huddle in a few shrunken cities and wait for the end of the world. The day of the dwarf has gone, never to return. We crawl like maggots through the work of elder days and the glory of what once was ours mocks us.'

He gestured out at the hall with his axe, as if he wished he could demolish it with one blow.

'This is what we must measure ourselves against!' he bellowed. The startled men looked at him. The echoes mocked him. Somewhere among them Felix Jaeger thought he heard the sounds of furtive movement. When he looked towards the noise he could almost swear he saw winking amber eyes receding slowly into the dark.

AS THEY PROGRESSED, the stone of the undercity took on a peculiar greenish tinge. They moved away from the lit hall into shadowy gloom, faintly illuminated by dim, flickering glowjewels. Occasionally Felix heard a tapping sound. Gotrek stopped and placed a hand against the wall. Out of curiosity Felix did the same. He felt a small, distant vibration pass through the stone.

Gotrek glanced at him. 'Gobbo wall-drumming,' he said. 'They know we're here. Best speed our pace to confuse any scouts.'

Felix nodded. The walls glittered like jade. He could see fat, red-eyed rats move away from the light. Their hides were pure black. Gotrek cursed and stamped at the nearest one but it evaded him.

He shook his head. 'Even here, so close to the surface, we see the taint of Chaos. It must be worse down below.'

THEY CAME TO a stairway running down into the dark. Great columns had fallen away. Piles of masonry lay in a heap. The stair itself seemed crumbled. They disturbed a nest of flitter-wings. The small bats took off like scraps of shadow and fluttered about. Uneasily Felix wondered how safe the stairs were.

They descended through galleries marked with the signs of orcish despoliation. Rats scuttled ahead of them from nests under broken stonework.

Gotrek gestured to halt and stood sniffing the air. From behind them Felix thought he heard the sound of footfalls further up the stairs.

'I smell gobbos,' the Trollslayer said.

'They are behind us, I think,' Jules said.

'All around us,' Gotrek said. 'This place has been used as an orc road for many years.'

'What shall we do?' Felix asked, exchanging worried looks with Zauberlich.

'Push on,' Gotrek said, consulting the map. 'We're going the way we want to anyway.'

Felix glanced back. He suspected they were being herded into a trap. Things look bad, he thought. Our way back to the surface has been cut off already, unless Gotrek knows another route.

The Trollslayer's expression assured him that Gotrek was giving no thought to such matters. The dwarf glanced around worriedly as if expecting to see a ghost.

Their pursuers' footsteps came ever closer. From ahead, echoing through the galleries, they heard a bellow that was deeper and louder than any orc's.

'What was that?' Zauberlich asked.

'Something big,' Aldred said quietly.

Gotrek ran his thumb along the blade of his axe until a jewel of blood glistened on its blade.

'Good,' he said.

'It must be close,' Felix said nervously, wondering if his face was as ashen as the sorcerer's and the scout's.

'Hard to say,' Gotrek said. 'These tunnels distort sound. Amplify it too. It could be miles away.'

The roar came again and there was the sound of running feet, as if goblins scuttled to obey an order.

'It's closer this time,' Felix said.

'Calm yourself, manling. As I said, it's probably miles away.'

IT STOOD WAITING in the next hall, near the foot of the long stairway. They passed under an archway carved with skeletal daemons' heads and saw the beast: an immense ogre, half again as tall as and four times the bulk of Aldred. A crest of hair emerged from its scaly scalp. Like Gotrek's crest, it was dyed. Unlike Gotrek's, it was patterned in alternating black and white bands. A huge spiked arm-guard, its fist a long, wicked scythe, covered its right arm. An enormous spiked ball and chain dangled from its left hand. It looked like it could demolish a castle wall.

The creature grinned, revealing spiked metal teeth. Behind it hunched a company of goblins, green skins glistening. They clutched metal shields emblazoned with the emblem of the skull. Scabs and boils and pock marks marked their leering, ugly faces. Some wore spiked collars round their necks. Some had metal rings pinching the flesh of their torsos. Their eyes were red and without pupils. Felix wondered if this was another sign of the taint of Chaos.

He glanced around. To his right was tumbled masonry. It looked as if old dwarfish stonework had been brought down and cleared to make way for newer and cruder carvings. Iron chains were set in the wall near him. To the left was a great chimney carved so that the fireplace was the maw of a gaping daemonic head. Brownish blood stained the stone. Have we stumbled into some goblin temple? wondered Felix. Just what we need, a man-hungry ogre and a horde of goblin fanatics. Well, he consoled himself, at least things can't get any worse.

He felt a tap on his shoulder and turned to look back up the stairs. Down it poured another company of goblins led by a

burly orc. In its left hand it clutched a scimitar and in its right
it held a standard whose banner depicted a stylised
representation of the tusked maw of the cursed moon,
Morrslieb. Stuck on the top of the standard was an embalmed
human head. Behind the bearer came more goblins armed
with maces and spears and axes.

Felix looked at Jules. The Bretonnian gave a shrug. What a
terrible place to die, thought Felix. For a long moment the three
groups exchanged glares. There was a brief peaceful silence.

'For Sigmar!' Aldred cried, raising his great sword high and
charging down the stairs with surprising nimbleness for a man
garbed in plate.

'Tanugh aruk!' Gotrek bellowed, as he followed. Overhead the
glowjewels seemed to glow briefly brighter. 'Kill the goblin-
scum!'

Felix brought his blade to the guard position. Beside him,
Jules Gascoigne stood at the ready. The standard bearer glared
at them but made no move to come closer. Felix was reluctant
to attack the goblins up the staircase. It was a stand-off.

Behind him Felix heard the clash of weapons and the screaming of battle-cries. The foul orc reek was strong in his nostrils.
Iron-shod feet rang on the stairs behind him. He whirled just
in time to parry a mace swung with considerable force by a
greenskin warrior. The force of the impact jarred up his arm.

He gritted his teeth and stabbed out. His blade cut a glittering arc through the gloom. The goblin skipped back and Felix
almost overbalanced. He moved as rapidly as he could down
the stairs, hampered by the uncertain footing.

'Jules, hold the stair!' he shouted.

'Anything for a friend.'

Felix pushed on after the goblin. He had some trouble pur-
suing his nimble foe over the broken ground. The gobbo stuck
out its tongue and yelled tauntingly. Overcome by stinging
anger, Felix rushed forward and tripped. He fell to his knees
and rolled, feeling pain where he had skinned flesh from his
knees. Something scurried over him. Tiny claws scratched him.
I've disturbed a nest of rats, he thought. For a moment he was
disoriented. As he struggled to his feet he caught sight of the
tableau of the battle.

Gotrek chopped into the chest of his foe. Mail exploded out-
ward from the goblin's breast where the huge axe impacted.

Aldred Fellblade charged within the sweep of the ogre's huge wrecking ball and stabbed upward through the creature's stomach. Felix saw his blade protruding from the ogre's back. Goblins swept past Felix to get at the dwarf, their ancient foe. Just out of reach of the struggle, Johann Zauberlich produced a scroll and chanted a spell. A ball of fire appeared in his left hand. Black rats swarmed everywhere. Shadowy flitterwings swooped agitatedly.

Felix fought for balance. His gaze shifted to Jules Gascoigne on the stair, bravely standing off a number of heavily armed foes. He had already killed one but more entered behind another standard bearer.

Pain surged through Felix as a club smashed into his shoulder. Flashing silver stars filled his field of vision. He fell on his face, letting go of his sword. Above him stood the goblin, its club raised, a leer of triumph on its face. Move, damn you, Felix told his protesting limbs as the club whistled down. It loomed like the trunk of a falling tree, moving with painful slowness to the man's panic-honed senses.

At the last moment Felix rolled to one side and the club hit rock with a loud crack. Felix twisted and lashed out with one foot, sending the goblin flying. Desperately Felix fumbled for his sword, feeling huge relief as his fingers closed over its hilt.

He dived forward, impaling the goblin before it could rise. The thing cursed as it died. Suddenly a titanic flash blinded Felix. He reeled back, covering his eyes as an inferno erupted before him. Hot air washed over his face. The air stank of sulphur. I'm dead, dead and in hell, he thought. Then understanding filled his mind. Zauberlich had unleashed his fireball.

He looked around. Gotrek and Aldred were clearing a path through the demoralised goblins. Behind them rushed the scout and the wizard. Jules grabbed Felix by the arm.

'Come on!' he yelled. 'We've got to get out while they're confused.'

They ran on down the long corridor. From behind them came the sounds of continuing conflict.

'What's happening back there?' he yelled.

'Different gobbo tribes,' Gotrek cackled. 'With any luck they'll slit each other's throats while they fight to see who gets to eat us.'

* * *

FELIX STARED DOWN into the chasm. Stars glittered in its depths. Aldred and Gotrek glanced back down the corridor. Jules prowled out onto the corroded metal bridge. The sorcerer, Zauberlich leaned against a cast-iron gargoyle, panting heavily.

'I fear I was not intended for the adventurous life,' he gasped. 'My studies did not prepare me for all this strenuous exercise.'

Felix smiled. The sorcerer reminded him of his old professors. The only conflicts they ever fought were struggles over the correct interpretation of the finer points of classical poetry. He was surprised and ashamed to find himself so contemptuous of those old men. Once it had been his ambition to become just like them. Had the adventuring life changed him so much?

Zauberlich was inspecting the gargoyle curiously. Felix revised his opinion of the wizard. He only superficially resembled those elderly academics. None of them would have survived the road to Karak Eight Peaks. The fact Zauberlich's sorcery was so adroit spoke volumes about the man's determination and intelligence. Magic was no art for a weakling or a coward. It held its own hidden perils. Curiosity overcame Felix. He suddenly wanted to ask the sorcerer how he had become involved with the Templar.

'I think we must have lost the goblins,' Aldred shouted. He and Gotrek clumped towards the others. The questions Felix had been about to ask Zauberlich died on his lips. As they crossed the bridge Felix sensed he would never get another chance to ask them.

THEY GAZED DOWN the long, dark corridor. For the first time the light from the glowjewels had failed. Felix had grown so accustomed to the dim greenish light that its sudden failure shocked him. It felt as if the sun had set in the middle of the day. Gotrek pushed on into the dark, seemingly oblivious to the lack of light. Felix wondered at how well the dwarf could see.

'Best break out the lanterns,' Gotrek said, shaking his head. 'The lights have been vandalised. Damn gobbos. Those jewels should have glowed forever but they just couldn't leave them alone. They can never be replaced now. The art has been lost.'

Jules prepared a lantern. Zauberlich lit it with a word. Felix watched them, feeling redundant until he heard Gotrek moan behind him. Felix turned to look.

Far down the corridor there was a faint greenishly glowing figure. It was an old bearded dwarf. Light poured from it and through it. It looked transparent, as tangible as a soap bubble. The ghostly figure wailed, a thin, reedy sound, and advanced towards Gotrek, arms outstretched. The Trollslayer stood transfixed. Terror overwhelmed Felix. He recognised the quality of the light. He had seen it before, on the mountainside and in the city above.

'Sigmar protect us,' Aldred muttered. Felix heard the Templar's blade ring as he pulled it from the scabbard.

Felix felt his hair stir as the ancient dwarf advanced. The air seemed cold. His flesh tingled. The figure's lips moved and Felix thought he heard a gibbering faraway voice. Gotrek stirred and moved forward, axe held up as if to ward off a blow.

The ghost redoubled its frantic pleas. Gotrek shook his head as if he did not understand. The ghostly dwarf hurried to meet him, looking over its shoulder as if pursued by a distant, invisible enemy.

Horror filled Felix. The ghost was falling apart. It was like a mist before a strong wind, parts of it just peeled away and vanished. Before Gotrek could reach it, it vanished entirely. As it went Felix heard a distant, despairing wail. It was the cry of a damned soul, vanishing into hell.

As Gotrek returned Felix saw the stunned look on his face. The Trollslayer looked appalled and bewildered. A tear gleamed beneath his single eye.

They hurried down the darkened corridor. Even after they reached an area where the glowjewels gleamed again, no one seemed in a hurry to extinguish the lantern. For long hours thereafter the Trollslayer never said a word.

FELIX WAS TEMPTED to drink from a spring flowing into the ancient carved trough. He bent over the greenly glowing water when he felt strong hands knot his hair and pull him back.

'Are you mad, manling? Can you not see the water is tainted?' Felix was about to object when Zauberlich looked down into the water and inspected the greenish glowing flecks.

'Warpstone?' he said, in a surprised tone. Felix felt his blood run cold. All he had ever heard about the dread substance was that it was the pure essence of Chaos, sought after by evil alchemists in certain grisly tales.

'What did you say, mage?' Gotrek asked curtly.

'I think this could be warpstone. It has the greenish luminescence that certain scholarly tomes attribute to that unpleasant substance. If there is even a trace of warpstone in the water that might account for the high level of mutation hereabouts.'

'There are old tales of the skaven poisoning the wells,' Gotrek said. 'Would even they be so foul as to do it with warpstone?'

'I have heard it said that the skaven subsist on warpstone. Perhaps this served a dual purpose. It gave them sustenance and made the wells unusable by their foes.'

'You seem very knowledgeable in the ways of Chaos, Herr Zauberlich,' Felix said suspiciously.

'The doctor and I have hunted our share of witches,' Aldred Fellblade said. 'It's a task that obliges you to learn much strange lore. Are you implying any companion of mine could be tainted by such foulness as trafficking with the Ruinous Powers?'

Felix shook his head. He had no wish to cross a warrior as deadly as the Templar. 'My apologies for my unjust suspicions.'

Gotrek guffawed. 'No need to apologise. Eternal vigilance is necessary in all foes of the dark.'

Aldred nodded in agreement. It seemed the Trollslayer had found a kindred spirit.

'We had best move on,.' Jules Gascoigne said, looking nervously back the way they had come.

'Best stick to drinking what we brought with us, manling,' Gotrek said as they moved off.

'WHAT IS THIS stuff?' Felix asked nervously. His question echoed off into the distance. Jules shone lantern light into the dark caverns. Giant, misshapen fungi cast long shadows against the white mould-covered walls. Spores drifted in the lantern's beam.

'Once we cultivated mushrooms for food,' Gotrek muttered. 'Now it looks like another victim of mutation.'

The Trollslayer marched into the room. His boots left prints in the sodden carpet of mould. Somewhere in the distance Felix thought he heard running water.

Foot-long splinters of whiteness detached themselves from the walls, enlarging as they came. They hurtled towards the startled adventurers. Gotrek chopped into one with his axe. It gave with a squishing sound. More and more splinters left the wall like a blizzard of giant snowflakes. Felix found himself surrounded by soft bloated bodies and fluttering wings.

'Moths!' Zauberlich shouted. 'They're moths! They're trying to get at the light. Kill it.'

It went dark. Felix had a last vision of Gotrek, his body covered in the giant insects, then he stood within a whirling snowstorm of wingbeats, his flesh crawling at the moths' touch. Then all was silence.

'Back out. Slowly,' Gotrek whispered, revulsion showing in every syllable. 'We'll find another way.'

FELIX PAUSED TO look back down the long hallway, wishing that the glowjewels were brighter. He was convinced he had heard something. He reached out and touched the smooth cold stone of the wall. A faint vibration thrummed through it. Wall drumming.

He strained his eyes. In the distance he could make out vague shapes. One carried a huge banner with what seemed to be a human head on top. He pulled his sword from its scabbard.

'Looks like they found us again,' he said. There was no reply. The others had disappeared round the corner. Felix realised that they had kept marching when he paused. He ran to catch up.

FILLED WITH DREAD, Felix opened one eye. He emerged from slumber. It was Gotrek's watch but he thought he heard eerie voices. He looked around the small chamber and his hair stood on end. His heartbeat sounded loud and fast in his ears and he thought that he was going to faint dead away. All power had fled from his limbs.

The strange green glow lit the area. It washed over the Trollslayer's haggard face, making him look like some ghastly zombie. Gotrek's shadow loomed huge and menacing on the wall. The entity from which the light emerged was on its knees in front of the Trollslayer, arms outstretched beseechingly. It was the ghost of some ancient dwarfish woman.

It was insubstantial and yet it had the presence of ages, as if it were a manifestation of the elder times made real. Its garb was regal and the face had once possessed authority. Its cheeks seemed sunken and the flesh seemed to have sloughed away and was pock-marked, like it was riddled with maggots. The eyes that lurked under cave-like brows were pools of shadow in which witch-lights burned. It was as if the ghost were being eaten away by some unworldly disease, a cancer of the spirit.

The aspect of the thing filled Felix with terror, and its suffering only intensified his awful fear. It hinted that there were things waiting beyond the grave from which even death was not an escape, dark powers which could seize a spirit and torment it. Felix had always been afraid of death but now he was aware that there were worse things. He felt himself on the edge of sanity, hoping for the release from this terrible knowledge that madness might bring.

Nearby Jules Gascoigne whimpered like a child enmeshed in a nightmare. Felix tried to avert his eyes from the scene being played out before him but could not; a compulsion lay on him. He was horribly fascinated by the confrontation.

Gotrek raised his axe and put it between him and the troubled spirit. Was it his imagination, Felix wondered, or did the runes that inlaid the huge blade glow with internal fire?

'Begone, abomination,' the Trollslayer rasped in a voice barely above a whisper. 'Depart, I am yet among the living.'

The thing laughed. Felix realised that it made no sound. He heard its voice within his head.

'Aid us, Gotrek, son of Gurni. Free us. Our tombs are desecrated and a terrible warping power rests within our halls.' The spirit wavered and seemed about to dissipate like mist. With a visible effort it maintained its form.

Gotrek tried to speak but could not. The great muscles in his neck stood out, a vein throbbed at his temple.

'We have committed no crime,' said the spirit in a voice that held ages of suffering and loneliness. 'We had departed to join our ancestral spirits when we were brought back by the desecration of our resting place. We were wrenched from eternal peace.'

'How can this be?' Gotrek asked, in a voice that held both wonder and terror. 'What can tear a dwarf from the bosom of the ancestors?'

'What else has the strength to upset the order of the universe, Trollslayer? What else but Chaos?'

'I am but a single warrior. I cannot stand against the Dark Powers.'

'No need. Cleanse our tomb of that which lies there and we will be free. Will you do this, son of Gurni? If you do not we shall not be able to rejoin our kin. We will gutter and vanish like candle-flames in a storm. Even now we fade. Only a few of us are left.'

Gotrek looked at the anguished spirit. Felix saw reverence and pity flicker across his face. 'If it is within my power, I will free you.'

A smile passed across the spirit's ravaged face. 'Others we have asked, including our descendant Belegar. They were too fearful to aid us. In you I find no flaw.'

Gotrek bowed, and the spirit reached out a glowing hand to touch his brow. It seemed to Felix as if sudden insight flooded into the Trollslayer. The ghost dwindled and faded as if receding to a vast distance. Soon it was gone.

Felix looked around at the others. They were all awake and gazing at the dwarf in astonishment. Aldred looked at the Trollslayer with something akin to reverence. Gotrek hefted his axe.

'We have work to do,' he said in a voice like stone grinding against stone.

LIKE A MAN in a trance, Gotrek Gurnisson led them down the long corridors in the depths below the old city. They passed into an area of wide, low tunnels lined by defaced statues.

'Greenskins have been here,' Felix observed to Jules Gascoigne next to him.

'Yes, but not so recently, my friend. Those statues were not broken recently. See the lichen growing on the breaks. I like not the way it glows.'

'There is something evil about this place. I can sense it,' Zauberlich said, tugging at the sleeve of his robe and peering around nervously. 'There is an oppressive presence in the air.'

Felix wondered whether he could sense it too or whether he was simply receptive to his companion's forebodings. They turned a corner and moved along a way lined by mighty stone arches. Strange runic patterns were carved between each archway.

'I hope your friend is not leading us into some trap laid by the Dark Powers,' the sorcerer whispered quietly.

Felix shook his head. He was convinced of the spirit's sincerity. But then again, he thought, what do I know of such things? He was so far beyond the realms of his normal experience that all he could do was trust to the flow of events. He gave a fatalistic shrug. Things were beyond his control.

'I hate to bother you, but our pursuers have returned,' Jules said. 'Why have they not attacked? Are they afraid of this area?'

Felix looked back towards the redly glowing eyes of the greenskin company. He made out the hideous standard.

'Whatever they were afraid of, they seem to have plucked up courage now.'

'Maybe they've been herding us here for sacrifice,' Zauberlich said.

'Yes, look on the bright side,' Jules said.

EVENTUALLY THEY PASSED over another chasm-bridge and into a further corridor lined with decorative arches. Gotrek halted at a particular huge open archway. He shook his head like a man waking up from a dream.

Felix studied the arch. He saw a great groove made for a barrier to slide along. On closer reflection, Felix thought that if the opening were closed it would be invisible, blending into the pattern of the way along which they passed. Felix lit his lantern, driving back the shadowy darkness.

Beyond the opening lay an enormous vault, lined on either side with great sarcophagi carved to resemble the figures of sleeping dwarfs of noble aspect. To the right were males, to the left females. Some of the tops of the stone coffins had been removed. In the centre of the chamber was a huge pile of gold and old banners mingled with yellowing, cracked bones. From the middle of the heap protruded the hilt of a sword, carved in the shape of a dragon.

Felix was reminded of the cairn they had built for Aldred's followers on the road to the city. A hideous stench came through the arch and made Felix want to gag.

'Look at all that gold,' the Bretonnian said. 'Why has no greenskin taken it?'

'Something protects it,' Felix said. A question crossed his mind. 'Gotrek, this is one of the hidden tombs of your people you spoke of, isn't it?'

The dwarf nodded.

'Why is it open? Surely it would have been sealed?'

Gotrek scratched his head and stood deep in thought for a moment. 'Faragrim opened it,' he said angrily. 'He was once an engineer. He would know the rune-codes. Ghosts only started appearing after he left the city. He abandoned the tomb to despoliation. He knew what would happen.'

Felix agreed. The prospector was greedy and would certainly have ransacked the tomb if he could. He had found the lost horde of Karak Eight Peaks. If that was true, then was the other part of his story true as well? Had he fled from the troll? Did he leave the Templar, Raphael, to fight the monster alone?

While they talked, Aldred entered the tomb and walked over to the treasure heap. He turned and Felix saw the look of triumph on the Templar's lean fanatic face.

No, get out, Felix wanted to shout.

'I have found it,' he cried. 'The lost blade, Karaghul. I have found it! Sigmar be praised!'

From behind the heap of treasure a huge horn-headed shadow loomed, twice as tall as Aldred, broader than it was tall. Before Felix had time to shout a warning, it tore off the Templar's head with one sweep of a mighty claw. Gore splashed the ancient stones. The thing lurched forward, pushing through the mound of treasure with irresistible power.

Felix had heard tales of trolls, and perhaps once this had been one. Now it was hideously changed. It had a gnarly hide covered in huge, dripping tumours and three enormously muscular arms, one of which terminated in a pincer claw. Growing from its left shoulder, like some obscene fruit, was a small, babyish head which glared at them with wise malign eyes. It chittered horridly in a language that Felix could not recognise. Pus dribbled down its chest from a huge leech mouth set below its neck.

The bestial head roared and the echoes reverberated through the long hall. Felix saw an amulet of glowing greenish-black stone hanging from a chain around its neck. Warpstone, he thought, placed there deliberately.

He did not blame Faragrim for running. Or Belegar. He stood paralysed by fear and indecision. From beside him he heard the sound of Zauberlich being sick. He knew warpstone had created this thing. He thought of what Gotrek had said about the long-ago war beneath the mountains.

Someone had been so insane as to chain warpstone to the troll, to deliberately induce mutation. Perhaps it was the rat-men, the skaven that Gotrek had mentioned. The troll had been down here since the war, a festering abomination changing and growing far from the light of day. Perhaps it was the desecration of their tombs by this warpstone-spawned monstrosity which had caused the dwarf ghosts to walk? Or perhaps it was the presence here of the warpstone, of pure undiluted Chaos.

The thoughts reverberated through his mind as the roar of the mad thing echoed through the vault. He stood unable to move, transfixed by horror, as the monster came ever closer. Its stench filled his nostrils. He heard the hideous sucking of its leech mouth. It loomed out of the gloom, its pain-wracked, bestial face hellishly underlit by its glowing amulet.

The troll was going to reach him and slay him and he could not make himself do anything about it. He would welcome death, having confronted this manifestation of the insanity of the universe.

Gotrek Gurnisson leapt forward between him and the monster, hunched in his fighting crouch. His shadow swept out behind him in the green light so that he stood at the head of a pool of darkness, axe held high, runes shimmering with witch-fire.

The Chaos-troll halted and peered down at him, as if aston-ished by the temerity of this small creature. Gotrek glared up at it and spat.

'Time to die, filth,' he said and lashed out with his axe, open-ing up a terrible wound in the thing's chest. The creature continued to stand there, studying the wound in fascination. Gotrek struck again at its ankle, attempting to hamstring it. Once again he drew green blood. The creature did not fall.

With blinding speed its huge pincer descended, clicking shut. It would have snipped off the Trollslayer's head if he had not ducked. The troll bellowed angrily and lashed out with a taloned hand. Somehow Gotrek managed to deflect it with a sweep of his axe. He avoided the hail of blows that rained down on him.

The Trollslayer and the troll circled warily, each looking for an opening. Felix noted to his horror that the wounds Gotrek had inflicted were knitting together again. As they did so they made a sound like slobbering mouths closing.

Jules Gascoigne rushed forward and stabbed the troll with his sword. The blade pierced the creature's leg and remained there. As the Bretonnian struggled to pull it out, the monster hit him with a back-handed sweep that sent him flying. Felix heard ribs break and the scout's head hit the wall with a terrible crack. Jules lay still in a spreading pool of his own blood.

While the creature was distracted, Gotrek leapt in and struck it a glancing blow to the shoulder. He sheared off the babyish head. It rolled over to near Felix's feet and lay screaming. Felix managed to put down the lantern, draw his sword and bring the blade down, chopping the head in two. It began to rejoin. He continued to hack until his sword was notched, blunted then broken from hitting the stone floor. He still could not kill the thing.

'Stand back,' he heard Zauberlich say. He leapt to one side. The air suddenly blazed. It stank of sulphur and burned meat. The tiny head was silent and did not heal.

As if sensing a new threat, the troll leapt past Gotrek and seized the sorcerer in its giant pincer. Felix saw the look of terror on Zauberlich's face as he was raised on high. Zauberlich struggled to cast a spell. A fireball erupted, and the shadows fled briefly. The monster screamed. With a reflexive action it closed the claw, chopping the mage in two.

The wizard fell to the ground, clothes blazing. Black despair overwhelmed Felix. Zauberlich could have hurt the thing, burned it with purifying fire. Now he was dead. Gotrek could only hack futilely at the troll but its Chaos-enhanced powers of healing made it all but invulnerable. They were doomed.

Felix's shoulders slumped. There was nothing he could do. The others had died in vain. Their quest had failed. The ghosts of the dwarfish rulers would continue to wander in torment. It was all futile.

He looked at Gotrek's sweating face. Soon the Trollslayer would tire and be unable to dodge the creature's blows. The dwarf knew this too, but he did not give up. A renewed determination filled Felix. He would not give up either. He looked over at the burning body of the sorcerer.

The fire had become more intense, more so than if simply the man's clothes were burning. Realisation dawned. Zauberlich had been carrying spare flasks of lantern oil in his coat. Swiftly Felix stripped off his pack and fumbled for an oil-flask.

'Keep it busy!' he yelled to Gotrek, unstoppering the ceramic bottle. Gotrek uttered a foul dwarfish curse. Felix flicked the flask at the monstrosity, showering it with glistening oil. The thing ignored him as it sought to pin down Gotrek. The dwarf redoubled his efforts, chopped away like a madman. Felix emptied a second flask over it and then a third, always keeping to the monster's blind side.

'Whatever you're going to do manling, do it quickly!' the Trollslayer yelled.

Felix ran over and picked up his lantern. Sigmar, guide my hand, he prayed as he threw the lamp at the creature. The lantern impacted on its back, shattering and spreading burning oil. It ignited the fuel with which Felix had already dowsed the creature.

The troll screamed shrilly. It reeled back. And now, when Gotrek's axe fell, the wounds did not heal. The dwarf drove the blazing troll back to the pile of gold. It stumbled and fell.

Gotrek raised his axe high above his head. 'In the name of my ancestors!' the Trollslayer howled. 'Die!'

His axe came down like a thunderbolt, severing the creature's foul head. The troll died and did not rise again.

Gingerly Gotrek picked up the warpstone amulet with the broken shard of Felix's sword. Holding the thing at arm's length, he took it outside to throw into the abyss.

Felix sat, drained of all emotion, on top of one of the sarcophagi. Once more it comes to this, he thought, sitting among ruin and corpses after terrible conflict.

He heard Gotrek's running footsteps coming closer. Panting, the dwarf entered the chamber.

'The gobbos come, manling,' he said.

'How many?' Felix asked.

Gotrek shook his head tiredly. 'Too many. At least I have disposed of that tainted thing. I can die happy here amid the tombs of my ancestors.'

Felix went over and picked up the dragon-hilted sword. 'I would have liked to have returned this to Aldred's people,' he said. 'It would give some meaning to all this death.'

Gotrek shrugged. He glanced to the door. The archway was filled with green-skinned marauders, advancing behind their grinning moon banners. Felix slid the Sigmarite sword smoothly from its sheath. A thrilling musical note sang out. The runes along its blade blazed brightly. For a second the goblins hesitated.

Gotrek looked over at Felix and grinned, revealing his missing teeth. 'This is going to be a truly heroic death, manling. My only regret is that none of my people will ever get to hear of it.'

Felix looked back at the oncoming horde, positioned himself so that his back was to a sarcophagus. 'You don't know how sorry I am about that,' he said grimly, making a few trial swipes with the blade. It felt good, light and well-balanced, as if it had been made for his hand alone. He was surprised to find he was no longer afraid. He had gone beyond fear.

The standard bearer halted and turned to harangue his troops. None of them seemed to be anxious to be the first to meet the Trollslayer's axe or the glowing runesword.

'Get on with it!' Gotrek bellowed. 'My axe thirsts.'

The goblins roared. The leader turned and gestured for them to advance. They surged forwards as irresistibly as the tide. This is it, thought Felix, steeling himself, preparing to lash out, to take as many foes as he could into the lands of the dead with him.

'Goodbye, Gotrek,' he said and stopped. The goblins had halted and stood, looking panic-stricken. What's going on? Felix wondered. Cold green light streamed over his shoulders. He looked back and hesitated at the sight. The chamber was filled with ranks of regal dwarfish spirits. They seemed fierce and terrible as they advanced.

The goblin standard bearer tried to rally his troops but the ghostly dwarf lords reached him and touched his heart. His face drained of colour, and he fell, clutching his breast. The spirits surged into the goblins. Spectral axes flickered. Greenskin warriors fell, no mark upon their bodies. A hideous keening filled the air, a thin reedy imitation of dwarfish war-cries. The remaining tribesmen turned and fled. The ghostly warriors swept after them.

FELIX AND GOTREK stood in the empty vault, surrounded by the towering sarcophagi. Slowly the air in front of them coalesced. Tendrils of greenish light drifted back through the entrance, took dwarfish shape. The spirits looked different.

The ghost who had spoken to Gotrek earlier stood there. She had changed somehow – as if a terrible burden had been lifted from her ethereal heart. She regarded Gotrek.

'The ancient enemies are gone. We could not leave them to despoil our tombs now that you have cleansed them. We are in your debt.'

'You have robbed me of a mighty death,' Gotrek said almost sourly.

'It was not your destiny to fall here this day. Your doom is far greater and its time is approaching.'

Gotrek looked quizzically at the ancient queen.

'I may say no more. Farewell, Gotrek, son of Gurni. We wish you well. You shall be remembered.'

The ghosts seemed to coalesce into one cold green flame that glowed like a star in the darkness. The light changed from green to warm gold and then became brighter than the sun. Felix averted his eyes and still was dazzled. When his sight returned he looked upon the tombs. The place was empty except for himself and Gotrek. The dwarf frowned thoughtfully. For a long moment a strange expression gleamed in his one good eye, then he turned and looked upon the treasure.

Felix could almost read his mind. He was considering taking the wealth, desecrating the tomb himself. Felix held his breath. After long minutes, Gotrek shrugged and turn away.

'What about the others? Shouldn't we lay them to rest?' Felix asked.

'Leave them,' Gotrek said over his shoulder as he strode away. 'They lie among the mighty. Their bodies are safe.'

They stepped through the arch, and Gotrek paused to touch the runes according to the ancient pattern. The tomb was sealed. Then they made their way up through the old darkness towards the light of day.

THE MARK OF SLAANESH

'As money was in short supply, we decided to return to the Empire and seek gainful employment of some sort. Our return from Karak Eight Peaks was in no sense an easy one. The weather was atrocious, the land bleak and empty, and my companion's mood even more savagely unreasonable than usual. Where we had come south in relative comfort and safety as part as a large, escorted caravan, our journey northwards was accomplished with no aid from anyone, and no means of transport other than our own legs. The people of the few villages we entered were understandably wary of two armed strangers, and the provisions they sold us were expensive and not of the best quality.

'It was perhaps unreasonable of me to expect any sort of respite from this seemingly unending chain of terrible adventures when we returned to my homeland, for it seems the Trollslayer and I were destined to forever be encountering minions of the Dark Powers. Even so, I

107

would scarcely have credited the extent of their sinister influence, had I not witnessed it with my own eyes. Furthermore, I was destined to wrestle with the forces of darkness alone for a period, for an odd fate befell the Slayer...'

—From *My Travels with Gotrek, Vol. II*, by Herr Felix Jaeger (Altdorf Press, 2505)

'BY GRUNGNI! What was that?' Gotrek Gurnisson bellowed, turning and raising his enormous axe defiantly.

As the second slingstone whizzed by his ear, Felix Jaeger ducked reflexively. The sharp stone splintered against the flat face of the nearest boulder, leaving a scar in its grey-green lichen covering. Felix threw himself behind the rock and glanced back with scared blue eyes, looking for the source of the attack.

The valley at the foot of Blackfire Pass was quiet. He could see only rolling tree-girt hills rising to the towering mountains beyond. He silently cursed the great rocks that filled the valley blocking his line of sight.

Suddenly movement caught Felix's eye. From high on his right, a tide of misshapen bodies teemed down the slope, dislodging a small avalanche of gravel and scree as they came. Shouting like maniacs, bestial figures leapt downhill towards him with the agility of mountain goats. The long, deep note of a hunting horn cut the air.

'No, not now,' Felix heard a voice whimper, and to his surprise, recognised it as his own. He was so close to civilisation. The long hard trail from Karak Eight Peaks to the southern borders of the Empire was nearly complete. He had fought goblins in the hills near the old dwarf city and skirmished with bandits prowling the ruins of Fort von Diehl. He had endured the cold heights of Blackfire Pass, shivered in the snow-covered trails leading to the old dwarfish routes under the peaks. He shuddered when he recalled the shadowy things that had lurked there and scuttled on many legs through the darkness. He had come so far and endured so much – and now he was within the borders of his homeland and still he was being attacked. It just wasn't fair.

'Stop cringing, manling. It's only a bunch of gods-forsaken mutants!' boomed Gotrek's deep coarse voice.

Felix threw the dwarf a nervous glance, wishing he shared the Slayer's confidence. Gotrek stood boldly on the open valley floor, disdaining the cover of the rocks, his great axe balanced negligently in one mighty fist. He seemed completely unworried by the hail of slingstones raising plumes of dust around his feet. An insane grin twisted his brutal features: unholy joy burned in his one good eye. Gotrek looked as if he was enjoying himself.

It was typical of the dwarf. The only time he seemed happy was in the thick of the fray. He had smiled when the goblins ambushed them, relishing the prospect of violence. He had actually laughed when the bat-winged monstrosities with a thirst for human blood and the faces of beautiful children had descended on them at the ford on Thunder River. The worse things looked the happier the Slayer became. He welcomed the prospect of his own death.

Gotrek thumped his chest with his fist and roared: 'Come on! My axe thirsts. She has not drunk blood in weeks.' A slingstone whistled past his head. The Slayer did not even blink.

Felix thought Gotrek's squat massive frame presented much less of a target than his own tall, spare form. He shook his head; his berserker comrade probably didn't take such things into consideration. Felix gave his attention back to their assailants.

They were indeed mutants; humans tainted and changed by the strange magic of Chaos. Some said this was because they had a trace of warpstone in their blood. Others said that they had been secret followers of the Dark, their appearance altered over time to reflect their inner corruption. A few sages maintained that they were innocent victims of a process of change overtaking all humanity. At that exact moment Felix did not care. He had a secret horror of the foul creatures which grew greater each time he encountered them. Fear filled him and provided fuel for murderous rage.

They were close enough now for Felix to distinguish individual members of the pack. The leader was a grossly fat giant with a belt of daggers stretched across his bulging belly. He was so obese that his body appeared to be made from dough. Great rippling folds of flesh bobbed up and down with each lumbering step. Felix was surprised that the earth did not shake under his monstrous tread. The leader's babyish grim revealed a multitude of chins and almost as many missing teeth as Gotrek's answering snarl. In one chubby hand he brandished a massive stone-headed mace.

Flanking the leader was a lanky creature taller than Felix. Its ear was notched from a vicious bite taken in some internecine squabble. A long thin strip of hair drooped like rotting lichen from atop its narrow, near-shaven skull. It howled a challenge as it raised its rusty scimitar high above its pointed head. Felix could see its incisors were fanged like a wolf's.

An elk-headed giant paused and raised a great curling horn to its lips. Another thunderous blast rang out across the blasted landscape, then the mutant let the instrument swing once more from the chain round its neck and continued to charge, head forward, antlers down.

Behind them came a ragged horde of surly faced followers. Each bore some stigmata of Chaos. Many were marked with weeping sores. Some had the faces of wolves, goats or rams. Some had claws or tentacles or great bludgeons of bone instead of hands. One had its head protruding from its belly, its neck a mere stump. Another had a hump on its back in which a great mouth glistened. The mutants brandished a motley assortment of crude weapons; spears and clubs and notched scimitars scavenged from forgotten battlefields. Felix estimated the number of attackers as somewhere above ten and below twenty. They were not odds that he relished, even though he knew the Slayer's awesome physical prowess.

Felix cursed silently. They had been so close to escaping from the Black Mountains to the lowlands of the Empire's southernmost province. From the brow of the pass the previous evening Felix had made out the lights of a town of men. He had been looking forward that very evening to a warm bed and a cold jack of ale. Now fear coursed through his veins like ice-water; he must fight for his life again. Involuntarily he let out a little moan.

'Get up, manling. Time for some bloodletting,' Gotrek said. He spat a huge gob of phlegm onto the rocks at his feet and ran his left hand through the massive red crest of hair that rose above his shaven tattooed skull. His nose chain tinkled gently; a strange counterpoint to his mad rumbling laughter.

With a sigh of resignation Felix threw his faded red cloak back over his broad right shoulder, freeing his sword arm for action, then he drew his longsword from its ornate scabbard. Reddened dwarfish glyphs blazed along the length of the blade.

The mutants were close enough now for him to hear the soft slap of their unshod feet and individual words in their harsh guttural voices. He could see greenish veins in yellowish jaundiced-looking eyes and count individual studs on the rims of leather shields. Reluctantly he raised himself from behind his cover and prepared to fight.

He glanced at Gotrek and to his horror saw a slingstone impact on the dwarf's massive skull. He heard the crack and saw the Slayer sway. Fear filled the man; if the dwarf went down he knew he had no chance of survival against the swarm of assailants. Gotrek reeled but remained upright then he reached up and felt the wound that the shot had left. A look of surprise passed over his face when he saw the blood on his fingertips. It was replaced in an instant by an expression of terrible wrath. The Trollslayer let out a mighty roar and charged towards the cackling mutants.

His ferocious attack took them off guard. The fat leader only just managed to duck back as the Slayer's axe whistled past his head. His agility surprised Felix. With a terrible crunch the axe tore through the chest of the thin lieutenant and then lopped off the head of a second attacker. The backstroke tore through a leather shield and sliced away an attached tentacle.

Without giving them time to recover Gotrek tore among them like a deadly whirlwind. The fat leader scuttled well out of the reach of the lethal axe as he gibbered orders to his followers. The mutants began to surround the dwarf, kept at bay only by the great figure of eight described by Gotrek's battleaxe.

Felix launched himself into the fray. The magical blade he had taken from the dead Templar Aldred felt as light as a willow wand in his hand. It almost seemed to sing as he clove a mutant's skull from behind. The runes glowed bright as it cut away the top of the head as easily as a butcher's cleaver cutting a joint of beef. The mutant's brains fountained messily forth. Felix grimaced as the jelly splattered his face. He forced himself to ignore his disgust and keep on hacking at another mutant. A shock passed up his arm as he rammed his blade underneath a mottled ribcage into the creature's rotten heart. He saw the mutant's eyes go wide with fear and pain. Its wart-covered face wore a look of horror and it whimpered what might have been a prayer or a curse to its dark god as it died.

Felix's hand felt wet and sticky now and he adjusted his grip on the sword to keep it from slipping as he was attacked simultaneously from either side. He ducked the swing of a spike-headed mace and lashed to the right. His blade cut the cheek of a barrel-like mutant, severing the earflap of its leather cap. The helm slid forward on the creature's face, covering its eyes and momentarily obscuring its vision. Felix kicked it in the stomach with the toe of his heavy Reikland leather boot and it doubled over, foolishly presenting its neck for the stroke that beheaded it.

Pain flashed through Felix's shoulder as the mace caught him a glancing blow. He snarled and turned, driven to frenzy by the agony. The accursed one caught the look on his face and froze for a heartbeat. It raised its weapon in what might have been a gesture of surrender. Felix shook his head and chopped the creature's wrist. Blood sprayed all over him. The mutant screamed and writhed, clutching at the stump of its arm, trying to staunch the flow of blood.

Everything seemed to be happening in slow motion now. Felix turned and saw Gotrek swaying like a drunk man. At his feet lay a pile of mangled bodies. Felix followed the slow sweep of the immense axe as it caught another victim, driving the ruined body back into two cringing foes. They fell in a tangled mass. His axe rose and fell in a bloody arc as Gotrek proceeded to hack them to pieces.

All vestiges of humanity and restraint fell away in a wave of bloodlust and fear and hatred. Felix leapt among the survivors. Swift as an adder's tongue the enchanted blade flickered, the runes growing brighter as it drank more blood. Felix barely felt the jar of impact or heard the howls of pain and anguish. Now he was a machine, intended only to kill. He gave no more thought to preserving his own life. Only to the slaughter of his foes.

As swiftly as it had begun it was over. The mutants were in retreat, fleeing as fast as their legs would carry them, their fat leader fleetest of all. Felix watched them go. As the last of them was beyond reach, he turned howling with frustrated murder-lust and began to hack up the bodies.

After a while, he began to shake. Noticing, as if for the first time, the terrible ruin which he and the Slayer had wrought, he bent double and proceeded to be sick.

THE CLEAR COLD water of the stream ran red with blood. Felix watched it swirl away and wondered at how numb he felt. It was as if the chill of the water had seeped into his veins. He realised how much he had changed since he had fallen into Gotrek's company and he was not sure he liked it.

He remembered how he had felt after he had killed the student, Krassner, the very first to fall to his sword. That had been an accident during what had been supposed to be a boyish duel on the field behind Altdorf University. The blade had slipped and the man had died. Felix could remember the look of disbelief on his face and his own feeling of horror and tearful remorse. He had ended a life and he had felt guilty.

But that had happened to someone else, a long lifetime ago. Since then, since he had sworn to follow the Slayer on his doomed quest for a heroic death, he had killed and killed again. With each death, he had felt a little less remorse; with each death, contemplating the next one had become a little easier. The nightmares that had once afflicted him came no more to trouble him. The sense of waste and revulsion had left him. It was as if Gotrek's madness had infected him and he no longer cared.

Once, as a student, he had studied the works of the great philosopher, Neustadt. He had argued in his great opus *De Re Munde* that all living creatures had souls. That even mutants were sentient beings capable of love and worthy of life. But Felix knew he had obliterated them without a second thought. They had been enemies, trying to kill him, and he could feel no real remorse at their deaths, only a wonder at his own lack of feeling. He asked himself where the change had occurred and could find no answer.

Was this why he loathed the altered ones so? Was it because he could see the changes happening in himself and feared that they might have an external manifestation? He found his new coldness sufficiently monstrous to justify it. How could it have happened and when?

Was it after Kirsten, the first great love of his life, died at the hands of Manfred von Diehl? He did not think so. The process was more subtle; a strange alchemy had transmuted him down all the long leagues of his wandering. A new Felix had been born here in these harsh lands by the world's edge, a product of the bleakness of the place and the hardness of his life and too many deaths seen from too close.

He looked across at Gotrek. The Slayer sat hunched on a flat plate of rock that jutted out into the stream. A piece torn from Felix's cloak was wrapped round his head, the red wool blotched a deep black by the dwarf's dried blood.

Will I become like that eventually, Felix wondered, hopeless and mad and doomed, dying slowly from a hundred small wounds, seeking only a magnificent death to redeem myself? The thought did not disturb him – and that in itself was disturbing.

What had he lost and where had he lost it, Felix wondered, listening to the rush of the water as if it carried some coded answer. Gotrek raised his head and slowly surveyed the scene. Felix noticed that the patch had come away from his ruined left eye, revealing the scarred and empty socket.

Felix himself looked at the tangle of leafless trees and thorny scrub that surrounded them and the cold grey of the rock. He felt dwarfed by the dismal titanic shadow of the great snow-capped mountains and asked himself how they had come to this god forsaken spot so many miles from his home. For a second it seemed he was lost in the endless immensity of the Old World, that he had no point of reference in time or space, that he and the Slayer were alone in a dead world, ghosts drifting in eternity bound by a chain of circumstance forged in Hell.

Gotrek glanced over at him. Felix returned his gaze with a feeling almost of hatred. He waited silently for the dwarf to start gloating about his pointless futile victory.

'What happened here?' the Slayer asked.

Felix looked at him open-mouthed.

THE LAND WAS greener now that they had left the mountains. The warm gold sun cast a mellow late afternoon light over the long coarse grass of the plains. Here and there patches of purple heather bloomed. Red flowers blossomed among the grass. Ahead of them, perhaps a league away, a great grey castle loomed above the flatlands, perched on the craggy hilltop. Beneath it Felix could see the walls of a town. Smoke drifted lazily skyward from its many chimneys.

He felt more relaxed. He estimated that they would reach the town before nightfall. Saliva filled his mouth at the thought of some cooked beef and fresh-baked bread. He was heartily sick of the dwarfish field rations they had picked up in the Border Princes; hard biscuits and strips of dried meat. Tonight, for the first time in weeks, he could lie safe beneath a real roof and enjoy the company of his fellow men. He might even sup some ale before retiring to bed. Tension began to ease out of him. He felt his shoulders relax and became aware of just how keyed up he had been during the journey, straining constantly to spot any hidden threat the dangerous mountains might conceal.

He glanced worriedly back at Gotrek. The dwarf's face was pale and he often stopped to look around them with a look of blank confusion, as if he could not recall quite why they were there, or what they were doing. The blow to the head had apparently taken a lot out of the Slayer. Felix could not tell why. In his time, he had seen Gotrek take a lot worse punishment.

'Are you all right?' he asked, half expecting the dwarf to snarl at him.

'Yes. Yes I am,' Gotrek said, but his voice was soft and reminded Felix of an old man's.

AFTER THE COOL, clear air of the mountains and the scented freshness of the plains, the town of Fredericksburg came as a shock to the senses. From a distance the high narrow houses with their red-tiled roofs and white-washed walls had seemed clean and orderly. But even the dim light of the setting sun could not conceal the cracks in the brickwork and the holes in the slate roofs.

The narrow, maze-like streets were piled high with garbage. Starving dogs wandered from pile of rotting vegetation to heap of ordure, defecating liberally as they went. The cobbled streets smelled of urine and mould and the fat dripping into cooking fires. Felix covered his mouth with his hand and gagged. He noticed the red blotch of a fresh flea-bite just above his knuckles. Civilisation at last, he thought ironically.

Vendors had set out lanterns to illuminate the market square. Loose women stood in pools of red light near the doorways of many houses. The business of the day was over, the atmosphere of the place changed as folk came to eat and be entertained. Storytellers gathered little circles round their charcoal braziers and competed with conjurers who made tiny dragons appear in puffs of smoke. A would-be prophet stood on a stool under the statue of the town's founder, the hero Frederick, and exhorted the crowd to return to the virtues of an earlier simpler time.

People were everywhere, their lively movements dazzling Felix's eyes. Hawkers tugged at his sleeve offering lucky charms or trays of small, cinnamon-scented pastries. Children kicked an inflated pig's bladder in the mouth of a narrow alley and ignored their mothers' cries to come inside out of the dark. Over their heads, ragged washing sagged on lines stretched from window to window across the narrow alleyways. Carts now empty of produce rumbled towards the draymen's yards, clattering over ruts and dislodging loose cobbles.

Felix stopped by an old woman's food stand and bought a piece of stringy chicken she had cooked over a charcoal burner. Warm juices filled his mouth as he gobbled it down. He stood for a moment trying to centre himself in the riot of colour and smell and noise.

Looking at the swarm of people he felt dislocated. Men-at-arms in the tabards of the local burgermeisters moved among the crowd. Richly dressed youths eyed the street-girls and exchanged quips with their bodyguards. Outside the entrance to the Temple of Shallya, beggars raised their scabrous stumps to passing merchants who kept their eyes carefully focused on the middle distance and their hands on their purses. Ruddy-faced peasants rolled drunkenly through the streets gazing in wonder at buildings more than a single storey high. Old women, heads wrapped in tattered scarves, stood on doorsteps and gossiped with their neighbours. Their wizened faces reminded Felix of sun-dried apples.

Fredericksburg was a mere hamlet compared to Altdorf, he told himself; there was no need to feel daunted. He had lived in the Imperial capital most of his life and never felt out of place. It was just that he had become used to the quiet and the solitude of the mountains. He was unused to feeling enclosed. Still, it should take him mere hours to adjust to being back among men.

Standing in the crowd he felt lonely, just one more face in a sea of faces. Listening to the babble of voices he heard no friendly words, just haggling over prices and rude coarse jokes. There was an energy here, the vitality of a thriving community, but he was not part of it. He was a stranger, a wanderer from the wilderness. He had little in common with these folk, who had probably never ventured more than a league from their homes in their lives. He was struck by how strange his life had become. He suddenly felt a tremendous longing to be at home, in the comfortable wood-panelled halls of his father's house. He rubbed the old duelling scar on his right cheek and cursed the day he had been expelled from university into a life of petty crime and political activism.

Gotrek wandered slowly through the marketplace, gazing stupidly at the stalls selling cloth and amulets and food, as if he did not quite understand what was going on. The Slayer's one good eye was wide and he seemed dazed. Disturbed by his comrade's behaviour, Felix took him by the shoulder and guided him towards the tavern door. A lazy-looking painted dragon beamed down at him from the sign above the door.

'Come on,' Felix said. 'Let's get a beer.'

WOLFGANG LAMMEL PUSHED the struggling barmaid from his knee. In her attempt to resist his kiss, she had marred the high velvet collar of his jerkin with rouge from her cheeks.

'Begone, slut,' he told her in his most imperious voice. The blonde girl stared at him angrily, her face flushed beneath its inexpertly applied mask of power and paint, annoyance distorting her peasant-pretty face.

'My name is Greta,' she said. 'Call me by my name.'

'I'll call you whatever I like, slattern. My father owns this tavern and if you would keep the job you so recently acquired you'll keep a civil tongue in your head.

She bit back a retort and hurried beyond his reach.

Wolfgang smirked. He knew she would be back. They always came back. Father's gold saw to that.

He brushed the rouge carefully from his clothing with one well-manicured hand. Then he studied his bearded aquiline features in his small silver hand-mirror, checking to make sure none of the girl's make-up marred his soft white skin. He ignored the titters of his sycophants and the amused looks of the bully-boys he employed as his bodyguards. He could afford to. By virtue of his father's wealth he was the undisputed leader of the clique of fashionable young fops who patronised this tavern. From the corner of his eye he could see Ivan, the tavern keeper, scolding the girl. The man knew he could not afford to offend the owner's son and heir. He saw the girl bite back an angry rejoinder and begin to come back across.

'I'm sorry for marring your raiment,' she said in a soft voice. Wolfgang noticed the two points of colour on her otherwise pale cheeks. 'Please accept my most humble apologies.'

'Of course,' Wolfgang said. 'Since your clumsiness is exceeded only by your stupidity and your stupidity is exceeded only by your plainness I must take pity on you. Your apology is accepted. I shall ask Ivan to deduct the cost of a new jerkin to replace the one you have ruined from your pay.'

The girl's mouth opened but she said nothing. Wolfgang knew that the jerkin cost more than the girl would earn in a month. She wanted to argue but knew it was futile. Ivan would have to side with him. Her shoulders slumped. Wolfgang noticed the way her bosom was revealed by her low-cut bodice and a thought occurred to him.

'Unless of course you would care to repay the debt in another way. Say... by visiting my chambers this evening at midnight.'

He thought at first she was going to refuse. She was young and fresh from the country and still held quaint ideas about virtue. But she was a thrall, one of the lowest classes of peasant owned by their liege lords. She had fled here to the town seeking escape from servitude. Losing her job would mean a choice between starving in the town or returning to her village and the wrath of her owner. If she lost her position here Wolfgang could see she never got another one. The realisation of her situation sank in and her head sank forward and she nodded once. The movement was so slight as to be almost imperceptible.

'Then get out of my sight until then,' Wolfgang said. The girl fled through the mass of his hangers on. Tears ran down her face. Coarse jibes followed her.

Wolfgang allowed himself a sigh of satisfaction then downed another goblet of wine. The sweet, clove-scented liquid burned down his throat and filled his stomach with fire. He stared across at Heinrich Kasterman. The fat pock-faced young noble stopped stuffing his face long enough to give him an ingratiating grin.

'Nicely done, Wolfgang. Afore this night is out, you'll have introduced young Greta to the secret mysteries of our hidden lord. May I join you later? Take my turn.'

Wolfgang frowned as Heinrich made the secret sign of Slaanesh. Even his father's wealth might not protect him if it got around that he and several of his trusted comrades were followers of the Lord of Vice. He looked around to see if anyone had paid any attention to the fat fool's remark. No one seemed to have noticed. He relaxed. He told himself he was unjustifiably nervous. In truth he had become a little uneasy since the stigmata had appeared on his chest. The books assured him that it was a sign of special favour from their patron power, a mark that showed he was one of the Chosen. Even so, if a witch-hunter ever found out…

Perhaps it would be wisest to deal with the girl after he had his way with her this evening.

'Maybe. Well that's tonight's amusement – but what shall we do till then to while away the long tedious hours in this dull, dull place?'

He could see no one worth tormenting. Most of the patrons were of similar status to himself, with their own bodyguards. In one corner sat an old man, plainly a sorcerer, leaning on a staff. The two corner booths were filled with cheery Sigmarite pilgrims. Only a fool would cross a mage and the pilgrims were too numerous to be easy prey. Torches flickered in the draught as the outer door opened.

'Or perhaps this evening's entertainment has just arrived.'

An oddly mismatched pair entered the Sleeping Dragon. One was a tall, gaunt blond-haired man, his bronzed and handsome face marred by a long scar. His clothing had obviously once been fine but was now stained and patched and tattered by long travel. From his dress he might have been a beggar but there was something about the way he carried himself, a nervous poise, that suggested he was not quite as down at heel as he seemed.

The other was a dwarf. A full head shorter than the man in spite of a great red crest of hair, he must nevertheless have outweighed the other by a considerable margin, judging from the great slabs of muscle which sheathed his big-boned frame. He carried an axe in one hand that a blacksmith might have strained to lift with two. His body was covered in strange tattoos. A crude leather patch covered one eye. Wolfgang had never seen his like before. The dwarf looked hurt and moved slowly. His gaze was blank and stupid and confused.

They moved to the bar and the man ordered two steins of beer. His accent and perfectly modulated High Reikspiel suggested an educated man. The dwarf set his axe down by the fire. The man looked shocked, somehow, as if he had never seen this happen before.

The tavern had gone quiet, anticipating what Wolfgang and his cronies would say. Wolfgang knew that they had seen him bait newcomers before. He sighed; he supposed he had a reputation to maintain.

'Well. Well. Has the circus come to town?' he said loudly. To his annoyance, the two at the bar ignored him. 'You, oaf! I said: Has the circus come to town?'

The man in the faded red cloak turned to look at him. 'Would you be talking to me, sir?' he inquired in a soft, polite voice at odds with the level cold stare he directed at Wolfgang.

'Yes, you and your half-wit friend. Are you perhaps clowns with some travelling troupe?'

The blond man glanced at the dwarf, who continued to stare around in bemusement. 'No,' he said and turned back to his drink. The man had looked confused, as if he had expected a response from the dwarf and got none.

Nothing infuriated Wolfgang more than being ignored. 'I find you surly and rude. If you do not apologise, I think I shall have my men give you a lesson in good manners.'

The man at the bar moved his head slightly. 'I think if anyone here needs a lesson in politeness it is yourself, sir,' he said quietly.

The nervous laughter of the tavern's other patrons fanned the sparks of Wolfgang's anger. Heinrich licked his lips and slammed a clenched fist into one pudgy palm. Wolfgang nodded.

'Otto, Herman, Werner. I can longer bear the odour of this tramp. Eject him from the tavern.'

Herman loomed over Wolfgang and rubbed one large knobbly knuckled fist through his unkempt beard. 'I don't know if this is wise, lord. Those two look tough,' he whispered.

Otto rubbed his shaven head, gazing at the dwarf. 'He has the tattoos of a Slayer. They're supposed to be vicious.'

'So are you, Otto. I don't keep you around for your wit and charm, you know. Deal with them.'

'I dunno,' Werner grumbled. 'It could be a mistake.'

'How much does my father pay you, Herman?' The big man shrugged in resignation and beckoned for the other bravos to follow him. Wolfgang saw him slip something hard and metallic over his fist. He leaned back in his chair to enjoy the show.

The blond man looked at the approaching bodyguards. 'We want no trouble with you, gentlemen.'

'Too late,' Herman said and swung. To Wolfgang's surprise, the stranger blocked Herman's punch with his forearm and then doubled the big man over with a blow to his ample paunch. The dwarf did nothing.

'Gotrek, help!' shouted the man, as the bodyguards raced towards him. The dwarf merely looked around bemusedly, flinching as Werner and Otto grabbed the young man's arms. He struggled viciously, sending Otto hopping with a kick to the shins and then butting Werner in the face. The burly bodyguard reeled back, clutching a profusely bleeding nose.

Karl and Pierre, two of Heinrich's hired louts, joined the fray. Karl caught the blond man on the back of the head with a chair and sent him sprawling. The others propped him up against the bar. Werner and Otto pinned him while Herman proceeded to take out his anger on the helpless stranger.

Heinrich winced every time a fist crunched into flesh. Wolfgang felt his own lips draw back in a snarl. He found himself panting with bloodlust. There was a real temptation to let Herman keep on hitting until the man was dead. He found his thoughts drifting to Greta. He was aroused. There was something about pain, particularly other people's, which appealed to him. Perhaps later he and the girl would follow this line of thought to its logical conclusion.

Eventually Wolfgang snapped out of it. The Reiklander was bruised and bloody when he signalled that he had seen enough and ordered him thrown into the street.

And still the dwarf did nothing.

FELIX LAY ON a pile of garbage. Every part of his body ached. One of his back teeth felt loose. Something wet ran down the back of his neck. He hoped it wasn't his own blood. A plump black rat sat atop a mound of mouldy food and gazed at him ironically. Moonlight made its red eyes glitter like malevolent stars.

He tried moving his hand. He put it down to brace himself on earth, preparing for the monumental task of rising to his feet. Something squashed under his palm. He shook his head. Little silver lights flickered across his field of vision. The effort of movement was too much for him and he lay back on the midden-heap. It felt soft as a warm bed beneath him.

He opened his eyes again. He must have fallen unconscious. He had no idea how long for. The greater moon was higher than it had been. Morrslieb, the lesser satellite, had joined it in the sky. Its eerie glow illumined the street fitfully. Mist had started to rise. In the distance a night-watchman's lamp cast a pool of sulphurous light. Felix heard the slow, painful movement of an old man's steps.

Someone helped him to his feet. A strand of long wavy hair tickled his face. Cheap perfume warred with the odour of refuse in his nostrils. It slowly filtered into Felix's brain that his benefactor was a woman. He began to slip and she struggled to support his weight.

'Herr Wolfgang is not a nice man.'

It was a peasant's voice, Felix decided. The words were pleasantly slurred and it had a husky, earthy quality. He looked up into a broad moon face. Large blue eyes gazed at him over high cheekbones.

'I'd never have guessed,' Felix said. Pain stabbed through his side as the tip of his scabbard caught in the garbage and the pommel of his sword connected with a tender patch of flesh under his ribs. 'My name is... ugh... Felix, by the way. Thank you for your assistance.'

'Greta. I work in the Sleeping Dragon. I couldn't leave you just lying in the street.'

'I think you should find a place with a better class of patron, Greta.'

'I'm starting to think that myself.' Her slightly too-wide mouth smiled nervously at him. The moon's light caught the white of her powdered face, making it look pale and sickly. If it wasn't for the make-up she would be beautiful, he decided.

'I can't believe no one came out to see how you were,' she was saying.

The tavern door opened. Automatically Felix reached for his sword. The movement caused him to gasp with pain. He knew he would be helpless if the bravos set on him again.

Gotrek stood in the door, empty handed. His clothes were splashed with beer. His crest was flattened and bedraggled as if someone had given him a ducking in an ale cask. Felix glared at him. 'Thank you for your help, Gotrek.'

'Who is Gotrek?' the Slayer said. 'Are you talking to me?'

'Come on,' Greta said. 'We'd better get both of you to a healer I know. He's a little strange but he's got a soft spot for me.'

THE OFFICE OF the alchemist Lothar Kryptmann smelled of formaldehyde and incense and the weirdroot he chewed constantly. The walls were covered in racks containing jars of chemicals: powdered unicorn horn, quicksilver, quicklime and dried herbs. On a stand in a corner huddled a mangy, glittering-eyed vulture; it was bald in places with no feathers on one wing. It took Felix some time to realise it was stuffed. On the heavy oak desk, amid a pile of papers scrawled in a crabbed illegible hand, was a massive bottle containing the preserved head of a goat-horned beastman. A mortar and pestle served as an impromptu paperweight to stop the notes floating away in the draught from the lazily shuttered windows.

Torches flickered smokily in niches and sent shadows scuttling into the cold recesses of the room. Leather bound volumes titled in fading gold leaf displayed the names of the great natural philosophers. Many were stuffed untidily into bookshelves which had bent dangerously under their weight. Wax from a taper set in a porcelain saucer dripped onto the topmost volume. In the grate a small heap of lit coals crackled. Felix saw some half-consumed sheets of paper jutting sootily from the hearth. He decided the whole place would be terribly dangerous if ever a fire broke out.

Kryptmann took another pinch of herbal snuff, sneezed, then wiped his nose on the sleeve of his filthy blue robe, adding another mark to the runes sewn into it. He threw a tiny measure of coal onto the fire with a small brass shovel and turned to look at his patients.

The alchemist reminded Felix of nothing so much as the stuffed vulture in the corner. His bald head was framed by wings of unruly grey hair. A great beak of a nose jutted over thin, primly pursed lips. Pale grey eyes glittered brightly behind small pince nez glasses. Felix saw that the pupils were huge, dilated, a sure sign that Kryptmann was addicted to hallucinogenic weirdroot. When the alchemist moved, his bulky robes flapped around his thin frame, he looked like a flightless bird attempting to take off.

Kryptmann moved over and perched on the edge of his desk. He pointed at Felix with a long bony finger. Felix noticed that the nail had been bitten and a fine sediment of dirt lay beneath it. When he spoke, Kryptmann's voice was high and grating, as irritating as a schoolmaster drawing his fingers down a blackboard.

'Feeling better, my young friend?'

Felix had to admit he did. No matter how unprepossessing his appearance, Lothar Kryptmann knew his job. The unguents he had applied had already reduced the swelling of the bruises and the vile tasting brew he had forced Felix to drink had caused the pain to evaporate like mist in the morning sun. 'You say that Wolfgang Lammel's bodyguards did this, Greta?'

The girl nodded. The alchemist tut-tutted. 'Young Wolfgang is a nasty piece of work. Still, "malum se delet", as it says in De Re Munde.'

'Perhaps in young Wolfgang's case, evil may indeed destroy itself. But I'm prepared to give it a helping hand,' Felix said.

'You understand Classical! Oh, that's excellent. I thought all respect for learning had died out in this benighted age,' Kryptmann said happily. 'Good. I'm only too pleased to have been able help a fellow scholar. If only curing your friend were so simple. It will be almost impossible I'm afraid.' He smiled dreamily. From the corner in which he sat, Gotrek stared back, his gaze as empty as a pit.

' Why exactly is that?' Greta asked. 'What's wrong with him?'

'It would seem that his mind has been disturbed by a blow to the head. His mnemonic lobes have been violently agitated and many memories have been shaken loose. He no longer knows quite who he is and his ability to reason has been impaired.'

Not that he ever had much of that, thought Felix.

'Moreover the humours which govern his personality have been thrown into a new configuration. I would imagine he had not been behaving quite like himself recently, has he, my young friend? I can see by his appearance that he is one of the cult of Trollslayers. They are not famed for their tolerance of pacifism.'

'True,' Felix acknowledged. 'Normally he would have torn those men's lungs out for insulting him.'

He noticed that Greta's broad pretty face brightened at the mention of violence towards his attackers and wondered what grudge she had to settle with them. Felix was forced to admit to himself that he had a yet more ignoble motive for wanting the dwarf cured: he wanted revenge on the men who had beaten him up. He knew it was unlikely he could exact it on his own.

'Is there nothing that can be done for him?' Felix asked, taking out his purse ready to pay for his treatment. Kryptmann shook his head sadly.

'Although… perhaps another blow to the head would help.'

'You mean just hit him?'

'No! It would have to be a powerful blow, struck in just the right way. It sometimes works but the chances are surely a thousand to one. It's possible that such a treatment would just make things worse, perhaps even kill the patient.'

Felix shook his head. He did not want to risk killing the Slayer. His heart sank. He was filled with a complex mixture of emotions. He owed the Slayer his life many times over and he was sorry for his state of bemusement and inability to remember anything, including his own name. It seemed wrong to leave the dwarf in such a state. He felt obliged to do something about it.

But on the other hand, ever since the drunken night when he had sworn to accompany Gotrek on his suicidal quest and record his end for posterity in an epic poem, he had had nothing but trouble. Gotrek's illness represented an opportunity to avoid keeping the promise. In his present state Gotrek seemed to have forgotten all about his doomed task. Felix could be free to return home and pursue a normal life. And perhaps it would be kinder to leave the dwarf like this, unaware of the crimes he had committed and the dark destiny that drove him to seek his doom.

But could he really abandon Gotrek to fend for himself with his present diminished faculties? And how would he get home to Altdorf across countless leagues of danger-infested wilderness and forest without the aid of the Slayer's mighty axe?

'Is there nothing else you can do?'

'Nothing. Unless…'

'Unless what?'

'No… it probably wouldn't work anyway.'

'What wouldn't work?'

'I have the formula for an elixir normally used by ageing magicians on the verge of senility. Among other things, it consists of six parts weirdroot to one part mountain sunblossom. It is said to be very good at restoring the humours to their proper configuration.'

'Perhaps you should try it.'

'If only I could, old chap. But sunblossom is rare and for maximum potency needs to be picked at the death of day on the highest slopes of Mount Blackfire.'

Felix sighed. 'I don't care what it costs.'

Kryptmann removed his glasses and polished them on the sleeve of his robe. 'Alas you misunderstand me, young man. I do not seek some petty pecuniary advantage. I simply mean I have no sunblossom in stock.'

'Well that's that then.'

'Wait,' Greta said. 'Mount Blackfire is not so far from here. The pass runs near its peak… Couldn't you go and pick some, Felix?'

'Go back into the mountains, at this time of the year, on my own? There are gangs of crazed mutants up there.'

'I never said it would be easy,' Kryptmann said.

Felix groaned and this time it was not simply with pain. 'Tomorrow. I'll think about it tomorrow.'

Kryptmann nodded sagely. 'I wouldn't recommend going back to the inn this evening. The temple of Shallya has a flophouse for indigents. You'll probably get a bed there for the night if you hurry. Now, about my fee. Given your obvious poverty I'll waive it if you bring me back a suitably large amount of sunblossom.'

Felix looked at his depleted purse and let his shoulders slump in defeat. 'Very well. I'll go.'

Gotrek sat and gazed blankly off into the distance. Felix wondered what was going on behind that one mad and empty eye.

WOLFGANG LAMMEL LAY drunk on his bed. From the Sleeping Dragon below came the muted sound of revelry. Even the thick Bretonnian rugs on the floor and the heavy, leaded Tilean glass in the windows could not entirely dampen it out. He drained the goblet of Estalian sherry in one gulp and stretched, enjoying the caress of satin sheets against his skin. With a nostalgic sigh he closed the old pillow-book from Cathay which had been his first purchase in that strange bookshop in Nuln. To tell the truth, he found the calligraphy rather simplistic now and the positions of the illustrated couples tediously unadventurous. Only one of them might have proved vaguely interesting but where was one to acquire a Lustrian devil-python in Fredericksburg at this time of the year?

He rose from the bed and drew his silk robe tight about him to conceal the stigmata on his chest. He smiled; the garment had been a gift from the fascinating traveller Dieng Ching, a guest of the Countess Emmanuelle's, and another patron of Van Niek's Exotic Books and Collectibles Emporium. He and Wolfgang had spent an interesting evening together in the Beloved of Verena, the famed brothel on the grounds of Nuln University. Their discussions had been wide ranging and covered many topics. The Celestial, as he styled himself, had proved to be knowledgeable in many esoteric philosophies and the hidden mysteries of many secret cults. In spite of his lack of interest in the finer points of the worship of Slaanesh, he had been a most stimulating companion – one of the many Wolfgang had met during his time in Nuln.

Wolfgang missed being at the university now. He deplored this tiny backwater town with its moon-faced peasant girls and its third rate courtesans who had simply no imagination at all. He often regarded his time in Nuln nostalgically as a golden period of his life to which he could never really return. It had not quite been the education his father had imagined when he sent him away to the Empire's finest university, but it had been one in which Wolfgang had excelled as a pupil. His teachers had been among the most debauched rakes and gallants of the age. It was just a pity that he had not done quite so well at his more conventional studies. Eventually his tutors had written to his father acquainting him with what they considered to be the truth about him.

Wolfgang laughed aloud. The truth! If those wizened old men had the vaguest inkling of the real truth of his activities they would have sent for the witch-hunters. If his father had any idea of the real truth then he wouldn't be simply threatening to disinherit him; he would have him banished to the woods to join Heinrich's bloated cousin, Dolphus, the one who had just kept on eating until he resembled a blob of dough. Rumour had it that he was caught trying to toast his own mother's ear. Such stories showed the paucity of imagination of the local townsfolk.

What could such unimaginative people know about the worship of Lord Slaanesh, the true god of pain and pleasure? He picked up the small statuette beside his bed and studied it. The jade carving was almost perfect; it showed the hermaphrodite figure, naked except for a cloak swept wide to reveal its single breast. One arm beckoned the viewer enticingly; a faint smile of lasciviousness or perhaps of contempt, flickered across its beautiful face. Wolfgang studied it with something like love. No, what could the petty money-grubbing fools know of the worship of a real god?

Their minds would have bent under the sanity-shattering impact of the secrets Wolfgang had learned in the catacombs beneath Nuln. Their feeble souls would have been blasted by the strange summonings which took place in the murder-houses of the Kommerzplatz. Not even in their wildest imaginings could they visualise what he had seen in the cemetery-bordello on the city's edge where mutant prostitutes serviced depraved noblemen at the so-called Night Circus.

Wolfgang had seen the truth: that the world was ending; that the Dark Powers gathered their strength; that man was a sick, depraved thing concealing his lusts behind a mask of propriety. He wanted nothing of such hypocrisy. He had turned to a god that offered ecstasy on earth rather than in an uncertain afterlife. He would know the ultimates of human life before the ending of all things. He smiled at the truths the wine had revealed to him. One more proof of the superiority of Slaanesh's way.

He replaced the pillow-book and statuette alongside his copy of Al-Hazim's Secrets of the Harem, took a stick of his special weirdroot from its jar then pulled the panel of the secret alcove securely into place. It wouldn't do for Papa to make a surprise visit and find this stuff. He was close enough to disinheriting Wolfgang as things stood. Only the hope of marrying his only son to Heinrich's pig-like sister, Inge, kept the old man from cutting Wolfgang off without a penny. Still, his father did have one great virtue: he might be a boring, dour, penny-pinching old miser but he was an incurable snob.

It was the only reason he sent Wolfgang away to university; it was the only reason he gave him enough money to live like an Imperial courtier. He wanted the Lammels to marry into the nobility and Heinrich's family, although inbred and poor, were definitely that. Yes, his father dreamed that his grandson might one day have the ear of the Emperor. Just think what that could do for business, he would often exclaim.

The weirdroot tingled on Wolfgang's tongue. He wondered whether Kryptmann had added more warpstone as he had ordered. It gave the drug extra savour. He could picture the alchemist's pale, nervous face even now, warning him of the dangers of warpstone exposure. Still his contacts in Nuln had provided him with some interesting information concerning the alchemist and so long as he knew Kryptmann's little secret he would do whatever he was told. It amused Wolfgang to see fear and hatred war on the old man's face. Perhaps it was time to trouble him for that poison – Papa had been getting rather tiresome of late.

The clock struck twelve and Wolfgang shivered. The weird-root made the sound seem like the tolling of the temple bell of Altdorf. He glanced at the clock. It was shaped like the House of Sigmar, built to resemble a tall gabled temple. The weirdroot blurred its outline and gave a strange animated quality to the little dwarfish figures who had emerged from within the machine's workings to strike the gong beneath its face.

The girl was late, Wolfgang realised. Perhaps it was excusable. Few people had access to clocks as precise as his. It was a work of art, precision-made by the finest dwarf craftsmen from Karak Kadrin. Still, the slut was late! He would make her pay for her tardiness later. His cupboard contained some of the finest orc-hide whips and some more sophisticated implements of pleasure.

He stumbled over to the fire, wine and weirdroot making him clumsy. For a final time he checked that the positioning of the bearskin rug was exactly right. He didn't know why he was going to such trouble for a peasant girl. But he knew that it wasn't for her he was doing it, it was for himself and his god. The more pleasure he granted himself, the better pleased the Lord of Hedonism would be.

He went to the window, pulled back the brocade curtains, and peered out through the thick dimpled glass panes. No sign of the girl. Wait – what was that? It looked like her coming down the street. Something nagged in his weirdroot-dulled brain. Shouldn't she be serving downstairs? What was she doing out at this time of night? The mist was thick, perhaps it wasn't her.

Anyway what did it matter, just so long as she arrived? Wolfgang heard the stairs creak under a light tread. He was glad he had pestered Papa to let him have the chambers over the Sleeping Dragon now. It simplified life so much. He guessed his father had given in to his entreaties because, despite his protestations, Papa really didn't care to know what his heir was up to.

Wolfgang tottered over to the door. He felt himself becoming aroused in spite of the drink and the drugs. The weirdroot made him tingle all over. He had to admit that the girl had a certain peasant prettiness that might conceivably be described as alluring in the dim light. Soon he would introduce her to the mysteries of Slaanesh in the proper and approved manner.

There was a faint, tentative knock on the door. Wolfgang threw it open. Fingers of mist drifted in. Greta stood there wrapped in her cheap cloak.

'Welcome,' Wolfgang slurred, letting the robe slip from his shoulders to reveal his naked body. 'Look what I've got for you.'

He was gratified when her eyes went wide. He was less gratified when she opened her mouth to scream.

FELIX AWOKE TO the smell of boiling cabbage and the stink of unwashed bodies. Chill had seeped into his bones from the cold flagstones. He felt old. When he sat upright he discovered that the aches from his battering the night before had returned. He fought back tears of pain and fumbled for the soothing lozenges the alchemist had given him.

Light filtered down from the vaulted ceiling, revealing the bodies crowding the temple vestibule. Poor wretches from all over the town had come here to shelter from the cold night and had been locked in together. The great double doors were barred, although the people here had nothing to steal. Felix wondered at the precautions. The doors at the far side of the room, in front of which priestesses were setting up a trellis table, had also been barred. He had heard the heavy bolts being slid into place last night after the main door had been locked. He wondered if there were really people who would steal from the lowest of the low. From what he had seen so far of Fredericksburg, he guessed so.

Icons of the sacred martyrs gazed down with melancholy wooden eyes onto their shabby flock. Although cheaply and crudely made, they had been hung too high for anyone in the vestibule to reach without a ladder. So little trust in the world, he thought. It's so sad when the servants of Shallya must protect themselves from those they aid. Looking at the folk around him he thought it was indeed sad – but wise. These people looked rough.

An old man lay on the floor crying. In the night his wooden leg had come detached from the stump of his knee. Someone had either stolen it or hidden it. He crawled around frantically asking people if they had seen it. An elderly woman, her face ravaged by the pox, sat coughing into a blood-spotted handkerchief. Two youngsters barely into their teens lay huddled together for warmth on the floor. Where were their parents? Were they runaways or orphans? One sat up and yawned and smiled. She had tousled blonde hair and the hopefulness of youth. Felix wondered how long it would be until that was knocked out of her.

The old madman who had spent the night howling that the end of the world was coming had at last fallen asleep. His babbling about cancers at the world's edges and rats gnawing at the foundations of the mountains had worked their way into Felix's dreams and given him nightmares about the things he had seen beneath Karak Eight Peaks. Felix pulled his cloak tighter about himself and tried to ignore the stabbing pains which shrieked through his shoulder blades.

Around him beggars picked themselves up from straw pallets and, scratching at fleabites, shuffled towards the makeshift table at the far end of the temple vestibule. There white clad priestesses of the goddess ladled cabbage soup into wooden bowls from a huge brass tureen.

'Best hurry if ye want breakfast,' said a filthy old warrior with a cauliflower ear. The smell of rotgut alcohol on his breath was nearly overpowering. 'Tis first come, first served. The bounty of the merciful goddess isn't unlimited.'

Felix lay back and studied the cracked plasterwork of the ceiling. A mural of the goddess healing the five thousand at the river in Nuln was slowly flaking away in the damp. The doves that perched on her shoulder were nearly shapeless blobs. The sight of it brought back memories from his childhood.

He could remember his mother's last long illness, when she had gone to the temple to pray. He had been nine at the time and he and his brothers could not understand why their mother coughed so much or spent so much time at the temple. It had bored them being there – they had wanted to be outside in the sun playing, not stuck inside with the calm old white-garbed women and their interminable chanting. Looking back he understood now his mother's pale features and her quiet recital of the Penitent's Litany. He was surprised by the force of the memory and the pain of it, although it had been nearly thirteen years. He forced himself to sit upright, knowing that he had to get out of this place.

Gotrek lay on a bed of straw across from him, snoring loudly. In sleep his face had a peculiar innocence. The harsh lines eroded into his craggy features vanished, leaving him looking almost young. For the first time Felix wondered about the Slayer's age. Like all dwarfs he had about him an aura of self-assurance that suggested great experience. Certainly everything about the Slayer hinted that he had endured suffering enough for a human lifetime.

Felix wondered about the life-spans of dwarfs. He knew they were not near immortal, as elves were said to be, but they were long-lived. How old was the Slayer? He shook his head. It was another mystery. It was surprising how little he knew of his companion, for all the time that they had travelled together. Certainly, in his present condition Gotrek would be unable to provide him with any answers.

He poked the Slayer with the toe of his boot, noticing how scuffed the once-fine leather had become. He cast a glance around at the score of tramps and beggars who had lined up in front of the priestess and filled the air with the sound of hawking and coughing and spitting. He looked at the shabbiness of his surroundings and of his clothing and realised to his horror that he fitted in here. The priestess did not give him a second glance. He and the Slayer looked at home amidst the beggars.

He thought of Gotrek's desire to be remembered as an epic hero. Would he want this mentioned in the poem, Felix wondered? Had Sigmar or any of the other great heroes endured this?

Certainly the balladeers never mentioned it. In those tales everything always seemed clean and clear-cut. The only time Sigmar ever visited a flophouse was in disguise as part of some cunning plan. Well, he thought, perhaps when I work this episode into the tale that is how I will tell it. He smiled ironically when he thought of all the tales of wandering heroes he had read as a youth. Perhaps the other storytellers had made similar decisions. Perhaps it had always been this way.

The old woman coughed loudly and long. It seemed to go on forever, rattling within her chest, as if bones had come loose. She was thin and pale and obviously dying and just for a second, looking at her, Felix saw his mother's face – though Renata Jaeger had been finely clad and married to a wealthy merchant.

He looked once more at the mural of the goddess overhead and offered her a silent prayer for the healing of the Slayer and the soul of his mother. If Shallya heard she gave no sign. Felix prodded Gotrek once more.

'Come, hero. It's time to move. We must get out of here. We have mountains to climb and a long way to go.'

THE TAVERN WAS nearly empty except for the innkeeper and a drunk in the corner still fast asleep, his body curled around the ashes of the fire. An old woman was on her hands and knees cleaning the wooden floor, her face obscured by the veil of grey hair falling across it. Gotrek's immense axe was still propped up by the fireside where he had left it.

In the daylight, filtering in through the small dimple-glass panes, the place looked completely different from the night before. The dozen tables that had initially appeared so welcoming looked abandoned. The cruel sun showed every scar and scratch on the bar top and revealed the dust on the clay grog bottles behind the counter. Felix thought he could see dead insects floating on the top of the ale barrel. Maybe they were moths, he decided.

No longer full of people, the tavern looked larger and more cavernous. The cloying scent of tallow candles and spitted, roasted meat filled the air. The place stank of stale tobacco and soured wine. The lack of babbling drunken voices made the place seem to echo when someone spoke.

'What do you two want?' the landlord asked coldly. He was a big man, running to fat, his hair swept sideways across his head to cover a bald patch. His face was ruddy and tiny broken veins showed in his nose and cheeks. Felix guessed he sampled too much of his own wares. Ignoring both the owner and the aching in his muscles, Felix walked over and picked up the axe. Gotrek stood where Felix had left him, gazing blankly around him.

Its weight surprised him. He could barely move it one handed. He shifted his grip so that he could use both hands to lift it and tried to imagine swinging it. He could not. The momentum of its massive head would have overbalanced him. Remembering how Gotrek could use it in short chopping strokes and change the direction of his swing in an instant, Felix's respect for the dwarf's strength increased greatly.

Moving it gingerly with both hands he studied the blade. It was made of star-metal, which resembled no steel of this earth. Eldritch runes covered the bluish-silver material. Its edge was razor keen although Felix could never recall having seen Gotrek sharpen it. Having satisfied his curiosity he gave the axe to the Slayer. Gotrek took it easily in one hand then turned it in his grip as if inspecting it to see what it was for. He seemed to have forgotten all about how to use it. It wasn't a good sign.

'I said what did you want?' The landlord stared at them. Felix could tell that beneath his bluster he was nervous. His face was flushed and a faint moustache of perspiration was visible on his upper lip. The slightest of tremors was evident in his voice. 'We don't need your sort here. Coming in and causing trouble with our regular patrons.'

Felix went over and leaned on the bar, resting himself on folded arms. 'I didn't start any trouble,' he said softly. There was menace in his voice. 'But I'm thinking about it now.'

The man swallowed. His eyes shifted so that he was looking over Felix's head but his voice seemed to gain some firmness. 'Hrmph… penniless vagabonds, come in from the wilderness, always causing trouble.'

'Why are you so afraid of young Wolfgang?' Felix asked suddenly. He felt himself getting angry now. He was not in the wrong. It was obvious that Wolfgang had some influence in this town and that the innkeeper was taking sides out of self-interest. Felix had seen such things before in Altdorf. He had not liked it there either. 'Why do you lie?'

The innkeeper put down the glass he was polishing and turned to look at Felix. 'Don't come in here to my own tavern and call me a liar. I'll throw you out.'

Felix felt the nervous flutter in his stomach he always got when he could see violence coming and was forewarned of it. He put his hand on the pommel of his sword. He wasn't really afraid of the innkeeper but in his weakened state he wasn't sure whether he could handle the big man. But his pride still smarted from the beating he had taken the night before and he wanted to pay back someone for it. 'Why don't you do just that?'

He felt a tug at his arm. It was Gotrek. 'Come on, Felix. We don't want any trouble. We've got to make a start for the mountains.'

'Yes, why don't you listen to your little friend and go, before I teach you a lesson in manners.'

He felt his fleet slide and fail to gain traction as Gotrek dragged him irresistibly towards the door.

'Why is it that everyone I meet around here offers me a lesson in manners?' Felix asked as he was dragged outside.

GRETA WAS WAITING for them on a street corner near the gate. She stood beside a striped canvas stall that a pastry maker was erecting in anticipation of the day's custom. Her eyes had a puffed, swollen look as if she had been crying. Felix noticed a bruise on her neck where someone had gripped her very tight. The scratch of nail marks was present too. Her hair was in disarray and her dress looked torn, as if someone had tried to remove it in a hurry.

'What's wrong?' Felix asked. He was angry with the innkeeper still and it came out too abruptly. She looked at him as if she wanted to cry but her face became set and hard.

'Nothing,' she said. The streets were starting to fill with freemen farmers come in to sell eggs and produce. The early morning passers-by stared at them; the beaten-up youth and the distressed tavern girl. A night-soil collector's cart rumbled by. Felix covered his mouth against the stench. Gotrek just stared blankly at the cart's wheels as they rumbled past, fascinated.

'Did someone attack you?' he asked, trying to sound more gentle, now that he saw how upset she was.

'No. No one attacked me.' Her voice was empty of expression. He had seen similar looks on the faces of survivors of the Fort von Diehl massacre. Maybe she was in shock.

'What happened last night?'

'Nothing!'

The anger smouldering within him began to focus on her, her deliberate lack of communication making her a target for his barely suppressed fury. He realised how upset he was by the beating he had taken. He was upset not just because of the pain but because of his own feelings of helplessness. He fought not to take his anger out on her.

'What do you want from me then, Greta?' His voice had an angry bitter edge. He wanted to be about his business and have nothing to do with someone else's problems. Pain and tiredness and anger had impaired his ability to sympathise.

'You're leaving town, aren't you? Take me with you.' It was almost a plea, as close to an expression of emotion as she had come since the conversation started.

'I'm going into the mountains to get the sunblossom for Kryptmann. It will be dangerous. The last time I was there we met hordes of mutants. I can't take you now. But I'm coming back to get Gotrek cured. We'll be going north then. You can come with us then if you like.'

He did not really like the thought of taking the girl with them on the long, dangerous route to Nuln. He did not like either the risk or the idea of having to watch over her en route but he felt he owed her something, that he had to at least make the offer. Even if she was going to be a burden to them.

'I want to come with you now,' she said. She was close to tears. "I can't stay here any longer.'

Again Felix felt the slow burn of anger and surprised himself with his own callousness. 'No. Wait here. We're just going to the mountain. We'll only be gone for a day. We'll come back for you. Looking out for Gotrek is going to be bad enough. I really can't take you with us now. It's too dangerous.'

'You can't leave me here, not with Wolfgang,' she said suddenly. 'He's a monster…'

'Go to Kryptmann's. He's your friend. He'll look after you till we get back.'

It looked like she wanted to say something more but she saw the unyielding expression on his face and turned and fled. The sight of her disappearing down the street made Felix feel guilty. He wanted to call out, to tell her to come back, but by the time he had come to that decision she was gone.

Felix shrugged and headed for the gate.

FELIX WAS GLAD to leave the town behind him. Once out in the rolling fields, Gotrek shuffling blankly alongside him, he sniffed the clean air and felt free from the corruption and poverty of Fredericksburg. Looking at the peasants at work in their long strips of land, he was glad he was not like them, shackled to the earth and a life of backbreaking toil.

Entire families worked the long, curving, cultivated strips. He saw stooped women, babies slung in pouches across their shoulders, bending to pick the crops. As he watched he saw a man stand up and rub his back; his entire spine seemed to be curved, as if the long years of working the fields had permanently affected his posture. A swineherd drove his bristle-covered pigs along the road in the direction of the distant village. From the unworked strips came the scent of excrement, fertiliser made from the town's night soil.

Felix lifted his gaze from the fields towards the distant horizon. Beyond the worked lands he could see the forest stretching to the mountains. In the daylight they were beautiful, mighty towers rising proud above the plain, piercing the cloud. They formed a barrier across the horizon, like a wall that the gods had raised to keep men out of the divine realm and penned within lands more suitable to them.

The peaks held the promise of silence and cold, of escape – of peace. Overhead a hawk soared, spread out on the thermals, a bright speck free from mortal concern. It drifted below the clouds and Felix saw it as a messenger of the mountains, part of their spirit; he wished that he could be up there with it, above the world of men, apart and free.

But even as he watched, the hawk swooped. Impelled by hunger or perhaps simple killing lust, it plummeted from the sky. A rabbit burst from the undergrowth and hurtled towards him frantically. The hawk struck it. Felix heard the crack of the animal's back breaking. Sitting atop its prey, the hawk gazed around with bright fierce eyes before it began to tear gobbets of flesh from the carcass.

He noticed the riders, oblivious to the damage their horses caused as their hooves churned the soil, thundering across the empty fields towards where the hawk had landed. He had been mistaken. The hawk was not a messenger of the mountains but part of the corruption about him, a wild thing trained to kill for sport.

Felix saw with a shudder that among the riders was Wolfgang, and the others were his cronies from the night before.

THE JUDDERING PACE of the horse was almost too much to bear. Wolfgang felt sick and not just from the after-effects of too much wine and too much weirdroot. He was nearly ill with fear. What had the girl seen when he removed his robe? Had she seen the mark of Slaanesh? By all the gods, if she had and she told someone the consequences could be simply dreadful.

He wished he could remember more. He wished he had not indulged in such a potent mixture of alcohol and narcotic drugs. His head felt as if it were an egg and some daemonic chick was pecking its way out. Slaanesh take them both, he wished that Otto and Werner would return soon with news of the girl. He wished he could forget the awful moment when he woke up from his drunken swoon and realised that she was not there.

Where had she gone when she had broken free of his fumbled first attempt at an embrace and left him sprawled on his bed? His groin still hurt from her well-placed knee and the movement of the horse wasn't helping any. He would make her pay for that injury a thousand times over.

Where could she be hiding? She definitely wasn't in the common rooms of the tavern or in the single room shared by three barmaids. Had she gone to the temples to seek a priest and report him? The thought made him tremble.

Get a grip, he told himself. Think.

Damn Heinrich! When would the fat fool stop his infernal prattling? Was the only time he shut his mouth when he chewed food? It had been an awful mistake to come hawking this morning. It had not distracted him from his worries, as he had hoped. It had merely forced him to endure the torture of Heinrich's company.

At dawn Heinrich had shown up with his offer of sport. He had really been hoping for a sniff at the peasant girl but, of course, she had not been there. Now he assumed that Wolfgang wanted to keep her to himself and had her hidden away somewhere. All morning Wolfgang had been forced to tolerate his inane innuendoes and schoolboy jokes. Pride kept him from asking for his associate's aid in finding Greta. Wolfgang could not abide losing face to such a loathsome toady as Heinrich.

'Look, Wolfgang, there are those two vagabonds you had ejected from the tavern. Didn't the dwarf look stupid when Otto and Werner threw him in the ale barrel? Come, let us have some more sport.'

Heinrich led the procession of horsemen towards the two strangers. By chance the hawk, Tarna, had landed near them and sat ripping flesh from her prey. Typical of fat Heinie's birds to be eating, thought Wolfgang. The whole damnable family has trouble with their appetites so why not their birds too?

He brought his steed to a halt as close to the blond-haired young man as possible. He got some slight satisfaction from watching him trying not to flinch as the massive beast loomed over him. The dwarf stepped back, obviously intimidated by the horse's bulk.

'Good morning,' Wolfgang said as cheerily as he could manage with his stomach heaving. 'Recovered, I see. We must have had equally rough nights. I trust you are not feeling so unsociable this morning.' Wolfgang glanced left and right at Heinrich's bodyguards just to let the worm know who was in control here.

Anger warred with common sense on the young man's face. 'I'm fine,' Felix said eventually.

Wolfgang heard the strain needed for self-control in the man's voice. The youth didn't like him, that was obvious.

'No need to worry about your girlfriend either. Wolfgang is taking care of her.'

By Slaanesh! Heinrich was repulsive when he was being triumphant, thought Wolfgang. Then what he had said percolated into Wolfgang's brain. Yes, Greta had left the tavern just after the stranger had been thrown out. And he had not seen her again until she had shown up at his door. Perhaps Heinrich was not so stupid after all.

'What girlfriend?' The blond-haired man looked genuinely puzzled. He rubbed the old duelling scar on his right cheek. A frown marred his smooth brow.

140   *William King*

'The lovely Greta,' Heinrich crowed. 'You must have thought she'd taken a shine to you when she followed you out into the street. Maybe you imagined her soft peasant heart had been warmed by your plight. Well she spent last night warming Wolfgang's bed.'

Wolfgang winced. If only it were true.

The tramp's hand moved to the pommel of his sword. It stayed there too, in spite of the fact that Heinrich's men had drawn their weapons. With what looked like a habitual motion he glanced at the dwarf. The dwarf had stopped inspecting the hawk. He glanced blankly up at the men on horse. The axe was held loosely in his hands, as if he didn't quite know what to do with it.

'We don't want any trouble,' the man said. He let his hand move away from his weapon.

The bodyguards guffawed. Wolfgang wished his head didn't hurt so much, so that he could think clearly. He badly wanted to ask the youth if he had seen the girl but pride kept him from asking in front of his cronies. He tried to see some way out of his dilemma but the solution just would not come to him. Life could be so hard sometimes, he thought.

He consoled himself with the thought that the girl could not have gone too far. If she was still in the town, Werner and Otto would eventually find her. And if she had decided to risk her lord's wrath and flee back to the peasant community she'd have to pass through these lands. So a sweep of the area surrounding the town would soon reveal her whereabouts. And this hawking party would provide a particularly fine excuse for it.

And, he reasoned, no one had come looking for him so she could not have told anybody yet. Even if she did, would anybody believe her; a peasant drab accusing the son of the town's most influential merchant? He allowed himself a smile. It was nice to know that one could still be brilliant, even with a simply dreadful hangover.

'Come, Heinrich,' he said magisterially. 'Let us leave these two clowns to return to their circus. It's too fine a morning to waste time in conversations with louts.'

He applied his spurs gently to the flanks of his mount and fought down the diminishing waves of nausea as it moved. Now that he had reassured himself, all seemed almost well with the world. He promised himself that when the girl was found she would pay for subjecting him to such excruciating, and what was worse, boring torment.

THE HILLS ROSE to meet the peak, the swell of their long curves reminding Felix of waves. Above them the mountains rose, tier upon massive tier, to block the horizon with their snaggle-toothed bulk.

Felix had feared that he would have some difficulty in locating the trail to Mount Blackfire but the path was obvious. It was a simple spur on the one he and Gotrek had followed the previous day while making their descent from the foothills of the range.

The strain on the back of his thighs and in his calves began to tell as the pathway continued to rise. It had been carved into the flank of the mountain by the passing of countless feet. Felix wondered whether the alchemist had ever followed this route or whether it was a way that had been left by less human passers-by. Some of the signs that had been scratched into the rock were in the form of a crude eye; but whether they were warnings of the goblins' presence or territorial claim markers left by the greenskins themselves he could not tell.

Gotrek looked like he was enjoying the walk. He hummed a broken tune to himself and took the slope in his stride without any noticeable effort. He picked his way along the slippery path with no difficulty, finding footholds where Felix could see none. Soon the man found it easiest to follow in the dwarf's footsteps. Gotrek was in an environment he was adapted to and it seemed wisest to let him lead.

Sweat rolled down Felix's back and his breathing became heavy. He had thought himself toughened by the long trip from Karak Eight Peaks but the effort of climbing these hills was a sore one. The beating he had taken and the alchemist's treatment had worn him out. He was worried about his ability to handle the tough climb. It would be worse if the clouds made good on their threat of rain.

The harshness of the landscape, all jutting rocks and windswept ground, matched the bleakness of his mood. Felix seethed with hatred for Wolfgang Lammel. He resented the wealthy young merchant's easy cruelty and spoiled arrogance. In his days in Altdorf, Felix had known dozens like him but had never had to contend with being the object of their cruelty.

His father's wealth and social status had shielded him from it. In his more honest moments, he was forced to admit that perhaps he too had once behaved a little like Wolfgang. Now he had seen injustice from the underdog's point of view and he did not like it.

He understood now why Greta had been so disturbed. He tried not to imagine what had happened between her and Wolfgang, but thoughts of Lammel forcing himself on the girl ran through his head and made him half-mad with fury. He swore that he would get Gotrek cured and make the brat pay. Cursing to himself he marched on. He fought down an urge to yell at the Slayer to stop his infernal humming.

Gotrek disappeared over the brow of a ridge. Felix swore as his feet slipped on the scree of the path and he fell, cutting his hand on the small stones. Pain stung him. He pulled himself up over the brow and found himself lying flat on soft turf.

Felix wondered why it was that sunblossom had to grow on the highest slopes just below the snowline; why couldn't it grow here in the foothills with all the rest of the blossoms. After a moment he shrugged. In his life he had found that few things were ever easy. Maybe the alchemists only used ingredients because they were difficult to find, to increase the mystique of their art. He would not be in the least surprised if that were the case.

He sat up and took another lozenge to dull the throbbing pain in his head. It was going to be a long day.

HARDY EVERGREEN trees lined the steep slopes of the narrow vale, like stubble on the upturned face of a giant. High to the right, a waterfall made a series of spectacular leaps over hundred-foot drops until it plunged into the small lake at the valley's centre. The mountains framed the valley and Felix had to crane his neck upwards to see their peaks. Looking down the vale was like looking down the sight of a crossbow, the eye focused by the line of grey peaks marching into the distance.

Here the pungent aroma of roses mingled with honeysuckle and bitterbriar. Tangled bushes fought with each other for space, the flower heads like the helmets of warring armies of colour. He wondered if there was any sunblossom present, then remembered what Kryptmann had told him about where the magical ingredient had to be picked.

A flicker of movement attracted his eye as the head of a huge elk, as high at the shoulder as a man, emerged from bushes overlooking a ledge of rock fifty yards above him. It gazed down warily as if judging whether it was safe to come down for water. Felix eyed the mighty sweep of its antlers with respect.

As the clouds parted, shafts of sunlight illuminated the valley. The chatter of birdsong reached his ears and mingled with the muted roar of the falling water. He bent to pick up a pine cone, enjoying the scaly roughness of its serrated edges beneath his fingers.

For a moment the beauty of the scene held him enthralled. Even his thoughts of revenge on the merchant's son evaporated. He felt relaxed and at peace, and the pain of his beaten body temporarily vanished. He was glad he had seen this place, that all the steps of his long journey had brought him here. He knew he would be one of the few men who ever saw this valley. The thought pleased him.

The presence of the elk was right. It made the scene look like a perfectly composed landscape painting. Then it struck him that perhaps it was rather odd that the deer was raising a horn to its lips with a massive, suspiciously human-looking hand. Then a blast of sound echoed down the valley and before it had faded the knowledge filtered into Felix's brain that he had not seen the head of an elk. It was the head of an altered one.

He lobbed the pine cone in the direction of the lake and, pulling his cloak around him against the increasing chill, he hurried onward and upward after Gotrek. He looked around for signs of pursuit but saw none. Even the elk-headed mutant was nowhere to be seen.

NOW FELIX KNEW for certain that they were being followed. Looking back down the winding trail he could see their pursuers, a band of mutants. All that long afternoon as he and Gotrek had climbed the flank of the mountain they had gathered behind them. The way back to Fredericksburg was blocked.

He stopped and let his breathing and heartbeat return to normal. He tried to count the number of their pursuers but it was difficult. The early evening gloom caused the creatures to blend in with the grey of the rock face. Felix made the sign of the hammer across his chest and commended his soul to Sigmar.

He had always known he would die in some out-of-the-way place. His participation in the dwarf's quest made it inevitable. He had just not imagined it would be so soon. It was all so stupid. Gotrek would not even get his heroic doom. The Slayer was too busy staring blankly into space, oblivious to their danger.

At first it had been easy to pretend that nothing was happening; that the horn-blowing beast was but a solitary creature too scared to tackle two well-armed travellers. But as the day wore on, the signs had mounted to tell them it wasn't so.

When Felix had seen the cloven-hoofed tracks mingling with clawed human footprints in the mud surrounding a ford he had managed to dismiss them as old spoor, something to which he did not need to pay too much attention. Yet even then he had loosened his sword in its scabbard.

Sometime later, as Felix clambered his way ever upwards after Gotrek's uncaring back, he had caught sight of scuttling shapes keeping pace with them. They flitted from tree to tree on either side of the path. He had tried to get a closer look but the shadow under the pines had defeated even his keen eyes. All he was left with was the impression of tentacled figures keeping carefully from view.

His nerves had begun to fray. He felt like charging under the canopy of the trees and seeking his foes. But what if he lost the path? Or what if there was more than one or two of them? Vague suspicion had kept him inactive. He had pushed aside his fears and kept climbing.

It had become almost unbearable when he had heard the horn blast away to his right and it had been answered by a similar one from the other side of the trail. He knew then that the accursed ones were closing in, that they were gathering for the feast. He was tempted to make a stand then, to get it over with – but some impulse had kept him going up towards the snowline.

He told himself it was the urge to keep trying, not to give up in the face of certain doom that drove him onwards, but he was honest enough with himself to know that it was just fear. He did not want to meet the mutants; he wanted to postpone the inevitable end for as long as possible.

Now he stood on the ridge near the snowline and looked back down the trail and knew it was finished. Here, in this frigid, windswept, barren place, his life would end along with the day. There would be no revenge on Wolfgang, no homecoming in Altdorf, no epic poem for Gotrek.

He looked at the Slayer who stood nearby, his axe drooping in his clumsy grip and watching the oncoming mutants. Felix counted about ten of them. The one in the lead was a familiar gross fat giant. His heart sank even further. He had envisaged perhaps begging for mercy or offering the prospect of a ransom, anything that would extend his life. Surely, though, the obese giant would want his revenge for the slaughter of the previous day.

Wait – what was growing at his feet? Small yellow flowers grew in clumps of thin soil in the shelter of the ridge. As the sun began to sink he realised it was what he had been sent to find. It seemed like a very slim chance but...

Swiftly he plucked a few blossoms and thrust them at Gotrek.

'Eat them,' he commanded. The Trollslayer stared at him as if he were truly mad. Slowly a frown passed across his scarred face.

'Don't want to eat flowers,' he said in bemusement.

'Just eat them!' Felix roared. Like an abashed child, the Slayer shoved them into his mouth and began to chew.

Felix studied him carefully, hoping to see signs of some change in the dwarf, the sudden, miraculous return of his old ferocity stimulated by the supposed magical quality of the flowers. He could see none.

Well, it had been a faint hope anyway, he told himself.

The mutants were close now. Felix could see that it was definitely the survivors of the band which had previously attacked them. Gotrek spat out a cud of yellow and moved behind Felix.

Oh well, Felix decided, best to meet death with a sword in his hand. At least this way he would take one or two of the warpspawned to Hell with him. As he unsheathed the sleek weapon, the fading sunlight caught the blade, and caused the runes to glow. Felix studied them as if for the first time. The approach of death made all of his senses keener. He appreciated the workmanship of those old dwarf craftsmen as he had never done before. He wondered what the runes meant, what their intricate symbolism signified. There was so much he would never know now and so much he wanted to find out.

The mutants had stopped not fifty paces away and their giant leader peered at Felix myopically. After a pause he cuffed the elk-headed mutant about the ear and advanced.

Felix wondered whether he should charge at the foul thing and hope to slay him. Perhaps that would break the morale of his confederates. Sword versus great stone club, he was sure he could win if only the others didn't intervene. With that thought some semblance of courage returned. There was some hope. He grinned a feral grin; fear had passed him and he almost started to enjoy the situation.

The leader paused ten paces from Felix; a great wobbling mound of fat, girded around with studded leather and many weapons. Waves of blubber cascaded from his chin like tallow melting on a candle. His huge hairless head was like a ball of meat with tiny holes poked in it for the eyes, nose and mouth. To the man's surprise he seemed quite nervous.

'I'm not fooled you know,' the mutant said at last. His voice sounded like the tolling of a great bell. It boomed out from within his vast chest. He was so close that Felix could hear his phlegmy, wheezing breaths.

'What?' Felix said, bemused. Was this a trick?

'I can see through your plan. Trying to get us within range of your friend's axe then slaughter us.'

'But–' The unfairness of the accusation mortified Felix. Here he was, standing waiting bravely for death and his disgusting opponent was claiming it was the other way about.

'You must think us complete idiots. Well the warpstone did-n't melt our brains along with our bodies. How stupid do you think we are? Your friend here pretends to be afraid but we recognise him. He's the one who killed Hans and Peter and Gretchen. And all the others. We know him and we know his axe and there's no way you're going to lure us within its sweep.'

'But–' Now that he had mustered his courage to make a brave last stand Felix felt cheated. He wanted to demand that they get on with their attack.

'I told Gorm Moosehead that I thought it was you, but he said "No". Well I was right and he was wrong, and I didn't gather the clan just so you and your nasty friend could collect the bounty on mutant heads.'

'But–' Slowly it dawned on Felix what was happening. They

had been reprieved. He forced his mouth firmly shut before it could betray him.

'No! You may think you're clever but you're not clever enough. This is one trap we're not going to fall into. We're too smart for you. I just wanted you to know that.'

So saying, the mutant leader backed slowly and cautiously away. Felix watched the foul band melt back into the gloom and only then did he let out his breath. He stood transfixed for a moment. The twilight on the nearby peaks was the most beautiful thing he had ever seen. He even rejoiced in the chill and the pain that throbbed in his hand. They were signs he was still alive.

'Thank you, Sigmar, thank you!' he shouted, unable to contain his joy.

'What are you shouting about?' Gotrek asked excitedly.

Felix resisted the sudden blinding urge to run him through with his sword. Instead he clapped the dwarf on the back. After a moment it struck him that they were stuck up here on the mountain until the morning. Even that thought was endurable.

'Quick, we must gather the flowers,' Felix said. 'The sun hasn't set yet!'

'WHO IS IT?' Lothar Kryptmann called warily from inside, as Felix banged upon his door. 'What do you want?'

It was just early evening and Felix was surprised by the elaborate precautions with which the alchemist greeted them.

'It's me. Felix Jaeger. I'm back. Open up!' Was it just his imagination or did Kryptmann sound more than usually nervous, Felix wondered? He turned and looked down the street. Lights glowed through the chinks in shuttered windows. In the distance he heard the clip-clop of horses hooves and the metalled wheels of a carriage on cobbles, heading towards the taverns of the town square. The wealthy out to play, he supposed.

'Hold on! Hold on! I'm coming.'

Felix stopped knocking. He coughed. Just his luck to have caught a chill on that pestilential mountain-top. He mopped the sweat of fever from his brow and drew his cloak tighter against the chill mist. He glared at Gotrek, who stood stupidly at the top of the steps leading down to the basement apartment, holding the flowers he had collected. As usual the Slayer showed no sign of illness.

Bolts snapped on the door. Chains were loosened. The door opened a little. Through the chink, light spilled out along with the pungent odour of chemicals. Felix pushed the door open despite the alchemist's resistance and forced his way within. He was surprised to see Greta standing in the room's other doorway. She had obviously been hiding in the other rooms.

'Do come in, Herr Jaeger,' the alchemist said tetchily. He stood aside to let Gotrek enter.

'Wolfgang is looking for you,' Felix said to the girl. She looked too scared to speak. 'Why?'

'Leave her alone, Herr Jaeger,' Kryptmann said. 'Can't you see she's terrified? She's had rather a nasty shock at the hands of your friend, Lammel.'

Swiftly Kryptmann outlined what Greta had seen when she ventured into the merchant's son's quarters the previous evening. Kryptmann was discrete about why she went but he mentioned the stigmata of Chaos she had noticed.

'I feared as much. I should have known when he made me add warpstone to his weirdroot. I would imagine that's when he started to develop the mark of the daemon.'

'You added warpstone to his weirdroot? Warpstone?'

'There's no need to look so shocked, my young friend. Its usage is not that uncommon in certain alchemical operations. Many respectable practitioners of my art make use of it in small doses. Why my old tutor at Middenheim University, the great Litzenreich himself, used to say...'

'I heard that Litzenreich was thrown out of the university for his experiments and that the Guild of Alchemists withdrew his license. There was quite a scandal. In fact, the last I heard he was an outlaw.'

'There is always malice among academics. Litzenreich was simply a man ahead of his time. I mean, look how long it took Eisenstern's theory that the sun goes round the earth to become commonly accepted. He was burned at the stake for claiming it originally.'

'Regardless of the philosophical merits of your argument, Herr Kryptmann, warpstone is a highly illegal and dangerous substance. If a witch-hunter was ever to hear–'

Kryptmann seemed to shrink in on himself. 'That's exactly what Wolfgang Lammel told me – though how he found out about my experiments is beyond me. I purchase the warp... the substance from a very small, very discrete emporium in Nuln. Van Niek's. I told him I didn't want to do anything illegal with it. All I wanted to do was learn how to transmute lead into gold – and warpstone is the very essence of transmutation.'

'So Wolfgang is about to find out, it would seem.' Try as he might, Felix could not keep an unseemly note of gloating from his voice. It was perfect. He would unmask the decadent swine as a mutant in front of the whole town. Thus would he repay him for the beating he had taken, and for what he had done to Greta too of course.

'You won't report me to the authorities will you, my young friend? After all, I did treat your wounds. I promise that if you don't report me, I'll never have anything to do with warpstone again.'

Felix glanced at the scared alchemist; he had nothing against him and Kryptmann might well have learned his lesson about dealing in illegal substances. But there was still the problem of the man's bodyguards to deal with. Still, he had the answer to that too.

'Herr Kryptmann, if you can cure my associate, I assure you that I will forget all about what you've done.'

FELIX TOYED IDLY with the pestle and mortar while Kryptmann proceeded with his work. The pungent fumes filled the laboratory, rising from the pot in which the alchemist had reduced the sunblossom to a yellow sludge.

The cool stone of the pestle was somehow comforting. The tang of the sunblossom perfume was noticeable even through his blocked nose. He had taken another two of Kryptmann's healing lozenges and he felt slightly distanced from everything. He wished his head would clear, that all of the aches and pains would go away.

'Felix?' a soft voice said, snapping him back to reality.

'What, Greta?' He was still snappish. Human contact closed the distance between himself and the world, broke the barriers around him that Kryptmann's medicine had built against the pain. It brought his anger back into focus.

'What will Wolfgang's men do if they find me here?'

'Don't worry about it. Soon Herr Wolfgang will have worries enough of his own.'

'I hope so. It's good of Lothar to hide me from him. It's at terrible risk to himself. You know what Wolfgang's bodyguards can be like.'

Privately, Felix thought that the alchemist had hidden the girl simply to spite Wolfgang. He had no reason to love the merchant's son. Or perhaps it was guilt for providing Wolfgang with the warpstone which had altered him. Had he always been a sadistic monster, Felix wondered, or had that transformation only come recently, with the mark of Chaos?

Other questions flickered through his dulled mind. Why did his enemy feel the need to use warpstone in the first place? And what about the sinister rumours Greta had claimed to have heard about him? He pushed them away. He would probably never know the answers. One thing was clear, though; he would be doing everyone in town a tremendous favour by disposing of the fellow.

'No! Put that down. That's acid!' Kryptmann shouted at Gotrek suddenly.

The Slayer stopped rooting about amidst the various jugs and beakers on Kryptmann's bench. He looked as if he were about to drink from one large silver flask. Gotrek shuffled his feet and returned the container to its proper place.

Felix glanced around the laboratory. He had never been in one before. It all looked so very arcane and incomprehensible. The benches were covered in intricate structures of pipework and beakers. Distillation equipment covered nearly half of one table. Several racks of stoppered glass tubes were stacked against one wall. Each contained liquids of cobalt blue or lime green or blood red. Some contained many layers of multi-coloured sediment. On one wall hung a framed certificate. Even at this distance Felix recognised the crest of the University of Middenheim, famed throughout the Empire for its schools of magic and alchemy.

Charcoal burners heated flasks and pots containing various substances. Kryptmann moved briskly from one to another, stirring, adjusting temperatures and occasionally tasting with a long glass spoon. He opened a great cabinet and produced a large padded white gauntlet covered in scorch marks. He pulled it over his right hand.

'Not long now,' he said, picking up a heated flask and pouring it into the central pot. The mixture bubbled and hissed. He

put a stopper on the second flask and shook it before uncork-
ing it and pouring it into the mix. A great cloud of pungent
green smoke billowed across the room. Felix coughed and
heard Greta do the same.

As the smoke cleared he saw Kryptmann carefully emptying
the contents of the third alembic into the mixture. With each
drop, a tiny puff of different-coloured smoke arose. The first
was red, the second blue, the third yellow. Each rose, a tiny
expanding mushroom-shaped cloud of vapour reaching
upward towards the ceiling.

The alchemist set down the alembic and adjusted the flame
under the pot. He picked up a small hourglass and turned it
upside down. 'Two minutes,' he said.

A sense of triumph filled Felix. Soon Gotrek would be cured
and they would visit the Sleeping Dragon. He would take out
all of the many tribulations he had suffered on Wolfgang
Lammel's hide.

No sooner had the last grain of sand fallen from the top of
the hourglass than Kryptmann removed the pot from the
flames. 'All done!'

He beckoned for Gotrek to come over, then ladled out a measure into a small china bowl. Felix saw that the inner rim was
marked with red circles and astrological signs. He presumed
these represented various levels of dosage. He was somehow
reassured when the alchemist filled it to the very top, then
handed it to Gotrek.

'Drink it all up now.'

The Slayer swilled it down. 'Ugh!' he said.

They stood and waited. And waited. And waited.

'How long should it take to work?' Felix asked eventually.

'Er, not long now!'

'You said that an hour ago, Kryptmann. How long exactly?'
Felix's knuckles whitened as his grip on the heavy pestle tightened.

'I told you that the process was, well, uncertain. There were
certain risks involved. Perhaps the sunblossom was not in
prime condition. Are you sure you picked it exactly at the death
of day?'

'How. Long?' Felix enunciated both words clearly and slowly,
allowing the measure of his irritation to show in his voice.

'Well, I – actually it should have worked almost instantly, jolting the mnemonic nodes and humours back into their old configuration.'

Felix studied the Slayer. Gotrek looked exactly as he had done when they entered Kryptmann's lab.

'How do you feel. Ready to seek out your doom?' Felix asked, very softly.

'What doom would that be?' Gotrek responded.

'Per–perhaps we should try another dose, Herr Jaeger?'

Felix let out an inarticulate howl of rage. It was not to be borne. He had endured a severe beating from Wolfgang's men. He had climbed that mountain along unspeakably difficult paths. He had narrowly escaped death at the hands of hordes of bloodthirsty mutants. He was tired and cut and bruised and hungry. What was worse, he was coming down with a pestilential flux. His clothes were torn. He badly needed a bath. And it was all the alchemist's fault.

'Calm down, Herr Jaeger. There's no need to growl like that.'

'Oh, there isn't, is there?' Felix snarled. Kryptmann had sent him for the flowers. Kryptmann had promised that he would heal Gotrek. Kryptmann had spoiled Felix's plans for glorious revenge. He had gone through hell for naught, at the foolish instructions of a foolish old man who did not know his own foolish business!

'Perhaps I could make you a nice soporific potion to calm your nerves. Things will look so much better after a good night's sleep.'

'I could have died getting those flowers.'

'Look, you're upset. Quite understandably so – but violence will solve nothing.'

'It will make me feel a lot better. It will make you feel a lot worse.' Felix threw the pestle at the alchemist. Kryptmann leapt to one side. The implement smacked into Gotrek's head with a great crunch. The Slayer fell over.

'Quick, Greta! Send for the watch!' the alchemist babbled. 'Herr Jaeger has gone mad! Help! Help!'

Felix darted round the work bench after Kryptmann, toppling him off his feet with a flying tackle. It gave him a great sense of satisfaction to get his fingers round the alchemist's throat. He began to tighten his grip, smiling all the while. He felt Greta try to pull him off Kryptmann. Her fingers locked in his hair. He tried to shake her off. The alchemist's face started to turn an interesting shade of purple.

'Not that I have anything against senseless violence, manling, but why exactly are you strangling that old man?'

The granite-hard voice was harsh and cracked and held an undercurrent of sheer cold menace. It took Felix a second to realise just who had spoken. He let go of Kryptmann's throat.

'And who is he? And where are we? And why does my head hurt, by Grimnir?'

'The blow from the pestle must have returned him to his senses,' Greta said softly.

'I, ah, prefer to think it was the delayed effect of my brew,' Kryptmann gasped. 'I told you it would work.'

'What senses? What brew? What are you talking about, you old lunatic?'

Felix picked himself up and dusted himself off. He helped Kryptmann to his feet, picked up the alchemist's glasses and handed them to him. He turned to face Gotrek. 'What is the last thing you can remember?'

'The mutant attack of course, manling. Some snotling-fondler caught me on the head with a slingshot. Now how did I get here? What magic is this?' Gotrek scowled majestically.

'This will take a lot of explaining,' his companion said. 'So first let's get some beer. I know a friendly little tavern just around the corner.'

Felix Jaeger smiled wickedly to himself, and the two of them set off for the Sleeping Dragon.

BLOOD AND DARKNESS

'After we exposed the cultists of Slaanesh in Fredericksburg, and incapacitated several of their minions, we ventured back onto the road to Nuln, leaving our former tormentors to the less than gentle mercies of their fellows. I have no idea why we settled on that mighty city as the terminus of our travels, other than perhaps because of the fact that my family had business interests there.

'During one roadside halt in a tavern, Gotrek and I decided, perhaps foolishly in hindsight, that we should avoid the main road. Inevitably, and perhaps predictably, our drunken decision to take a circuitous route through the forest led to disaster.

'In our desire to avoid any possible encounter with the agents of law, we wandered far from the normal haunts of man, and ended up deep in the forests, in an area long thought to be the site of a Black Altar of Chaos. Little did we suspect when we set out that we would soon meet with startling proof of that dire fane's existence, and also that we

**would soon do battle with the most powerful of all of the
followers of Darkness we had yet encountered...'**

— From *My Travels with Gotrek, Vol. II,* by Herr
Felix Jaeger (Altdorf Press, 2505)

WHEN SHE HEARD the approaching footsteps, Kat concentrated
on making herself smaller. She squeezed even more tightly into
the tiny space between the stone blocks of the tumbledown
building, hoping that the beasts had not come back. She knew
that if they had, and they found her, this time they would kill
her for certain.

She wriggled further into the shadowy recess until her back
was against stone. The rock was still warm from the fire which
had burned down the inn. She felt a small measure of safety.
No adult could squeeze into so small a hiding place, certainly
nothing as large as the beasts. But they could always reach in
with their spears or swords. She shuddered when she remembered the one with tentacles instead of arms, imagining the
long leech-mouthed limbs questing like great snakes to find
her in the darkness.

She grasped the hammer shaped amulet that old Father
Tempelman had given her and prayed to Sigmar to deliver her
from all snake-armed things. She tried hard to block out her
last memory of the priest, fleeing down the street, carrying little Lotte Bernhoff. A horn-headed giant had impaled him with
a spear. The weapon had pierced both Tempelman and the five
year old, lifting them into the air as though they were weight-
less.

'Something terrible has happened here, manling,' a voice
said. It was deep and gruff and harsh, but it did not sound like
the feral snarling of a beast. The accent was foreign, as if
Reikspiel were not the native tongue of the speaker. It
reminded Kat of the strangers she had once served in the inn.

Dwarfs, Old Ingmar – who fancied himself a traveller
because he had once been to Nuln – had called them. They had
been short, not much taller than herself but far broader and
heavier than any man. They had worn cloaks of slate grey and,
though they had called themselves merchants, they carried axes
and shields. They spoke sadly in low musical voices and when
drunk joined the villagers in singing. One had shown her a

clockwork bird which flapped its metal wings marvellously and spoke in a metallic voice. She had begged bald-pated Karl, the innkeeper, to buy it for her but, but though he had loved her like she was his own daughter, he had just shaken his head and continued to polish the glasses, saying there was no way he could afford such workmanship.

She shivered when she thought of what had become of Karl and fat Heide and the others in the inn who she had called family. She had heard screams as the bestial horde ravaged through the village led by the strange warrior in black armour. She had seen the lines of villagers being marched to the great bonfire in the village square.

'Perhaps we should leave, Gotrek. By the looks of it, this is not a healthy place to linger,' said another voice from close by. This one definitely belonged to a human, Kat decided. It was soft spoken and gentle, with a cultured accent similar to old Doctor Gebhardt's. A brief spark of hope flickered in Kat's mind. There was no way a beast could sound like that.

Or was there? Like many other villagers who had grown up in the depths of the wild woods, Kat was familiar with the stories. Of wolves who looked like men until let in by unsuspecting villagers. Of children who looked normal until they grew up into hideous mutated monsters that slew their own families. Of woodcutters who had heard a child's cry in the deep forest at twilight and who went to investigate and never returned. The servants of the Dark Powers were devilish and clever, and found many ways of luring the unwary to their doom.

'Not until I've found out what happened here. By Grungni, this place is an abattoir!' The first voice spoke again, unnaturally loud in the silence.

'Whatever force could do this to a walled village could surely squash us like bugs. Look at the holes in the walls of the keep! Let us be away.' There was an undercurrent of fear in the cultured voice which echoed the terror in Kat's own breast.

Once again the memory of the previous night rose before her. It had begun with a great thunderclap of sound although the sky had been empty. She recalled the tolling of the alarm bell and the splintering of the gate. She recalled rushing to the inn door and seeing the beastmen pouring down the street, torching the village and putting everyone to the sword.

One huge figure with the head of a goat had lifted Johan the miller clean over its head and pitched him into a burning cottage. Little Gustav, Johan's son, had driven a pitchfork through its chest before being torn to pieces by two deformed creatures in beggars' clothes whose faces showed wattled crests and lizard-like skin. She wished she could forget the way they tore the gobbets of flesh from the corpse and stuffed them greedily into fanged mouths.

She remembered wondering why Count Klein and his soldiers had not come to defend them but when she gazed at the castle she knew the answer. The towers were ablaze. Silhouetted against the flames, figures dangled from the lord's gibbet. She guessed they were Klein's men.

Karl had forced her inside and barred the door, before stacking the tables in front of the entrance. Karl and Ulf the potboy and even Heide, Karl's wife, had clutched knives and other kitchen implements; a pitiful defence against the foul rabble that whooped and gibbered in the streets outside.

They had stood around, pale-faced and sweating in the flickering light of the flambeaux, while outside the sounds of killing and destruction continued. It had seemed like all their darkest fears has come true, that finally the monstrous, mythical forces lurking in the forest's heart had erupted forth to claim what was theirs.

For a time it seemed like the inn was going to be left untouched but then the door was knocked from its hinges by a mighty blow and several immense beastmen had pushed aside the piled furniture. Kat remembered so vividly the taste of the smoky air that accompanied the opening of the door.

With a whimpering cry, Ulf had charged the leading monster. It brought a huge club down on his head, splitting his skull and splattering brains about the room. Kat had screamed as the jelly-like material hit her face and slid down her cheek.

When she opened her eyes she looked into the face of death. Over her loomed a huge creature. It was man-shaped but goat-headed, its horns twisted to resemble a strange X-shaped rune. Ruddy fur covered its mighty body; Ulf's brains covered its massive club.

The beastman had looked down on her and she saw that it had no eyes, only a blank expanse of flesh where the sockets should have been. Even so, she somehow knew that it could see her as well as any sighted thing. Perhaps the circlet of desiccated eyeballs dangling from its neck gave it sight. It had inspected her with a puzzled expression, then reached down and touched her long black hair, running its finger through the white streak that ran from her forehead to the back of her neck. It shook its head and backed away almost fearfully.

Nearby Karl bled to death, whimpering piteously as he failed to staunch the blood pumping from the stump where his left hand had been. Kat couldn't see what was happening behind the tumbled table where two beasts had Heide pinned but she could hear the old woman's screams. She had fled out into the night.

And there she had met the beautiful white-faced woman who was mistress of the beasts. She was sitting astride a great red-eyed steed whose flesh was as black as her ornate armour. The woman looked at the destruction, her smile revealing fanged incisors drawn back over ruby-red lips. Her hair was long and black with a white strip running down the middle. Kat wondered whether it was the mark of Chaos – and whether that was the reason the beastman had spared her.

The woman held a black sword in one hand, runes glowed the colour of blood along its length. She noticed Kat and looked down at her. For the second time that night, the girl thought she was dead. The woman had raised her blade as if to smite her. Numbed with terror, Kat had just stood there looking up at her, her gaze had locked with the warrior's.

The woman paused as their eyes met. Kat thought she detected a faint glimmer of sympathy there. The woman mouthed the word 'No', and nudged her mount into motion with a touch of her spurs. She rode off down the street, not looking back. Kat noticed the bonfire and the beaten villagers being pushed towards it and scurried into hiding.

Soon the sound of bestial chanting rose over the village. The burnt meat smell of roasting flesh, both tantalising and sickening, filled the air. The hideous screams of the dying villagers filled the night.

Kat had hidden until morning, praying for the souls of her friends, praying she wouldn't be found. When the sun came up, the beasts were gone as if they had never been there. But the smoking ruins of the village, and the piles of charred skulls and cracked bones in the still-smouldering embers of the bonfire showed it had not been a nightmare.

Suddenly it was all too much for Kat. She started to cry with great choking sobs. Tears ran down her soot-blackened face.

'What was that, manling?' the deep voice said nearby.

Kat stifled her sobs as stealthy footfalls approached. Something blocked the sunlight in the entrance to her hiding place. She stared up at a man's face, framed by long golden hair. The eyes that looked at her were scared and tired and world-weary. A long scar marred the man's cheek. She found herself looking at the sharp point of a longsword. Faint markings were etched into the blade.

'Come out slowly,' he said. His soft, cultured voice was cold now and held no hint of mercy. Kat crawled slowly out into the daylight. She could tell she was near to death at this moment. Fear of the unknown had made the man desperate.

She stood up. The man was much taller than she was and dressed like a bandit. A shabby cloak of faded red wool was thrown back over his right shoulder, leaving his sword arm free. His clothes were stained and patched and very travel-worn. His high leather boots were cracked and scuffed. He glanced around with an edgy wariness that seemed habitual.

'It's only a little girl,' he shouted over his shoulder. 'Maybe a survivor.'

The figure that stomped into view past the tumble-down remains of Frau Hof's bakery was just as terrifying in its own way as the beasts had been. It was a dwarf – but one which bore little resemblance to the travelling merchants Kat had known.

He stood halfway between Kat and the bandit in height but he was heavy, maybe as heavy as Jan the blacksmith had been and certainly more muscular. A patchwork of intricate tattoos covered his whole body. A huge crest of red-dyed hair rose over his shaven skull. A crude leather patch obscured his left eye and a gold chain ran from his nose to his left ear. In one ham-sized fist he carried the largest axe Kat had ever seen.

The dwarf glared at her belligerently. There was a sense of barely restrained wrath about him that was desperately frightening. He showed none of the obvious fear his companion did.

'What happened here, child?' he demanded brusquely in a voice like scraping stones.

Staring into that one mad, inhuman eye, Kat could think of no response. The man touched her gently on the shoulder.

'Tell us your name,' he said softly.

'Kat. Katerina. It was the beasts. They came from the forest, killed everybody. I hid. They left me alone.'

Kat found herself babbling the story of her encounter with the beastmen and the woman in the black armour to the astonishment of the two adventurers. By the time she had finished the dwarf looked at her wearily. His ferocious expression had softened a little.

'Don't worry child. You're safe now.'

'I HATE TREES. They're like elves, manling,' Gotrek said. 'They make me want to take an axe to them.'

Felix Jaeger peered into the shadowy forest nervously. All around, the great trees brooded, ominous presences whose branches met over the trail, intertwined like the fingers of a giant at prayer, blocking out the sun until only a few solitary shafts of light illuminated the way forward. Moss covered the branches and the scaly bark of the trunks reminded him of the withered hides of dead serpents. A stillness as old as the vast primeval forest surrounded them, broken only by occasional stirrings in the undergrowth. The sound spread across the silence until it vanished as mysteriously as ripples from the surface of a pool. Here in the forest's ancient, evil heart no birds dared to sing.

He was forced to agree with Gotrek. He had never really liked woods, not even as a child. He had never shared his brother's passion for hunting. He had always preferred to be left at home with his books. Forests for him were scary places, the haunt of beastmen and trolls and nightmare creatures from darkest legend. They were the places to where those who showed the stigmata of Chaos were banished too. In their depths he had always pictured werewolves and witches, and ferocious struggles between mutants and other exiled followers of the Ruinous Powers.

Up ahead Gotrek vaulted the log which had fallen across the path then turned and helped Kat to climb over it, easily lifting the child one-handed. Felix stopped in front of the obstruction, seeing that the bole was rotten and blotched with some strange fungus. Segmented insects scuttled along it, blindly burrowing into the reeking mould. Felix shuddered as he felt the damp wood under his hand, bracing himself for his jump. His boots almost slipped on the wet moss of the other side. He was forced to spread his arms to keep his balance. As he did so his fingers touched a cobweb stretched from the lower branches. He swiftly pulled his hand away and tried to brush off the sticky substance.

No, Felix had never liked forests. He had hated the summer retreats to his father's manor in the wood. He had detested the pine-walled house surrounded by the timberlands which provided the raw materials for Gustav Jaeger's drayage and shipping interests. By day it hadn't been too bad if he didn't stray far from the buildings, but by night his overactive mind peopled even the open, managed woodlands with a host of monstrous inhabitants. The goblins and daemons of his imagination found a ready home beneath the swaying trees.

He had at once envied and pitied the fur-clad woodsmen who kept his father's estate. He had envied them their bravery, seeing them almost as heroes facing the terrors of the untamed land. He had pitied them for having to live constantly on their guard. It had always seemed to him that anyone who lived in a settlement in the woods lived in the most precarious environments imaginable.

He could remember standing at his window and looking out into the green, and picturing it stretching away to the very end of the world, to those wastes where the foul minions of Chaos roamed. The strange noises and the clouds of fluttering moths attracted to the building's lights did nothing to diminish his unease. He was a child of the city, of Altdorf's urban sprawl. Getting lost in the woods was a nightmare, one that had recurred often in those long summer nights.

Of course it had been a joke: the Jaeger estate was ten leagues from Altdorf in the most cleared area of the Empire. The wood was thinned by ceaseless logging. It was tamed, cultivated land that bore no resemblance to the dense, tangled Drakwald in which he found himself now.

Gotrek paused suddenly and sniffed the air. He turned and looked back at Felix. Felix cocked his head to one side enquiringly. Gotrek made the sign for silence, frowning as if he were concentrating on hearing some distant sound. Felix knew that the dwarf's hearing and sense of smell were better than his. He waited expectantly. Gotrek shook his head and then turned to move on. Was the malign presence of the forest getting on even the Slayer's iron nerves?

What he had seen this morning was justification for anyone's fears. These woods did indeed shelter forces inimical to humankind; Kat's story confirmed it. He looked down at his hands and saw that they were trembling. Felix Jaeger thought himself a hard man but what he had seen in the ruined village would make even the hardest shudder.

Something had rampaged through Kleinsdorf like an irate giant through an anthill. The little village had been levelled with appalling malevolence and thoroughness. The attackers had not left a single building untouched, and no inhabitant save Kat had survived. The sheer senseless brutality of it astonished him.

He had seen things there that he knew he would see again in nightmares. A bonfire in the village square piled high with skulls. Fused ribs sticking out of the smouldering ash like unconsumed wood. Some had come from the skeletons of children. A disgusting scorched meat smell had filled his nostrils and he had tried to keep from licking his dry lips for fear of what the windblown ash might contain.

He had stood stunned in the silence and desolation of the ruined village. Everything about him was ash-grey or soot-black, save for the few fires which still flickered here and there. He had flinched in alarm as the roof collapsed on the devastated town hall. It had seemed like a dark omen. He had felt like a tiny atom of life in an endless empty desert. Slowly, a bit at a time, memory of that moment had etched itself into his brain.

High on the hill, the scorched walled castle stood, a stone spider clutching the hilltop with blasted stone feet. Before the gaping maw of its broken gate, hanged men dangled on gibbets, flies caught in its single-strand web. The village below was the playground of daemon children, idiot giants who had grown bored with their toy town and kicked it to flinders.

Little things filled the street. A broken pitchfork, its prongs crusted with dried blood. A temple bell lying half-melted in the rubble of the toppled church. A child's wooden rattle and a shattered cradle The printed pages of the Unfinished Book, the Sigmarite testament, floating on the breeze. Trails in the dirty street where bodies had been dragged, all leading to the central fire. A beautiful dyed dress, never worn, lying incongruously untouched in the street. A human femur, cracked for marrow.

He had seen violence before but never on such a scale and never so wantonly mindless. Even the carnage at Fort von Diehl had been a battle, fought by opposing sides for their own reasons. This had been a massacre. He had heard of such slaughters but to confront the hard, tangible evidence was altogether different. The reality, the implication that such things could and did happen, had always happened, scared him. How could Sigmar, how could any of the Gods, permit such things?

He was disturbed too that Kat had survived. Looking at the little girl walking in front of him, her shoulders slumped, her hair grimy and her clothing soot-stained, he wondered how she could have been allowed to live. That too made no sense – why had she, alone out of all the inhabitants of that sleepy community, been spared?

Was she a changeling, some slave of Darkness, luring them to their doom? Did he and the Slayer escort something evil towards its next set of victims. Normally he would have dismissed such a thought as utterly ridiculous; obviously she was just a frightened young child who had the good fortune to live where others had died. Yet here in the gloom of the deep forest such suspicion came easily. The stillness and silence of their surroundings worked on the nerves, and bred watchfulness and mistrust of strangers.

Only the Slayer seemed undisturbed by their predicament. He marched along boldly, avoiding the clutching tree roots that threatened to trip him, his easy pace eating up the miles. The dwarf moved with uncanny quietness for one so squat and heavy. In the shadows of the forest he seemed at home, somehow; he stood taller and looked more alert. His habitual slouch vanished, perhaps because his under-mountain dwelling people were adapted to darkness and the feeling of being enclosed. He never stopped, as Felix did, to survey the undergrowth whenever he heard rustling. He seemed quite confident in his ability to discern any threat.

The young man sighed, remembering the arguments he had had to use to prevent the dwarf from investigating the village further. The girl had at least proved a useful excuse for moving on and seeking a place of safety, where they might find her refuge. It had been that and the possibility that the creatures might be marching on the next village that had convinced the Slayer to take the road to Flensburg.

Felix paused, bidden by some buried instinct. He stood quite still and strained to hear anything out of the ordinary. Perhaps it was just his imagination, but it seemed to him that the very stillness of the woods had a quality of menace about it. It hinted at the presence of old evils, biding their time, waiting for victims. Anything could lurk in those long shadows and now he knew that something did.

It was getting colder. A slight deepening of the gloom hinted that night was falling above the shroud of leaves. Felix glanced back over his shoulder, dreading the silence but dreading the sound of pursuit more. When he looked round again, Kat and Gotrek had vanished, disappearing round a curve in the path. Somewhere in the distance a wolf howled. Felix hurried to catch up.

FELIX LOOKED ACROSS the campfire at the Slayer. Gotrek sat propped up against the fallen tree trunk, gazing into the depths of the fire, watching the flickering flames as if he could divine some mysterious truth in their depth. His hands toyed idly with the flints of his firemaker. Lit from below, the stark angles of his face looked as rough hewn as the face of a granite cliff. The flickering of their fire made shadows chase each other across the planes of his cheeks. His tattoos were shadowy blotches, like the signs of the last stage of some terminal disease. Light caught the pupil of his one good eye. It glittered inhumanly in its socket, a star reflected in the depths of a shadowy pool. Close to him Kat lay still, her breathing regular, apparently asleep. Gotrek sensed Felix watching him and looked up.

'What ails you, manling?'

Felix looked away from the fire. The bright after-image of the flame ruined his night vision. Still, he scanned the shadows under the trees, looking for signs of hidden watchers. The image of the villagers of Kleindorf going to sleep with the forces of Chaos creeping up on them unawares came unbidden to his mind. He cast around for something to say, decided upon the truth.

'Actually I'm… I'm a little worried, Gotrek. For some strange reason what we saw in that village back there frightened me. The gods alone know why.'

'Fear is for elves and children, manling.'

'You don't really believe that, do you?'

Gotrek smiled. His few remaining teeth looked even yellower in the firelight. 'Yes.'

'You don't seriously expect me to believe that dwarfs are never afraid, do you? Or is it Slayers who never know fear?'

'Believe what you like, manling. That's not what I said, though. Only a fool or a maniac is never afraid; only a child or a coward lets his fear master him. It is the mark of a warrior that he masters his fears.'

'Didn't the destruction of that village frighten you? Aren't you afraid now? Something's out there, Gotrek. Something evil.'

The Slayer laughed. 'No. I am a Slayer, manling. Born to die in battle. Fear has no place in my life.'

Felix shook his head, unsure of whether Gotrek was mocking him. He was used to the dwarf's erratic mood swings and starting to suspect that there were times when the Slayer possessed something close to a sense of humour. Gotrek put his flints back into his pouch and grasped the handle of his axe.

'Rest easy, manling. There's nothing you can do for the dead, and if whatever killed them is fated to find us there's nothing you can do about that either.'

'Is that supposed to reassure me?'

Suddenly the atmosphere of camaraderie evaporated as swiftly as it had formed. Anger blazed in the dwarf's voice. 'No, manling, it is not. But believe this: if I find the killers, there will be a reckoning in blood. Such evil as we witnessed this day will not go unpunished.'

There was no trace of human feeling in Gotrek's voice now. Looking into the dwarf's alien eye, Felix saw the madness there, the inhuman molten violence waiting to erupt. Just for a second he believed the dwarf, shared his mad conviction that he could stand against the dark power that destroyed the village. Then he recalled the sheer scale of the havoc that had been wrought and the moment passed. No warrior, not even one as mighty as Gotrek, could withstand that. He shuddered and drew his cloak tighter about him.

To cover his anxiety, he leaned forward and tossed more wood on the fire. Little stalks shrivelled and caught ablaze. Sparks drifted lazily upward. Acrid smoke stung his eyes as the lichen-covered branches smouldered. He wiped away the smoke tears and spoke to fill the silence. 'What do you know of the man-beasts? Do you believe the girl's story about them attacking the village?'

'Why not? The beasts have inhabited these woods since my people drove the elves out nigh on three thousand years ago. Many times in history huge hordes of them have marched forth to attack the cities of dwarf and man.'

Felix felt some wonder at the way the dwarf so casually alluded to events three thousand years ago. The war he referred to preceded the founding of the Empire and recorded human history by many centuries. Why had not human scholars paid more attention to the dwarfs when they compiled their records? The part of Felix which had been a student regarded the dwarf as a first-rate repository of obscure lore. He listened carefully, trying to memorise all that Gotrek said.

'I thought the beasts were simply mutants, human exiles devolved into man-beasts, altered by the power of warpstone. Certain of our learned professors claim as much.'

Gotrek shook his head as if despairing at the folly of mankind. 'Such mutants follow the hordes as lackeys or camp followers but the beastmen proper are a separate race, with origins back in the Age of Woe. They date from the time of the first incursions of Chaos into this world, from when the Dark Powers first ventured through the Polar Gates to trouble this sad planet. They may well be the first-born children of Chaos.'

'I have heard tales of them aiding human champions of Chaos. It is said they made up the bulk of the troops that assaulted Praag two centuries ago. Part of the great host driven off by Magnus the Pious.' Felix remembered to make the sign of the Hammer when he mentioned the Sainted One's name.

'That is not surprising, manling. Beastmen worship strength almost as much as they worship Chaos. The champions of the Ruinous Powers are among the greatest warriors to walk this world, Grimnir damn them! I hope the girl-child's tale is true and that I may soon face this black armoured she-devil. It would be a worthy trial of arms and if ordained, a worthy death.'

'That it would be.' Felix fervently hoped it would not come to that. Any circumstance he could imagine which involved Gotrek dying at the hands of the Chaos Warrior would surely involve his own demise fairly soon thereafter.

'And what of the girl?' he whispered. 'Do you think she is what she claims? Could she not be in league with the attackers?'

'She is only a child, manling. She has not the stink of the Dark about her. If she had, I would already have killed her.'

To his horror Felix noticed that Kat's eyes were wide open, and she studied the two of them fearfully. Their gazes met. Felix was ashamed to see such fear in the eyes of one who had already suffered so much. He got up and walked around the fire. He placed his worn cloak over her and wrapped it round her.

'Go to sleep,' he said. 'You're safe.'

He wished he could believe it himself. He saw that Gotrek's eye was closed but his axe was gripped firmly in one hand. Felix lay down on the leaves he had piled for bedding and for a long moment gazed upwards at the stars glittering coldly through the branches. He slept fitfully and old nightmares stalked him.

'YOU HAVE FAILED, beloved,' the Daemon Prince Kazakital said calmly. He looked at her through his stolen eyes and Justine felt a shock pass through her to the core of her being.

She flinched, knowing well the punishments her patron could inflict when displeased. Instinctively her fingers closed on the ruby pommel of her black war-blade. She shook her head. Her great mane of white-striped black hair swayed. She felt powerless. Even though she had a small army of beastmen within earshot, she knew they could not help her. In her master's presence no one could help her, no one. She was glad that the old beastman shaman, Grind, and his acolytes had withdrawn beyond the black altar after the summoning. She wanted no one to witness her discomfiture.

'Everyone in the village is dead. As we both desired,' she lied, knowing even as she did so that it was futile. Her ornate armour already felt clamped around her like a vice. Faint hints of pain tickled her nerve endings. If the daemon so desired she knew that she would soon swim in an ocean of agony.

'The child lives.' The daemon's beautiful voice remained flat, uninvolved, emotionless.

Justine tried to keep from looking at it, knowing the effect that the sight of it would have upon her. She knew that it would already have started to change the body of the sacrificial victim into something that more resembled its true form.

She gazed around. Overhead the two moons glared down in evil conjunction. Morrslieb, the Chaos moon waxed full. Mannslieb was at its smallest. For tonight and the next two nights, the power of Chaos would be strong in the land, strong enough to summon her daemonic patron from his hellish home in the realms beyond reality. Strong enough to let it possess the body of the man which they had offered up on its altar here in the deep woods.

Through the thick red cloud surrounding the altar she could see the campfires of her followers, the flames smudged by the sweet red mists that stained the night. They were tiny stars compared to the bright sun of the daemon's aura. She heard it shift its weight, recognised the leathery creak of the wings emerging from the corpse's back. She focused her attention on the impaled heads that flanked the altar. The pale faces of Count Klein and his son, Hugo, looked back at her. They brought back the memory of last night.

The old count had been a fighter. He had come to meet her in the courtyard wielding a spiked mace, half-garbed in hastily thrown-on mail. He had cursed her for a hell-damned whelp of darkness. She had seen the fear written on his face, as he saw the bestial horde of gors and ungors at her back, pouring through the shattered gate of his castle. She had felt almost sorry for the moustached old fool. She had always liked him. He had been worthy of a warrior's death and she had granted him it quickly.

The youth stood behind his father, pale faced with terror. He had turned and fled through the blood-soaked courtyard where her followers were slaughtering the half-awake men-at-arms. She had followed him easily, relentlessly, the black armour fused to her flesh granting her extra endurance as well as strength.

The chase through the darkened castle had ended in Hugo's bedchamber, where she had always known it must. That, after all, was the place where it had all begun. He had bolted himself inside and howled for the gods to save him. She had splintered the door with one kick of her armoured foot and strode in like an avenging daemon.

The place looked much the same as she remembered it. The same huge bed dominated it. The same fine Bretonnian rugs covered the floor. The same stags' heads and hunting trophies filled the walls, along with the same pennants and weapons.

Only Hugo had changed. The intense thin-faced youth had grown into a blubbery man. Sweat ran down his jowled cheeks. His face looked babyish even as the eyes squinted in terror. Yes, he had changed. Another might not have recognised him after so much time but Justine did. She would never forget his eyes, those glassy eyes which had followed her from the very first day she had arrived in the castle, over seven years before.

A long sword was grasped awkwardly in his pudgy paw. He raised it feebly and she effortlessly batted it aside, sending the blade spinning across into the corner. She put the point of her sword to his chest and pushed slightly. He had been forced to back away until he had tripped over the foot of the bed and lay sprawled on the sheets. The smell of excrement pervaded the air.

The bloated pink maggot wet his lips.

'You are going to die,' she said.

'Why?' he managed to gasp. She removed her helmet then. He moaned aloud as he recognised – at last – her face, her long distinctive hair.

'Because I told you that you would, seven years ago. Do you remember? You laughed then. Why are you not laughing now?' She pushed on her blade a little harder. Blood blossomed on the white silk of his shirt. He stretched out his hand in entreaty.

For the first time in years, tears of passion stung her eyes. She felt again the hot surge of rage and hatred. It raced through her veins and transformed her face into a mask. She pushed the sword down, revelling in the shock of impact and the clean slice of hell-metal through flesh. She leaned forward pinning him to the bed where he had forced himself upon her seven years before. Once again blood stained the sheets.

She had surprised herself. After long years of planning so many, slow, deliberate, delicious tortures she had dispatched him with a single stroke. Revenge had seemed less important somehow. She had turned and left the chamber and went to oversee the sacking of the town. She had ignored the pleas of the two men that the beasts were raising on the gallows in one of their incomprehensible macabre jokes. It had been down there, in the village, that she had encountered the child.

She strove to forget the child.

'You should not have spared the girl, beloved.' The daemon allowed a hint of its anger to glitter in its voice. The promise of eternities of pain emphasised its every word.

'I did not spare the child. I left it for the beasts. I am not responsible for the slaying of every dreary village urchin.'

The lash of the daemon's words stung her. 'Do not lie, beloved. You spared it because you were too soft. For a moment you allowed mere human weakness to stay your hand, to push you from your chosen path. That I cannot allow. Nor can you, for if you change course now you have lost everything. Believe me, if you let the girl live, you will have cause to regret it.'

She looked up at it then and, as always, was struck by the thing's polished chitinous beauty. She saw its black armoured form, the brutally beautiful face glaring out from beneath the rune-encrusted helmet. She met its redly glowing eyes and saw its strength. It knew no weakness, no mercy. It was without flaw. One day she could be like it. It plucked the thought from her mind and smiled in apparent pleasure.

'You understand, beloved. You know the nature of our pact. The path of the Chaos Warrior is but a trial. Follow the path to the end and you will find power and immortality. Deviate from it and you will find only eternal damnation. Great Khorne rewards the strong but he abhors the weak. The battles we fight, the wars we wage are but tests, crucibles to burn out our weakness and refine our strengths. You must be strong, beloved.'

She nodded now, hypnotised by the beauty of its molten voice, seduced by the promise of knowing neither pain nor weakness, of being flawless, perfect, of allowing no chink in her armour for the horror of the world to seep through. The daemon reached out with one clawed hand and she touched it.

'An age of blood and darkness is coming, an era of terror and rage. Soon the armies of the four Great Powers will march forth from the polar wastes and the fate of this world will be decided with steel and dark sorcery. The winning side will own this world, beloved. To the victors will belong eternal dominion. This planet will be cleansed of filthy humanity. We shall remould everything in our own image. You can be on the victorious side, beloved, one of its privileged champions. All you must do is be strong and lend our lord your strength. Do you wish that?'

That moment gazing into the creatures burning eyes, hearing the silken persuasiveness of its voice she felt no doubt.

'Do you wish to join us beloved?'

'Oh yes,' she breathed. 'Yes.'

'Then the child must die.'

JUSTINE MARCHED THROUGH the crowds of her followers to take her place on the carved wooden throne. She placed her bare blade across her knees, confronting the mightiest of her followers, the gors. The sword was a reminder to them all of how she ruled here, a naked symbol of her power. She had the favour of their daemon god and the expression of that favour was her might. The beastmen might not like it but they would have to tolerate it until one of them could, according to their primitive code, best her in single combat. And none would challenge her if they had any sense: they all knew of Kazakital's prophecy, made when she had been elevated to the ranks of the Chaos Warriors. They all knew what the daemon had said – that no warrior would ever overcome her in battle. They had all witnessed its truth. Yet they were beastmen, and challenging their leader was an instinct.

This night she almost hoped that one of them would try; the bloodlust was strong in her tonight as it always was after she confronted her patron. She glanced at what the beastmen rested upon: a huge tapestry she remembered once covering an entire wall. It depicted scenes of battle and hunting from Klein's family's past. Now it was covered in mud and leaves from the floor of the forest glade and the filth of the beastmen's own excrement. She would order it burned. She wanted nothing left to remind anyone of the Klein family.

Seeing the huge animal-headed forms of her followers lolling on Lord Klein's favourite possession was a reminder to her of how her world had changed since that fatal morning when she fled Hugo's chamber into the depth of the woods.

The scene that confronted her now was like something from the nightmare engravings of the mad artist, Teugen. Great horned animals clad in armour walked among the twisted trees of the darkened forest. They looked like an evil parody of the chivalric ideal, an upset in the natural order of things, as if the brutes of the forest had risen to oust upstart man. As one day they would. The servants of Chaos would send all the kingdoms of men toppling into the dust. She had made a small start here. It would grow. As word of her victories spread, more and more servants of Chaos would flock to her banner. Soon she would have a great army and all the mighty of the Empire would tremble. Somehow that prospect did not excite her as once it would have. Disgruntled, she pushed the thought aside.

She gazed on the captains of her future army and wondered what orders she should give them. She ran her measuring gaze over them, wondering when and from where the challenge to her leadership would come from. It could be from any of them. They were all gors, the largest and most powerful type of beast-man, and the most violently ambitious.

She saw posturing Hagal, his goat-horns burnished with gold, his brilliant blond fur gleam in the firelight. Of all the beasts who followed her she thought him most likely to challenge her, to instigate the Clashing of Horns. Her spies told her that it was he who grumbled most loudly round the campfires, complaining that it was unnatural to have a female lead them. He was the most surly, always questioning her orders but never to the point where she would have to initiate the challenge. At the moment, though, he was biding his time until perhaps she weakened. If it came to a fight now he knew that she would win.

Against Lurgar she would have been less certain of victory, had it not been for the prophecy; the great red-furred bull head was the most savage of her warriors in battle, a blood-drinking berserker whose appetite for carnage was exceeded only by his hunger for man-flesh. He was a deadly fighter when battle madness came on him. She almost feared a challenge from him, but thought it unlikely unless someone put him up to it. The man-bull was too stupid to have much ambition and was content to follow any leader who promised him foes to face and food to eat. Not a leader himself, he would be the perfect tool for someone to rule from behind.

Beside him sat one who obviously thought so: the old shaman, Grind. For a beastman, Grind was clever, possessed of low cunning and much of what passed for learning among the warped ones. He could cast bones and read omens, talk to spirits and intercede with the Ruinous Powers. In the time before Justine came to power it had been he who made the sacrifice to the Daemon Prince, Kazakital. But the fat, white-maned bull was too old now to father many sons in the Great Rut and so could not become leader of the warband. Justine knew it didn't stop him from resenting her pre-empting his position of spiritual authority in the tribe or simply hating her for being female. Justine could not afford to underestimate him, that much she knew. The shaman was full of spleen and malice, and his words swayed many of the rank and file beasts in her army.

Tryell the Eyeless was no real threat; a great warrior of heroic stature but marked by warpstone. He had no eyes yet he could see as well as anyone. As one who had been marked by Chaos he had a great fear of Justine, who he saw as specially favoured by it. He lived only to kill and add new eyes to his collection.

Then there was Malor Greymane, whose father she had killed to assume leadership of this horde. If the youngling felt any resentment he hid it well. He followed her instructions to the letter, fought well and exercised sound judgement. Often his plans were better than those of war-leaders twice his age. He was already a great warrior, although not yet come into the full strength of his prime. Let the others grumble that he was a member of the council only because of his friendship for her. She knew that some had even been whispering the abominable lie that, secretly, he was her mate. She knew that he had earned his place on merit and his position was justified by his prowess.

Of all those she commanded, she felt she could place a measure of trust only in the black-armoured Chaos Warriors that she had recruited in the Wastes, long before she had returned here. They were sworn to her service. In a way she wished they were here now, to provide her with a measure of support, but they were not. This evening they were off in the depths of the woods, performing their own rites, propitiating the daemonic engine which they crewed with blood and souls, making it ready for the hard battles to come.

The beastmen looked up at her expectantly, a half-circle of animal faces whose eyes held both human intelligence and inhuman lusts. She was suddenly glad that her blade was easily accessible. She felt isolated and out of place here. As always, before she began the council she felt a sense of anticipation. Would it happen now? Would the challenge come?

Justine wondered what orders she should give them. She had never thought past this point. The doubts that she had felt earlier returned, redoubled. She had lived for her vengeance. Now that it was achieved she felt empty. When she spoke to Kazakital it was easy to be firm of purpose, to feel allegiance to his cause. The Daemon Prince had an almost hypnotic effect

on her. But when he wasn't there, doubt set in. She wondered
whether she wanted what he wanted. Her major purpose had
been achieved with the death of Hugo.

It was simply the fulfilment of a long-held desire that left her
feeling so, she told herself. For seven years she had been driven
by her desire for vengeance. Now it had left her, snuffed out
with the life of her tormentor. It was bound to leave a gap after
so many years. She forced herself to concentrate, to feel the
desire for power and immortality that came so easily in the
presence of her daemonic patron. She managed to summon up
a faint shadow of it. It was enough.

'We have destroyed our first victims,' she said to them, voice
strong. 'But there is one survivor. It is ordained that she must
die. Our master demands it.'

'Should find other man-places. Kill more,' Hagal said, glancing round with his golden eyes. 'Why worrying about one
survivor?'

Grind tapped his wand of carved human thighbone on the
flagstones. 'Let them live. Spread word to others. With word
comes fear. Fear is our friend.'

Always this constant testing, she thought. Always this constant circling and searching for a weakness. Even simple
matters became minor skirmishes as the beasts sought to
enhance their status at the cost of others. Their society was
based on a hierarchy of strength; showing weakness, any weakness, diminished prestige.

'Because our lord demands it. Because red Kazakital, Chosen
of Khorne, says we must.'

Malor turned his grey gaze on Grind and Hagal. 'And because
our leader, Justine, demands it!'

'Who are you to question what our leader demands?' Tryell
asked directly of Hagal. So the rumours of bad blood between
them were true. Good. It strengthened her position.

'I do not question our leader. I question need to find single
human when could find dozens more. Are you so anxious to
find girl because you spared her last night?'

'Who told that?' Tryell said, too quickly. 'Do you seek challenge?'

Justine sensed that Tryell was trying to cover this up, not that
she cared. She, too, had spared the girl. Or was this what Hagal
was getting at? Was this a subtle criticism of her? It did not suit

her to allow the fight to continue. If Tryell killed Hagal, fine; but if it went the other way she would have one less true ally among the beasts' leaders and she doubted if she could find a replacement.

'There will be no challenge,' she said softly, but loud enough to be heard by all present. 'Unless it is with me!'

The gathering fell silent, waiting to see if anyone would call her to the clashing of horns. She saw Grind lick his lips in anticipation. She locked glances with Hagal. For a moment he was tempted, she could tell. For a moment he met her gaze full on and the killing lust came into his eyes. His hand reached to rest on the pommel of his weapon. She smiled, hoping to goad him into making the call, but at the last he seemed to think the better of it and lowered his head.

'Good,' she said with finality. 'Tryell, take your warriors and find me the girl with hair like mine. Take trackers, search the area, find her and bring her to me. I will offer her to Kazakital myself. The rest of you assemble your forces. We will march onto the next human town and find merit by slaughtering more men.'

They nodded agreement and approval and rose to depart. Justine was left alone in the chill hall with her thoughts, wondering just what she would do when they brought the girl to her.

'WAKE UP, MANLING! Something's coming!'

Felix roused himself from sleep. Wisps of eerie dreams still shrouded his mind. He shook his head to clear it, and felt the ache in his neck and back from lying on the cold forest floor. Chill had eaten through the insulation of the leaves and leeched strength from his body. He rose slowly to his feet and rubbed the sleep from his sticky eyes. As quietly as he could, he unsheathed his sword and glanced around.

Gotrek stood nearby; a squat, massive statue frozen in the dim light of the fading fire. The red glow of the embers reflected from his axe blade. The dwarf carried a weapon of blood.

Felix looked at the sky. The moon's were almost down. Good. Dawn was not far off.

'What is it?' he asked. His words caught in his throat and came out as a rasping whisper. He did not need the dwarf's posture of alertness to tell him something was wrong. There was an air of quiet menace about the wood that even he could feel.

'Listen!'

Felix listened. He strained his ears to pick up any unusual sounds. At first all he heard was the thumping of his heart. He could hear nothing unusual, only the chirping of the night insects and the quiet rustle of leaves. Then somewhere far off, so quiet he might only have imagined it, he heard the low muttering of voices. He looked over at the Slayer. Gotrek nodded.

Felix glanced around to see what had become of Kat. She was awake as well, sitting hunched up by the fire. Her eyes looked huge and scared in the firelight. Felix prayed for the sun to rise quickly. He turned from the fire and peered out into the shadows, resolving not to look back and spoil his night sight again.

'Kat, put more wood on the fire,' he said quietly. There was an almost overwhelming temptation to turn and see if she was obeying. He fought it and was relieved when he heard movement behind him and the crackling of wood catching light. Shadows raced away from the fire and the island of light in which they stood expanded to encompass the near forest. The trees looked like monochrome titans in the dim illumination.

Felix stood absolutely still. In spite of the chill, sweat ran down his spine and made his clothing clammy. His palms were slippery and it felt like strength was draining from his limbs. He felt an urge to flee from whatever approached.

It was definitely coming closer, making no attempt at stealth. He could hear heavy footsteps in the distance and once a short yelping bark of what sounded like pain. There was a tautening of the muscles in his stomach and a fluttering, excited feeling in his belly. The incautious approach of their foes spoke of overwhelming self-confidence. Was he about to meet the destroyers of Kleindorf?

Strangely he began to feel the urge to move in the direction of the noise, to investigate, to not simply stand here by the fire like a sheep waiting to be slaughtered. To calm himself he made a few experimental swipes with his sword. It hissed as it cut the air. The runes on its blade grew brighter as if in anticipation of the coming conflict. The loosening of his muscles and the readiness of his enchanted dragon-hilted blade relaxed Felix a little. A smile grafted itself to his lips. If he died here he would not die alone.

The confidence vanished as a chorus of howls echoed through the woods, erupting triumphantly from half a dozen bestial throats. In the pre-dawn gloom they were echoes from his nightmares. Things were out there – things he did not wish to face. Their pursuers knew they were close and were prepared to close in for the kill. Felix wanted to drop his blade and run. Strength ran from him like wine from a spilled goblet. Behind him Kat whimpered and he heard the sound of stealthy movement, as if she crept for cover.

'Steady, manling. They do that to frighten their foes. Weaken them for the kill. Don't let your fear master you.'

Gotrek's calm rumbling voice was almost reassuring but Felix could not help but think that whatever happened would be an acceptable outcome for the Slayer. Either he would vanquish his foes or, more likely, he would find his heroic death. Felix wondered if perhaps now was the time to point out that if he himself did not survive there would be no one left to record it. His humour made him laugh a little. He heard the Slayer move closer.

Their pursuers were nearly on top of them. Felix could hear the sandy rasping of their tread upon the trail. They could not be more than a hundred paces away. He glanced around looking for cover. There was a patch of bushes under the largest of the trees. He wondered about the advisability of hiding among them and then leaping out from ambush. Or perhaps not leaping out at all and simply hoping that the Chaos spawn did not find him. He realised that for him it was a slender hope.

He pointed to the briar patch with the tip of his sword and whispered, 'Kat, hide yourself there. If anything happens to Gotrek and I, stay hidden!'

He was gratified to see the small figure rush over, throw herself flat on her belly and wriggle into the undergrowth. She might have some chance if the two of them fell.

How had they been found, he wondered? Was it simply ill luck – was this just a party of scouts which had stumbled upon them? Or was there some malevolent sorcery at work? Where Chaos was concerned you could never tell. For a moment he allowed himself the fantasy that it was all a mistake – that this was a party of merchants who would shelter them. But he knew that only the dead or their killers would take the night road from Kleindorf, and that thought made him shudder.

The sound of footsteps was so close now that he felt their pursuers must soon come into view. He wished that the dying moons would break free from cloud and grant him some more light. As if Sigmar had answered his prayer, there came a break in the cloud cover. He wished that it had not.

The eerie silver light of Mannslieb mingled with the blood-tinged glow from the witch-moon, Morrslieb. It washed down through the rents in the treetops and fell on the faces of their pursuers; aberrations from the wildest reaches of his night-mares.

To the fore was a leashed mutant. It crouched close to the ground, sniffing the trail. It was the maker of the snuffling sound Felix had heard. It had a hairless dog-like face and a huge nose. A spiked collar round its neck was joined to a heavy steel chain, the other end of which was held by a mighty, goat-headed beast. It was enormously muscular and it had a leather cloak over its shoulders. There was a necklace of what appeared to be dried eyes round its neck. It had no eyes of its own, only a blank expanse of flesh where the sockets should have been. Yet it walked as if it could see perfectly. Felix wondered what trick of Chaos sorcery permitted that. In one hand it held an enormous spike-headed club around whose tip were smeared congealed substances the nature of which Felix preferred not to think about.

Behind came its lackeys: smaller versions cut from the same monstrous template; hunched muscular giants carrying spears and rusty swords. Bestial eyes glared from goat-heads and stag-heads, turned red by the firelight. Aside from their leader none bore any obvious stigmata of further mutation. The sight of them made Felix's flesh crawl. The thought of what they had done in the village the night before filled him with both fear and rage.

The eyeless leader halted and gestured to his followers with one immense knuckled hand. They filtered into the clearing and formed a large half circle facing the man and dwarf. Felix moved into his fighting stance, willing his muscles to relax as his fencing masters had taught him. He tried to clear his mind, to be calm but facing these massive monsters it was impossible.

For long moments man and beast glared at each other across the shadowy clearing. Felix willed himself to meet the gaze of the nearest goat-head. I am going to kill you, he thought, hoping that he could intimidate the creature. Its animal mouth opened and its tongue lolled out. Faint flecks of foams appeared on its lips. It looked as if it were mocking him. Well, perhaps I won't then, thought Felix and smiled.

He wanted to look at Gotrek, to see what the Slayer was going to do but dared not take his eyes off his opponents. He feared that they might attack with supernatural speed if he looked away. This was the worst of facing foes of unknown quality; who knew what they might be capable of?

The beasts held their position, as if uncertain what to do in the face of two undaunted opponents. They looked at each other as if amused or uncertain. Perhaps they were deciding who would have the first choice of their prey's flesh, Felix decided. It struck him as odd that things with such dire reputations as eaters of man-flesh should have the heads of herbivorous animals. Perhaps it was a joke of the Ruinous Powers.

'Ready, manling?' Gotrek sounded remarkably lucid for a berserk on the verge of battle, Felix thought. His deep voice was calm, even and held no hint of any emotion.

'As I'll ever be.' Felix tightened his grip on the hilt of his blade until it was almost painful. The muscles of his forearm went as rigid as steel bands. When he heard the Slayer's wild laughter he, too, charged forward to face the foe.

KAT WRIGGLED UNDER the bushes. She did not want to, but fascinated horror forced her to look out again. She knew the beasts were closing in. She could feel it. There was the same sense of presence in the air that there had been the previous night. She looked out at her two benefactors and felt sorry for them. They were going to die. They may have been frightening, but they had tried to help her and they did not deserve the death the beasts would give them.

She looked at Felix. His handsome features wavered between an expression of hopeless fear and one of wild exultation. She understood how that could happen. She had often felt the same way when Karl had driven too fast along the rutted road in his cart. A sort of tingly feeling, of being excited and scared and happy all at once. Felix didn't look very happy, though, which was the difference.

The dwarf did. His brutal features were twisted into a grim smile that revealed his missing teeth. Kat was sure that he noticed her looking at him, because he turned and winked in her direction. Either he was not afraid or he was a very good actor, she decided.

They both looked brave in their own way. And looking at their well-used weapons, she knew they must both be great warriors. The runes on Felix's sword glowed with an inner fire like some enchanted blade in a story. Gotrek's axe looked as if it could knock down a tree with one sweep. But in the end she knew it would not matter; they were doomed. The beasts would see to that.

Despite herself she gasped when they entered the clearing. The leader, the one who held the snuffling mutant on the end of his chain, was the same one who had spared her in the inn the previous evening. She knew he had come looking for her, just for her, to rectify his error. His followers were some of those she had seen rampaging through the village. They were all massive; taller than Felix, heavier than Gotrek. Seeing the two warriors standing by the fire she realised what an unequal contest it was. Man against monster; outnumbered and outmatched, they would have no chance.

For a second they stood frozen, facing each other. Caught up in the drama of the situation Kat forgot her own fears. She held her breath. Gotrek crouched like a great gargoyle, his axe held lightly in one hand. Felix stood in the classic pose of the fencer that she had once seen the noble Hugo use at practice. Massed against them were the misshapen beasts, slouching confidently, weapons at ease.

She heard Gotrek's rumbled 'Ready, manling?', and Felix's answering 'As I'll ever be.' She saw the Slayer run his thumb over the blade of his axe until a bead of blood glistened on its tip. She heard his mad laughter and saw him charge. Felix followed in his footsteps. Unable to watch them get cut down, she closed her eyes.

She heard a great crunch and a howl of pain. That was the dwarf, she knew. He was the first to die. She heard the ring of steel on steel and the hoarse grunts of exertion followed by more cries of pain. Felix had gone too. But still the sound of fighting went on, longer than she would have thought possible. But eventually the sound of battle faded, as she had

known it would. Burned hollow with terror, she opened her
eyes to face her fate.

FELIX CHARGED. Ahead of him he saw the Slayer leap to one side
as a spear lashed out at him. Gotrek caught the shaft with his
left hand and moved forward, sliding his grip along the spear's
length, holding it immobile as he closed. Once within striking
distance he lashed out with his axe, splitting the astonished
beastman's skull like a melon. There was a crunch and a stran-
gled howl of pain. Good, thought Felix; one less to worry
about.

He engaged blade to blade with a scimitar wielding monstrosity. His sword rang against it, notching the rusted steel of
his opponent's weapon. The thing was strong but unskilled.
With a life of its own, Felix's enchanted blade found its way
through the creature's guard. Within a matter of seconds he
had it bleeding from several small cuts. It let out an angry bellow and hewed at him with a stroke that could have cut Felix
in half. He leapt back, parrying wildly. Sparks flew as the blades
made contact. His arm felt numb from the impact.

He looked up into the beastman's face. Foam flecked its lips
and madness danced in its eyes. It lashed out again, its blade a
blurring arc. Reflexively Felix ducked beneath it and stepped
forward, his blade skewering up. The beast's warm entrails
poured out over his hands. It reeled back trying to hold in its
intestines with one hand, whimpering like a stuck pig. The
other beastman had recovered from the surprise of being
attacked and leapt into the fray.

It charged forward, head down, spear aimed at a point six
inches behind Felix's back. The beastman slipped on his companion's guts and fell at Felix's feet. The young warrior offered
up a prayer of gratitude to Sigmar and beheaded it with one
easy stroke. He turned, sword sweeping, and put the other one
out of its misery.

Gotrek had disposed of his two lesser foes and was engaged
in a duel with the beastman leader. The mutant-tracker was
nowhere to be seen. It had fled. Looking at the scene of carnage
Felix reconstructed what must have happened. The Slayer's sudden charge, two great rending strokes, the first of which had
split a skull, the second of which had staved in rib cages. The
eyeless beast was made of sterner stuff.

Axe and club flickered back and forth with sight-blurring speed. Sparks flew as starmetal bit into the steel studs covering the bludgeon's head. The beast was larger but slower. The impact of the Slayer's axe drove him back with every stroke. Felix wondered whether he should help Gotrek but decided against it. Gotrek wouldn't thank him and the possibility of being accidentally caught by a stroke of his axe was too frightening to contemplate.

The beast made a massive desperate swing at the Slayer's head. Gotrek skipped back out of reach and caught the head of the club in the curve of his axe blade. With a swift twist he jerked the weapon from the beastman's hand, disarming it.

The dwarf's face held an expression of cold fury such as Felix had never seen before. There was no mercy written there, only anger and grim determination. Gotrek struck it on the leg, knocking it over. Blood flowed from the tendon-cutting wound. The creature gave a shrill screech of pain and rolled over. As it did so, the ancient axe descended like that of an executioner. The eyeless beastman's head parted from his shoulders and the thing tumbled lifeless to the ground.

The Slayer spat on the corpse then shook his head as if in disgust. 'Too easy,' he said. 'I hope that Chaos Warrior is tougher.'

Privately Felix hoped they would never find out.

FELIX MARCHED ALONG with a spring in his step. He was not tired, despite his lack of sleep the previous evening and the rough terrain through which they passed didn't daunt him. He breathed in deeply, enjoying even the still air and the musty forest scents. At least he was still capable of breathing.

He was still alive! The sun filtered down through the leaves, catching spinning motes of dust, making them dance like fairy lights. He wanted to reach out and collect a handful of them, as if it were some kind of magic powder. For a moment the forest was transformed; they moved through an enchanted grove where foot-high mushrooms sprouted in the shadow of the great trees. Just then they did not look sinister; they were a promise of the continuity of life.

He was still alive. He repeated it to himself like a mantra. He had passed through terror and come out the other side. His foes, the monsters who had wanted to kill him, were dead. And he was still here, to feel the sunlight and drink in the air and watch Gotrek and Kat pick their way downhill, feeling their way from stone to stone set in the mud of the steep and slippery trail.

His senses were keener and he felt more alive, more full of energy, than he had ever been. It was simply a joy to be there.

Webs glistened with early morning dew. Birds sang. All around the forest was pregnant with the stirrings of life. Small animals moved through the undergrowth. Felix paused to let a snake cross the path and made no attempt to kill it. This morning he had a feeling of how precious life was, how fragile.

The fight with the beasts had brought home to him how tentative his grip on living was, how easily the cord of his life could be severed. It could have been him lying cold in an unmarked grave, or more likely filling the stomach of the beastman. The difference had been some luck, a bit of skill and the correct use of his blade. It could all have gone so much differently. One mistake and he might not have been here to enjoy this glorious morning. He could be wandering in Morr's misty grey kingdom or pitched into the oblivion which some scholars claimed was the only thing after death.

He knew the thought should frighten him – but it did not. Here and now he was too happy. In his mind he replayed every stroke of the fight, remembered every move with something close to love. He felt exalted; he had matched himself against mighty foes and come away the master. The forest could not frighten him today.

He knew that the feeling was artificial; he had felt something like it before on many occasions after he had fought. He knew that it would fade and be replaced by a horror at and guilt about what he had done but for the moment he could stop himself. He was forced to admit that, in a strange way, he had enjoyed the battle. The violence had appealed to something dark in him, something that he usually kept hidden even from himself. For a moment he felt he could almost understand those who followed the Blood God, Khorne, who were addicted to bloodshed, combat and excitement. There could be no greater thrill than gambling with your life. There was no stake higher, except perhaps your soul.

That thought stopped him. He could see that his thoughts had been leading him down the path of sin. Perhaps all those who sold themselves to the Ruinous Powers started this way, taking pleasure in their own dark side. He had seen where that road led, and so he let his mind veer.

Ahead Gotrek stooped to inspect some tracks in the mud. Perhaps, Felix speculated, he was too addicted to battle. Perhaps this was why he followed his peculiar vocation – perhaps it was as much for his own gratification as for the atonement of the sins he had committed. Why else would anyone follow such a strange path, that led down such dark roads. Perhaps the Slayer's motives were less noble and tragic than he pretended.

Felix sighed; he would never know. The dwarf was alien to him, the product of a different society with a different code of ethics, perhaps even a different picture of the world looked at through different senses. He doubted that he would ever understand Gotrek. Every time he felt close to it, the understanding eluded him. The dwarf was different – strong in ways that Felix could never hope to be, brave beyond sanity, seemingly oblivious to pain and weariness.

Was that why Felix followed him? Out of admiration and a wish to be like him? To have his certainty and his strength? Certainly his life would have been much different now if he had not sworn his oath to follow the dwarf that drunken night in Altdorf. Perhaps he would have been happier. On the other hand, he would not have seen half of what he had seen, for good or for ill. There were times when the Slayer seemed like his own personal daemon sent to upset his life and lead him to the darkness.

He made his way carefully down the slope, watching where he placed his feet, feeling the hard rocks under the thin leather soles of his boots. When he reached the bottom of the hill he saw what Gotrek and Kat were looking at. The path had divided at a fork. There was a league marker by the right hand way – not the usual stone slab left to mark the Empire's highways but a simple block cut from the trunk of a tree. Felix read it.

'We'll be in Flensburg in a couple of hours then,' he said.

'If it's still standing, manling,' Gotrek said and spat.

'I WISH I WAS brave like you, Felix,' Kat said.

Felix surveyed the open glade. The woods were thinner here and there was evidence of logging. Stumps littered the forest floor. Tangles of vegetation grew round them. Here and there saplings sprouted. The air had a hint of the fresh smell of new-cut wood about it. In the distance he thought he could hear the roar of a river. Overhead, through the break in the branches, the sky was bright and clear and blue. Far to the east, though, they could all see great storm clouds gathering. Thunderclouds piled one on the other, huge, insubstantial moving mountains drifting ever closer. Another evil omen.

He glanced down at the girl. Her soot-covered face was serious. 'What did you say?'

'I said, "I wish I was brave like you".'

He laughed at that. Something about her openness and transparent desire to be liked touched him. 'I'm not brave.'

'Yes you are. Fighting those beasts was brave – like something a hero in a tale would do.'

He tried to picture himself as a hero from one of the sagas he had been fond of as a youth, a Sigmar or an Oswald. Somehow he couldn't quite manage it. He knew himself too well. Those men had been god-like, flawless. In fact Sigmar had become a god, the patron deity of the Empire he had founded. People like that never knew fear or doubt or venality.

'I was scared. I was only trying to stay alive. I'm not brave – Gotrek is.'

She shook her head emphatically. 'Yes, he is – but so are you. You were scared and fought anyway. I think that's why you're brave.'

She was completely serious. Felix was amused and not a little flattered. 'No one's ever accused me of that before.'

She turned and pouted, thinking he was making fun of her. 'Well I think you are, anyway. It doesn't matter what no one says.'

He stood a little taller and pulled his ragged cloak tight. Strange – he had become used to seeing Gotrek as the hero of an epic tale, the one he was supposed to write on the Slayer's death. He had never imagined himself as a part of that tale before. He had always pictured himself more as an invisible observer, a chronicler of the dwarf's exploits, unmentioned in the text. Maybe the child had a point. Maybe he should devote some space to his own adventures as well.

The Saga of Gotrek and Felix. No – My Travels with Gotrek. By Herr Felix Jaeger. He could picture it as a leather-bound book, printed in immaculate Gothic script on one of his father's printing presses. It would be written in Reikspiel of course, a popular work. Classical was too stuffy, the language of scholars and lawyers and priests. Maybe it would be read all across the Known World. He might become as famous as Detlef Sierck or the great Tarradasch himself.

He would put in all their various adventures. The destruction of the coven on Geheimnisnacht; their skirmishes with wolf riders in the land of the Border Princes. All the events leading up to the destruction of Fort von Diehl. Their ventures into the dark beneath the world. Their battles with the Horned Man and their journey through the plague pits below Altdorf.

He tried to imagine how he would portray himself in the story – of course he would be brave, loyal, modest. Reality began to intrude on his daydream almost immediately. Brave? Maybe. He had faced some scary situations without dishonour. Loyal? If he stuck with the Slayer until the end he would certainly be that. Modest? Unlikely, since how modest was it to include oneself in the saga of someone else's adventures? Perhaps it wasn't such a good idea after all. He would just have to wait and see.

'If you're not a hero and Gotrek is, why do you travel with him?'

'Why do you ask such difficult questions, little one?' Felix asked, hoping the Slayer couldn't hear. Gotrek had wandered far ahead across the glade, wrapped up in his own dour thoughts.

It was a difficult question, Felix decided. Why did he follow the Slayer? The simple answer was because he was sworn to. He had taken an oath that drunken night after the Slayer had pulled him out from underneath the hooves of the Emperor's cavalry. He was honour-bound to keep his promise. He owed the dwarf a debt for saving his life.

In the beginning he had thought that was why he had stuck by Gotrek but now he had another theory. The dwarf had presented him with the perfect excuse to adventure, to see far places and dark things. Things that interested and excited him. He could have stayed at home and become a boring merchant like his older brother, Otto. He had never wanted that, had always rebelled against it. The Slayer's quest had provided him with a reason to leave Altdorf. One that he had used to rationalise his own wish to go anyway. Since then he had lived an extraordinary life, one not so very different from that of the hero of a saga. He no longer knew what he would do if he ceased to travel with Gotrek. He couldn't imagine going back to his old life.

'I'm damned if I know,' Felix said eventually.

THE ARROW HIT the tree trunk beside Gotrek and stayed there, quivering. The Slayer glared around, sniffing the air and peering into the long grass. Had the beasts caught up with them again? Why had they not just shot them?

Felix looked at the black feathers attached to the shaft. It couldn't be beastmen, he thought. It didn't look like their type of weapon. Kat hadn't mentioned seeing any of them armed with bows. His skin crawled with the threat of danger. He strained his senses to hear any sound. All he could hear was the wind in the branches, the singing of birds and the sound of the distant river.

'That was a warning shot,' said a voice, coarse and untutored. 'Don't come any closer.'

Downwind, Felix thought, the archer is downwind. Very professional. The same thought undoubtedly occurred to Gotrek as he glared at where the words had come from.

'I'll give you a warning shot all right. Come out and face my axe,' he said. 'Are you warriors or weaklings?'

'Doesn't sound like a beastman,' another voice said, off to the left. It sounded hearty. There was a hint of mirth so great that it could not be kept in check, no matter how serious the situation.

'Who can tell – these are strange times. Certainly doesn't look like a man.' This from a woman somewhere behind them. Felix turned to look but could see nothing. The area between his shoulder blades crawled. He expected an arrow to plant itself between them at any moment.

Gotrek's voice was full of wrath. 'Are you implying that I could of your weak race? I'll make you eat those words, human. I'm a bloody dwarf!'

'Perhaps you should restrain yourself until we can see our ambushers,' Felix whispered, then he shouted: 'Forgive my friend. He is a great enemy of the Ruinous Powers and takes insult easily. We are not beastmen or mutants as you can undoubtedly see. We are simple swords for hire, en route to Nuln and work. We mean no harm to you whoever you are.'

'He's fair spoken an' that's for sure,' the first voice said. 'Hold your fire, lads. Until I give the word.'

'Could be he's a sorcerer – they're said to be educated men,' the woman's voice said. 'Maybe the child's his familiar.'

'Nah, that's Kat from the Kleindorf Inn. She's served me often enough. I'd know that hair anywhere.' The jovial voice sounded thoughtful for a moment. 'Maybe they've kidnapped her. I hear there's a good market for virgin sacrifices in Nuln.'

Felix thought that things could easily turn very nasty here. These people sounded scared and suspicious, and it wouldn't take much to convince them to fill him full of arrows and question the child later. He wracked his brains looking for a way out. He hoped Gotrek could restrain his natural inclination to go diving headlong into trouble or they might both be finished.

'Is that you, Herr Messner?' Kat said suddenly.

Sigmar bless you child, thought Felix. Keep them talking. Every word spoken increases the human contact, makes it harder for them to think of us as faceless foes.

'Don't kill them. They protected me from the beasts. They're not warlocks or Chaos-lovers.' She looked up at Felix with bright eyes. 'It's Herr Messner, one of the old Duke's rangers. He used to sing me songs and tell me jokes when he came to the inn. He's a nice man.'

That nice man is probably only a few seconds from putting an arrow between my eyes, thought Felix. 'Kat's right. We did kill beasts. We may have to kill many more. They destroyed Kleindorf – they may be on the march right now. They're led by a warrior of Khorne.'

A large paunchy man emerged from the woods to Felix's right. He was garbed in leathers and a mottled cloak of green and brown. Felix was surprised. He must have looked at the man several times and never known he was there. He had a bow in one big hand but he did not point it at either Gotrek or Felix. His movements were uncannily quiet for such a big man.

He stopped ten paces from the side of the trail and stared at them as if measuring them. His face was battered and his grey hair thinning. His nose looked broken and flattened. He had cauliflower ears like an ageing prize-fighter. His eyes were as grey and cold as steel.

'Nah – you don't look like hellspawn an' that's for sure. But if you're not you've certainly picked a fine time to go wandering in the woods – what with every warped soul from here to Kislev on the move.'

'Then why are you here?' Gotrek asked. His face was dark, his anger barely held in check.

'Not that I have to answer your questions, mind, but it's my job. Me an' the lads keep an eye on things in these woods for the old Duke. An' I can tell you just now I don't like what I've been seein'.'

He rubbed his nose with his knuckles and stood staring at them. Felix tried to gauge the man. He sounded like a peasant but there was a keenness to his eye and a humour to his lazy drawl that suggested a clever man cunningly concealed. He looked slow to anger but Felix guessed that, once aroused, he would be a formidable foe. In his quiet way he was frightening. The way he stood casually facing the Slayer suggested one who was sure of his authority. Felix had seen his sort before – trusted retainers who had their lord's confidence and who often dispensed instant justice on their holdings.

'We are not your enemies,' Felix said. 'We are just passing on the Emperor's road. We want no trouble.'

The man laughed as if Felix had said something amusing. 'Then you're in the wrong place, lad. Something's got the old beastmen stirred up like I ain't seen them in a score of years. They've left a trail of destruction from wood to mountain an' from what you're saying they've done for Kleindorf as well. Pity – I always liked the place. What of Klein an' his soldiers? Surely they must have done somethin'.'

'Died,' Gotrek said and laughed caustically. The forester looked at him. Anger was in his eyes.

'Nah – there was the castle. That's been there nigh on six hundred years. Beasts never attack fortifications. Don't have the strategy. It's what's kept us alive in these cursed lands.'

'It's true. What Gotrek says is true,' Kat said. She sounded like she was about to cry.

'I'd watch out for the next village if I were you,' Gotrek said, then added sardonically, 'for sure.'

Messner turned and shouted into the forest: 'Rolf – head west an' see what you can see. Freda – round up the rest of the lads an' meet us in Flensburg. I'll take our friends there. Looks like things are about to turn nasty.'

The others didn't respond. Felix didn't even hear a rustle of the bushes but he sensed that their watchers were gone. He shivered. He had been standing so close to death and never even seen its deliverers. He felt his dislike for the woods returning; he preferred a place where a man could see danger approaching.

Messner gestured for them to follow him. 'Come on. You can tell me what you know along the way. By the time we get to Flensburg I want to know exactly what happened.'

AN OLD MAN sat cross-legged on a rush mat near the door of a blockhouse, smoking a long curved pipe. He and a young boy were playing draughts with pebbles on a board scratched in the earth. He looked up from his game and eyed Felix with the finely honed suspicion of the woodsman for the stranger, before blowing out several lines of smoke rings into the air. Messner waved to him, a kind of curt salute, and the old man returned it with a convoluted gesture of his left hand. Was he warding off the evil eye, Felix wondered, or communicating in some sign language?

He studied the little town with interest, paying special attention to the burly men carrying large two-handed axes. Their faces were covered with multicoloured scar-tattoos. Their eyes were narrow and watchful. They stomped through the muddy streets in high fur-trimmed boots with all the arrogant assurance of a Middenheim Templar. Sometimes they paused to exchange gossip with the fat fur-hatted traders or to leer at a pretty nut-brown girl carrying pails from the river to the drinking water barrels.

A pot-bellied man shouted Messner over to inspect a pile of furs spread out on wicker mats in front of him. They were obviously the pick of some trapper's haul. Messner shook his head in a friendly manner and strolled on. He stopped only to let laughing barefoot children chase a pig in front of him.

They passed a smokehouse in front of which hung great hams and half carcasses of boar. The smoky smell of the meat made Felix's mouth water. Chickens hung by their necks from thongs attached to the eaves. Felix was reminded uncomfortably of the men hanging from the gibbet outside Kleindorf and he looked away again.

Messner wandered over to the house of a scribe and after a brief consultation took a brush and ink and inscribed something on a tiny piece of paper. Then they marched over to a coop outside one of the blockhouses in which were six fat grey pigeons. Messner rolled the paper up and put it in a steel ring. Then he reached into the coop and took out one of the birds. He ringed it, released it and watched with some satisfaction as it fluttered skyward.

'Well, duty done an' the old Duke warned,' he said. 'Maybe Flensburg will be safe yet.'

Felix thought it might be; it was certainly defensible enough and there must be nearly seven hundred people here. Flensburg lay near the bend of the river, and resembled a great logging camp more than a village or town. It was walled on two sides with a ditch and a wooden palisade. The curve of the river protected the other two sides. From jetties, rafts and great piles of lumber were poled out into the stream to drift to the-gods-knew-what market – probably Nuln eventually, Felix thought.

As they approached, they had seen dozens of the square wooden blockhouses within the thick wooden walls, each built like a miniature fort, with their stout log walls and their flat turf ceilings. The place spoke of the functional; he imagined some of the buildings were storehouses and trading posts. One had a crude hammer shape made from two logs stuck onto the roof – a temple to Sigmar.

Once through the heavy fortified gate, he had seen that the people of Flensburg were like their town: dour, spare, functional. Most of the men were garbed in fur; they were sullen, hard faced and hard eyed. They looked at the strangers warily. Their watchfulness seemed inbred. Most carried heavy woodsman's axes. Some, the ones garbed in functional rangers clothing, carried bows. The women wore gayer colours, thick multi-layered skirts, padded jerkins; their hair was wrapped in red spotted scarves. Matrons marched down the muddy streets carrying baskets of produce, trailed by processions of children like mother ducks leading a line of young.

The people here near the southern border of the woods were shorter than the citizens of the Empire's cities. Their hair was predominantly sandy-brown and their complexions darker and more tanned. Felix knew that they had a reputation as a gloomy, god-fearing folk, superstitious, poor and ill-educated. Looking at these people he could believe it, but he knew that his city-bred prejudices told only half the story.

He had not been prepared for their pride and fearlessness. He had expected something like the downtrodden serfs of a noble's estate. He had found people who looked him fearlessly in the eye and stood tall and straight in the frightening shadows of the great forest. He had thought Messner exceptional but he could see he was typical of his folk. Felix had expected serfs and found freemen, and for some reason that pleased him.

Gotrek looked at the walls and the blockhouses, and turned to Messner. 'Best call your people and tell them what to expect. It won't be good.'

FELIX STARED OUT from the watchtower across the cleared area surrounding the village towards the woods beyond. Now that he was out of their shadow, the trees seemed threatening again: giant, alien, alive, their gloom giving shelter to something inimical. He watched the last stragglers of the day filter in through the gates. Beside him, Messner kept watch with his cold grey eyes.

'Things look bad an' that's for sure,' he said.

'I would have thought you often had to deal with the beasts, living in these woods.'

'Right enough we fight them and the outcasts and other things every now and again. But it's always been skirmishes. They steal a child, we kill a few. They raid for pigs, we hunt them down. Sometimes we have to send to the old Duke for troops an' mount an expedition when the raids get too fierce. Ain't seen nothin' like this before though. Somethin's got them stirred up bad an' that's for sure.'

'Could it be this woman, this champion?'

'Seems more than likely. You hear about them in the old stories – the Dark Ones, the champions of Chaos – but you never expect to come across them.'

'There have been times when I've thought that those old stories contain much truth,' Felix said. 'I've seen a few strange things in my travels. I'm not so quick to doubt these days.'

'That's right true, Herr Jaeger. An' I'm glad to hear an educated man like yourself admit as such. I've seen a few strange things myself in these woods. An' there's many an old tale of me da's I don't doubt either. They say there's a Black Altar in those woods somewhere. A thing dedicated to the Dark Ones

where humans are sacrificed. They say beastmen and other...
things... worship there.'

They lapsed into uneasy silence. Felix felt gloom settle over
him. All this talk of the Dark Ones had unsettled him and left
him deeply uneasy. He glanced out once more into the clearing.

The women and children had stopped working in the fields
and were returning to the safety of the walls, their baskets full
of potatoes and turnips. Felix knew that they would take them
to the storehouses. The village was preparing itself for a siege.
The other women, who had been gathering nuts and herbs in
the wood, had returned hours ago when the great warning
horn was blown.

The foresters and woodsmen were within, checking the water
barrels were full, whittling stakes and attaching the metal heads
to spears. From behind him he could hear the continuous whiz
and thunk of arrows impacting on targets as the archery practice continued.

Felix wondered whether it made more sense for him to stay
or slip off into the woods. Maybe he could take a raft and drift
away downriver. He did not know which was worse – the
thought of being alone in the forest or of being trapped here
with the forces of Chaos closing in. He tried to dismiss these
thoughts as unworthy, to remember Gotrek's words about mas-
tering fear, but the terror of being trapped in the maze of trees
nagged constantly at the back of his mind.

As he looked out, a group of rangers hurried across the fields;
Felix could see that they were carrying someone wounded. One
kept glancing back over his shoulder as if expecting pursuit.
Two of the remaining women moved to help him.

'That's Mikal and Dani,' Messner said. 'Looks like there's been
trouble. Better go and find out what's happened. Stay here,
keep your eyes peeled; if anything happens blow the horn.'

He thrust the great instrument into Felix's hand and before
he could raise any objections Messner had swung himself
down through the trapdoor and was halfway down the ladder.
Felix shrugged and stroked the smooth metal of the horn with
his fingers. The cool weight was reassuring even if he was uncertain as to his ability to sound it. He glanced down at the top of
the hunter's head, noticing for the first time the bald spot on
the top of his skull. He gave his attention back to the fields.

The men reeled forward bearing their companion. The gates creaked open and villagers rushed forward to help them, Messner in the lead. Felix saw the way they all jumped to obey the duke's man's orders. That Messner was something of a leader in the community had become obvious at the great public meeting held in the village square that afternoon. Burly lumberjacks and old men, stout housewives and slim girls alike had listened to his soft jovial voice as he outlined the danger approaching.

No one had argued with him or doubted him. With Messner to vouch for them, there had been no questioning of Gotrek or Felix's story. They had even listened respectfully to Kat, though she was just a child. He could remember all that had been said and done even now, after they had stopped speaking. The silence, the grim fatalistic expressions on the folk's faces, the warm afternoon sun on the back of his neck. He remembered the way the women with babies had turned and taken them to the central blockhouse, the Temple of Sigmar. The crowd had parted wordlessly to let them pass.

Equally wordlessly, the men had divided into squads of archers and axe-men. It was obvious to Felix that he was watching a well-practised routine devised for just this eventuality. Messner had given orders in his usual calm voice. There was no shouting here nor any need for it. These people had the discipline of those for whom discipline represented the only means of survival in a harsh land.

In a way, he had envied them their sense of community; they relied on each other implicitly. As far as he could tell, no one doubted the ability or loyalty of anyone else. It must be the flip side of the coin of living in an isolated community, he realised. Everyone here had known each other for most of their lives. The bonds of trust must be hard and strong.

For a time it had seemed to Felix that he was the only one out of place here, then he noticed Kat. She too stood slightly apart from the crowd, marked among the children present as much by her strange hair as by her grubby clothing. He had felt a strong sense of sympathy for her then and wondered what would become of her. From what Messner and she had discussed en route, he had gathered she was an orphan. Felix's own mother had died when he was still a child and this had strengthened his feeling of sympathy for her.

Was she important to the Dark Warrior, he wondered? Had the beastmen he had fought been simple scouts or had they been seeking Kat? Not for the first time in his life he found himself wishing he knew more of the ways of Darkness. Knowing that to be a sinful thought, he pushed it aside.

He heard the wounded man groaning below as they brought him through the gate.

KAT HURRIED TO the base of the watchtower, feeling a need for solitude. She had grown tired of sitting near the big central fire. Even the presence of Gotrek did not reassure her. She felt very lonely here amidst all the busy adults. There was no one, really, to talk to and for the first time it was coming home to her that she knew no one in this world now and had no place in it. The flames reminded her too much of the burning of Kleindorf. The ladder creaked slightly under her bare feet. She ascended, nimble as a monkey, to the watchpost.

Felix was sitting alone, staring out into the darkness. The sun had long ago set, like a bloody smear on the horizon. The greater moon had drifted skyward. Silver light washed down. A slight breeze chilled Kat's cheeks and made the forest whisper and rustle menacingly. Felix watched it as if hypnotised, lost in his own dark thoughts. She scuttled swiftly over and sat cross-legged beside him.

'Felix, I'm scared,' she said. He looked down at her and smiled.

'Me too, little one.'

'Stop doing that!'

'Doing what?'

'Calling me "little one". The same as Gotrek does. He never calls anyone by their proper names does he? My name is Kat. You should call me that.'

Felix smiled at her. 'All right, Kat. Could you do something for me. It might be important for us all.'

'If I can.'

'Tell me about your parents.'

'I don't have any.'

'Everyone has a mother and father, Kat.'

'Not me. I was found by Heidi, Karl's wife, in a basket where she always picked berries.'

Felix laughed. 'You were found under a berry bush?'

'It's not funny, Felix. They say there was a she-monster nearby. The villagers killed it. They wanted to kill me too but Heidi wouldn't let them.' Felix struggled to keep his face straight. His mirth vanished when he saw how serious her expression was.

'No, you're right. It wasn't funny.'

'They took me in and looked after me. Now they're dead.'

'Did Karl and Heidi have any idea who your parents were? Any idea at all?'

'Why are you asking this, Felix? Is it really important?'

'It could be.'

Kat thought back, to that night when old Karl had got drunk. He and Heidi had thought she was asleep. She had slipped down to the kitchen to get a drink of water and overheard them talking. When she had realised that they were talking about her, she had frozen in place on the other side of the door. The memory of that evening came flooding back. She had wanted to ask them more, ask them what they had meant but she had been too scared to. Now she realised she would never get the chance.

'I once heard them talk about a young girl at the castle who had hair like mine,' she said quietly, struggling to remember it all. 'Her name was Justine. She was a distant cousin of Lord Klein or something, a poor relation who had come to live with the family. She vanished the year before I was born. No one ever found out what happened to her.'

'I think I know,' Felix said softly.

Footsteps approached the bottom of the tower. The ladder trembled and Messner's head poked through the trapdoor.

'There you are, Herr Jaeger. I've come to relieve you. Go below and get something to eat. You too, child. No sign of Rolf? He's still missing.'

'I haven't seen anything,' Felix said.

'I wonder what could have happened to him.'

'WHAT IS YOUR name?' Justine asked. The bearded man whom her scouts had captured spat at her. She nodded to Malor. The beastman brought his fist forward. There was a crack as ribs broke. The man slumped. If it had not been for the two beasts supporting him he would have fallen.

'What is your name?'

The man opened his mouth. Blood trickled down his chin and onto his leather jerkin. Justine reached out and took some on her fingertip. When she tasted it, it felt warm and salty and strength flowed through her.

'Rolf,' he said eventually. Justine knew then that he would tell her whatever she asked. She knew that it had not been the foresters who had killed Tryell's band. The tracker who had survived the assault on the camp had told her about the girl's guardians.

'There is a dwarf and a blond-haired man travelling with a young girl. Tell me about them.'

'Go to the hell that spawned you.'

'That I will... eventually,' Justine said. 'But you will be there to greet me.'

He shrieked as one of the beastmen dislocated his shoulder. His entire body stiffened with pain. The muscles in his neck stood out like taut wires. Eventually the tale of how he had met with the dwarf, the man and the girl in the forest came tumbling from his cracked lips. At last the man stopped speaking and stood before her, drained by his own confession.

'Take him to the altar!' Justine commanded.

The man tried to struggle as they carried him towards Kazakital's cairn. His efforts to escape were futile. The beasts were too strong and too many. He wept with terror when he saw what awaited him. He was more daunted by the sight of that great cairn and the black altar atop it than he had been when he was taken captive by the beasts. He must know what's coming, Justine thought. The sight of the heads of Lord Klein and Hugo seemed to scare him most of all.

'No! Not that!' he shrieked.

She saw to his binding herself and carried him to the altar easily. The army gathered in anticipation of what was coming. As the moon broke through the clouds she gestured for the drummers to begin. Soon the great drum sounded rhythmic and slow as a heartbeat.

She stood atop the cairn and sensed the slow gathering of forces. She looked out and down at a sea of animal faces. They were upturned, eyes bright with anticipation. She drew her sword and brandished it above her head.

'Blood for the Blood God!' she shouted.

'Skulls for the skull throne!' The answering cry was torn from a hundred throats.

'Blood for the Blood God!'

'Skulls for the skull throne!' The response was even louder this time. It rumbled like thunder in the woods.

'Blood for the Blood God!'

'Skulls for the skull throne!'

The blade came down and parted Rolf's ribs. She reached forward and stuck her gauntleted hand into the sticky mass of the man's innards. There was a hideous sucking noise as she tore the heart free and held it high over her head.

Somewhere, in a space beyond space, in a time beyond time, something stirred and came in answer to her call. It flowed inwards, spiralling from beyond. In the space over the altar a red pulsing darkness gathered. It flowed in to the heart she held above her and it began to beat once again. She reached out and placed the heart back within the sacrifice's chest.

For a moment, nothing happened and all was silence, then a great scream emerged from the throat of the thing that had once been Rolf. The flesh of the corpse's chest flowed together and began to smoke. The corpse sat upright on the altar. It eyes opened and Justine recognised the intelligence which peered out from within. The body was temporarily possessed by the mind of her daemonic patron, Kazakital.

Smoke rose from the corpses as flesh flowed beneath skin. A smell of rot and burning flesh combined filled her nostrils. The mind and the power contained within the deathless frame was moulding it into a new shape, a shape that bore some resemblance to the Daemon Prince's inhumanly beautiful form. Justine knew that the body would be burned out within minutes, unable to contain the power which pulsed within it, but that did not matter. She needed only a few minutes to commune with her lord and seek his council.

Swiftly she outlined what Rolf had told her. 'I will go to this place and kill everyone there.'

'Do that, beloved,' the Daemon Prince's lovely voice tolled like a bell from within its corrupting form. Once again she felt the sense of certainty and of worship that she always did in his presence.

'I will kill the girl. I will give you the hearts of the dwarf and the man if they try to protect her.'

'Best kill them quickly. They are a fell pair, ruthless and deadly. The dwarf carries a weapon forged in ancient days to be the bane of gods. They are both killers without mercy.'

'They are both as good as dead. I stand armoured in your prophecy. No warrior will ever overcome me in battle. If you what you have spoken is the truth.'

'Search your heart, beloved. You know I have never spoken anything but the truth to you. And know you this also – if you do this thing, immortality and a place among the Chosen will most certainly be yours.'

'It will be done.'

'Go then with my blessing. Spread chaos and terror and leave none of your chosen prey among the living.'

The sense of presence ended. The corpse fell headlong into the dirt, already starting to crumble to dust. Justine turned to her troops and gave them the signal to move out.

FELIX LOOKED UP at the ornate golden hammer. The sun's rays fell on it through the open door of the temple, making it shimmer in the early morning light. The runes that encrusted the hammerhead reminded him of those which adorned his own blade. He was not too surprised. His sword had been the prized possession of the Order of the Fiery Heart, a group of Sigmarite Templars. It seemed only natural that the blade should have holy markings.

There were few other people present; just some old women who sat cross-legged on the floor and prayed. Babes and their mothers were outside taking in the fresh air while they could. Felix imagined that it could get very stuffy in here with the door barred.

The temple was a simple shrine. The altar was bare save for the hammer used to sanctify weddings and contracts. Sigmar was not so popular a deity here. Most woodsmen looked to Taal, Lord of the Forests, for protection, but he imagined that the Cult of the Hammer would find some favour. Few wanted to willingly offend the gods. The shrine would also provide a link with the distant capital. It was a sign that there was an Empire, with laws and those who would enforce them. The state cult was the link which bound the disparate, distant peoples of the Empire together.

The walls bore none of the friezes and tapestries so popular in richer areas. The altar itself was carved from a block of wood not stone. He was tempted to touch the hammer, to find out if it were gilded or simply painted. The carving of the altar was of no ordinary quality, however. He admired the coiling around the edges and a representation of the First Emperor's head that would not have been out of place among the icons in Altdorf cathedral. He wondered who was responsible for the wood-work. He also wondered whether it would burn when the beasts came.

Felix bowed his head and made the Sign of the Hammer and prayed. He prayed that the town would be delivered, and that his life and the lives of his friends would be spared. He touched his hand to the hammer and then to his forehead for good luck and then rose to depart. He stretched, feeling his joints click. He had spent last night in the blockhouse of Fritz Messner and his family. The floor had been marginally preferable to a cold pile of leaves. He had to admit there were times when he missed his down-mattressed bed in Altdorf; there were times when being the son of a wealthy merchant had been not altogether bad. Right now for instance, he could be sleeping off a hangover in his chambers rather than wait-ing the attack of Chaos in some village no one had ever heard of.

'Felix...' It was the girl, pale and unsmiling. 'Herr Messner told me I would find you here.'

'He was right, Kat. What can I do for you?'

'I had a nightmare last night, Felix. I dreamt that something came out of the forest and dragged me away. I dreamt I was lost in the dark and things were chasing me...'

Felix could sympathise with that. Many times he had endured similar bad dreams.

'Hush, little one. They're not real. Dreams can't hurt you.'

'I don't think that's true, Felix. I had the same dream the night before the beasts attacked my home.'

Felix suddenly felt chilled to the bone. In his mind's eye, he could picture the forces of Chaos marching ever closer, bring-ing their inevitable doom.

JUSTINE SAT HIGH in the saddle on the back of her immense, mid-night-black charger. Overhead the storm clouds gathered, huge dark thunderheads that seemed to echo the mood of violent rage that boiled within her. This trail, part of the Imperial

Highway, was clear. It had been constructed over the years to allow the Emperor's messengers to pass quickly.

She thought it ironic that such paths would speed the Empire's inevitable destruction by Chaos. Invaders from the wastes could use them to move quickly westward. She likened this process to the way diseases used the body's own bloodstream to spread. Yes, she thought, the Empire was dying and Chaos was the disease which would kill it. Secret cabals of cultists spreading corruption in the cities; bands of beastmen and mutants bringing terror in the forests; champions of the Ruinous Powers crossing the border from Kislev and the wastes beyond. She knew these were not unrelated occurrences but symptoms of the same blight. First the Empire and then all the kingdoms of men would fall prey to it. No – she mustn't think of it as a disease, she told herself. It was a crusade to scourge the earth.

She looked back on the small army that followed her. First the squads of beastmen; huge, deformed and mighty, each led by its own champion. After them rumbled the great black bulk of her secret weapon, the Thunderer, the long-snouted daemonic cannon which had destroyed the gates of Castle Klein and would make it possible for her to take other fortified towns. It was pulled by teams of captured slaves driven by the black-armoured artificers who would man it. Bringing up the rear were the scavengers, the ill-organised rabble who followed like jackals following a pride of lions. Mutants, malformed and demented, driven from their villages and homes by the hatred of their normal kin. They were driven by hate and ready to revenge themselves on humanity.

All the elements of her own life were there, she thought. This road, the route to death and destruction, was simply an extension of the path she had followed all her days. That thought saddened her. Today more than ever she felt riven. It was as if she were two souls inhabiting the same body. One was dark, driven, fed on slaughter and carnage; it gloried in its strength and despised others their weaknesses. It despised her own weakness. She knew this was the side of her Kazakital cultivated as carefully as the gardeners of Parravon nurtured their hellflowers. It possessed the seeds of daemonhood and of immortality. It was a pure hateful being, driven, determined, strong.

The other soul was weak and she hated it. It was sickened by the unending violence of her life and just wanted it to stop. It was the side of her that felt pain, and the urge to give in to pain and not allow pain to befall others. It had been long submerged and twisted almost out of all recognition by the events of her life. Up until the death of Hugo, she had not even allowed herself to know that it still existed. The thought was too horrible, her need for revenge too strong and urgent. She had made her pact with the daemon seven long years ago; and she had needed to keep it in order to gain vengeance. Now her purpose had been fulfilled and once again she knew doubt.

The doubt centred upon the child. She could remember carrying it within her. She could remember feeling it grow and kick. She had born it during the long, sick period of wandering in the wild, when she had scrabbled for roots and grubs, drunk from streams and slept in the hollows beneath trees. It had been her only companion in the wild days after she had run off in fear and horror. It had been a growing presence within her as hunger, hardship and horror had driven her slowly mad.

She doubted that she or it would have survived if she had not encountered the beastwomen in the forest. If they had not taken her in and guarded her and fed her. She remembered them as being oddly shy and gentle compared to the gors and ungors. They had acted on the instruction of their daemonic patron, that was now clear, but she was no less grateful to them for that. They had taken the child away from her on the day of its birth and she had not seen it from that day to this. She knew now, had earned the right to know through long years of tests and battle, that this had all been part of her patron's plan, a daemonic strategy designed to allow her to transcend her mere humanity and join the ranks of the Elect. She knew it was her last tie with frail humanity and she despised it – and wondered at it too.

She recalled how it had all began. The beasts had dragged her before that great black altar in the forest. They had brought her to bow before the black stone inscribed with dreadful runes. They had laid her down on the rock and Grind had slashed her throat and wrists with his razor-edged obsidian blade while his acolytes chanted the praises of the Blood God.

She had expected to die then, and she would have welcomed it as an end to her suffering. Instead she had found the darkest of new lives. Her blood had burst forth, to be caught in the depression on the altar's surface. She had somehow pushed herself upright, kept on her feet by rage and defiance and a strangely serene hatred that blossomed within her. That was when she had sensed the presence. That was when she had seen the face.

In the pool of her own blood she had seen the daemon's form take shape. Crimson lips had emerged from the red liquid and mouthed questions and answers and promises. It had asked her whether she wanted revenge on those who had brought her to this. It had told her that the world was as corrupt and evil as she thought. It promised her power and eternal life. It had spoken its prophecy. Somehow she had stood, swaying and filled with pain, throughout the ordeal. Afterwards she seemed to remember her own blood, blackened and smoking, had somehow flowed back from the altar and returned to her veins. The wounds slurped shut, while poison and power blazed through her.

For days she had lain in burning dreams while her body changed, touched by the daemonic essence carried within her own tainted blood. Darkness twisted her and made her strong. Her fangs grew in her mouth. Her eyes changed so that they could see in the dark. Her muscles grew far stronger than a mortal man's. She had emerged from her trance knowing that it was not chance which had brought her to this concealed altar in the forest's depths, it was a dark destiny and the malign whim of a daemon's will.

From somewhere the beastmen produced a suit of black armour, covered in runes. At the following full Morrslieb they had repeated the ritual. Once more her wrists had been cut, once more the daemonic presence appeared. This time the armour was fixed to her body. The blood had flowed and congealed between its plates, forming a network of muscles, veins and fleshy pads which made the armour a second metal skin. The process had left her weak. Once more she had dreamed, and in that dream she had seen what she must do.

She had left the beasts for long years of wandering. Her trek took her ever northwards, through Kislev, through the Troll Country, to the Chaos Wastes and the long eternal war fought between the followers of Darkness. She had battled and fought for the favour of her dark gods and in every combat Kazakital's prophecy had proven true. She had overcome Helmar Ironfist, the bull-horned champion of Khorne. She sacrificed Marlane Marassa, the flame-hearted priestess of Tzeentch, on her own altar. She had torn Zakariah Kaen, the grossly obese champion of Slaanesh, limb from perfumed limb. She had fought in minor battles and great sieges. She had stalked her humanoid prey in the ruined mines beneath the lost dwarf citadel of Karag Dum. There she had recruited the servants of the Thunderer.

Each skirmish had brought her new gifts and powers. She had acquired her steed, Shadow, by challenging its owner, Sethram Schreiber, to single combat and tearing out his heart as an offering to Khorne. She had taken her hellblade from the mangled corpse of Leander Kjan, the leader of the Company of Nine, after the great battle at Hellmouth. She had overcome mutated beasts and monsters, and grown in skill and power until her patron had told her the time was right to return and take vengeance. And during all that time, as she felt the thrill of triumph and the exultation of victory and the sheer joy of battle sing in her tainted blood, she had sometimes wondered what became of the child, and whether the beasts had spared it.

It was nothing to her now, she knew. There was no connection. It was just another piece of flesh cast loose to live and die hopelessly amid the flotsam of this terrible world. It was the final pawn to be sacrificed in the game which would win her immortality. That was all.

So she told herself. But she knew that Kazakital did nothing without reason, and that the child had been spared for a reason. Perhaps this was the final test. Perhaps the daemon hoped to reveal some ultimate flaw within her for its own perverse reasons. In that case, it was doomed to disappointment. She would prove in the end that she was harder than stone. And let the Dark Gods take any who thought to stand in her way.

FELIX WATCHED THE clouds overhead. They bolted across the sky, a tumbling billowing mass driven by the fierce wind. The hue of the forest changed from light green to a darker, more ominous shade. It seemed that the trees, like everything else, were waiting.

He stood on the parapet atop the wooden barricade. He stared out over the fields straining to catch any sight of movement in the undergrowth. He guessed that it was late afternoon. Beside him stood Gotrek, studying his axe disinterestedly. Every ten paces along the walls edge stood an archer – one of the foresters, men who could hit a bullseye at two hundred paces. Beside each were three quivers full of arrows. Measuring the distance to the edge of the trees Felix realised that the space was a killing ground. Any attackers would get bogged down in the ploughed fields and be easy prey for the archers.

He tried to let the thought reassure him; it did not. Night in the forest was not like the night in the well-lit thoroughfares of Altdorf. When darkness came it was absolute. A man six paces away was a blurred outline. After dark, only the moons provided any light to see by and the clouds would block them out.

Earlier that day the foresters had lined the forest's edge with traps: sharpened branches bent back and tied that would snap forward when a tripwire was triggered; pits to trap the ankles of the unwary, some filled with sharpened stakes and covered with patches of turf; bear traps and mantraps, spring-driven steel jaws ready to bite any interlopers were there too. If the villagers survived the attack they would have their work cut out disarming their own devices. Perhaps the thoroughness with which they had saturated the wood reflected a belief that they would not survive, he thought.

Felix drummed his fingers on the top of the wall, feeling the rough touch of the lichen-covered wood against his fingers. Gotrek hummed tunelessly to himself, ignoring the irritated stares of the woodsmen. The waiting was always the worst of it. No fight he had ever faced had been as bad as the premonitions he had before it. Once action began he would be fine. He would be scared but the simple business of keeping alive would occupy his mind. For now he had nothing to do but stand and wait, and face the spectres his imagination conjured.

He pictured himself wounded, a great beastman standing over him. He imagined himself facing the woman in black and shuddered. He remembered the slaughter at Kleindorf and his terror strained against its leash of self-control. To comfort himself he tried to remember how he had felt after surviving the battle with the beastmen; the memory was pallid. He tried to envisage a scene after the battle with himself and the Slayer as the heroes who had rallied the troops and driven off the beasts. It seemed unconvincing.

'They'll be here soon enough, manling,' Gotrek said. He sounded almost happy.

'That's what I'm worried about.'

NIGHTMARE SHAPES drifted to the edge of the wood. In the pale light, Felix thought he could see a great horn-headed figure among the trees. An arrow rushed out from the parapet and fell short. Yes, they were there. More beast silhouettes became visible. Something disturbed the undergrowth. It rustled and moved like water displaced by great behemoths beneath its surface. The clouds parted and the moons leered down. Their glow illuminated a hellish scene.

'Grungni's bones!' Gotrek cursed. 'Look at that!'

'What?'

'There, manling! Look! They've got a siege machine. No wonder Kleindorf fell.'

Felix saw the black-armoured figures. They surrounded a great long-snouted machine, like a many-barrelled siege cannon. With whips they drove back a crowd of snarling mutants. As he watched he saw their twisted leader climb up into a seat at the engines back. Other dark warriors hurried round the machine's base, pulling out metal legs to secure the thing in place. As the leader turned a great crank the weapon swivelled to bear on the village. Its barrel was moulded in the shape of a dragon's head. Even at this distance Felix could hear the creaks from its mounting. More arrows hurtled towards it but again they fell short. Jeering cries echoed from the woods.

'What is it, Gotrek? What will it do?'

'Damn them – it's a cannon of some sort! Now we know what did for the fortifications at Kleinsdorf.'

'What can we do?'

'Nothing! After full dark they'll breach the walls and then charge us. The beasts can see in the dark. The villagers cannot.'

'That sounds too sophisticated for beasts.'

'It's not just beasts we fight, manling. It's a Chaos Champion and her entire retinue. They do not lack intelligence. Believe me, I have fought their kind before.'

Felix tried to estimate the number of beastmen in the forest but could not. They kept too well out of sight, knowing that lack of knowledge of their numbers would frighten the defenders even more. Fear of the unknown was another weapon in their armoury. Felix felt his heart sink.

'Maybe we should sally forth and spike the cannon,' Felix suggested.

'That's just what they're waiting for. The killing ground out there will work just as well for them as it would for us.'

'Do they have bows, though – they're beasts.'

'Doesn't matter. There's too many traps out there for comfort. Someone would be bound to blunder into them.'

'I thought you wanted a heroic doom?'

'Manling, if I just stand here and wait it will come to me. Look!'

Felix glanced in the direction indicated by the dwarf's stubby outstretched finger. He saw the black-armoured Chaos Warrior ride up to beside the huge cannon. He could see now that a horde of bestial faces glared out from under the edges of the trees. As he watched, a veritable tide of horned figures flowed out from under the eaves of the forest, and began to form up in units, just out of bow-shot. Somewhere deep in the forest a huge drum began to beat. It was answered by the blast of a horn and the beating of another drum somewhere off to the south. A chorus of screams and bellows filled the night. Somehow, within the rhythmic cadences of the strange words he began to sense a meaning. It was as if the understanding had been bred into his ancestors in ancient times, and it had taken only this event to waken it. Blood for the Blood God. Skulls for the skull throne. He shook his head to clear the hallucination but it did not matter. Whatever he did, it seemed like the thread of understanding would come back.

The noise reached a crescendo, fell silent for a moment and then started again. It grated on the nerves and set the butterflies fluttering in Felix's stomach. Looking out Felix could see that the chanting served a dual purpose. It worked to undermine the morale of the beastmen's enemies and it helped work the followers of Chaos up into a frenzy. He could see them clashing their weapons against their shields, gnawing the edges of their blades, slashing themselves. They danced insanely, raising their legs and then stomping the earth as if they were crushing the skulls of an enemy beneath their hooves.

'I wish they would just come on and get it over with,' Felix muttered.

'You're about to get your wish,' Gotrek said.

The Chaos Warrior raised her sword. The horde fell suddenly silent. She turned and spoke to them in their own bestial tongue and they answered her with cheers and growls. She turned to the armoured figures atop the siege engine and gestured with her blade. One of them capered for a moment then lit a fuse. After five long, silent heartbeats the mighty war engine spoke with a voice of thunder. There was a loud whistling sound and then a section of the wall near to Felix exploded, sending fragments of wood, torrents of earth and gobbets of flesh erupting into the air. The beastmen cheered and howled like the hordes of hell unleashed from torment.

Felix flinched as the cannon's barrel began to traverse on its mount. He could see that there was no way these wooden walls could withstand the sorcerous power of that awful weapon. They had just not been built to stand up to anything like this sort of punishment. Perhaps the best thing to do would simply be to leap down from the wall and take cover deeper within the township.

Gotrek seemed to sense his thoughts. 'Stay where you are, manling. They will hit the watchtower next.'

'How can you be so sure?'

'I have worked with cannons in my time, and this one is no different from any other. I can tell the trajectory they are shooting at.'

Felix forced himself to stand where he was, despite the way the flesh crawled down his back. He felt certain that he was virtually looking down the muzzle of the weapon. It spoke once more. Flame and smoke gouted from the barrel. Once more the whistling noise sounded. One of the legs of the great wooden watchtower was blasted away as the shot smashed a hole in the palisade in front of it. The tower teetered backwards and fell. One of the sentries fell from his post, arms wheeling, to crash to the ground below. His long wailing cry, audible even above the noise of the beasts, was cut off by his sudden impact on the earth below.

Felix smelled smoke and heard the crackle of burning from behind. He cast a glimpse over his shoulder and saw that one of the buildings and the remains of the tower had started to blaze. He could not tell whether it was as a result of the blast or not. Somewhere in the distance someone started shouting to others to bring water. He cast a glance along the wall where what seemed like a pitifully few defenders waited with their bows clutched near at hand. He exchanged glances with the nearest, a lad of not much more than sixteen years, his face white with dread.

Felix stared out desperately in the gloom, wondering how much longer this could go on, before either the morale of the defenders was broken or the town was reduced to a flattened ruin.

JUSTINE WATCHED AS the great cannon smashed a third gap in the town's wall. It was enough, she judged. They needed to save powder for the next fortress they came to. The gaps were large enough for her force to flow through. The defenders were tired and rattled. It was time. She gestured to her trumpeter. He sounded the call to advance. Marching in step to the beat of their human-skinned drums, the beastmen started forward.

Justine felt the bloodlust grow within her, and her desire to offer souls to the Blood God along with it. Tonight she would make him a mighty offering.

FELIX WATCHED AS the tide of beastmen advanced across the open ground. From the walls the archers began to fire. Calmly, methodically and efficiently they chose their targets, and let fly. Arrows flashed through the gloom and found homes in bestial breasts and throats and eyes. The blood-crazed Chaos worshippers came on relentlessly, their infernal drums beating. They chanted their call to their foul god in time to the music. Once again, he thought he could pick out the words: Blood for the Blood God. Skulls for the skull throne!

His grip felt slick on the hilt of his sword. Felix felt useless crouched here behind the parapet while others did the fighting and killed their advancing foes. His heart beat faster in his chest. His breath came in short gasps as if he had already run a mile. He fought down a sense of panic. He knew that soon enough it would be time to descend into combat. For now he had a bird's eye view of the struggle. In the distance he saw the black-armoured she-devil urging them on. She looked like a daemonic goddess from the dawn of time come to exact tribute in blood and souls.

He saw one goat-headed beastman fall, his legs caught in the steel jaws of a bear-trap. His companions did not even slow down. They marched on, crushing him to bloody pulp beneath their iron-shod hooves. Casualties did not seem to affect them. They showed no sign of fear. Perhaps it was true. They were soulless daemons immune to all normal emotion. Or perhaps, he told himself, they simply knew that their chance for revenge would soon come.

THE BEASTS WERE almost upon them now. Felix could see the gleam of firelight reflected in their eyes. He could see the bloody froth on their lips where they appeared to have bitten their own cheeks and tongues in their frenzy. He could smell the musty, furry stench they emitted. He could almost make out the crude runes etched into individual weapons.

All around the archers were letting fly with their last shafts and seizing up their swords and axes. Some had already taken to the ladders and moved to join the units of axe-men on the ground between the buildings. Some were lowering themselves down from the platform on which they stood, dangling at arm's length before dropping the last few strides to the earth below.

'Come, manling,' Gotrek said. 'It's time for bloodletting.'

Felix forced his locked limbs to move. It seemed to take some time to get them to obey him.

JUSTINE SMILED AS the beastmen picked up their pace and surged into through the gaps the great cannon had blown in the walls. She heard the sound of weapon on weapon, steel on steel as they encountered the defenders within. She touched her knees to her steed's flanks. It responded at once with its more than animal intelligence and bore her towards the fray.

FELIX BLOCKED THE sweep of a beastman's axe. The shock felt like it would dislocate his arm. He dropped to one knee and stabbed upwards, taking the surprised beastman under the ribs and putting the ancient Templar's blade through his victim's heart. Ripping the weapon free, he jumped back just in time to avoid being knocked over by a ranger and a beastman locked in a deadly wrestling match. The two of them fell to the ground in front of him, grunting with effort.

It was obvious to Felix that, given time, the beastman's superior strength would prevail. For a moment he watched appalled unsure of what he should do. He did not want to simply flail into the combat with his sword. Instead, he came to an instant decision. He ripped his dagger left-handed from the scabbard, dropped down and stabbed it into the beastman's broad back. It rose from the fight, howling its agony, and as it did so Felix slashed its head from its shoulders with his blade.

Its former opponent rose to his feet, nodding his thanks to Felix. It was the pale-faced boy Felix had seen on the battlements. He had just time to shrug before another wave of beastmen raced towards them. Somewhere in the distance he thought he heard the sound of thunderous hoofbeats.

JUSTINE CHARGED INTO the mass of bodies around the middle entrance, lashing about her with her hell-blade, killing a man with every stroke. Her horse trampled the wounded beneath its hooves, and whinnied triumphantly as the smell of blood filled its nostrils. She held herself easily in the saddle, knowing that nothing could stand against her.

'To me!' she shouted, and the beasts rallied about her, forming a wedge and driving their human opponent's back into the streets of their town. Behind her reinforcements poured through and began to flood through the lanes and alleys. She felt triumphant. Many souls would be offered screaming to the Lord of Battles this evening.

The sense of triumph diminished slightly as her horse vented a bestial scream. She looked down to see an arrow protruding from its eye. Even dying, with uncanny discipline the animal did not rear and try to throw her; instead it sank down on its haunches, allowing her time to vault clear from her saddle.

Blazing rage filled her. Shadow had carried her all the way from the Chaos wastes and finding another steed would not be easy. She swore that whoever killed it would pay with his life, even if she had to slay every living thing in this pitiful dungheap. Then she smiled, revealing her long wickedly sharp teeth. Mad laughter bubbled from her throat. She was merely swearing to do what she had already decided upon, long before the battle.

* * *

FELIX PAUSED IN the shadow of a building and glared around desperately. His breath came in ragged gasps. His clothing was soaked with blood and sweat. His sword arm felt numb. Where was Gotrek? They had become separated earlier in the battle without him realising it, when the fury of the action had prevented him from noticing anything except the movements of his current foe.

Now, he had a breathing space and the Slayer was nowhere to be seen. Felix knew that it was important that he find the dwarf, that his chances of surviving would be greatly increased in the presence of the Slayer's mighty axe. And if all else failed, he felt called upon to be present when the dwarf made his last stand, to perform his sworn task to witness it, even if he himself died shortly thereafter.

All around the buildings were alight, and the flames added a hellish illumination to the scene. Amid billowing, reeking clouds of smoke the battle raged on. Felix saw shadowy beastmen fighting with the wraiths of human warriors in the mist. He could hear the bellow of the monsters, the screams of the dying and the clash of weapon upon weapon. All semblance of formations had been lost in the vast melee. It was kill or be killed, in a brutal struggle to the death.

Somewhere off in the distance, he thought he heard the Slayer's warcry. He gathered his strength and courage and forced his legs to move in the direction from which he thought it had come. He offered up a brief hopeless prayer to Sigmar, asking the Lord of the Hammer would protect himself, the Slayer, Kat and all the others. For a moment, he wondered where the girl was.

LOST IN THE howling madness of the battle, Kat could see no escape. She had not wanted to remain within the Temple, knowing as she did that it was doomed. She needed a place to hide from the beasts. She still had not found it.

She ducked to one side and crouched behind a rain barrel. Nearby, two young men wrestled with a beast. One held it round the legs while the other dashed its brains out with a large boulder. Kat had never witnessed anything like this; the sheer insensate ferocity was appalling. All of the participants seemed possessed by a kind of madness that drove them to acts of hideous cruelty and lunatic bravery.

No quarter was given. No quarter was asked.

A great tide of warriors swept down the main street, carried along by their own fury and bloodlust. Screams of dying men and beasts filled the air. The clash of steel on steel rang out through the burning night. The muddy earth, churned by the feet and hooves of the mob, became slippery with blood.

A beast howled with triumph as it spitted a man on its spear. Its cry turned to a bellow of rage and fear as the man's friends chopped it to pieces. A circle of men surrounded a bull-headed giant. As it reached for one, another would leap in from its blind side and stab it. Soon it bled from a dozen small cuts; with a fierce bellow, it charged at the nearest warrior and by sheer weight bowled him off his feet, breaking out of the circle and into the mob.

Kat nearly screamed when the black-armoured woman strode through the throng. She feared that the Chaos Champion had come from her. Then Gotrek stepped from the shadows to issue his challenge. The woman snarled, revealing bloodstained fangs and lashed out at the Slayer. The blow was a blur, nearly too fast for the eye to follow. She did not know how the Slayer got his axe in the way but he did. Black steel clashed with blue starmetal. Red sparks flew amidst the smoke.

The Slayer returned the woman's blow with one of his own. The axe flashed towards her with the irresistible force of a thunderbolt. The woman ducked beneath the stroke and thrust forward. Somehow the Slayer's axe was there, blocking the blow. They stood straining against each other, blade pressed against blade, inhuman strength measured against daemonic power. Neither gave. Great ropes of muscle bulged in Gotrek's arms and shoulders. Sweat ran down his face, great veins standing out in his neck and forehead. The woman stood as immobile as an ebon statue. Her armour seemed locked in place. Her pale face was a bone white mask, a frozen image of bloodlust. The whites of her eyes had vanished; her eye sockets shone with red balefire.

Seconds raced by as the two of them stood locked in titanic conflict, each unable to budge the other. From the corner of her eye Kat spied a host of beastmen approach. They raced towards the battle, clearly intent on butchering the Slayer. Without thinking, Kat screamed a warning. Gotrek glanced to one side as the beastmen reached him. At the last moment he stepped back and parried a swing which would have split him in two. Kat feared that the woman would take the opportunity to stab him but she need not have worried. The tide of battle swirled around the combatants and the Champion of Khorne and the Slayer were dragged apart in the melee. Kat breathed a sigh of relief.

Then she noticed that the woman was staring at her. She met the red gaze straight on and her heart nearly stopped. She wanted to scream but when she opened her mouth no sound came out. The dark-clad warrior-woman marched closer.

THE KILLING LUST thundered in Justine's brain. The darkness rooted in her soul threatened to take over completely. Madness bubbled through her veins. The bloodlust filled her like a drug; she took ecstatic pleasure in the carnage. She wanted to find the dwarf and kill him. Of all the foes she had ever faced he had been the mightiest. A worthy offering to the Blood God indeed. At the last second, as she had been going to push aside his axe and slaughter him, fate, in the shape of her own idiotic followers, had intervened and torn them apart. She wanted to find him again and end the struggle.

Then she saw the girl. As if against her will, she saw the small scared face peeking out from its hiding place. She knew what she had to do. It was time to end this thing once and for all, to set her foot on the path that would end in eternal life, to seize her chance at a glorious destiny in the sight of Khorne. The dark thing that had been growing within her howled in triumph, knowing that its moment had come at long last.

Forgetting all about the dwarf, she marched towards her destiny.

FELIX TORE AROUND the corner. He was instantly thrown into battle once more. The heat of the burning buildings warmed him. The acrid smell of smoke filled his nostrils. The clangour of battle rang in his ears. He could hear Gotrek's shouts as he hewed his foes down but his eyes were drawn with instinctive, unthinking horror to the Chaos Warrior – and the child who cowered in the darkness before her.

He could see the resemblance as plain as day now. It went beyond the white stripe in the hair. They had similar features: the same wide eyes, the same narrow jawline. Seeing the warrior raise her blade to strike, he ran forward, bellowing, knowing in his heart that he was going to be too late.

JUSTINE WATCHED HER shadow fall on the child in front of her. She saw the look of fear in its eyes. The pallor of the face. She saw the resemblance to herself and wondered how it was that after all these years she truly felt nothing.

'What is your name, girl?' she asked quietly.

'Kat. Katerina.'

Justine nodded, surprised that she felt nothing whatsoever at this information.

In a flash of insight, she finally understood the ways of daemons. She saw all the tests, all the rituals, all the sacrifices for what they were, preparations for this one crucial moment. She knew now that all of this killings, and all of the bloodletting had been for a purpose. It had been a process which had changed her into something other than the human she had once been. She had been tempered by the process the way a blade is tempered by a master smith. She finally understood, after all the violence and all the massacres, that a human being could get used to anything, even to the destiny that made them a Chaos Warrior. She knew that at this moment, she could turn away from the child, that it would make no difference, she had finally and truthfully confirmed to herself that she was on the path of damnation. Killing the girl would make no difference now. She could do it if she wanted to, but it was meaningless – a piece of book-keeping, nothing more. She had passed the point of no return when she had decided to kill her a few moments ago. Still, she thought, it was always best to leave things tidy. With no more feeling now than if she was about to chop a log of wood, she raised her blade high.

And there was a flash of pain in her side as something crashed into her.

FELIX LEAPED, CROSSING the distance between himself and the Chaos Warrior in one bound. He smashed into the woman just as she raised her blade, overbalancing her and sending them both toppling to the ground. Knowing that he would never get another opportunity he lashed out with his blade, piercing the woman's side. She gave no sign of pain beyond a small grunt.

As they rolled over on the trampled earth, locked in a deadly embrace, Felix knew at once that he was overmatched. The woman reached up with mailed hands and grasped him by the throat. He reached up to try to dislodge them, grateful at least that she had dropped her blade, and at once knew that he had made a mistake. The Chaos Warrior was far stronger than he, possessed of a supernatural strength which was as superior to his own as his was to that of a child. He fought to slacken her grip but it was like trying to pry loose the fingers of a troll.

She was on top of him now, and the weight of her armour knocked all the breath from him. He rolled, trying to raise his shoulders from the earth, to throw her off, but it was useless. She seemed to anticipate his every move with ease. In that moment, he knew he was going to die. He was faced with an opponent who was simply too strong for him, and Gotrek was not there to save him.

Darkness pressed on him, sparks flashing before his eyes. Somewhere in the distance he heard Gotrek's battle-cry and part of him, infinitely remote and infinitely detached, thought it ironic that the Slayer would witness his doom, and not the other way around.

'Now, mortal, you die,' the woman said calmly, and her hands began to twist his neck.

Felix strained as hard as he could, as the terrible pressure mounted, knowing that if he gave way his neck would snap like a twig, and death would come to him instantaneously. He felt the veins bulge and muscles began to tear as he tried to resist, knowing that it was futile and that in a moment it would all be over. The darkness deepened. He saw everything as a shadow. It was quiet save for the thunder of his breath within his chest and the distant tolling of his heartbeat. He knew he was beaten, that he could take no more, and his muscles started to relax in surrender.

KAT LOOKED OUT on the terrible battle. She knew the Chaos Warrior had been about to kill her. She knew that Felix had tried to save her. She knew that the black-armoured woman was going to kill him. She knew she must do something.

Something glittered on the ground nearby. She saw it was the black sword which the Chaos Warrior had dropped. Its edge glittered brightly in the firelight. Perhaps there was something she could do. She reached out and tried to pick it up but it was too heavy. Maybe if she used both hands. Slowly, the blade started to rise. It twisted in her hands. The runes on its blade glowed bright red and she sensed the terrible power within it.

Now if only she could—

SUDDENLY FELIX FELT the terrible pressure cease. The Chaos Warrior looked down at him and then further, at her own chest. Felix followed her burning gaze and saw the blade of black metal which protruded there. The red runes glowed. Smouldering blood dripped from the wound and evaporated into poisonous smoke as it hit the ground. The Chaos Warrior stood upright, reeling to her feet, and turned to look in the direction the blow had come from.

Frantically Felix forced himself to move. Leadenly his limbs responded. He looked around seeking his blade, and reached out to grab it. His fingers folded round the hilt and he tried to raise it. It felt like he was trying to lift the weight of that great cannon outside the gate but somehow he forced himself to do it. He pushed himself upright and saw that there was no one else around, only the Chaos Warrior, himself and Kat. The woman's eyes were locked on the girl's, her lips twisted into a terrible ironic smile. Mad laughter bubbled from her lips. She took a step forward, the blade still protruding from her chest and Kat took a step backwards, eyes wide with horror and fear.

Slowly it filtered into Felix's brain what must have happened. Kat had lifted the heavy blade and driven it into the warrior's back while they fought. She had saved his life. Now it was up to him to save hers. Slowly he forced his battered body to move. He dragged himself along the ground after the Chaos Warrior.

The woman's step faltered. Slowly she began to topple forwards.

JUSTINE LAUGHED INSIDE even as the pain ate away at her consciousness. It was the final terrible joke. She had been killed by the one she had come to kill. A little girl had succeeded where mighty warriors had failed.

It was true, as the daemon has always said. A warrior had not

killed her. Her own child had done it instead. She stumbled
forward and fell into the waiting darkness.

FELIX WATCHED AS the vile Chaos Warrior fell. Flesh melted,
decomposing with horrid rapidity to leave only a reeking skeleton within the black armour. Somehow, without being told,
Felix knew that he looked upon the body of someone who had
died a long time ago. The sight of it made him want to vomit.

Something wet hit his face. The storm had broken at last and
rain was starting to fall. Sizzling sounds from nearby told him
that the raindrops were at war with the blaze. Good; perhaps
the town would not burn to the ground after all.

Suddenly Kat was there, huddling beside him. 'Is it over
now?' she asked.

Felix listened to the sounds of carnage all around him and
nodded.

'It soon will be,' he said softly. 'One way or another.'

FELIX SLUMPED ON a tree-stump looking back towards the town.
Messner and Kat sat nearby, watching him reproachfully. Both
of them thought he should not be up and about. His throat
was still bruised and he had trouble speaking and eating, but it
looked like he was going to be all right. He was just grateful to
still be alive.

So were the two hundred or so villagers who had survived
the great battle and its aftermath. He could still hear them
chanting prayers of thanksgiving for their deliverance in the
Temple of Sigmar.

A knight rode by, one of the mighty force despatched by the
Duke in answer to Messner's message. He had the head of a
beastman spiked on his lance. Felix and Messner watched him
pass, and Felix could tell that the man was thinking the same
as he was. There was a faint look of contempt on the woodsman's face. It was all very well for the knight to pose with his
trophy now – but where were they when the real fighting was
being done? The conquering heroes had arrived the morning
after the battle.

'So you found the cannon?' he asked. His voice came out in
a croaking whisper.

'Yes,' Messner said. 'It's an eerie thing. They say it feels as
warm to the touch as flesh. Dark sorcery involved, for sure.

We've sent for a priest to exorcise it. If that doesn't work, the old duke will send a wizard.'

'But the beasts are all dead.'

'Yes, we've hunted down every one of them. Gotrek just got back at dawn. He says that's the last.'

The two of them were just talking to keep Kat quiet and they both knew it. Neither wanted to let her get a word in. Still, this news gladdened Felix. It seemed that the beasts had lost heart and fled when word of their foul leader's death had got out. The rout had turned into a massacre as the foresters had pursued them. Now it looked like Kat had saved the whole town by her actions. She was a heroine and everybody told her that. Right now, she didn't sound much like one.

'I still want to go with you,' the girl said. Even after two days of argument she hadn't given up.

'You can't, Kat. Gotrek and I are bound for dangerous places; we can't take you. Stay with Messner.' He didn't want to tell her there was a price on his and Gotrek's heads. Not with a ranger present.

'You do that, girl,' Messner added. 'There's a place for you here with me and Magda and the kids. And you'll have friends among the other little ones, for sure.'

Kat looked at Felix imploringly. He shook his head and forced his features to remain stern and calm. He was not sure how much longer he could manage it when he heard the Slayer clump up. Gotrek grinned evilly. From his look Felix guessed he had added to the huge tally of deaths he had inflicted in the battle.

'Time's a-wasting, manling. We'd best be off.'

Felix got up slowly. Messner advanced and shook hands. Kat hugged first Felix and then the Slayer. Messner had to pull her away in the end.

'Goodbye,' she said tearfully. 'I'll always remember you.'

'You do that, little one,' Gotrek said softly.

They turned and walked away from Flensburg. The path was steep and the road rocky. Ahead lay Nuln and an uncertain future. At the top of the slope Felix turned and looked back. Below them Messner and Kat were two small figures, waving.

THE MUTANT MASTER

'It must sometimes occur to the readers of these pages that my companion and I were under some sort of curse. Without any effort on our part, and without any great desire on my part, we somehow managed to encounter all manner of worshippers of the Dark Ones. I myself have often suspected that we were somehow doomed to oppose their schemes without ever really understanding why. This sort of speculation never seemed to trouble the Slayer. He took all such events in his stride with a grunt and a fatalistic shrug, and dismissed any speculation along these lines as vain and useless philosophising. But I have thought long and hard on this matter, and it seems to me that if there is a power in this world which opposes the servants of Chaos, then perhaps it sometimes guided our steps, and even shielded us. Certainly, we often stumbled across the most outrageous and wicked schemes perpetrated by the most unlikely of evildoers...'

— From *My Travels with Gotrek, Vol. II*, by Herr
Felix Jaeger (Altdorf Press, 2505)

WHEN HE HEARD the snap of the twig, Felix Jaeger froze on the spot. His hand groped instinctively for the hilt of his sword, as his keen eyes searched his surroundings and spotted nothing. It was useless, Felix knew – the light of the fading sun barely penetrated the thick canopy of leaves overhead and the forest's dense undergrowth could have hidden the approach of a small army. He grimaced and ran his fingers nervously through his long blonde hair. All of the peddler's warnings came back to him in a flash.

The old man had claimed there were mutants on the road ahead, packs of them, preying on all who travelled this route between Nuln and Fredericksburg. At the time, Felix had paid no attention to him, for the peddler had been attempting to sell him a shoddy amulet supposedly blessed by the Grand Theogonist himself, a sure protection for pilgrims and wanderers – or so the merchant had claimed. He had already bought a small throwing dagger in a concealable wrist sheath from the peddler, and he had not felt inclined to part with more money. Felix rubbed his forearm where the sheath chafed, making sure the knife was still secure.

Felix wished he had the amulet now. It had most likely been a fake but at times like this any weary traveller on the dark roads of the Empire would feel the need for a little extra protection.

'Hurry up, manling,' Gotrek Gurnisson said. 'There's an inn in Blutdorf and my throat is as dry as the deserts of Araby.'

Felix regarded his companion. No matter how many times he looked upon the dwarf, the Trollslayer's squat ugliness never ceased to astonish him. There was no single element that made Gotrek so outstandingly repulsive, Felix decided. It wasn't the missing teeth, the missing eye or the long beard filled with particles of food. It wasn't the cauliflower ear or the quiltwork of old scars. It wasn't even the smell. No, it was the combination of them all that did it.

For all that, there was no denying that the Trollslayer presented a formidable appearance. Although Gotrek only came up to Felix's chest, and a great deal of that height was made up of the huge dyed crest of red hair atop his shaved and tattooed skull, he was broader at the shoulders than a blacksmith. In one massive paw, he held a rune-covered axe that most men would have struggled to lift with both hands. When he shifted his massive head, the gold chain that ran from his nose to his ear jingled.

'I thought I heard something,' Felix said.

'These woods are full of noises, manling. Birds chirp. Trees creak and animals scuttle everywhere.' Gotrek spat a huge gob of phlegm onto the ground. 'I hate woods. Always have. Remind me of elves.'

'I thought I heard mutants. Just like the peddler told us about.'

'That so?' Gotrek showed his blackened teeth in what could have been a snarl or a smile, then he reached up and scratched under his eye-patch, rubbing the socket of his ruined left eye with his thumb. It was a deeply disturbing sight. Felix looked away.

'Yes,' he said softly.

Gotrek turned to face the woods.

'Any mutants there?' he bellowed. 'Come out and face my axe.'

Felix cringed. It was just like the Trollslayer to tempt fate like this. He was sworn to seek death in battle with deadly monsters in order to atone for some unmentionable dwarfish sin, and he wasted no opportunity to complete that quest. Felix cursed the drunken night he had sworn his oath to follow the Trollslayer and record his doom in an epic poem.

Almost in answer to Gotrek's shout there was a further rustling in the undergrowth, as if a strong wind had disturbed the bushes – only there was no breeze. Felix kept his hand clasped on his sword hilt. There was definitely something there and it was getting closer.

'I think you might be right, manling,' Gotrek smiled nastily. It occurred to Felix that he had known there was something there all along.

A horde of mutants erupted from the undergrowth, screaming oaths and curses and the vilest of obscenities. The sheer horror of their appearance threatened to overwhelm Felix's mind. He saw a repulsive slimy-skinned creature that hopped along like a toad. Something vaguely female scuttled along on eight spidery legs. A creature with the head of a crow and greyish feathers screeched a challenge. Some of the mutants had transparent skin through which pulsing organs were visible. They brandished spears, and daggers and what looked like rusty kitchen implements. One of them launched itself towards Felix, swinging a notched, blunt-edged cleaver.

Felix reached up and caught the creature's wrist, stopping the blade a moment before it crunched into his skull. He jabbed a knee into the monster's groin. As it bent double, he kicked it in the head, knocking it over. Its greenish vomit spewed all over Felix's boots before it rolled back into the undergrowth.

In the brief respite, Felix ripped his blade from its scabbard, ready to lay about him. He need not have bothered.

Gotrek's mighty axe had already cleaved a path of red ruin through their attackers. With one blow he cut down three more. Bones splintered under the impact. Flesh parted before the razor-sharp edge. The Trollslayer's axe flashed again. Two halves of a severed torso flopped down, and, briefly unaware that it was already dead, tried to crawl away from each other. Gotrek's axe completed its upswing, severing the head of another mutant.

Appalled by the sudden carnage, the mutants fled. Some of them rushed past Felix into the woods on the far side, others turned and ran back into the dark undergrowth from which they had come.

Felix looked at Gotrek speculatively, waiting to see what the Trollslayer did. The last thing he wanted was for them to separate and pursue the creatures into the darkening forest. Their victory had been too easy. It all smacked of a trap.

'Must've sent the runts of this litter after us,' Gotrek observed, spitting on a mutant corpse. Felix looked down to see the Trollslayer was right. Very few of the dead looked as if they would have come up to Gotrek's chest, and none of them looked taller than the Trollslayer.

'Let's get out of here,' Felix said. 'These things smell awful.'

'Hardly worth the killing,' Gotrek grumbled back. He sounded deeply disappointed.

THE HANGED MAN was one of the most dispiriting inns Felix had ever visited. A tiny cheerless blaze flickered in the fireplace. The taproom smelled of damp. Mangy dogs gnawed at bones that looked as if they had been lost for generations in the carpet of filthy straw. The landlord was a villainous-looking individual, his face tracked with old scars, a massive hook protruding from the stump of his right hand. The potboy was a wall-eyed hunchback with an unfortunate habit of drooling into the beer as he poured it. The locals looked thoroughly miserable. Every one of them glanced at Felix as if he wanted to plunge a knife into the youth's back but were just too depressed to summon up the energy.

Felix had to admit that the inn was appropriate for the village it served. Blutdorf was as gloomy a place as he had ever seen. The mud huts looked ill-tended and about to collapse. The streets seemed somehow empty and menacing. When they had finally intimidated the drunken gatekeeper into letting them enter, weeping crones had watched them from every doorway. It was as if the whole place had been overcome with grief and lethargy.

Even the castle brooding on the crags above the village appeared neglected and ill-cared for. Its walls were crumbling. It looked as if it could be stormed by a group of snotlings armed with pointed sticks, which was unusual for a town which appeared to be surrounded by a horde of menacing mutants. On the other hand, Felix thought, even the mutants about here seemed a particularly unfearsome bunch, judging by the attack they had attempted earlier.

He took another sip of his ale. It was the worst beer he had ever tasted, as thoroughly disgusting a brew as had ever passed his lips. Gotrek threw back his head and tipped the entire contents of the stein into his mouth. It vanished as fast as a gold purse dropped in a street of beggars.

'Another flagon of Old Dog Puke!' Gotrek called out. He turned and glared at the locals. 'Try not to deafen me with the sound of your mirth,' he bellowed.

The customers refused to meet his eye. They stared down into their beers as if they could discover the secret of transmuting into lead into gold there, if they only studied it hard enough.

'Why all the happy faces?' Gotrek enquired sarcastically. The landlord placed another flagon on the counter before him. Gotrek quaffed some more. Felix was gratified to note that even the Trollslayer made a sour face when he finished. It was a rare tribute to the nastiness of the ale. Felix had never seen the dwarf evince the slightest discomfort or hesitation in drinking anything before.

'It's the sorcerer,' the landlord said suddenly. 'He's a right nasty piece of work. Things never been the same since he came an' took over the old castle. Since then we've 'ad nothin' but bother, what with the mutants on the road and all. Trade's dried up. No one comes here anymore. Nobody can sleep safe in their beds at night.'

Gotrek perked up at once. A nasty grin revealed the blacked stumps of his teeth. This was more to his liking, Felix saw.

'A sorcerer, you say?'

'Aye, sir, that he is – a right evil wizard.'

Felix saw that the customers were all glaring at the landlord strangely, as if he was speaking out of line, or saying something they had never expected to hear him say. Felix dismissed the thought. Maybe they were just frightened. Who wouldn't be, with a servant of the Dark Powers of Chaos in residence over their village?

'Mean as a dragon with toothache, he is. Ain't that right, Helmut?'

The peasant who the landlord addressed stood frozen to the spot, like a rat petrified by the gaze of a snake.

'Ain't that right, Helmut?' The landlord repeated.

'He's not so bad,' the peasant said. 'As evil sorcerers go.'

'Why don't you just storm the castle?' Gotrek asked. Felix thought that if the dwarf couldn't guess the answer to that from the whipped-dog look of these poor clods, he was stupider than he looked.

'There's the monster, sir,' the peasant said, shuffling his feet and staring down at the floor once more.

'The monster?' Gotrek asked, more than a hint of professional interest showing in his one good eye. 'A big monster, I suppose.'

'Huge, sir. Twice as big as a man and covered in all sorts of nasty mut… mut… mut…'

'Mutations?' Felix suggested helpfully.

'Aye, sir, those things.'

'Why not send to Nuln for help?' Felix suggested. 'The Templars of the White Wolf would be interested in dealing with such a follower of Chaos.'

The peasants looked at him blankly. 'Dunno where Nuln is, sir. None of us ever been more than half-a-league from Blutdorf. Who'd look after our wives if we left the village?'

'An' then there's the mutants,' another villager chipped in. 'Woods is full of them and they all serve the magician.'

'Mutants as well?' Gotrek sounded almost cheerful. 'I think we'll be visiting the castle, manling.'

'I feared as much,' Felix sighed.

'You can't mean to attack the sorcerer and his monster,' one of the villagers said.

'With your help, we will soon rid Blutdorf of this scourge,' Felix said shakily, ignoring the nasty look Gotrek threw him. The Trollslayer wanted no assistance in his quest for glorious death.

'No, sir, we can't help you.'

'Why not? Are you unmanly cowards?' It was a stupid question, but Felix felt he had to ask. It wasn't that he blamed the villagers. Under normal circumstances he would have been no more keen than they were to confront a Chaos sorcerer and his pet monster.

'No, sir,' the villager said. 'It's just that he has our children up there – he's keeping them as hostages!'

'Your children?'

'Aye, sir, every last one of them. His monster and he came down and rounded them all up. There was no resisting either. When Big Norri tried, the creature tore his arms off and made him eat them. Nasty, it was.'

Felix did not like the glint that had entered the Trollslayer's eye. Gotrek's enthusiasm for getting to the castle and fighting the monster radiated across the room like heat from a large bonfire. Felix wasn't so certain. He found that he shared the villagers' lack of enthusiasm for the direct approach.

'Surely, you must want to free your children?' Felix asked.

'Aye, but we don't want to kill them. The magician will feed them to his monster if we gave him any lip.'

Felix looked over at Gotrek. The Trollslayer jerked his thumb meaningfully in the direction of the castle. Felix could see he was keen to be off, hostages or no hostages. With a sinking feeling, Felix realised that there would be no getting out of this. Sooner or later, he and the dwarf were going to end up paying Blutdorf Keep a visit.

Desperately, he searched for a way of staving off the inevitable. 'This calls for a plan,' he said. 'Landlord, some more of your fine ale.'

The landlord smiled and fussed about at the bar pouring some more ale. Felix noticed that Gotrek was eyeing him suspiciously. He realised that he wasn't really showing the proper enthusiasm for their quest. The landlord came back and thumped down two more steins with an enthusiastic smile.

'One for the road,' Felix said, raising his ale jack. He swigged away at the beer, which tasted even fouler than it had previously. Because of the taste, he wasn't quite sure, but he thought there was a faint chemical tang to the beer. Whatever it was, a few more sips left him feeling dizzy and nauseous. He noticed that Gotrek had finished his ale and was calling for another. The landlord obliged and the dwarf swigged it back in one gulp. His eyes widened, he clutched his throat and then he fell back as if pole-axed.

It took Felix a moment to register what had happened and he stumbled forward to examine his companion. His feet felt like lead. His head swam. Nausea threatened to overwhelm him. There was something wrong here, he knew, but he couldn't quite put his finger on it. It was something to do with the ale. He had never seen the Trollslayer fall over before, no matter how much beer he drank. He had never felt so bad himself, not after so few beers. He turned and looked at the landlord. The man's outline wavered, as if Felix was seeing him through a thick fog. He pointed an accusing finger.

'You drudged… I mean drunk… no, I mean you drinked our drugs,' Felix said and fell to his knees.

The landlord said, 'Thank Tzeentch for that. I thought they would never go down. I gave that dwarf enough skavenroot to knock out a horse.'

Felix fumbled for his sword but his fingers felt numb and he fell forward into the darkness.

'Cost me a crown a pinch, as well,' the landlord muttered. His peevish voice was the last thing Felix remembered before unconsciousness took him. 'Still, Herr Kruger will pay me well for two such fine specimens.'

WAKE UP, MANLING!' The deep voice rumbled somewhere close to Felix's ear. He tried to ignore it, hoping that it would go away and let him return to his slumber.

'Wake up, manling, or I swear I will come over there and strangle you with these very chains.' There was a threatening note to the voice now that convinced Felix he'd better pay attention to it. He opened his eyes – and wished that he hadn't.

Even the dim light of the single guttering torch illuminating their cell was too bright. Its feeble glow hurt Felix's eyes. In a way, that was alright, because it made them match the rest of his body. His heartbeat thumped in his temples like a gong struck with a warhammer. His head felt like someone had used it for kickball practice. His mouth was desert dry and his tongue felt like someone had sandpapered it.

'Worst hangover I ever had,' Felix muttered, licking his lips nervously.

'It's not a hangover. We were dru–'

'Drugged. I know.'

Felix realised that he was standing up. His hands were above his head and there were heavy weights attached to his ankles. He tried to bend forward to see what they were but found that he could not move. He looked up to see that he dangled from manacles. The chains were attached to a great loop of iron set in the wall above him. He confirmed this by peering across the chamber and seeing that Gotrek was held the same way.

The Trollslayer dangled from his chains like a side of beef in a butcher's shop. His legs were not chained, though. His frame was too short to reach the ground. Felix could see that there were leg irons set in the wall at ankle height but the dwarf's legs did not stretch that far.

Felix looked around. They were in a large chamber, paved with heavy flagstones. There were a dozen sets of chains and manacles set in the walls. An oddly distorted skeleton dangled from the farthest set. In the wall to the far left was a huge bench covered in alembics and charcoal burners, and other tools of the alchemist's trade. A huge chalk pentagram surrounded by peculiar hieroglyphics was inscribed in the centre of the room. At each junction of the pentacle was set a beastman skull holding an extinguished candle made from black wax.

At the far right of the room, a flight of stone steps led up to a heavy door. There was a barred window in the door, through which a few shafts of light penetrated down into the gloom. Near the foot of the stairs Felix could see his sword and Gotrek's axe. He felt a brief surge of hope. Whoever had taken their weapons had not been very thorough. Felix could still feel the weight of the throwing dagger in the hidden sheath on his forearm. Of course, there was no way he could use it with his arms manacled, but it was somehow comforting to know it was there.

The air was thick and fetid. From the distance Felix thought he heard screams and chants and bestial roars. It was like listening to a combination of a lunatic asylum and a zoo. Nothing about their situation reassured Felix.

'Why did the landlord drug us?' Felix asked.

'He was in league with this sorcerer. Obviously.'

'Or he was afraid of him.' If he could have, Felix would have shrugged. 'No matter, I wonder why we're still alive?'

A high-pitched tittering laugh answered that question. The heavy door creaked open and two figures blocked out the light. There was a brief flare as a lucifer was struck, then a lantern was lit and Felix could see the source of the mocking laughter.

'A good question, Jaeger, and one I will be only too pleased to answer.'

There was something very familiar about this voice, Felix thought. It was high-pitched and nasal and deeply unpleasant. He had heard it before.

Felix squinted across the chamber and made out the voice's owner. He was just as unpleasant as his voice. A tall, gaunt man, he wore faded and tattered grey robes, patched at the sleeves and elbows. Around his scrawny neck hung an iron chain bearing a huge amulet. His long thin fingers were covered in rune-encrusted rings and tipped with long blackened nails. His pale, sweating face was framed by a huge turned-up collar. He wore a skull-cap trimmed with silver.

Behind the man stood an enormous creature. It was huge, half again as tall as a man, and maybe four times as heavy. Perhaps once it had been human but now it was the size of an ogre. Its hair had fallen out in great clumps, and massive pustules erupted from its scalp and flesh. Its features were twisted and hideous. Its teeth were like millstones. Its arms were even more muscular than Gotrek's, thicker around than Felix's thighs. Its hands were the size of dinner plates. Its callused, sausage-sized fingers looked like they could crush stone. It glared at Felix with eyes full of insane hatred. Felix found he could not meet the thing's gaze and he turned his attention back to the human.

The man's features were gaunt and lined. His eyes were the palest blue and bright with madness. They were hidden only slightly by his steel-framed pince-nez glasses. His nose was long and thin and tipped with an enormous wart. A drip of mucous hung from his nose. He tittered again, sniffed to draw the drip back into his nostrils and then wiped his nose on his sleeve. Then, recovering his dignity, he threw his head back and strode purposefully down the stairs. The effect of impressive sorcerous dignity was spoiled a little when he almost tripped on the hem of his robe and fell headlong.

It was this last touch which stirred Felix's memory. It brought everything else into focus. 'Albericht?' He said. 'Albericht Kruger?'

'Don't call me that!' The robed man's voice approached a scream. 'Address me as "Master"!'

'You know this idiot, manling?' Gotrek asked.

Felix nodded. Albericht Kruger had been in a few of his philosophy classes at Altdorf University before he had been expelled for duelling. He had been a quiet youth, very studious, and was always to be found in the libraries. Felix has probably never exchanged more than a dozen words with him in the whole two years that they had studied together. He remembered also that Kruger had vanished. There had been a bit of a scandal about it – something to do with books missing from the library. Felix could remember that a few witch hunters from the Temple of Sigmar has shown interest.

'We were students together back in Altdorf.'

'That's enough!' Kruger screeched in his thin and annoying voice. 'You are my prisoners and you will do as I say for what remains of your pitiful lives.'

'We will do as you say for what remains of our pitiful lives?' Felix stared back at Kruger in astonishment. 'You've been reading too many Detlef Sierck melodramas, Albericht. Nobody speaks like that in real life.'

'Be quiet, Jaeger! That's enough. You were always too clever for your own good, you know. Now we'll see who's the clever one – oh yes!'

'Come on, Albericht, a joke's a joke. Let us out of here. Quick, before your master comes.'

'My master?' Kruger seemed puzzled.

'The sorcerer who owns this tower.'

'You idiot, Jaeger! I am the sorcerer.'

Felix stared in disbelief. 'You?'

'Yes, me! I have probed the mysteries of the Dark Gods and learned the source of all magical power. I have plumbed the secrets of Life and Death. I wield the mighty energies of Chaos and soon I will have total domination over the lands of the Empire.'

'I find that a little hard to believe,' Felix admitted honestly. The Kruger he had known back then had been virtually a non-entity, ignored by all the other students. Who would have guessed at the depths of megalomania that lurked in his head.

'Think what you will, Herr-clever-clogs-Jaeger with your la-di-da accent and your my-father-is-a-rich-merchant-and-I'm-too-good-for-your-sort manners. I have mastered the secrets of life itself. I control the alchemical secrets of warpstone and understand the innermost secrets of the Art of Transmutation!'

Out of the corner of his eye, Felix could see Gotrek's huge muscles beginning to bulge as he strained against the chains that held him. His face was red and his beard bristled. His body was contorted, arched to brace his feet against the wall. Felix did not know what the dwarf hoped to achieve. Anyone could see that these huge chains were beyond the strength of man or dwarf to break.

'You've been using warpstone?' That explained a lot, Felix thought. He did not know much about warpstone but what he did know was disturbing enough. It was the raw essence of Chaos, the final and ultimate source of all mutations. Just a pinch of it was enough to drive a normal man mad. By his tone, it sounded like Kruger had consumed a barrel of it. 'You're insane!'

'That's what they told me back in Altdorf, back at their university!' Spittle dripped from Kruger's mouth. Felix could see that his eyes glowed an eerie green, as if there were tiny marsh-lights behind the pupils. Vampire-like fangs protruded from his gums. 'But I showed them. I found their forbidden books, all wrapped up in the vault. They said that they were not meant for the eyes of mortal man but I've read them, and they've done me no harm!'

'Yes, I can see that,' Felix muttered ironically.

'You think you're so clever, don't you, Jaeger? You're just like all the rest, all of them who laughed at me when I said I would be the greatest sorcerer since Teclis. Well, I'll prove you wrong. We'll see how smart you act once I have transformed you, the way I transformed Oleg here!'

He tapped the monster on the shoulder with paternal pride. It grinned like a dog whose stomach has been scratched by its master. Felix found the sight very disturbing. Behind them Gotrek was practically standing against the wall. His arms were at full stretch, the chains holding firm, leaving him parallel to the floor. The Trollslayer was blue in the face. His features were contorted in a grimace of rage and fury. Felix felt that something would have to give soon. Either the chains would break or the Trollslayer would burst a blood vessel. That might prove to be a mercy, Felix thought. He did not see how Gotrek could overcome the monster without his axe. The Slayer was strong, but this creature made him look like a scrawny child.

Kruger raised his arm, brandishing his staff. At the tip, Felix could see that a sphere of greenish warpstone held in a lead claw. Felix could not help but notice that the hand that held the staff was scaly, and that its fingernails resembled the talons of a wild beast.

'It took me years to perfect the Spell of Transmutation, years,' Kruger hissed. 'You have no idea how many experiments I did. Hundreds! I laboured like a man possessed but at last I have the secret. Soon you will know it too.' The sorcerer tittered. 'Alas, it will do you no good, for you will not be clever enough to speak. Still, you'll provide fine company for Oleg.'

The glowing tip of the man's staff came ever closer to Felix's face. He could see strange lights in its depth. Its surface seemed to shimmer and swirl like oil dropped on water. He could sense the terrible mutating power emerging from it. It radiated out of the warpstone like heat from a glowing coal.

'I don't suppose begging for mercy would help?' Felix asked breezily. He was proud that he managed to keep his voice even.

Kruger shook his head. 'It's too late for that. Soon you will be even more of a witless dullard than you are now.'

'In that case, I have to tell you something.'

Gotrek's muscles bulged as he made one last superhuman effort, throwing himself forward like a swimmer diving headlong off a cliff.

'What's that, Jaeger?' Kruger leaned close to Felix's mouth.

'I never liked you either, you madman!'

Kruger looked like he was going to strike Felix with the staff but instead he just smiled, revealing his feral teeth.

'Soon, Jaeger, you will learn the true meaning of madness. Every time you look in the mirror.'

Kruger began to chant in a strange, liquid-sounding tongue. It was not elvish but something even older and considerably more sinister sounding. Felix had heard it before, at other times when he and Gotrek had interfered with rites being performed by the followers of Chaos. Well, it looked as though this time the forces of Darkness were going to have the last laugh. He and the Trollslayer would soon be joining their ranks, however unwillingly.

With every word Kruger chanted, the warpstone glowed ever brighter. Its greenish glow drove back the gloom of the chamber and washed everything in its eerie light. Ectoplasmic tendrils emerged from the warpstone. At first they resembled glowing mist, then congealed into something more solid. There was about them the suggestion of something loathsome and diseased. As Kruger brandished his staff, its ectoplasmic emissions trailed behind it like the tail of a comet. He waved it around with grand sweeping gestures, as if with every wave the evil device gathered power.

His chanting now resembled insane shrieking. Sweat beaded the Chaos sorcerer's forehead and dripped down his glasses. Oleg, the mutated monster, howled in unison with his master's chanting. His bass rumbling providing an eerie counterpoint to the spell. Felix felt his hair stand on end, when the chanting stopped and an eerie silence blanketed the dungeon.

For a moment, everything was still. Felix could hardly see, so dazzled was he by the light of the Chaos staff. He could hear his own heartbeat and Kruger's frantic breathing as he gasped for breath after completing his invocation. There was a strange metallic creaking, and a grinding of metal on stone. He opened his eyes to see one of Gotrek's chains whip free from the wall, then the Trollslayer tumbled forward with a curse, ending up dangling above the flagstones.

Kruger turned at the sound. The monster opened his mouth and let out an enormous bellow.

Felix groaned. He had hoped the Slayer would be able to make a run for his axe. With his weapon in his hand, Felix would have backed the Trollslayer against any monster. However, Gotrek still hung from one of the chains. All he could do was dangle there, while the monster ripped him limb from limb.

Kruger seemed to realise this at the same time as Felix. 'Get him!' he yelled to his monster.

Oleg surged forward and Gotrek lashed out with his chain. The heavy metal links whipped towards the huge mutant's eyes. Oleg howled with pain as the chain hit his face, then reeled backwards, crashing into Kruger. There was a snapping sound as Gotrek used his moment's grace to break his other chain free from the wall. Kruger's face went white. He lurched to his feet and scuttled for the stairs. The last Felix saw of him was his departing backside.

'Now there will be a reckoning!' Gotrek pronounced, his flinty voice guttural with rage.

The monster surged forward to meet the Trollslayer, reaching out with one ham-sized hand. Gotrek brought the chain flashing forward and down, hammering the metal into the creature's hand. Once more it backed off. Gotrek's one good eye squinted sideways as though measuring the distance between himself and his axe. Felix could almost read his mind. The distance was too far. If he turned his back and ran for his weapon, the monster's longer stride would enable it to overhaul him.

Perhaps he could back towards it. As always, Felix misread the strength of the dwarf's lust for combat. Instead of backing off, he ran forward, swinging his chain in an eye-blurring arc. It smashed into the monster's chest, then a moment later Gotrek caught Oleg across the face with the second chain.

This time Oleg expected the pain. Instead of retreating, he advanced on towards the Trollslayer, scooping him up in a bear hug. Felix winced as he watched the giant mutant's arms constrict. Oleg's flexed biceps looked the size of ale-barrels. Felix feared that the Trollslayer's ribs would snap like rotten twigs.

Gotrek brought his head forward, butting Oleg in the face. There was a sickening crunch as Oleg's nose broke. Red blood spurted over Gotrek. Oleg howled with pain and cast the dwarf across the room with one thrust of his huge arms. Gotrek smacked into the wall and fell to the ground with a clattering of chains. After a few seconds, the Trollslayer staggered unsteadily to his feet.

'Get your axe!' Felix shouted.

The dazed dwarf was in no condition to take his advice. Besides, Gotrek was out for blood. He staggered towards Oleg. The giant stood there, howling and clutching his nose. Then, hearing the dwarf's reeling footsteps, he looked up and gave a mighty bellow of rage and pain. He rushed forward, hunkered down, arms outstretched, once more intending to catch the Trollslayer in his death grip. Gotrek stood on swaying legs as the monster thundered towards him, irresistible as an runaway wagon. Felix did not want to look – the mutant was big enough to crush the Slayer beneath his elephantine feet. Horror compelled him to watch.

Oleg reached for Gotrek, his enormous arms closing, but at the last second the Slayer ducked and dived between his legs, turned and lashed out with the chain. It wound around the monster's ankle. Gotrek heaved. Oleg tripped and sprawled, and the chain unwound like a serpent.

Gotrek looped a length of chain around the mutant's throat. Oleg pushed himself to his feet, pulling Gotrek with him. The Trollslayer's weight tightened the grip of the chain around his neck. Using it to hold himself in place, Gotrek pulled himself up to behind Oleg's neck and continued to tighten the chain. The flesh turned white around the mutant's windpipe as the metal links bit into flesh. Felix could see that Gotrek intended to strangle the monster.

Slowly the thought percolated into the mutant's dim mind, and he reached up with both hands to try and unloose the grip of the metal noose that was killing him. He grasped at the chain and tried to work his fingers into the links but they were too big and the chain was gripped too tight. Then he tried to reach behind his head to grasp Gotrek. The Trollslayer ducked his head and pulled himself in tight. He pulled the chain backwards and forward like a saw now. Felix could see droplets of blood emerging where the links had bit.

Now Oleg's hand fastened in Gotrek's crest of hair. It held fast for a moment as Oleg tugged, then his fingers slipped loose on the bear fat ointment that held the crest together. Felix could see fear and frustration begin to appear in the monster's eyes. He could tell that the mutant was weakening. Now Oleg panicked, throwing himself backward at the wall, slamming Gotrek into the stone with sickening force. Nothing could loosen the Slayer's grip. Felix doubted that death itself would make the dwarf loose his hold now. He could see a fixed glazed look had entered Gotrek's eyes, and his mouth was half-open in a terrifying snarl.

Slowly Oleg weakened as his strength drained from him. He tumbled forward onto his hands and knees. A ghastly rattle emerged from his throat and he sank to the ground and was still. Gotrek tightened the noose one last time to make sure of his prey and then stood up, gasping and panting.

'Easy,' he muttered. 'Hardly worth the killing.'

'Get me down from here,' Felix complained.

Gotrek fetched his weapon. In four strokes of the axe, Felix was free. He raced over and retrieved his sword. From up above, he heard the sound of windlasses turning, great metal doors being raised, and the howling of a bloodthirsty horde. Felix and Gotrek had just time to brace themselves before the door to the laboratory was thrown open and a tide of frenzied mutants swept down the stairs. Felix thought he recognised some of the creatures from the earlier battle. This was the place where the mutants came from.

One dived from the landing, its reptilian eyes glazed with bloodlust. Felix used a stop-thrust to take it through the chest, and then let his arm slump forward under the weight so that its corpse slid free from his blade. The tide of mutants flowed on, inexorably, pressed forward by their own bloodlust and the weight of those behind them. Felix found himself at the centre of a howling maelstrom of violence, where he and the Trollslayer fought back to back against the chaos-spawn.

Gotrek frothed at the mouth and lashed out in a great figure-of-eight with his blood-stained axe. Nothing could stand in his way. With the chains still hanging from his wrists, he carved a path of red ruin through the howling mob. Felix waded along in his wake, dispatching the fallen with single thrusts, stabbing the few mutants who got past the flailing axe.

On the landing above, Felix could see Kruger. The sorcerer had caught up his staff once more. A greenish glow played around his face, and illuminated the whole scene with an infernal light. Kruger chanted a spell and suddenly viridian lightning lashed out. It arced downwards and narrowly missed Felix.

The mutant standing in front of Felix was not so lucky. Its fur singed and eyeballs popped. For a moment it danced on stilts of pure sorcerous power and then fell to earth, a twisted, blackened corpse. Felix dived to one side, not wanting to be the target of another such bolt. Gotrek surged forwards, cleaving a mutant in two as he hacked his way to the foot of the stairs.

The lightning lashed out, aiming for Gotrek this time. He was not so lucky as Felix has been. The green bolt hit him head on. Felix expected to see the Trollslayer meet his long-threatened doom at last. Gotrek's hair stood even more on end than usual. The runes on his axe blade glowed crimson. He howled what might have been a final curse at his gods, then something strange happened. The green glow passed right through his body and along the length of the iron chain still attached to his wrist. It hit the ground in a shower of green sparks and dissipated harmlessly.

Felix almost laughed out loud. He had heard of such a thing before in his natural philosophy classes. It was called earthing: the same thing that let a metal lightning rod conduct the force of a thunderbolt harmlessly into the ground had saved Gotrek. He gave himself a moment to consider this, then flipped his hidden dagger from its sheath and cast it at Kruger.

It was a good throw. It aimed straight and true and buried itself in the foul sorcerer's chest. It hung there for a moment, quivering, and Kruger stopped his chanting to peer down at it. Kruger dropped his staff and clutched the wound. Greenish blood oozed from the gash and stained the wizard's fingers. He glared down at Felix in hatred – then turned and fled.

Felix gave his attention back to the melee but it was all over. The small mutants had again proved no match for the Slayer's axe. Gotrek stood triumphant, his muscular form covered in blood and ichor. A faint glow faded from his axe. Bear fat sizzled and spluttered on his hair.

Felix raced past him up the stairs and out into the corridor. A trail of greenish blood led off down the passage. It wound past a mass of open, empty cages. Felix guessed that it was from these that the mutants had come. They had been the products of Kruger's foul experiments.

'Let's free the children and get out of here.' Felix said.

'I want that sorcerer's skull for my drinking cup!' Gotrek spat.

Felix winced. 'You don't mean that.'

'It's just an expression, manling.'

From the look on Gotrek's face, Felix wasn't so sure about that.

THEY ADVANCED DOWN the corridor towards their goal. The thought of saving the children gave Felix some comfort. At least he and the Slayer would be able to do some good here, and return the young ones to their parents. For once, they would actually manage to act like real heroes. Felix could already picture the tear-stained faces of the relieved villagers as they were reunited with their offspring.

The rattling of the chain on Gotrek's wrist began to get on Felix's nerves. They turned the corner and came to a door. A single sweep of Gotrek's axe reduced it to so much kindling. They entered a chamber which had obviously once been Kruger's study.

The massive silver moon shone in through its single huge window. The Chaos-corrupted sorcerer lay slumped over his desk, his greenish blood staining the open pages of a massive leather-bound grimoire. His hands still moved feebly as if he were trying to cast a spell that might save him.

Felix grabbed his hair from behind and pulled Kruger upright. He looked down into eyes from which the greenish glow was fading. Felix felt a surge of triumph. 'Where are the hostages?'

'What hostages?'

'The villagers' children!' Felix spat.

'You mean my experimental subjects?'

Cold horror filled Felix. He could see where this was leading. His lips almost refused to frame his next question. 'You experimented on children.'

Kruger gave Felix a twisted smile. 'Yes, they're easier to transmute than adults and they soon grow to full size. They were going to be my conquering army – but you killed them all.'

'We killed... them all.' Felix stood stunned. His visions of being feted by joyful villagers evaporated. He looked down at the blood that stained his hands and his tunic.

Suddenly blind rage, hot as the fires of hell, overwhelmed Felix. This maniac had transformed the village children into mutants, and he, Felix Jaeger, had taken a hand in slaughtering

them. In a way that made him as guilty as Kruger. He
considered this for a moment, then dragged Kruger over to the
window. It looked down onto the sleeping village, a drop of
several hundred feet down a sheer cliff face.

He gave Kruger a moment to consider what was about to
happen and then gave him a good hard shove. The glass shattered as the sorcerer tumbled out into the chill night air. His
arms flailed. His shriek echoed out through the darkness and
took a long time to fade.

The Trollslayer looked up at Felix. There was a malevolent
glitter in his one good eye. 'That was well done, manling. Now
we'll have a few words with the innkeeper. I have a score to settle with him.'

'First let's torch the castle,' Felix said grimly. He stalked off to
turn the accursed place into a giant funeral pyre.

ULRIC'S CHILDREN

'In spite of all our efforts, yet somehow unsurprisingly, we failed to reach Nuln before winter set in. Worse yet, lacking a compass, or any other means of navigating in the deep forest, we were soon lost once more. I can think of few circumstances more frightening or hazardous to the traveller than to be lost in the woods in the winter snows. Unfortunately, by some quirk of the dark destiny that dogged our steps, it seemed we were just about to encounter one of those "few circumstances"...'

— From *My Travels with Gotrek, Vol. II*, by Herr Felix Jaeger (Altdorf Press, 2505)

THE HOWLING OF the wolves echoed through the forest like the wailing of damned souls in torment. Felix Jaeger pulled his threadbare red Sudenland wool cloak tight and trudged on through the snow.

Over the past two days he had seen their pursuers twice, catching glimpses of them in the shadows beneath the endless pines. They were long, lean shapes, tongues lolling, eyes blazing with ravenous hunger. Twice the wolves had come almost within striking distance and twice they had withdrawn, as if summoned, by the howling of some distant leader, a creature so frightful that it had to be obeyed.

When he thought of that long wailing call, Felix shuddered. There had been a note of horror and intelligence in its cry that brought to mind the old tales of the darkened woods with which his nurse had frightened him as a child. He tried to dismiss his evil thoughts.

He told himself he had merely heard the howling of the pack leader, a creature larger and more fearsome than the others. And, by Sigmar, the howling of wolves was a dismal enough sound without letting his mind populate the forest with monsters.

The snow crunched below his feet. Chilly wetness seeped through his cracked leather boots and into the thick woollen socks he wore beneath them. This was another bad sign. He had heard of woodsmen whose feet had been frozen solid within their boots who had to have their toes paired off with knives before gangrene set in.

He was not really surprised at finding himself lost deep in the heart of the Reikwald just as winter was setting in. Not for the first time, Felix cursed the day he ever encountered the dwarf, Gotrek Gurnisson, and sworn to follow him and record his doom in an epic poem.

They had been following the tracks of a large monster that Gotrek swore was a troll when the snow had started to fall. They had lost the trail in the whiteout and now were completely lost.

Felix fought down a surge of panic. It was all too possible that they would trudge around in circles until they died of exhaustion or starvation. It had happened to other travellers lost in the woods in winter.

Or until the wolves picked them off, he reminded himself.

The dwarf looked just as miserable as Felix. He trudged along using the haft of his huge axe like a walking stick to test the depth of the snow ahead of him. The great ridge of red dyed hair that normally towered above his shaved and tattooed head drooped like the crest of some bedraggled bird. The sullen madness that glittered in his one good eye seemed subdued by their dismal surroundings. A great blob of snot dripped from his broken nose.

'Trees!' Gotrek grumbled. 'The only things I hate more than trees are elves.'

Another piercing howl broke Felix out of his reverie. It was like those earlier howls, full of malign intelligence and hunger, and it filled Felix with blind primordial fear. Instinctively he flicked his cloak over his shoulder to free his sword arm and reached for the hilt of his blade.

'No need for that, manling.' Malicious amusement was evident in the dwarf's harsh flinty voice. 'Whatever it is: it's calling our furry little friends away from us. It seems like they've found other prey.'

'The Children of Ulric...' Felix said fearfully, remembering his nurse's old tales.

'What has the wolf-god of Middenheim got to do with it, manling?'

'They say that, when the world was young, Ulric walked among men and begat children on mortal women. That those of his bloodline could shift shapes between that of man and wolf. They withdrew to the wild places of the world long ago. Some say their blood grew tainted when Chaos came and now they feast on human flesh.'

'Well, if any of them should come within reach of my axe I will spill some of that tainted blood.'

Suddenly Gotrek raised his hand, gesturing for silence. After a moment he nodded and spat on the ground.

Felix paused fearfully, watching and listening. Nowhere could he make out any sign of pursuit. The wolves had vanished. For a moment all he could hear was his own pounding heart, and the sound of his rasping breath then he heard what had caused the Trollslayer to stop: the sounds of a struggle, battle-cries and the distant howling of wolves drifted on the wind.

'Sounds like a fight,' he said.

'Let's go kill some wolves,' Gotrek said. 'Maybe whoever they are attacking knows the way out of this hell-spawned, tree-infested place.'

PANTING FROM THE run through the thick snow drifts, face stinging from where branches and briars had torn at him, Felix bounded into the clearing. A dozen crossbows swung to cover him. The smell of ozone filled the air. The corpses of men and wolves lay everywhere.

Slowly Felix raised his hands high. His gasping breath clouded the air in front of him. Sweat ran down his face despite the cold. He would have to remember that it was not a good idea to run through the winter woods in heavy clothing. That was if he was still alive to remember anything after this. The heavily-armed strangers looked anything but friendly.

There were at least twenty of them. Several were garbed in the rich furs of nobles. They held swords and gave orders to the others: tough-looking, watchful, men at arms. For all their obvious competence there was an air of deep unease about all these men. Fear was in their eyes. Felix knew that he was instants away from being pin-cushioned by crossbow bolts.

'Don't shoot!' he said. 'I'm here to help.'

He wondered where Gotrek was. He had run for quite a distance. In the heat of the moment he had let his excitement and his longer legs carry him in front of the dwarf. Right now that might prove to be a fatal mistake, although he was not sure what even the Trollslayer could do faced with this glittering array of missile weapons.

'Oh you are, are you?' said a sarcastic voice. 'Just out for a walk in the woods, were you? Heard the sounds of a scuffle. Come to investigate this little disturbance, did you?'

The speaker was a tall nobleman. Felix had never cared much for the Empire's nobility, and this man seemed like a prime example of the worst of that pox-ridden breed. A trim black beard framed his narrow face. Startling dark eyes glared out of his pale features. A great eagle beak of a nose gave his face a predatory air.

'My friend and I were lost in the forest. We heard the wolves and the sounds of battle. We came to help, if we could.'

'Your friend?' the nobleman asked ironically. He jerked a thumb towards a tall, beautiful young woman who stood chained nearby. 'Do you mean this witch?'

'I have no idea what you're talking about, sir,' Felix said. 'I've never seen that young lady before in my life.'

He glanced around him. The dwarf was nowhere to be seen. Perhaps it was just as well Felix thought. The Trollslayer was not known for his tact. Doubtless right now, he would be saying something that would get them both killed.

'I was travelling with a companion...' It dawned on Felix that it might not be such a good idea to mention Gotrek right now. The Trollslayer was a conspicuous figure and an outlaw, and perhaps these men might want to claim the bounty, if they recognised him.

'He appears to have got lost,' Felix finished off weakly.

'Put down your sword,' the noble said. Felix complied. 'Sven! Heinrich! Bind his hands!'

Two of the men-at-arms raced forward to obey. Felix found himself kicked to the ground. He fell face first into the snow, and felt the cold wetness of it begin to seep into his tunic.

He opened his eyes and found he was lying in front of the corpse of a wolf. As he gazed into the creatures death-clouded eyes, the soldiers swiftly and efficiently bound his hands behind his back. Felix felt cold metal bite into his wrists and was surprised to find that they were using more than mere rope to hold him.

Then someone tugged down the hood of his cloak and pulled his head up by the hair. Foul breath assaulted his nostrils. Coldly crazy eyes gazed deep into his own. He looked up into a lined face framed by a greyish beard. A gnarled hand made a gesture in front of his face. As it swept through the air it left behind a trail of glittering sparks. Quite obviously this old man was a magician.

'He seems untouched by the taint of Darkness,' the sorcerer said in a surprisingly mellow and cultured voice. 'It may be that he tells the truth. I'll know more when we get him back to the lodge.'

Felix was allowed to slump forward into the snow once more. He recognised the voice of the noble speaking.

'Even so, take no chances with him, Voorman. If he is a spy for our enemies, I want him dead.'

'I'll find out the truth once I have my instruments. If he's a spy for enemies of the Order, we'll know!'

The noble shrugged and turned away, obviously dismissing the matter as beneath his concern. A boot hit Felix in the ribs again and knocked all the air out of his lungs.

'Get up and get on the sledge,' a burly sergeant said. 'If you fall off, I'll kill you.'

Felix drew his legs underneath himself and reeled to his feet. He glared at the sergeant, trying to memorise every line of the man's face. If he got out of this alive, he would have vengeance. Seeing his look one of the men-at-arms drew back the butt of his crossbow as if to brain Felix. The magician shook his head mildly.

'None of that. I want him undamaged.'

Felix shivered. There was something more frightening in the magician's calm detachment than there was in the soldier's unthinking brutality. He climbed on to the back of the sledge.

As far as Felix could tell, the party consisted of the nobleman, some of his toadies, the men at arms, and the mage. The nobles rode in horse-drawn sledges. The soldiers clung to the running boards or sat up front driving.

Beside him sat the young woman. Her hair was pure silver in colour and her eyes were golden. She had a sleek predatory beauty and a naturally haughty bearing that was in no way diminished by the collar and chain that attached her to the back railing of the sledge or the strange rune-encrusted metal shackles that bound her hands behind her back.

'Felix Jaeger,' he murmured by way of introduction. She said nothing, merely smiled coldly and then seemed to withdraw within herself. She gave no further acknowledgement of his presence.

'Be silent,' the magician sitting opposite them said, and there was more menace in his calm, quiet tone than there was in all the angry glares of the guardsmen combined.

Felix decided there was nothing to be gained by defying the old man. He cast another look around the forest, hoping to see some sign of Gotrek but the Trollslayer was nowhere in evidence. Felix lapsed into morose silence. He doubted that the dwarf could overtake them now, but he could at least follow the tracks of the sleds – providing it didn't snow too heavily.

And then what? Felix did not know. He had every respect for Gotrek's formidable powers of slaughter and destruction but he doubted that even the Trollslayer could overcome this small army.

Occasionally he risked a glance at the woman beside him, noting that she too was casting anxious glances towards the trees. He could not decide whether she was hoping that friends would come to her rescue or was simply measuring the distance of a dash for freedom.

A wolf howled in the distance. A strange inhuman smile twisted the woman's lips. Felix shuddered and looked away.

FELIX WAS ALMOST glad when the manor house loomed out of the gathering storm. The low, massive outline of the lodge was partially obscured by the drifting snowflakes. Felix could see that it was built from stone and logs in the style they called half-timbered.

He felt weary beyond belief. Hunger, cold and the long trudge through the snow had brought him almost to the end of his strength. It occurred to him that this was their destination and that here he would be prey for whatever foul schemes the wizard had in mind, but he simply could not muster the energy to care. All he wanted was to lie down somewhere warm and to sleep.

Someone sounded a horn and the gates were swung open. The sleds and the accompanying men-at-arms passed through into a courtyard, and then the gates were closed behind them.

Felix had a chance to glance around the courtyard. It was flanked on all four sides by the walls of the fortified manor house. He revised his earlier opinion. It was not so much a hunting lodge as a fortress, built in to withstand a siege if need be. He cursed: his chances of escape seemed slimmer than ever.

All around the party climbed down from the sledges. The nobles called for hot mulled wine. Someone ordered the drivers to see that the horses were stabled. All was bustling disorder. The breath of men and beasts emerged from their mouths like smoke.

The guards pushed Felix into the building. Inside it was cold and damp. It smelled of earth and pine and old woodsmoke. A massive stone fireplace filled the centre of the entrance chamber. The warriors and nobles stamped about inside, windmilling their arms and hugging themselves against the chill. Servants rushed forward bearing goblets of hot spicy wine. The scent of it made Felix's mouth water.

One of the warriors hastily laid kindling in the fire and then set to work, striking sparks from a flint. The damp wood refused to catch.

The wizard watched with growing impatience, then shrugged, gestured and spoke a word in the ancient tongue. A small burst of flame leapt from the end of his pointed index finger to the wood in the fireplace. The wood hissed, then roared. Ozone stink filled the air. Blue flames flickered around the wood then the logs all caught fire at once. Shadows danced away from the fireplace.

The nobles and the wizard passed through one of the doors into another chamber, leaving the warriors and the prisoners alone. Tense silence reigned for a moment then all the men began to speak at once. All the words that they had held in during the long trek to the lodge tumbled from the soldiers' mouths.

'By Sigmar's hammer, what a fight that was. I thought those wolves were going to have our nuts for sure!'

'I was never been so frightened as when I saw the hairy beasts loping out of the trees. Those teeth looked plenty sharp.'

'Yeah but they died quick enough when you put a crossbow bolt through their eyes or twelve inches of good Imperial steel through their mangy hides!'

'It wasn't natural though. I've never even heard of wolves attacking such a large party! I've never seen wolves fight so hard or long either.'

'I think we can blame the witch for that!'

The girl returned their stares impassively until none of them could meet her gaze. Felix noticed that her eyes were odd. In the gathering gloom, they reflected the light of the fire the way the eyes of a hound would.

'Yeah, just as well we had the wizard with us. Old Voorman showed them what real magic is and no mistake!'

'I wonder why the count wants her?'

At this a chill smile passed over the girl's face. Her teeth were small and white and very, very sharp. When she spoke her voice was low and thrilling and strangely musical.

'Your Count Hrothgar is a fool of he thinks he can hold me here, or kill me without my death being avenged. You are fools if you think you will ever leave this place alive.'

The sergeant drew back his hand and struck her with his gauntleted fist. The outline of his palm stood out stark and pink on her cheek where the blow fell. Anger blazed in the girl's eyes so hot and hellish and fierce that the sergeant shrank back as if he himself had been the one struck. The girl spoke again and her words were cold and measured.

'Hear me! I have the gift of the Sight. The veils of the future do not blind me. Every one of you, every single miserable lackey of Count Hrothgar, will die. You will not leave this place alive!'

Such was the compelling certainty in her voice that every man present froze. Faces went white with fear. Men glanced at each other in horror. Felix himself did not doubt her words. The burly sergeant was first to rouse himself. He slid his dagger from its sheath and walked over to the girl. He held the blade before her eyes.

'Then you will be the first to die, witch,' he said. The girl looked at him unafraid. He drew back his blade to strike. Filled with sudden anger Felix threw himself forward. Weighed down with chains he cannoned into the man and knocked him from his feet. He heard a low gurgle come from the man he had hit and felt a stab of savage exultation at taking some small revenge on the man who had struck him.

The other soldiers dragged him to his feet. Blows slammed into his body. Stars danced before his eyes. He fell to the ground, curling himself into a ball as heavy booted feet crunched into him. He pulled his head against his chest and drew his knees up to his stomach as the pain threatened to overwhelm him. A kick caught him under the chin, throwing his head back. Darkness took him momentarily.

Now he was really scared. The angry soldiers were likely to keep up this punishment until he was dead and there was nothing he could do about it.

'Stop!' bellowed a voice he recognised as belonging to the sorcerer. 'Those two are my property. Do not damage either of them!'

The kicking stopped. Felix was manhandled to his feet. He looked around him wildly then he noticed the spreading pool of red liquid on the floor that surrounded the recumbent form of the sergeant.

One of the soldier's turned the man over and Felix noticed the knife protruding from the sergeant's chest. The sergeant's eyes were wide and staring. His face was white. His chest did not rise and fall. He must have fallen on the blade when Felix had knocked him over.

'Throw them in the cellar,' the sorcerer said. ' I will have words with them both later.'

'The dying has begun!' the girl said with a note of triumph in her voice. She looked at the spreading pool of blood and licked her lips.

THE CELLAR WAS damp. It smelled of wood and metal and stuff contained in barrels. Felix caught the scent of smoked meat and cheeses as well. It just made him hungrier than already was, and he remembered that he had not eaten in two days.

A clink of chains reminded him of the girl. He sensed her presence in the dark. He heard her shallow breathing. She was somewhere close by.

'What is your name, lady,' he asked. For a long time there was silence, and he wondered if she was going to answer.

'Magdalena.'

'What are you doing here? Why are you in chains?'

Another long silence.

'The soldiers believe you are a witch. Are you?'

More silence, then: 'No.'

'But you have the second sight and the wolves fought for you.'

'Yes.'

'You're not very communicative, are you?'

'Why should I be?'

'Because we both appear to be in the same boat and perhaps together we can escape.'

'There is no escape. There is only death here. Soon it will be night. Then my father will come.'

She made the statement as if she was convinced that it was a complete answer. There was the same mad certainty in her voice, as convincing as it had been when she predicted death for all those armed men upstairs.

In spite of himself, Felix shuddered. It was not pleasant to think that he was alone in a dark basement with a madwoman. It was less pleasant to consider the alternative to her being mad.

'What do they want with you?'

'I am bait in a snare for my father.'

'Why does the Count want you dead?'

'I do not know. For generations my people have lived at peace with the Count's. But Hrothgar is not like his forefathers. He has changed. There is a taint about him, and his pet wizard.'

'How did they capture you?'

'Voorman is a sorcerer. He tracked me with spells. His magic was too strong for me. But soon my father will come for me.'

'Your father must be a mighty man indeed if he can overcome all the occupants of this castle.'

There was no answer except soft, panting laughter. Felix knew that the sooner he got out of here the better.

THE DOOR LEADING into the cellar was thrown open. A shaft of light illuminated the darkness. Heavy footsteps marked the approach of the wizard Voorman. He held a lantern in his hand and leaned on a heavy staff. He twisted his head up to look Felix in the face.

'Having an interesting chat with the monster, were you, boy?'

Something in the man's tone rankled. 'She's not a monster. She is only a sad, deluded young woman.'

'You would not say that if you knew the truth, boy. If I were to remove those shackles binding her, your sanity would be blasted in an instant.'

'Really,' Felix said with some irony. The magician tittered.

'So sure of yourself, eh? So ignorant of the way the world really is. What would you say, boy, if I told you that cults devoted to the worship of Chaos riddle our land, that soon we will overthrow all that exists of order here in the Empire.'

The wizard sounded almost boastful.

'I would say that you are, perhaps, correct.' He could see that his reply surprised the sorcerer, that Voorman had expected the usual casual denial of such things one expected from the educated classes of the Empire.

'You interest me, boy. Why do you say that?'

Felix wondered why he had said that himself. He was admitting to knowledge that could get him burned at the stake if a witch-hunter overheard him. Still, right now, he was cold and tired and hungry and he did not like being patronised by this irritating and supercilious mage.

'Because I have seen the evidence of it with my own eyes.'

He heard a sharp intake of breath from the wizard, and sensed now that perhaps for the first time he had got his full attention.

'Really? The Time of Changes is coming, eh? Arakkkai Nidlek Zarug Tzeentch?' Voorman paused as if expecting a reply. His head tilted to one side. He rubbed his nose with one long bony finger. His foul breath filled Felix's nostrils.

Felix wondered what was going on. The words were spoken in a language he had heard before, during the rituals of depraved cultists that and Gotrek had interrupted one Geheimnisnacht. The name 'Tzeentch' was all too familiar and frightening. It belonged to one of the darkest of dark powers. Slowly the air of expectancy passed from Voorman.

'No, you are not one of the Chosen. And yet you know the words of our Litany, or some of them. I can see that in your eyes. I don't think you are part of the Order. How can this be?'

It was obvious that the sorcerer did not expect an answer, that the last question was asked more of himself than of Felix. Suddenly there came the sound of the baying of many wolves outside the keep. The wizard flinched and then smiled. 'That will be my other guest arriving. I must go soon. He slipped through the net earlier but I knew he would come back for the girl.'

The wizard checked the chains that held Magdalena. He inspected the runes on them closely, and then apparently satisfied with what he saw, he smirked and turned and limped away. As he passed he looked at Felix. The younger man felt his flesh crawl. He knew that the wizard was deciding whether or not to kill him. Then the sorcerer smiled.

'No – there's time enough later. I would talk more with you before you die, boy!'

As the wizard shut the door behind him, the light died. Felix felt horror mount within his soul.

FELIX WAS NOT aware of how long he lay there with despair growing in his heart. He was trapped in the dark with no weapons and only a madwoman for company. The wizard intended to murder him. He had no idea where the Trollslayer was or if he had any hope of rescue. It was possible that Gotrek was lost in the woods somewhere. Slowly it dawned on him that if he was going to get out of this, he was going to have to do it for himself.

It did not look good. His hands were chained behind his back. He was hungry and tired and ill with cold and weariness. The bruises from the beating earlier pained him. The key to his chains was on the belt of the wizard. He had no weapon.

Well, one thing at a time, he told himself. Lets see what I can do about the chains. He hunkered into a squat, drawing his knees up to his chest. The chains pooled around his ankles, then by dint of wriggling and squirming, he drew his arms underneath him so that he they were in front of his body. The effort left him breathing hard and he felt like he had pulled his arms from his sockets, but at least now he could move more freely and the length of heavy coiled chain he held in his hands could be used as a weapon. Experimentally he swung it before him. There was a swishing noise as it cut through the air.

The girl laughed as if she understood what he was doing. Now he moved forward cautiously, placing one foot ahead of him gently testing the ground like a man might who was on the edge of a cliff. He did not know what he might stumble over in the darkness, but he felt it was wisest to be careful. This would be a bad time to fall and dislocate an ankle.

His caution was rewarded when he felt a stairway under his foot. Slowly, carefully he worked his way up the steps. As far as he remembered they had not curved in anyway. Eventually his outstretched hands struck wood. The chains clinked together softly as they swung. Felix froze and listened. It seemed to him that somewhere far off he could hear sounds of men fighting and wolves howling.

Wonderful, he thought sourly. The wolves had somehow got inside the manor. He pictured the long lean shapes racing through the hunting lodge, and a desperate battle between man and beast taking place mere paces from where he stood. It was not a reassuring thought.

For long moments he stood undecided and then he pushed against the door. It did not move. He cursed himself and fumbled for a handle. His fingers clutched a cool metal ring. He twisted and pulled towards himself and the door opened. He was looking up a long flight of stairs dimly illuminated by a guttering lantern. He reached out for the lantern, then thought about the girl.

However strange she was, she was also a prisoner here. He was not going to abandon her to the tender mercies of Voorman. He edged back down the stairs and gestured for her to follow him. He caught sight of her face. It was pale and strained and feral. Her eyes definitely did catch the light like those of some animal. There was a ferocious inhuman aspect to her whole appearance that did not reassure Felix in the slightest. He moved towards the head of the stairs but the girl pushed past him into the lead.

Felix was glad not to have those fierce eyes burning into his back.

THE SOUNDS OF fighting became clearer. Wolves bayed. War-cries rang out. Magdalena opened the door at the head of the stairs. They found themselves once more amid the mansion's corridors. The place was deserted. All the guards appeared to have been drawn towards the sounds of battle. A line of doorways edged the corridor. At one end a flight of stairs moved upwards. At the other there was a doorway beyond which was the sound of battle. Felix's nostrils twitched. He thought he smelled burning. Somewhere in the distance horses whinnied with terror.

Discretion told him to head for the stairs, to get away from the sounds of fighting. He was not part of either faction here, and discovery might prove fatal for him. The longer the others fought the more the odds against him were whittled down, and the more chance he had of escaping.

Magdalena, however, felt differently. She moved towards the doorway at the end of the corridor. The one that led towards the battle. Felix grabbed her chains and tugged. She did not stop. Although he was taller and heavier, she was surprisingly strong, stronger perhaps than he was.

'Where are you going?'

'Where do you think?'

'Don't be stupid. There's nothing you can do there.'

'What do you know?'

'Let us look around. Perhaps upstairs we can find a way to remove these chains.'

For a moment, she stood undecided but the last point appeared to sway her. Together they moved up the stairs. Behind them the sounds of howling and war-cries reached a crescendo and then abruptly ceased. For a moment, Felix wondered what had happened. Had the wolves overcome the defenders?

Then he heard men at arms begin to shout at each other once more. He heard noble voices tell the men to take the wounded inside and he realised that the men had won – for a while.

* * *

AT THE TOP of the stairs a window looked down into the court-yard of the lodge. He could see that there were dozens of dead wolves down there and maybe five dead men. Blood reddened the snow.

'How the hell, did that gate get open?' he heard Count Hrothgar ask. Felix wondered the same himself, for he could see that the wooden gate lay wide open. The wolves had come right through it. Then he saw the thing, and he wondered no more.

On the roof of the stables lay a grey shape, half-man and half-wolf. The hairs on the back of Felix's neck prickled. The man-wolf rose and dropped back out of sight, leaving Felix wondering if he had imagined the whole thing. He offered a prayer to Sigmar that he had done so but somehow, in his heart of hearts, he doubted it. It looked like Ulric's Children were here.

'Let us go on,' he muttered and turned and headed down the corridor.

THEY ENTERED A library. Bookcases so high that one would need a ladder to reach the highest volumes lined the walls. Felix was surprised by the size of it. Count Hrothgar had not seemed to him to be a scholar but this was worthy of the chambers of one of Felix's former professors at the University of Altdorf. His guess was that this was the wizard's place.

Felix ran his eyes over the titles. Most seemed to be written in High Classical, the tongue of scholars across the Old World. The ones he could see mostly concerned voyages of explo-ration, ancient myths and legends and lorebooks compiled from the dwarfish.

On the desk ahead of him was an open book. Felix walked over and picked it up. The tome was leather bound and no title was embossed on its spine. The parchment pages were thick and coarse and obviously ancient. For the thickness of the book there surprisingly few pages. It was not a printed volume set in the movable typefaces perfected by the Guild of Printers. It was done in the old style, hand-copied and illuminated around the borders. Felix picked it up and began to read and soon wished he had not.

Magdalena obviously noticed the look on his face. 'What is it? What is wrong? What does it say?'

'It's a grimoire of sorts… it deals with magic of a certain type.'

Indeed it did. Felix laboriously translated the Classical and a thrill of horror made him shiver. As far as he could tell it appeared to be a spell of soul transmutation, an invocation designed to let a man switch his very essence with that of another, to steal their shape and form. If the claims of the book were true, it would allow the wizard to take possession of another's body.

In another time, at another place Felix would have found the whole thing ludicrous. In this out of the way place, it all seemed rather likely. The madness of it did not seem out of place here.

None of this reassured Felix. He was trapped in an isolated keep by a group of mad cultists and their men at arms. The keep was surrounded by hungry wolves and cut off by a winter blizzard. As if that weren't bad enough, if his suspicions were true, there were not one but two werewolves within the walls of the fortress. And one of them was behind him.

Felix's flesh crawled.

THEY MOVED ON through the second floor of the castle, down corridors lit by flickering torches and echoing with the howling of wolves. A faint unpleasant odour, as of wet fur and blood, reached Felix's nostrils just before they turned a corner. He poked his head round cautiously and saw the corpse of a man-at-arms lying there. The soldier's eyes were wide open. Great talon gouges ripped his chest. His face was white as that of a vampire. Blood poured from where huge jaws had ripped out his jugular.

A sword lay near the dead man's hand. There was a dagger at his belt. Felix turned to look at the girl. She was smiling evilly. Felix felt like taking up the sword and striking her but he did not. The thought occurred to him that maybe he could use her as a hostage and strike a deal with the man-wolf. He turned it over in his mind and then dismissed it as being at once impractical and dishonourable.

Instead he bent over the man and fumbled for his dagger. It was a long needle-sharp blade as thin almost as a stiletto. He considered the lock of his chains. It was large and cumbersome and crudely made. He picked the blade up with his right hand and thrust it down into the lock of the manacle on his right wrist. He felt mechanisms move as the point went home. For long tense moments, he twisted and prodded. There was a click and the manacle opened. A weight fell from Felix's shoulders as the chain slid from his wrist. He tried repeating the process for the right hand chain but his left hand was clumsier and it took him longer.

Seconds stretched into minutes and he kept imagining that awful wolf-headed shape creeping up on him as he did so. Eventually there was a click and his other hand was free. He turned smiling triumphantly and the smile faded from his lips.

The girl was gone.

FELIX MOVED CAUTIOUSLY through the manor house. The wolves were quiet once more. The sword felt heavy as death in his hands. He had come across two more dead guards in his wanderings through the hall. Both their throats were torn out. Both had died with looks of horror on their face. The strange musk smell filled the air.

Felix considered his options. He could make a run for it out through the courtyard. That did not seem sensible. Outside snow covered the ground and wolves filled the woods. Even without their malevolent presence he doubted he would get very far without food or winter gear.

Inside the mansion was a sorcerer who wanted to kill him and the Children of Ulric. Plus a whole crew of scared men at arms to whom he was a stranger. That did not look too promising either.

Common sense dictated that he find some place to hide and wait for one side to slaughter the other. Maybe upstairs he could find an attic in which to hide, or maybe there was some quiet room in which–

Voices approached. The door at the end of the corridor started to open. Swiftly Felix pushed the door beside him open and ducked through, pulling it closed behind him. He realised he must be in Count Hrothgar's study. A massive desk sat under the window. Family portraits glared down from the walls. A burnished suit of armour stood sentry in an alcove. Curtained drapes covered the windows.

Some instinct prodded Felix to race across the room and dive behind the drapes. He was just in time. The door to the chamber swung open. Two men talked loudly. Felix recognised their voices. One was the count. The other was the sorcerer.

'Damn! Voorman, I thought you said your chains held them fast as the clutches of demons. How could they have disappeared?'

'The spells were not broken. I would have sensed it. I suspect some more mundane means. Perhaps one of your people…'

'Are you suggesting that one of my men could be in league with those things.'

'Or one of your servants. They stay here all year round. Who knows? The Children of Ulric have lived in this area longer than you. They say the folk about here used to worship them or at least sacrifice to them.'

'Maybe. Maybe. But can you find the prisoners. They can't just have disappeared into thin air. And what about my men. Over half are dead and the other half are frightened out of their wits, jumping at shadows. You'd best do something soon, wizard, or you will have some explaining to the Magister Magistorum. Things are not going as you promised the Order they would.'

'Don't panic, excellency. My magic will prevail and the cause will be stronger for it. The Time of Changes is coming, and you and I will have worked some of blessed Tzeentch's strongest magic. We will be immortal and unkillable.'

'Perhaps. But right now, at least one of the beasts is lose within these walls. Maybe two if you were wrong about the youth.'

'No matter. The spell of Transmutation is ready. Soon final victory will be ours. I go to find our vessel.'

'You go to find our vessel, do you wizard? You plan treachery more like. Be careful! The Magister gave me the means to deal with you, should you prove unfaithful to the Order!'

There was a ringing of steel as a weapon was drawn.

'Put it away, count.' The wizard sounded nervous now. 'You do not know the power of such a thing. There will be no need for its use.'

'Make sure that is so, Voorman. Make sure that is so.'

The door opened then closed. Felix heard the nobleman slump down into his chair. Briefly he wondered about this Order. Who was this mysterious Magister? Mostly likely the head of some unspeakable cult. Felix dismissed the thought. He had other things to worry about.

He pulled the curtain to one side and saw the bald spot at back of the count's head. A dagger lay on the desk in front of him. It was covered in strange glowing runes. Trying to follow their lines hurt Felix's eyes. Still, he thought, the dagger might be useful.

The nobleman rubbed his neck, feeling the cold draft from the window behind him. He began to reach for the dagger. Felix leapt from his place of concealment and brought the pommel of sword down on Count Hrothgar's skull. The nobleman fell like a pole-axed ox.

Gingerly Felix reached out for the dagger. His skin prickled as he brought his hand near the blade. A dangerous energy radiated from the thing. He picked it up by the hilt and noticed that the handle was wrapped with dull metal: lead. He realised that he had seen a glow like that from the blade before.

It looked like warpstone had been used in the creation of this dagger. This was a weapon that could be as dangerous to its user as to its victim. He reached down and found the sheath the count had drawn the weapon from. It was lined with lead. Felix felt a bit better after he had returned the weapon to its sheath.

Briefly he considered discarding the dagger but only briefly. In this hellish place, it might prove the only protection he might find. He buckled the sheath around his waist and got ready to move on.

THERE WERE THREE dead servants in the kitchen. They too had their throats torn out. It looked like the man-wolf intended to slay everyone in the mansion. Felix did not doubt that he would be included in that reckoning.

Looking at the dead bodies was almost enough to put Felix off his food. Almost. He had found fresh made bread on the table and cheese and beef in the larder. He gulped them down hungrily. They seemed like the best food he had ever tasted.

The door opened and two wild-eyed men-at-arms entered. They looked at the corpses and then looked at him. Fear filled their eyes. Felix reached for the naked sword on the table.

'You killed them,' one of the men said, pointing an accusing finger.

'Don't be stupid,' Felix said, his words muffled by the bread and cheese filling his mouth. He swallowed. 'Their throats were ripped out. It was the beast.'

The men paused, undecided. They seemed too afraid to attack and yet filled with fear-fuelled rage.

'You've seen it?' one asked eventually. Felix nodded.

'What was it like?'

'Big! Head like a wolf. Body of a man.'

An eerie howl echoed through the halls. It sounded close. The men turned and bolted for the door into the courtyard. As they did so, lean grey shapes sprang on them and pulled them down. Wolves had been waiting silently outside.

Felix raced forward but was too late to help the men. Looking out, he saw that the main gate was once again open. What looked like the girl stood near it. Her head was thrown back. She appeared to be laughing.

Hastily Felix closed the door shut and threw the bolts. He was trapped but at least whatever had howled had not come any closer. He sat back down at the table, determined to finish what might be his last meal.

FELIX CREPT THROUGH the corridors once more, sword in one hand, glittering dagger in the other. He had sat in the kitchen as long as he dared while fear made a home in his gut. Eventually it seemed like a better idea to go meet his doom head on than to sit their like a frightened rabbit.

He entered a great hall. The ceiling was high. Banners with the crest of Count Hrothgar hung from the ceilings. The heads of many animals, taken as hunting trophies covered the walls. Two figures were present. One was the sorcerer, Voorman. The other was the man-wolf. It was monstrous, half again as tall as Felix, its chest rounder than a barrel. Great claws flexed at the end of its long arms. Undying hatred glittered in its red-wolf eyes.

'You came, as I knew you would,' the wizard said. At first Felix wondered how the sorcerer had known he was there but then he realised that Voorman was talking to the man-wolf.

'And now you will die.' Lips never meant for human speech mangled the words. The sorcerer stepped back. His cloak billowed and light flared around his staff. The wolf stood frozen to the spot for a moment then reached out and tore Voorman's head off with one massive claw. The sorcerer's body stumbled forward. Blood gouted from his severed neck and sprayed the beast-thing.

From outside came the sound of wolves howling, and combat. Doubtless, the last survivors were being mown down Felix thought. He eyed the beast warily.

The sorcerer's blood steamed. A cloud of vapour rose over his corpse, taking on the outline of the mage. It stretched its arms triumphantly and flowed towards the Child of Ulric. The mist entered the creature's mouth and nostrils and it stood there for a moment, clutching its throat and seemingly unable to breath. The light vanished from its eyes and then a hellish green glow flickered there.

When the creature spoke again, its voice was Voorman's.

'At last,' it said. 'The spell of Transmutation is a success. Immortality and power are mine. The beast's strength is mine. I will live until Lord Tzeentch comes to claim this world. All things are indeed mutable.'

Felix stood aghast. A horrified understanding of what he had witnessed filled his brain. Voorman's plan had come to fruition. The trap was sprung. The corrupt soul of the wizard had taken possession of the man-wolf's body. His malign intelligence and sorcerous power would live on its monstrous shape. Voorman now possessed the strength and invulnerability of the Children of Ulric as well as his own evil powers.

Slowly the terrible green gaze came to rest on Felix. He felt the strength leech of him under that baleful glare. Outside he heard the wolves whimper in fear and the bellow of a warcry that sounded strangely familiar. The man-wolf gestured and, hypnotised, Felix stepped closer until he was within striking distance of its massive blood-spattered claws. Voorman reached out, his massive talons closing...

Throwing off his fear, Felix ducked and lashed out with his sword. He might as well have struck a stone statue. The keen edge of the blade bounced. The man-wolf's return slash tore Felix's jerkin. Pain seared his side where the razor edged claws bit deep. Felix sprang away. Only the fact that his reflexes were on a knife-edge had saved him from being gutted.

Things seemed to happen in slow motion. The man-wolf wheeled to face him. Felix circled. The beast sprang. Its rush was as irresistible as a thunderbolt. It bore Felix over, its enormous arms encircling him in a hug that threatened to snap his ribs like twigs. Frantically Felix stabbed downwards with the dagger in his left hand. To his surprise it pierced fur. There was a smell like rotting meat and the man-wolf through back its head and howled.

Felix kept stabbing. Where he stabbed the flesh became soft. The wolf's grip was weak now. Felix pulled himself clear and kept stabbing. Pockets of blackness appeared in the man-wolf's fur like spots of rot in overripe fruit. He kept stabbing. The man-wolf fell and the rot spread across its body, consuming it completely. The mighty form simply withered, overcome by the baneful runes on the dagger. Then the hellish glow left the weapon. It felt inert in Felix's grasp. He opened numb fingers and let it fall to the floor.

It was a long time before he pulled himself to his feet to look around the hall. The girl stood sullenly in the doorway. Gotrek stood behind her like an executioner. The blade of his massive axe lay against her neck.

'Thought I'd never get to the end of those damn tracks. Had to kill about fifty wolves to get in too,' the Trollslayer said, inspecting the scene of carnage with a professional air.

'Well, manling, it looks like you've had a busy night. I hope you've left me something to kill.'

The adventures of Gotrek and
Felix continue in
SKAVENSLAYER and
DAEMONSLAYER.

Here is a preview of
just one of those adventures.

From SKAVENSLAYER:

GUTTER RUNNERS

'Needless to say, we could not tell the authorities the whole truth of our encounter with the skaven, for in doing so we would implicate ourselves in the murder of a high official of the court of the Countess Emmanuelle. And murder, no matter how deserving the victim, is a capital crime.

'We were dismissed from service and forced to seek alternate employment. As luck would have it, during a drunken spree we happened upon a tavern, the owner of which had been a companion of the Slayer's in his mercenary days. We were employed to eject undesirables from the bar, and believe me when I tell you that people had to be very undesirable indeed to warrant being thrown out of the Blind Pig.

'The work was hard, violent and unrewarding but at least I thought we were safe from the skaven. Of course, as was so often the case, I was wrong. For it seemed that one of them at least had not forgotten us and was plotting revenge...'

— From *My Travels With Gotrek, Vol. III*, by Herr Felix Jaeger (Altdorf Press, 2505)

FELIX JAEGER DUCKED the drunken mercenary's punch. The brass-knuckled fist hurtled by his ear and hit the doorjamb, sending splinters of wood flying. Felix jabbed forward with his knee, catching the mercenary in the groin. The man moaned in pain and bent over, Felix caught him around the neck and tugged him towards the swing doors. The drunk barely resisted. He was too busy throwing up stale wine. Felix booted the door open then pushed the mercenary out, propelling him on his way with a hard kick to the backside. The mercenary rolled in the dirt of Commerce Street, clutching his groin, tears dribbling from his eyes, his mouth open in a rictus of pain.

Felix rubbed his hands together ostentatiously before turning to go back into the bar. He was all too aware of the eyes watching him from beyond every pool of torchlight. At this time of night, Commerce Street was full of bravos, street-girls and hired muscle. Keeping up his reputation for toughness was plain common sense. It reduced his chances of taking a knife in the back when he wandered the streets at night.

What a life, he thought. If anybody had told him a year ago that he would be working as a bouncer in the roughest bar in Nuln, he would have laughed at them. He would have said he was a scholar, a poet and a gentleman, not some barroom brawler. He would have almost preferred being back in the Sewer Watch to this.

Things change, he told himself, pushing his way back into the crowded bar. Things certainly change.

The stink of stale sweat and cheap perfume slapped him in the face. His squinted as his vision adjusted to the gloomy, lantern-lit interior of the Blind Pig. For a moment he was aware that all the eyes in the place were on him. He scowled, in what he hoped was a fearsome manner, glaring around in exactly the fashion Gotrek did. From behind the bar, big Heinz, the tavern owner, gave a wink of approval for the way in which Felix had dealt with the drunk, then returned to working the pumps.

Felix liked Heinz. He was grateful to him as well. The big man was a former comrade from Gotrek's mercenary days. He was the only man in Nuln who had offered them a job after they had been dishonourably discharged from the Sewer Watch.

Now that was a new low, Felix thought. He and Gotrek were the only two warriors ever to be kicked out of the Sewer Watch in all its long and sordid history. In fact they had been lucky to escape a stretch in the Iron Tower, Countess Emmanuelle's infamous prison. Gotrek had called the watch captain a corrupt, incompetent snotling fondler when the man had refused to take their report of skaven in the sewers seriously. To make matters worse, the dwarf had broken the man's jaw when he had ordered the pair of them horsewhipped.

Felix winced. He still had some half-faded bruises from the ensuing brawl. They had fought against half of the watch station before being bludgeoned unconscious. He remembered waking up in the squalid cell the morning after. It was just as well his brother Otto had got them out, wishing to hush up any possible scandal that might blacken the Jaeger family name.

Otto had wanted the pair of them to leave town but Gotrek insisted that they stay. He was not going to be run out of town like some common criminal, particularly not when a skaven wizard was still at large and doubtless plotting some terrible crime. The Trollslayer sensed an opportunity to confront the forces of darkness in all their evil splendour and he was not going to be robbed of his chance of a mighty death in battle against them. And bound by his old oath, Felix had to remain with the dwarf and record that doom for posterity.

Some mighty death, Felix thought sourly. He could see Gotrek now, huddled in a corner with a group of dwarfish warriors, waiting to start his shift. His enormous crest of dyed orange hair rose over the crowd. His enormously muscular figure hunched forward over the table. The dwarfs slugged back their beer from huge tankards, growling and tugging at their beards, and muttering something in their harsh, flinty tongue. Doubtless they were remembering some old slight to their people or working through the long list of the grudges they had to avenge. Or maybe they were just remembering the good old days when beer was a copper piece a flagon, and men showed the Elder Races proper respect.

Felix shook his head. Whatever the conversation was about, the Trollslayer was thoroughly engrossed. He had not even noticed the fight. That in itself was unusual, for the dwarf lived to fight as other folk lived to eat or sleep.

Felix continued his circuit of the tavern, taking in every table with a casual sidelong glance. The long, low hall was packed. Every beer-stained table was crowded. On one, a semi-naked Estalian dancing girl whirled and pranced while a group of drunken halberdiers threw silver and encouraged her to remove the rest of her clothes. Street-girls led staggering soldiers to dark alcoves in the far wall. The commotion from the bar drowned out the gasps and moans and the clink of gold changing hands.

One whole long table was taken up by a group of Kislevite horse archers, guards for some incoming caravan from the north. They roared out drinking songs concerning nothing but horses and women, and sometimes an obscene combination of both, while downing huge quantities of Heinz's home-distilled potato vodka.

There was something about them that made Felix uneasy. The Kislevites were men apart, bred under a colder sun in a harsher land, born only to ride and fight. When one of them rose from the table to go to the privy, his rolling, bow-legged walk told Felix that here was a horseman born. The warrior kept his hand near his long-bladed knife – for at no time was a man more vulnerable than when standing outside in the dim moonlight, relieving himself of half a pint of potato vodka.

Felix grimaced. Half of the thieves, bravos and muscle boys in Nuln congregated in the Blind Pig. They came to mingle with newly arrived caravan guards and mercenaries. He knew more than half of them by name; Heinz had pointed them out to him on his first night here.

At the corner table sat Murdo Mac Laghlan, the Burglar King who claimed to be an exiled prince of Albion. He wore the tartan britches and long moustaches of one of that distant, almost mythical island's hill-warriors. His muscular arms were tattooed in wood elf patterns. He sat surrounded by a bevy of adoring women, regaling them with tales of his beautiful mountainous homeland. Felix knew that Murdo's real name was Heinrik Schmidt and he had never left Nuln in all his life.

Two tall hook-nosed men of Araby, Tarik and Hakim, sat at their permanently reserved table. Gold rings glittered on their fingers. Gold earrings shone in their earlobes. Their black leather jerkins glistened in the torchlight. Long curved swords hung over the back of their chairs. Every now and again, strangers – sometimes street urchins, sometimes nobles – would come in and take a seat. Haggling would start, money would change hands and just as suddenly and mysteriously the visitors would up and leave. A day later someone would be found floating face down in the Reik. Rumour had it that the two were the best assassins in Nuln.

Over by the roaring fire at a table all by himself sat Franz Beckenhof, who some said was a necromancer and who others claimed was a charlatan. No one had ever found the courage to sit next to he skull-faced man and ask, despite the fact that there were always seats free at his table. He sat there every night, with a leather bound book in front of him, husbanding his single glass of wine. Old Heinz never asked him to move along either, even though he took up space that other, more free-spending customers might use. It never pays to upset a magician was Heinz's motto.

Here and there, as out of place as peacocks in a rookery sat gilded, slumming nobles, their laughter loud and uneasy. They were easy to spot by their beautiful clothing and their firm, soft flesh; upper-class fops out to see their city's dark underbelly. Their bodyguards – generally large, quiet, watchful men with well-used weapons – were there to see that their masters came to no harm during their nocturnal adventures. As Heinz always said, no sense in antagonising the nobs. They could have his tavern shut and his staff inside the Iron Tower with a whisper in the right ear. Best to toady to them, look out for them and to put up with their obnoxious ways.

By the fire, near to the supposed necromancer, was the decadent Bretonnian poet, Armand le Fevre, son of the famous admiral and heir to the le Fevre fortune. He sat alone, drinking absinthe, his eyes fixed at some point in the mid-distance, a slight trickle of drool leaking from the corner of his mouth. Every night, at midnight, he would lurch to his feet and announce that the end of the world was coming, then two hooded and cloaked servants would enter and carry him to his waiting palanquin and then home to compose one of his blasphemous poems. Felix shuddered, for there was something about the young man which reminded him of Manfred von Diehl, another sinister writer of Felix's acquaintance, and one which he would rather forget.

As well as the exotic and the debauched, there were the usual raucous youths from the student fraternities, who had come here to the roughest part of town to prove their manhood to themselves and to their friends. They were always the worst troublemakers, spoiled, rich young men who had to show how tough they were for all to see. They hunted in packs and were as capable of drunken viciousness as the lowest dockside cutthroat. Maybe they were worse, for they considered themselves above the law and their victims less than vermin.

From where he stood, Felix could see a bunch of jaded young dandies tugging at the dress of a struggling serving-wench. They were demanding a kiss. The girl, a pretty newcomer called Elissa, fresh from the country and unused to this sort of behaviour, was resisting hard. Her struggles just seemed to encourage the rowdies. Two of them had got to their feet and began to drag the struggling girl towards the alcoves. One had clamped a hand over her mouth so that her shrieks would not be heard. Another brandished a huge blutwurst sausage obscenely.

Felix moved to interpose himself between the young men and the alcoves.

'No need for that,' he said quietly.

The older of the two youths grinned nastily. Before speaking he took a huge bite of the blutwurst and swallowed it. His face was flushed and sweat glistened on his brow and cheeks. 'She's a feisty wench – maybe she'd enjoy a taste of a prime Nuln sausage.'

The dandies laughed uproariously at this fine jest. Encouraged he waved the sausage in the air like a general rallying his troops.

'I don't think so,' Felix said, trying hard to keep his temper. He hated these spoiled young aristocrats with a passion, had done ever since his time at the University of Altdorf where he had been surrounded by their sort.

'Our friend here thinks he's tough, Dieter,' said the younger of the two, a crop-headed giant larger than Felix. He sported the scarred face of a student duellist, one who fought to gain scars and so enhance his prestige.

Felix looked around for some help. The other bouncers were trying to calm down a brawl between the Kislevites and the halberdiers. Felix could see Gotrek's crest of dyed hair rising above the scrum. No help from that quarter, then.

Felix shrugged. Better make the best of a bad situation, he thought. He looked straight into the duellist's eye.

'Just let the girl be,' he said with exaggerated mildness – then some devil lurking at the back of his mind prompted him to add, 'and I promise not to hurt you.'

'You promise not to hurt us?' The duellist seemed a little confused. Felix could see that he was trying to work out whether this lowly bouncer could possibly be mocking him. The student's friends were starting to gather around, keen to start some trouble.

'I think we should teach this scumbag a lesson, Rupert,' Dieter said. 'I think we should show him he's not as tough as he thinks he is.'

Elissa chose this moment to bite Dieter's hand. He shrieked with pain and cuffed the girl almost casually. Elissa dropped as if pole-axed. 'Bitch took a chunk out of my hand!'

Suddenly Felix had just plain had enough. He had travelled hundreds of leagues, fought against beasts, monsters and men. He had seen the dead rise from their graves and slain evil cultists on Geheimnisnacht. He had killed the city of Nuln's own chief of secret police for being in league with the wretched skaven. He didn't have to take cheek from these spoiled whelps, and he certainly didn't need to watch them beat up an innocent girl.

Felix grabbed Rupert by the lapels and swung his forehead forward, butting the duellist on the nose. There was a sickening crunch and the big youth toppled backward, clutching his face. Felix grabbed Dieter by the throat and slapped him a couple of times just for show, then slammed the student's face into the heavy tabletop. There was another crunch. Steins toppled.

The spectators pushed their chairs backwards to avoid being soaked. Felix kicked Dieter's legs out from under him and then, after he hit the ground, kicked him in the head a couple of times. There was nothing pretty or elegant about it, but Felix was not in the mood to put up with these people any more. Suddenly they sickened him and he was glad of the chance to vent his anger.

As Dieter's friends surged forward, Felix ripped his sword from its scabbard. The razor-sharp blade glittered in the torch-light. The angry students froze as if they had heard the hissing of a deadly serpent.

Suddenly it was all deathly quiet. Felix put the blade down against the side of Dieter's head. 'One more step and I'll take his ear off. Then I'll make the rest of you eat it.'

'He means it,' one of the students muttered, Suddenly they did not look so very threatening any more, just a scared and drunken bunch of young idiots who had bought into much more trouble than they had bargained for. Felix twisted the blade so that it bit into Dieter's ear, drawing blood. The young man groaned and squirmed under Felix's boot.

Rupert whimpered and clutched his nose with one meaty hand. A river of red streamed over his fingers. 'You broke my node,' he said in a tone of piteous accusation. He sounded like he couldn't believe anyone would do anything so horribly cruel.

'One more word out of you and I'll break your fingers too,' Felix said. He hoped nobody tried to work out how he was going to do that. He wasn't quite sure himself, but he needn't have worried. Everybody took him absolutely seriously. 'The rest of you pick your friends up and get out of here, before I really lose my temper.'

He stepped away from Dieter's recumbent form, keeping his blade between himself and the students. They hurried forward, helped their injured friends to their feet, and hurried towards the door. A few kept terrified eyes on Felix as they went.

He walked over to Elissa and helped her to her feet.

'You all right?' he asked.

'Fine enough. Thanks,' she said. She looked up at him grate-fully. Not for the first time Felix noticed how pretty she was. She smiled up at him. Her tight black ringlets framed her round face. Her lips pouted. He reached down and tucked one of her jet-black curls behind her ear.

'Best go and have a word with Heinz. Tell him what happened.'

The girl hurried off.

'You're learning, manling,' the Trollslayer's voice said from behind him.

Felix looked around and was surprised to see Gotrek grinning malevolently up at him. 'I suppose so,' he said, although right at this moment he felt a little shaky. It was time for a drink.

GREY SEER THANQUOL perched on the three-legged bone stool in front of the Farsqueaker and bit his tail. He was angry, as angry as he could ever remember being. He doubted he had been so angry even on the day he had made his first kill, and then he had been very, very angry indeed. He dug his canines into his tail until the sensation made his pink eyes water. Then he let go. He was sick of inflicting pain on himself. He felt like making someone else suffer.

'Hurry-fast! Scuttle-quick or I will the flesh flay from your most unworthy bones,' he shrieked, lashing out with the whip he carried for just such occasions as this.

The skaven slaves squeaked in dismay and scuttled faster on the lurching treadmill attached to the huge mechanisms of the Farsqueaker. As they did so, the powerglobes began to glow slightly. Their flickering light illumined the long musty chamber. The shadows of the warp engineers of Clan Skryre danced across the walls as they made adjustments to the delicate machine by banging it lightly with sledgehammers. A faint tang of warpstone and ozone became perceptible in the air.

'Quick! Quick! Or I will feed you to the rat-ogres.'

A chance would be a fine thing, Thanquol thought. If only he had a rat-ogre to feed these slaves too. What a disappointment Boneripper had proved to be – that cursed dwarf had slain him as easily as Thanquol would slaughter a blind puppy. Just the thought of that hairless dwarf upstart made Thanquol want to squirt the musk of fear. At the same time, hatred bit at Thanquol's bowels and stayed there, gnawing as fiercely as a newly born runt chomping on a bone.

By the Horned Rat's fetid breath, he wanted revenge on the Trollslayer and his henchman! Not only had they slain Boneripper and cost Thanquol a lot of precious warptokens, they had also killed von Halstadt and thus disrupted the Grey Seer's master plan for throwing Nuln and the Empire into chaos.

True, Thanquol had other agents on the surface but none so highly placed or so malleable as the former head of Nuln's secret police. Thanquol wasn't looking forward to reporting the failure of this part of the scheme to his masters back in

Skavenblight. In fact, he had put of making his report for as long as he decently could. Now he had no option but to talk to the Seerlord and report how things stood. Warily he looked up at the huge mirror on top of the Farsqueaker, as he waited for a vision of his master to take form.

The skaven slaves scuttled faster now. The light in the warp-globes became brighter. Thanquol felt his fur lift and a shiver run down his spine to the tip of his tail as sparks leapt from the globes at either end of the treadmill, flickering upwards towards the huge mirror at the top of the apparatus. One of the warp engineers rushed over to the control panel and wrenched down two massive copper switches. Forked lightning flickered between the warpglobes. The viewing mirror began to glow with a greenish light. Little flywheels began to buzz. Huge pistons rose and fell impressively.

Briefly Thanquol felt a surge of pride at this awesome triumph of skaven engineering, a device which made communication over all the long leagues between Nuln and Skavenblight not only possible but instantaneous.

Truly, no other race could match the inventive genius of the skaven. This machine was just one more proof, if any was needed, of skaven superiority to all other so-called sentient races. The skaven deserved to rule the world – which was doubtless why the Horned Rat had given it into their keeping.

A picture took shape in the mirror. A towering figure glared down at him. Thanquol shivered again, this time with uncontrollable fear. He knew he was looking on the features of one of the Council of Thirteen in distant Skavenblight. In truth, he could not tell which, since the picture was a little fuzzy. Maybe it was not even Seerlord Tisqueek. Swirls and patterns of interference danced across the mirror's shimmering surface. Perhaps, Thanquol should suggest that the engineers of Clan Skryre should make a few adjustments to their device. Now, however, hardly seemed the time.

'What have… to… report… Seer Thanq…' The majestic voice of the Council member emerged from the machine's squeaking trumpet as a high-pitched buzzing. Thanquol had to strain to make out the words. With his outstretched paw he snatched up the mouthpiece, carved from human thighbone and connected to the machine by a cable of purest copper. He struggled hard to avoid gabbling his words.

'Great triumphs, lordly one, and some minor setbacks,' Thanquol squeaked. His musk glands felt tight. He fought to keep from baring his teeth nervously.

'Spea... up... Grey... I... hardly hear you... and...'

Thanquol decided there were definitely a few problems with the farsqueaking machine. Many of the Seerlord's words were being lost, and doubtless his superior was only catching a few of Thanquol's own words in return. Perhaps, thought the Grey Seer, this could be made to work to his advantage. He must consider his options.

'Many triumphs, lordly one, and a few minor setbacks!' Thanquol bellowed as loud as he could. His roaring startled the slaves and they stopped running. As the treadmill slowed, the picture started to flicker and fade. The long tongues of lightning dimmed. 'Faster, you fools! Don't stop!'

Thanquol encouraged the slaves with a flick of his lash. Slowly the picture returned until the dim outline of the gigantic skaven lord was visible once more. A cloud of foul-smelling smoke was starting to emerge from the Farsqueaker. It smelled like something within the machine was burning. Two warp engineers stood by with buckets of foul water drawn directly from the nearby sewers.

'...setbacks, Grey ...eer Thanquol?'

If ever there was time for the machine's slight irregularities to prove useful, now was that time, thought Thanquol. 'Yes, master. Many triumphs! Even as we speak our warriors scout beneath the man-city. Soon we will have all information we need for our inevitable triumph!'

'I said... setbacks... Seer Thanquol.'

' It would not wise be to send them back, great one. We need every able-bodied skaven warrior to map the city.'

The Council member leaned forward and fiddled with a knob. The picture flickered and became slightly clearer. Thanquol could now see that the speaker's head was obscured by a great cowl which hid his features. The members of the Council of Thirteen often did that. It made them seem more mysterious and threatening. Thanquol could see that he was turning and saying something to someone just out of sight. The Grey Seer assumed his superior was berating one of the engineers of Clan Skryre.

'...and how is... agent von Halstadt...'

'Indisposed,' Thanquol replied, a little too hastily for his own liking. Somehow it sounded better than saying he was dead. He decided to change the subject quickly. He knew that he had better do something to save the situation and fast.

No matter how cunningly he stalled his masters on the Farsqueaker, he knew that word of von Halstadt's death would get back to them eventually. Every skaven force was full of spies and snitches. It was only a matter of time before the news of his scheme's failure reached Skavenblight. By then Thanquol knew he had better have some concrete successes to report.

'We have news... change of plans... we send army to Nuln... when ready... ttack city...' The Seerlord's words made Thanquol ears rise with pleasure. If an army was being dispatched to Nuln, he would command it. Taking the city would increase his status immeasurably.

'Warlord Vermek Skab will command... render him all... sible assistance...'

Thanquol bared his teeth with disappointment. He was being replaced in command of this army. He sniffed as he considered the matter. Maybe not. Vermek Skab might have an accident. Then Grey Seer Thanquol could rise majestically to claim his full and rightful share of the glory!

Thanquol's nose twitched. The billowing cloud of smoke from the machine almost filled the chamber now, and Thanquol was pretty sure that the device was not supposed to be emitting great showers of sparks like that. The fact that two of the warp engineers were running for the door wasn't a good sign either. He considered following them.

'I have foreseen the presence... ill-omened elements in your future, Than... I predict disaster for you unless... do something about them.'

Suddenly Thanquol was rooted to the spot, torn between his desire to flee and his desire to hear more. He almost squirted the musk of fear. If the Seerlord prophesied something then it had almost as good as happened. Unless, of course, his superior was lying to him for purposes of his own. That happened all too often, as Thanquol knew only too well.

'Disaster, lordly one?'

'Yes... see a dwarf and a human... destinies are intertwined with yours... you do not slay them then...'

There was a very loud and final bang. Thanquol threw himself off his stool and cowered on the floor. An acrid taste filled his mouth. Slowly the smoke cleared and he saw the fused and melted remains of the farsqueaking machine. Several dead skavenslaves lay in its midst, their fur all charred and their whiskers burned away. In one corner a Warp Engineer lay curled up in a ball, mewling and writhing in a state of shock. Thanquol was unconcerned about their fate. The Seerlord's words filled him with a great fear. He wished he had been able to speak with his superior a little longer but alas he had not that option. He raised his little bronze bell and tinkled it.

Slowly members of his bodyguard entered the chamber. Clawleader Gazat looked almost disappointed to see him alive, Thanquol thought. Briefly the idea that the warrior might have sabotaged the Farsqueaker crossed Thanquol's mind. He dismissed it – Gazat did not have the imagination. Anyway, the Grey Seer had more important things to worry about.

'Summon the gutter runners!' Thanquol squeaked in his most authoritative tone. 'I have work for them.'

For a moment silence fell over the chamber. A foul smell made Thanquol's whiskers twitch. Just the mere mention of the dreaded assassins of Clan Eshin had caused Clawleader Gazat to squirt the musk of fear.

'Quick! Quick!' Thanquol added.

'Instantly, master,' Gazat said sadly and scuttled off into the labyrinth of sewers.

Thanquol rubbed his paws in glee. The gutter runners would not fail, of that he was assured.

FELIX UNLOCKED THE door of his chamber and entered his room. He yawned widely. He wanted for nothing more than to lie down on his pallet and sleep. He had been working for more than twelve hours. He put the lantern down beside the straw-filled mattress and unlaced his jerkin. He tried to give his surroundings as little attention as was possible, but it was difficult to ignore the loud moans of passion coming from the next room and the singing of the drinkers downstairs.

The chamber wasn't good enough for paying guests but it suited him well enough. He had occupied better, but this one had the great virtue of being free. It came with the job. Like a minority of old Heinz's staff, Felix chose to live on the premises.

Felix's little pile of possessions stood in one corner, under the barred window. There was his chainmail jerkin and a little rucksack which contained a few odds and ends such as his fire-making kit.

Felix threw himself down on the bed and pulled his old, tattered woollen cloak over himself. He made sure his sword was within easy reach. His hard life on the road had made him wary even in seemingly safe places, and the thought that the skaven they had recently encountered might still be about filled him with dread.

He recalled only too well the huge corpse of the slain rat-ogre lying at the foot of the stairs in von Halstadt's mansion. It had not been a reassuring sight. Somehow he was unsurprised that he had heard nothing at all about the fire at von Halstadt's mansion. Perhaps the authorities had not found the skaven bodies, or perhaps there was a cover-up. Right now, Felix didn't even want to consider it.

Felix wondered how men could ignore the tales of the skaven. Even as a student he had come across scholarly tomes proving that they didn't exist, or that if they had ever existed they were now extinct. He had come across a few references to them in connection with the Great Plague of 1111 and of course the Emperor of that period was known as Mandred Skavenslayer. Yet that was all. There were innumerable books written about elves and dwarfs and orcs, yet knowledge of the rat-men was rare. He could almost have suspected an organised conspiracy to cloak them in secrecy but that thought was too disturbing, so he pushed it aside.

There was a soft knock at the door. Felix lay still and tried to ignore. Probably just one of the drunken patrons lost and looking for his room again, he told himself.

The knock came again, more urgently and insistently this time. Felix rose from the bed and snatched up his sword.

A man could never be too careful in these dark times. Perhaps some bravo lurked out there, and thought a sleep-fuddled Felix would prove easy prey. Only two months ago Heinz had found a murdered couple lying on bloodstained sheets a mere three doors away. The man had been a prominent wine merchant, the girl his teenage mistress. Heinz suspected that the merchant had been slain by assassins on order of his harridan of a wife, but claimed also that it was none of his business.

Felix had got his new tunic all covered in blood when he dumped the bodies in the river. He hadn't been too thrilled about having to use the secret route through the sewers either.

The knocking came a third time, and he heard a woman's voice whisper, 'Felix.'

Felix eased his blade from its scabbard. Just because he heard a girl's voice didn't mean that there was only a girl waiting for him out there. She might have brought a few burly friends who would set about him as soon as he opened the door.

Briefly he considered not opening the door at all, of simply waiting till the girl and her friends tried to batter the door down then he realised quite how paranoid he had become. He shrugged. Since the deaths of Hef and Spider and the rest of the Sewer Watch he had every reason to be paranoid. Still, was he going to wait here all night? He slipped the bolts and opened the door. Elissa was waiting there.

She looked up at him nervously, brushing a curl from her forehead. She was very short but really very pretty indeed, Felix decided.

'I... I wanted to thank you for helping me earlier,' she said eventually.

Felix thought that it was a bit late for that. Couldn't she have waited till the morning? Slowly, though, realisation dawned on him. 'It was nothing,' he muttered, feeling his face flush.

Elissa glanced quickly left and right down the corridor. 'Aren't you going to invite me in, I wanted to thank you properly.'

She had to stand on her tiptoes to kiss his lips. He stood there dumbfounded for a second then pulled her into the room and slammed the door, slipping the lock into place.

As HIS HENCHLING Queg reached twelve in his muttered count, Chang Squik of Clan Eshin twitched his nose and sampled the smells of the night.

Strange, he thought; so like the stinks of the man-cities of Far Cathay and yet so unlike. Here he could smell beef and turnip and roast pig. In the east it would have been pickled cabbage and rice and chicken. The food smelled different but everything else was the same. There was the same scent of overflowing sewers, of many humans living in close proximity, of incense and perfume.

He opened his ears as his master had trained him as well. He heard temple bells tolling and the rattle of carriage wheels on cobbles. He heard the singing of drunks and the call of the night watchmen as they shouted the hour. It did not trouble him. He could not be distracted. He could, if he so wished, tune out all extraneous sound and pick out one voice in a crowd.

The skaven squinted out into the darkness. His night-vision was keen. Down there were the shadowy shapes of men and women leaving the taverns arm in arm, heading for brief liaisons in back alleys and squalid rooming houses. Chang did not care about them at all. His two targets were in the building that humans called a tavern.

He did not know why the honourable Grey Seer had selected these two, out of all the inferior souls in this city, for inevitable death. He merely knew it was his task to ease the passing of their souls into the maw of the Horned Rat. He had already offered up two sticks of narcotic incense and pledged their immortal essence for his dark god's feast. He could almost, but not quite, feel sorry for the doomed ones.

They were there in that tavern, under the sign of the Blind Pig, and they did not know that certain doom approached. Nor would they, for Chang Squik had trained for years in the delivery of silent death. Long before he had left the warm jungles of his eastern homeland to serve the Council in these cold western climes, he had been schooled to perfection in his clan's ancient art of stealthy assassination. While still a runt, he had been made to run bare-pawed through beds of white hot coals, and snatch coins from the bowls of blind beggars in human cities. Even at that early age he had learned that the beggars were often far from blind, and often viciously proficient in the martial arts.

By the time of his initiation he had become proficient in all forms of unarmed combat. He was a third degree adept in the way of the Crimson Talon and held a black belt in the Path of the Deadly Paw. He had spent twelve long months being trained in silent infiltration in the jungles, and a month in fasting and meditation high atop Mount Yellowfang with only his own droppings for food.

Since that time he had killed and killed again in the name of the Council of Thirteen. He had slain Lord Khijaw of Clan

Gulcher when that mighty warlord had plotted the downfall of Throt the Unclean. He had served as personal assistant to Snikch when the great assassin had killed Frederick Hasselhoffen and his entire household, and he had been rewarded with one-on-one instruction by the Deathmaster himself.

Chang Quik's list of triumphs was long, and tonight he would add another to it. It was his task to slay the dwarf, Gotrek Gurnisson, and his human henchling, Felix Jaeger. He did not see how he could fail.

What chance had a one-eyed dwarf and his stupid human friend against a mighty skaven trained in every art of death-dealing? Chang Squik felt confident that he could take the pair himself. He had been almost insulted by Grey Seer Thanquol's insistence that he take his full pack of gutter runners.

Surely the dire rumours of this dwarf were exaggerated. The Trollslayer could not possibly have slaughtered a unit of stormvermin single-handed. And it seemed well nigh unbelievable that he could have slain the rat-ogre Boneripper without the aid of an entire company of mercenaries. And, of course, it was impossible that this could be the same dwarf who five years ago had slain Warlord Makrik of Clan Gowjyer at the battle of the Third Door.

Chang exhaled in one long controlled breath. Perhaps the Grey Seer was right. He had often proved to be so in the past. It was simple prudence to assign the task of slaying the dwarf to Slitha. Chang would slay the human, and if there were any difficulties he would race to the assistance of his henchling's squad. Not that there would be any difficulties.

Queg stopped counting at one hundred and tapped his superior on the arm. Chang lashed his tail once to show that he understood. Slitha and his team, with the clockwork precision which characterised all skaven operations, would be in position at the secret entrance to the tavern by now. It was time to proceed.

He loosened his swords in their scabbards, checked to make sure that his blowpipe and throwing stars were ready at paw, and whistled the signal to advance.

Like a dark wave, the pack of gutter runners surged forward over the rooftop. Their blackened weapons were visible only as shadowy outlines in the moons' light. Not a weapon clinked. Not an outline was visible; well, almost.

HEINZ MADE HIS last rounds of the night, checking the doors and windows of the lower floor to make sure they were securely barred. It was amazing how often thieves tried to break in to the Blind Pig and steal from its cellars. Not even the reputation for ferocity of Heinz's bouncers could keep the desperately poor and alcoholic denizens of the New Quarter from making the attempt. It was quite pathetic really.

He made his way down into the cellars, shining his light into the dark corners between the great ale barrels, and wine racks. He could have sworn he heard a strange scuttling noise down here.

Just his imagination, he told himself.

He was getting old, starting to hear things. Even so, he went over and checked the secret door that led down into the sewers. It was hard to tell in this light but it looked undisturbed. He doubted anybody had used it since he and Felix had dumped those bodies two months back and saved everybody quite a scandal. Yes, he was just getting old, that was all.

He turned and limped back to the stairwell. His bad leg was playing up tonight. It always did when there was going to be rain. Heinz smiled grimly, remembering how he'd got the old war wound. It had been stamped on by a Bretonnian charger at the battle of Red Orc Pass. Clean break. He remembered lying there in the bloody dirt and thinking it was probably a just payback for spiking the horse's owner on his halberd. That had been a bad time, one of the worst he had faced in all his years of soldiering. He'd learned a lot about pain that day. Still there had been good times as well as bad during his career as a mercenary, he was forced to admit that.

There were occasions when Heinz wondered whether he had made the right decision, giving up the free-spirited life of the mercenary companies for the life of a tavern keeper. On nights like this he missed the camaraderie of his old unit, the drinking round the campfires, the swapping of stories and recounting of tales of heroism.

Heinz had spent ten years as a halberdier, and had seen service on half the battlefields of the Empire, first as a lowly trooper and later as a sergeant. He had risen to captain during Emperor Karl-Franz's campaigns against the Orc hordes in the East. During the last Bretonnian scrap he had made enough in plunder to buy the Blind Pig. He had finally given in to old

Lotte's promptings to settle down and make a life for the two of them. His old comrades had laughed when he had actually married a camp follower. They had insisted she would run off with all his money. Instead the two of them had been blissfully happy for five years before old Lotte had to spoil it all by going and dying of the Wasting Sickness. He still missed her. He wondered if there was anything to stay here in Nuln for now. His family were all dead. Lotte was gone.

As he reached the head of the stair, Heinz thought he heard the scuttling sound again. There was definitely something moving down there.

Briefly he considered calling Gotrek or some of the other lads, and getting them to investigate, then he spread his huge hands wide in a gesture of disgust. He really was getting old if he would let the noise of some rats scrabbling round in his cellar upset him. He could just imagine what the others would say if he told them he was scared to go down there himself. They would laugh like drains.

He drew the thick cosh from his waistband and turned to go back down. Now he really was uneasy. He would never have drawn the weapon normally. He was too calm and easy tempered. Something definitely did have him spooked. His old soldier's instincts were aroused, and they had saved him on more than one occasion.

He could still remember that night along the Kislevite border when he had somehow been unable to get to sleep, filled with a terrible sense of foreboding. He had risen from his bed and gone to replace the sentry, only to find the man dead at his post. He had only just roused the camp before the foul beastmen attacked. He had a similar feeling in the pit of his stomach now. He hesitated at the top of the stair.

Best go get Gotrek, he thought. Only the real hardcore drinkers were still in the tavern by now. The rest were asleep, under the tables, in the alcoves, in the private rooms, or else gone home.

There it was again, that skittering sound, like the soft scrabble of padded claws on the stone stairs. Heinz was definitely worried now. He pulled the door closed and turned, almost running down the corridor until he came out in the main bar area. A handful of the bouncers chattered idly with a few of the barmaids.

'Where's Gotrek?' Heinz asked. A burly lad, Helmut, jerked his thumb in the direction of the privies.

SLITHA REACHED THE head of the staircase and flung the door open. So far, so good. All was going like a typically well-oiled Clan Skryre machine. Everything according to plan. They had entered the tavern undetected; now it was simply a case of searching the place until they came upon the dwarf and killed him. And furthermore killed anything else that got in their way, of course.

Slitha felt a little irritated. It was typical of his superior to take the easy task. They had already found out where the human Jaeger slept, and their leader had taken the task of killing him for himself. Surely that was the only explanation. It could not be that the great Chang Squik was afraid of an encounter with the Trollslayer. Not that Slitha cared. When he dispatched the feared dwarf it would simply reflect all the more to his credit. He gestured for his fellows to go in first.

'Quick! Quick!' he chittered. 'All night we haven't got!' The gutter runners moved quickly into the corridor.

The story continues in
SKAVENSLAYER by William King,
the next instalment in the
adventures of Gotrek and Felix
from the Black Library.

Also from the Black Library

SKAVENSLAYER
A Gotrek & Felix novel
by William King

'BEWARE! SKAVEN!' Felix shouted and saw them all reach for their weapons. In moments, swords glittered in the half-light of the burning city. From inside the tavern a number of armoured figures spilled out into the gloom. Felix was relieved to see the massive squat figure of Gotrek among them. There was something enormously reassuring about the immense axe clutched in the dwarf's hands.

'I see you found our scuttling little friends, manling,' Gotrek said, running his thumb along the blade of his axe until a bright red bead of blood appeared.

'Yes, Felix gasped, struggling to get his breath back before the combat began.

'Good. Let's get killing then!'

SET IN THE MIGHTY city of Nuln, Gotrek and Felix are back in Skavenslayer, the second novel in this epic saga. Seeking to undermine the very fabric of the Empire with their arcane warp-sorcery, the skaven, twisted chaos rat-men, are at large in the reeking sewers beneath the ancient city. Led by Grey Seer Thanquol, the servants of the Horned Rat are determined to overthrow this bastion of humanity. Against such forces, what possible threat can just two hard-bitten adventurers pose?

Also from the Black Library

DAEMONSLAYER
A Gotrek & Felix novel
by William King

THE ROAR WAS so loud and so terrifying that Felix almost dropped his blade. He looked up and fought the urge to soil his britches. The most frightening thing he had ever seen had entered the hall and behind it he could see the leering heads of beastmen.

As he gazed on the creature in wonder and terror, Felix thought: this is the incarnate nightmare which has bedevilled my people since time began.

'Just remember,' Gotrek said from beside him, 'the daemon is mine!'

FRESH FROM THEIR adventures battling the foul servants of the rat-god in Nuln, Gotrek and Felix are now ready to join an expedition northwards in search of the long-lost dwarf hall of Karag Dum. Setting forth for the hideous Realms of Chaos in an experimental dwarf zeppelin, Gotrek and Felix are sworn to succeed or die in the attempt. But greater and more sinister energies are coming into play, as a daemonic power is awoken to fulfil its ancient, deadly promise.

Also from the Black Library

FIRST & ONLY
A Gaunt's Ghosts novel
by Dan Abnett

'THE TANITH ARE strong fighters, general, so I have heard'. The scar tissue of his cheek pinched and twitched slightly, as often did when he was tense. 'Gaunt is said to be a resourceful leader.'

'You know him?' The general looked up, questioningly 'I know *of* him sir. In the main by reputation'.

GAUNT GOT TO his feet, wet with blood and Chaos pus. His Ghosts were moving up the ramp to secure the position. Above them, at the top of the elevator shaft, were over a million Shriven, secure in their bunker batteries. Gaunt's expeditionary force was inside, right at the heart of the enemy stronghold. Commissar Ibram Gaunt smiled.

IT IS THE nightmare future of Warhammer 40,000, and mankind teeters on the brink of extinction. The galaxy-spanning Imperium is riven with dangers, and in the Chaos-infested Sabbat system, Imperial Commissar Gaunt must lead his men through as much in-fighting amongst rival regiments as against the forces of Chaos. First and Only is an epic saga of planetary conquest, grand ambition, treachery and honour.

Also from the Black Library

INTO THE MAELSTROM

An anthology of Warhammer 40,000 stories, edited by Marc Gascoigne & Andy Jones

'THE CHAOS ARMY had travelled from every continent, every shattered city, every ruined sector of Illium to gather on this patch of desert that had once been the control centre of the Imperial Garrison. The sand beneath their feet had been scorched, melted and fused by a final, futile act of suicidal defiance: the detonation of the garrison's remaining nuclear stockpile.' – **Hell in a Bottle** *by Simon Jowett*

'HOARSE SCREAMS and the screech of tortured hot metal filled the air. Massive laser blasts were punching into the spaceship. They superheated the air that men breathed, set fire to everything that could burn and sent fireballs exploding through the crowded passageways.' – **Children of the Emperor** *by Barrington J. Bayley*

IN THE GRIM and gothic nightmare future of Warhammer 40,000, mankind teeters on the brink of extinction. INTO THE MAELSTROM is a storming collection of a dozen action-packed science fiction short stories set in this dark and brooding universe.